TO FIND A CROOKED SIXPENCE

Terry White

Published by New Generation Publishing in 2016

Other titles by the author in paperback:
TILL THE FAT LADY'S SUNG
WITH GENTLY SMILING JAWS
THERE CAME A BIG SPIDER
TRESPASSERS WILL BE MUTILATED
A DONKEY UP A MINARET
THE HORNS OF THE MOON

ISBN13: 978-1-78507-871-2

Cover design by Jacqueline Abromeit

www.newgeneration-publishing.com

 New Generation Publishing

TO FIND A CROOKED SIXPENCE

There was a crooked man who walked a crooked mile
He found a crooked sixpence against a crooked stile
He bought a crooked cat, which caught a crooked mouse
And they all lived together in a little crooked house

PROLOGUE

Nobby Garside MP was a contented man. He eased his large bulk into a comfortable position in the first-class seat on the Intercity Express from Doncaster to Kings Cross, put his briefcase on the table in front of him to block off any other passenger and opened that morning's copy of the *Sheffield Telegraph* containing details of the latest parliamentary expenses scandal. He smiled to himself; he'd got away scot-free in that brouhaha because, sticking to his policy of never killing the goose that lays the golden eggs, he hadn't milked the system like many of his colleagues, just filtered out small amounts here and there which hadn't attracted official attention. Some Members of Parliament were even facing jail now, stupid sods – or greedy sods – or both.

The ticket inspector paused briefly beside him.

'Morning Mr Garside, off back down to the big smoke to put the country to rights again?'

'Morning George, the railway company not twigged about you and that blonde attendant in the buffet car yet?'

'You're a bugger Mr Garside, that you are! They don't make 'em like you no more.' And with a big smile across his face he waved away Nobby's travel pass and wandered off down the train.

1

Nobby was contented because he was going to be rich; no, he corrected himself, he was rich – theoretically. The beautifully engraved, gold-embossed Certificate of Deposit, which had been stowed in that briefcase on the journey north, was effectively cash and was now safely lodged in the hidden safe in his house in Cadeby. It hadn't been easy, but he had pulled it off at last.

For a coal miner's son he had to admit that he had done very well for himself.

****

APRIL 2010 – BEAUREGARD ISLAND, COMORANTES GROUP, INDIAN OCEAN.

The sun blazed down from directly overhead and the humidity was high at this time of year in Port Mahon. At midday you stood in your own shadow at that latitude. In spite of the air conditioning, the bead of sweat forming on Jack Fourie's nose broke its surface tension and dropped on to the papers in front of him. His light blue shirt was stained black under the arms and down his back from just half-an-hour outside. He wiped his face with a tissue from the box on his battered desk and looked again at the quantity surveyor's monthly figures and at the record photographs of the site spread out damply in front of him.

There was something very wrong about this project; it had been coming on for some time. The people working on it had become listless and uninspired; some of the hired heavy plant had been shipped out – allegedly for repair, but had not come back. When he pushed Bannerjee hard he became evasive, his head wobbled from side to side like a toy dog in the rear window of a Ford Escort. Things were getting worse not better as promised. He had had strong suspicions for a couple of months now and these documents confirmed that he was correct. The dredging and the building of the breakwater and jetty had started five months ago, but both the cost plan and the programme indicated that twice as much work should have been done as these monthly reports cited. Mumbai Construction just didn't have enough plant, equipment or men on the site. He reached for the intercom to speak to Bannerjee, the company's Site Manager, but paused when he heard the sound of heavy boots coming purposefully down the corridor towards his office. He recognised Bannerjee's footsteps.

There was a cursory tap on the wide open door and the huge figure of Raul Bannerjee blocked out the entrance. He was wearing his hard hat with "MUMBAI CONSTRUCTION" stencilled across the front, a ragged blue shirt with the sleeves rolled up, cotton trousers stained with diesel oil and dusty site boots. He puffed out his cheeks and nodded good morning to Jack.

'Morning Raul, I was just going to contact you.' Jack's voice was neutral and noncommittal, his face hard. He waved Bannerjee to a chair.

The big Indian took off his hard hat and sat down heavily, his face bore its usual angry worried look.

'What's going on Raul? What the fuck are you playing at – and no bullshit this time!?'

Bannerjee scowled and mopped his brow. 'Frankly, it's the money Jack. There's still no payment from the government. I phoned The National Bank of Comorantes this morning and not a brass riyal has been paid! Can CONDES help?'

Jack frowned and shook his head. 'Hugo Elmes, our senior director confirmed three months ago that the Department for International Development have definitely made the funds available at The National Bank and that weasel Rouget at the Ports and Harbour Authority assured me last week that the down payment was on its way. I'll phone him again.'

Bannerjee raised a warning finger. 'Jack, I am telling you this. This is now serious! You know and I know that ve are veeks behind programme. This is entirely because of money. The contract says ve get a tventy per cent down payment vhen ve start on site. Ve have put up a bank bond of thirty million dollars to cover this as required and – not one damn riyal. Ve cannot afford to continue funding this project and my boss in Mumbai, B K Menon, is breathing down my neck to keep expenditure as low as possible. He is threatening to shut down the site now.'

Jack chewed his lip thoughtfully. 'Look Raul, let's put some meat on this bone. Set out what Mumbai Construction's exact position is and I'll contact London again and the Ministry of Ports here in St George's and lay it on the line.'

Bannerjee wobbled his head. 'Vill that be officially or unofficially?'

'Officially. It's been five months since you started on site, you should have had your down payment plus payment for at least two monthly certificates – allowing for the usual bureaucratic delays that always take place. So give me an official letter saying that you are unable to fund the Port Mahon project any further and will close down the site until payment is received.'

The Indian rubbed his forehead nervously. 'I am not sure about that Jack. Ve don't vant to fall foul of the government here. Stir up the bees nest, do ve?'

Jack shrugged. 'Well the ball is in your court, mate. I must report to London that the project is running at least two months behind programme. I'll mention the lack of payment, but I suspect that all the blame will fall on your head without an official complaint from you.'

Bannerjee picked up his hat and stood up grumbling. 'Oh crikey, oh blimey, ve are in a right kettle of pickle. I'll have to be talking to Mumbai about it.'

Jack gave a faint grin. 'You've been listening to the BBC overseas broadcasts again haven't you?'

The grin disappeared as soon as Bannerjee left the office. Something was definitely not right here. Ignoring the Comortel phone – any conversation on that was not secure – he picked up his satellite phone and punched in CONDES' London number.

'Hugo Elmes please. It's Jack Fourie from Port Mahon.'

CHAPTER ONE

Norbert Garside was a big burly florid-faced man, a hail-fellow-well-met type of person with a broad South Yorkshire accent, a booming voice to go with it and big teeth that could crack walnuts. He liked to be known as Nobby, and when asked why by people who were too dim to work it out for themselves, would slap his large backside and say 'It takes a big hammer to knock in a big nail.' Of course the folk who were too dim too work it out in the first place were totally lost the second time so his joke usually fell flat on its face.

He tried hard to cultivate popularity amongst his fellow Members of Parliament, but he was treated warily by the upper echelons of the Party – the Islington socialists, who, whilst mixing vinaigrette and discussing Marcuse's views on Hegelian philosophy in the privacy of their salons, referred to people like Nobby as 'The Flat Cap Brigade'. The Tories didn't like him either but tolerated him because he posed no intellectual threat and told the best dirty jokes in Westminster.

He was the second of three boys born to Mr and Mrs Ron Garside of Maltby, South Yorkshire, an active mining village before the demise of the coal industry. The Nye Bevan Comprehensive School was responsible for his education. By careful cheating he held a place near the top of the 'B' stream, but his main achievement was running the unofficial school betting shop round the back of the metalwork building.

It was expected that after leaving school Norbert would follow his father and older brother and go 'down t' pit', but Nobby Garside could already see the writing on the wall spelling out the decline of the mining industry, and he was ambitious. Collieries were closing in the area and nuclear and gas were taking over from coal to generate increasing amounts of the nation's electricity. The day after he shook the dust of 'Nye Bevan's' from his feet he signed on at the local job centre as a precaution, then caught the bus into Rotherham. He presented himself at the works offices of James Maddison & Sons Steel Fabricators, and demanded to 'see t' gaffer.'

'Gi' us a job? Teach us to cut steel and weld and I'll work for nowt. Do anything, go anywhere any time,' he told the receptionist when she demanded to know why he was there.

The works manager happened to be in the next office and overheard this exchange; he was intrigued. Nobby was a well-built lad and it just so happened that one of the apprentice fabricators had broken an arm the previous day when a heavy steel joist had slipped out of a crane sling and fallen across it, leaving him shorthanded.

He asked Nobby a few question and was satisfied that the lad was both serious and intelligent.

'Ah can't take thee on for nowt lad, it's agin t'law, but I can take thee on as an apprentice. Come back next Monday wi' a letter from thi' parents giving their approval and we'll sign thee up.'

Nobby was duly enrolled for the princely wage of £70 per week and was given one day off a week to attend the local technical college.

On the bus back to Maltby after his first day at work he reflected on life. A working-class lad from a Yorkshire pit village did not have an easy start up the wealth ladder – and that's what Nobby dreamt about. He wanted to be rich; not just rich but rich and respected.

James Maddison & Sons was a fully unionised firm so he automatically joined the National Union of Metalworkers. Being a sharp lad, it wasn't long before he spotted opportunities there for making a few pounds on the side, but to do this he had to become a union official. Most of the men who worked there were only interested in taking home their weekly wage, having a few pints of John Smith's in the Furnace and Ladle on a Friday night and supporting Rotherham United on Saturday afternoon. It was a life without ambition; they were content to work 8.00am to 5.00pm five days a week and let the union negotiate their working conditions and wages. Within three years Nobby Garside had replaced the current shop steward, an elderly and lazy man called Brumpton, who followed the suggestion that he should retire – possibly because it was attached to the brick that was posted through his bedroom window one dark night. Nobby became union representative for the fabricating shop. This gave him a seat on the works committee at the relatively young age of nineteen and access to their union dues.

Nobby liked to think he represented the friendly face of unionism and his endeavours came to the notice of the regional office. At the age of twenty-four, he was offered a full-time job as regional negotiator for the union in South Yorkshire.

He thought about this carefully. It would mean giving up his job at Maddison and the shop steward sinecure, but the potential for making more money obviously existed in the bigger job. It would also put him closer to the political side of unionism and open up a much larger range of additional activities than skimming off a few pounds from union dues.

He handed in his notice, and one week later started work at his new office. Very soon steel fabrication firms in the area found that slipping Nobby a brown envelope every now and then ensured that they had no union problems when erecting buildings or adjusting shift patterns. The one or two that hesitated about this began to have strikes, go-slows and other labour troubles until the message sank in.

One cool spring day, after he'd had a couple of lunchtime pints and a pie with his mates in Rotherham Workingmen's Club, he was sitting in his small, gas-fire heated office with his feet on the desk reading *The Sun* when an article about a local man who had made a shedload of money caught his eye. He suddenly threw down the paper and sat silently for a couple of minutes.

Where are you going, Nobby, he thought to himself? *What do you really want out of life?* He reviewed his situation; his job was alright – not too taxing, but he wasn't going anywhere. The steel industry was consolidating. He was having to negotiate harder to preserve men's jobs or get adequate redundancy money.

Staying as a union official for the rest of his life seemed a dismal prospect at that moment. *Who am I? Nobody really! I make a reasonable living, and with what I can skim off the top, it gives me a week each year on the Costa Brava with the lads and a council allotment down the road – but is that the be-all and end-all of my existence?*

He answered his own question aloud. 'No it fucking isn't! There's thousands of people out there just waiting to be screwed, and thousands of others elbowing their way upwards, cutting deals and making money. I can do better than this so let's have a look at what other possible prospects there could be.'

Working his way further up the union hierarchy was out; union power was shrinking in the steel industry. There was no real future there for either obtaining power or making money. What else did he know? Not much, it turned out on reflection. What talents did he possess? He was tough, he was ruthless – both of which he concealed under a veneer of bonhomie. Politics was the only other route he could think of where these three attributes would be useful, and that might enable him to fulfil his ambitions.

He considered the runners and riders in the area. The local Labour MP for Sheffield Brightside was a young and enthusiastic thruster from North London – stiff collar and shiny shoes, already earmarked for a place in government, he would be difficult to dislodge. Pontefract and Wakefield

11

had two old sweats, both of whom were well established. Any case, they were a bit too far away from his stamping ground in the Don Valley. Then a spurt of excitement went through him. Of course, old Willie McArdle at Mexborough East could be the answer to his problem. He gave that some thought. Willie's local constituency party was based at Wath-on-Dearne Labour Club. That was within easy reach of Nobby's office and his home in Cadeby. He'd noticed Willie coughing and spluttering a few times at local functions and he must be pushing eighty. There could be a crack in that door that could be eased open. He flicked on his computer and looked up Willie McArdle on the net. It turned out Willie was seventy-seven; he'd been shot through the lungs in the Korean war and his last contribution to parliamentary debate had been eight years ago when he'd supported a miner's strike. Nobby frowned thoughtfully; Willie couldn't last that much longer, the next election was in three years and if he didn't fall off his perch before then he surely would retire at that time.

Young Tottie Teasdale brought in his afternoon mug of tea and put it on his desk with a flash of her cleavage. He gave her bottom a quick pinch and she squeaked 'Oh Mr Garside!' and grinned as she swayed out of the door provocatively. He pulled his thoughts back to Willie McArdle. The first thing to do was to transfer his membership from Rotherham Labour Club to Wath-on-Dearne. This was simple. His reason for moving was that the latter was much closer to his home for meetings. Nobby called Tottie back and drafted out a glowing testimonial letter to be sent by the secretary of the Rotherham Labour Club to the secretary of Wath.

His transfer was accepted and he duly turned up at the next meeting of Wath to a friendly welcome. Nobby was a hard and ruthless worker and, with his jovial air, it didn't take him long to manoeuvre himself into a key position as assistant secretary.

Willie McArdle was a decent old stick, a die-hard left-winger who'd never varied in his trust of the Labour Party. It was obvious that his lungs were giving him trouble so Nobby took him under his wing, ostensibly to look after him, but principally to ease him into a quiet retirement – one way or another. Initially there was a set-back to his plans: Willie told him he had no intention of retiring. This rocked Nobby back on his heels momentarily. He gave the matter considerable thought. As a result Willie was lined up to speak at various constituency and union meetings around South Yorkshire, all to be held in the evening in pit yards open to the weather in December, January and February. This turned out to be a waste of time because that winter's Asian flu epidemic solved Nobby's problem for him.

The by-election caught Labour's Central Committee on the hop and they sent a twenty-five year old public relations executive to be interviewed as the potential local candidate. He didn't stand a chance! He sat there in his Gieves and Hawkes suit, his Old Paulines tie, starched collar and loafers quoting figures dreamed up by Labour Party Central Office which just didn't relate to South Yorkshire. He was murdered by questions about local schools, coal-cutting machinery, miners' welfare, the staggeringly high local unemployment figures and attracting new business for the area.

'We want jobs in this area, squire, not a load of bloody statistics, so what would tha do about that lad, eh?'

'Ah, well I think we would seriously consider putting out a 'Green Paper' on unemployment in the North and incentivise the demographic to reflect the imbalance between regional hegemonies.'

'Would yer by 'eck? And how many bloody jobs would that create, eh? Thank you lad, that'll be all. Send in t' next candidate!' The public relations guy was shot out of the door and back on the London train before he could utter a protest.

The only other candidate was Norbert Garside.

'Na then, Nobby lad, tha knows what we need here,' said the chairman, a grizzled old steelworker, 'so what's tha going to do about it?'

Nobby gave them an explanation about regional assistance funds to create jobs and European Union money that, if he was elected, he would ensure was spent in depressed areas, of which South Yorkshire would be his primary focus.

'Tha knows me, fellers – when ah say ah'm going to do summat ah do it!'

Nobby's next problem was that he had also 'done it' to Tottie Teasdale. In fact, he had 'done it' to most of the secretaries at the Union offices, but Tottie was the one who apparently drew the most energetic sperm and was showing distinct signs of enlargement. When he was picked as the prospective candidate for Mexborough East with the certainty of becoming an MP, Tottie woke up to the fact and began to fancy herself as an MP's wife – so she put the squeeze on Nobby. She refused a termination or even to see a doctor; she 'just knew' who the baby's father was and threatened to sell her story to the 'meeja' if he didn't do the honourable thing.

At first he was furiously indignant, but on reflection he calmed down. She wasn't bad looking, she was a cheerful soul and a hard worker; he decided he 'could do worse'. It might help his career to be married – at least people wouldn't think he was queer. So Mr and Mrs Norbert Garside were spliced four weeks later at Wath Registry Office on the 3rd June, 2008.

On 10th June, 2008 Tottie Garside was diagnosed as having a pseudocyeis – a false pregnancy.

Nobby was not best pleased to say the least but, after a blazing row, eventually cooled down and began to see the positive side of things. There had been a worm of doubt nagging in his mind in the first place that he might not be the father. There were several contenders for the position – in fact a lot more than he was aware of. However, being married would help him in his constituency work and prevent rumours about his sexuality. On the positive side, it could be said without question that Tottie was an enthusiastic, if unaccomplished shag. Horizontal intercourse was unfamiliar to her; she was more used to a vertical arrangement in the alley, leaning up against a wall at the back of The Miner's Arms. However, she adapted to the more domestic positions with alacrity.

****

The returning officer strode to the rostrum, adjusted his spectacles, cleared his throat and with an appropriate sense of theatre, read from a single sheet of paper the number of votes cast for each candidate concluding, 'Norbert Arthur Garside is therefore duly elected Member of Parliament for the Mexborough East Constituency'.

There were cheers and flag waving from the small crowd in Mexborough Town Hall at two o'clock in the morning. Nobby was embraced by his now slim wife; the Conservative candidate gave a resigned smile and hoped he'd done enough to get a better, more right-wing constituency to challenge next time and the Liberal Democrat woman burst into tears as she realised that her deposit had gone up in smoke. National television didn't bother to cover the by-election, it being a foregone conclusion, and *The Mirror* gave it a small paragraph on some inner page next to an advert for 'Blastolax for Constipation'.

****

JUNE, 2008 – CITY OF YORK, ENGLAND

I turned off the A1 at Brotherton, and headed the MG TF towards Tadcaster on the A162 instead of continuing up the A1 as far as Bramham. Zoe wanted to see the site of the Battle of Towton which took place in 1461 between the Yorkists and the Lancastrians. She had read something in the paper that five skeletons had been dug up recently by a local farmer, and the local policeman, fed up with yet more old bones being stored in his garage until somebody decided what to do with them, had complained to the council.

I explained to her that Towton was the biggest and bloodiest battle ever to take place on English soil. Of the 50,000 participants, 28,000 were killed; they didn't take prisoners in those days. Relics of the battle were still being dug up to this day.

'Who won?' she asked.

I glanced down modestly at my finger nails. 'We did,' I told her.

She burst out laughing. 'What do you mean "*we* did"? That was six hundred years ago. You Yorkshiremen are impossible; no wonder Lancashire always beats you at cricket. You're still mentally carrying spears and wearing skins!'

'No they don't and we're not,' I replied, huffily.

There was very little to be seen at the site; it was a typical piece of rural England basking in the Saturday afternoon sun. Grassland and copses; it was very hard to picture thousands of demented, enraged men in a snowstorm slashing each other to pieces with swords and axes, and the stream meandering through the meadows running red with blood.

We arrived at my parents' house in time for tea. It was one of our twice yearly Moon family gatherings; Zoe and I were staying with my married sister, her husband Geoffrey and their little twin girls. My younger sister had come over from Liverpool where she was a nurse in a children's hospital and was staying with our parents. I liked my sisters, and although there was the usual banter, we got on well together. My mother was annoyed with me because I turned down her offer of accommodation, but I knew my mother – she would have insisted that Zoe and I had separate rooms. My sister was more broadminded and put us together with a cheeky warning that she'd oiled the bed-springs and not to frighten the children.

They had all met Zoe several times before so she slotted in very easily.

Whilst they all chattered away round the china teacups and cucumber sandwiches I slid away quietly into my father's study with my two little three-year-old nieces and taught them to shout a couple of rude words for use when they got home.

This was payback for the 'oiled bed-springs' remark.

We rejoined the mob just in time to hear my mother announce proudly to everyone that my father had been promoted to area manager of the bank. 'It's a great honour for him – and not before time I might add,' she said with a touch of acerbity.

'And,' my father chipped in, 'your mother has been elected ladies vice-captain at the golf club.'

Reflected glory flickered in the air – and was instantly extinguished. The self-satisfied looks on their faces were wiped off in a flash when little Emily suddenly stood up and shouted 'Bum!'

There was a short, stunned silence whilst this was digested, my mother reacted first, wagging a finger crossly at Emily and telling her that she shouldn't say naughty words like that, whereupon both the twins started to shout 'Bum! Bum! Bum!' at the top of their voices.

My mother glared at my sister and snapped. 'I don't know where they pick up such things, I really don't, but it's not in this house I can tell you!' Implying that it must be their home life that was at fault.

My sister glared at me because she knew.

'One all' I mouthed at her.

She switched off the glare and turned a sweet smile on to Zoe instead. 'You do realise that your boyfriend is an infant at heart, don't you Zoe? Unfortunately Marcus' behaviour has stayed at the age of five ever since he was five.'

Zoe looked puzzled; she had missed the 'in' situation.

'I assumed that all men stopped progressing at the age of five so what's different about Marcus?'

At this my sister became all defensive, concerned that Zoe might have got the wrong impression about her husband.

'Geoffrey's not, Geoffrey's responsible. He does the washing up, bathes the twins, goes down to the supermarket, even helps with the cleaning.'

'And earns the money,' I added. 'Don't forget that. So what do *you* do, sister mine?'

Before she could answer there was a cry of pain from the direction of the twins. She spun round ready to leap to the defence of whichever of them was being attacked, but seeing that it was one of them who had bitten Geoffrey for putting his hand over her mouth to stifle cries of 'Bum' and it was him calling out and hopping about clutching his thumb, she turned back to me, but was too late.

Geoffrey bundled the twins out of the room leaving my mother still holding the floor. My remark about earnings rekindled an old complaint from her.

'Marcus, I worry about you. Why don't you get yourself a proper job, like your father, instead of all this airy-fairy design and gadding about with foreigners and the like. No good will come of it, you'll see.'

I sighed, it was going over old ground yet again, but mother's are like that, aren't they? Once they get a bee in their bonnet it stays there.

'Mother, I have told you a thousand times I *have* got a proper job as you put it. I am a director of a large and reputable firm of consulting engineers working all over the world. For example, at this very moment we are working on a design for a $150 million port in the Indian Ocean—'

She cut me off. 'Yes, yes I know all that, but *who* pays your salary? The bank pays Daddy's and has always done so and always will, but who pays yours?'

'The firm does.'

'But it's *your* firm! How can you pay your own salary?'

It was no use; she'd never understand it, and I found her faith in banks touching. I just hoped they didn't live to regret it.

My father caught my arm. 'All this bloody tea makes me want to pee! D'you fancy a small Scotch to brace up the appetite before dinner? I wanted to have a word with you anyway.'

He led me back to his study where Geoffrey was trying to persuade the twins that 'bum' was a very naughty word, and by doing so was unwittingly convincing them to use it gleefully whenever possible. They were ejected and my father closed the door. He poured me a miniscule Scotch.

I grinned at him. 'Come on, Dad I'm not one of your customers, you can push the boat out a bit more than that! Well done about your promotion, by the way. That'll help the pension.'

He apologised with a rueful grin and topped up my glass. 'Force of habit you know.' He poured himself an equally stiff one. So this was to be a real heart-to-heart talk, was it? I guessed what it would be about and I was right.

'Your mother is very worried about your... er... arrangements.'

'Arrangements?'

'Yes, you know, with Zoe. We like her very much; she's a beautiful girl and we think she would be very good for you.'

'Would she?'

'Your mother thinks so.'

'Does she? And what do *you* think?'

'Yes, well I agree.'

'Do you?'

He gave me his practised bank manager's look, the sort of look a recalcitrant customer would get if he exceeded his overdraft limit by a pound for the second time.

'You're not making this easy, are you?'

I decided to put him out of his misery. My mother had obviously put him up to this and he was very half-hearted about it.

'Look Dad, Zoe and I are both grown adults; we know what we're doing and what we want for the future, but that's our business. If we have anything to tell, you and Mum will

21

be the first to know. Until then, we are blissfully happy together and see no reason why that cannot continue. Let's leave it at that.'

The relief that appeared on his face made me smile. I put my hand on his shoulder. For the first time I saw that behind this lay my parents' real concerns for their children's futures. Concerns they would like to be resolved so that they could settle down to a satisfying late middle and old age without worries about their offspring.

'Don't worry Dad, everything's fine, let's go and join the happy band.'

Sunday was to be the day of the big family lunch. My mother had made the Yorkshire pudding mix and left it overnight to do whatever it was supposed to do. The big joint of beef was being slow roasted in the oven and the ingredients for the beef and onion gravy prepared.

In the morning Zoe and I intended to go for a walk round the old walls of York, but after breakfast my mother said to Zoe, 'Would you like to see some photographs of Marcus when he was younger?'

There was danger here, I could sense it. 'No she wouldn't,' I said. 'We're going for a walk.'

'Yes I would!' Zoe contradicted. 'We have plenty of time for a walk later.'

So we sat round the coffee table, them to look at the photos, me to try to sensor anything embarrassing. This went on for half an hour whilst the women oohed and aahed over Marcus on a fur rug, Marcus in his training pants and

Marcus in the bath. 'You can see he has a funny little birthmark just there,' pointed out my mother.

'He still has it,' Zoe said, innocently. My mother gave her a sharp look and I had had enough.

I gathered up all the photos and put them back in their case. 'Right, time for our walk,' and I grabbed Zoe's arm and led her out of the house ignoring any protests about 'my hair, my make-up, my shoes.'

'It's chilly today, Marcus, are you wearing your vest?' Words that followed me into the distance from my mother as we headed off down the drive.

'I didn't know you wore a vest. I've never seen you in one?' Her eyes sparkled cheekily.

'Not since I was ten, then we had central heating put in. Let's change the subject!'

'For the moment,' she murmured and I had a very nasty feeling that 'Marcus on a fur rug' and 'Marcus being potty-trained' was going to be brought up at some future date.

She looked at me questioningly. 'Also, I didn't know CONDES had got a big port design job in the Indian Ocean?'

'Just a few days ago – well it's Hugo's job really, he's the port expert. It's only a preliminary study, but the government will appoint us to do the whole lot if they decide to allocate aid funds to it.'

'So you're not involved?'

'No way! It's on some insect-infested hell-hole in the Comorantes Islands, hundreds of miles from anywhere. He's welcome to it. It's not my cup of tea.

23

CHAPTER TWO

Nobby Garside was not really concentrating on the papers spread out on his desk. He was thinking about financial matters – *his* financial matters.

His small nest egg was accumulating in a Swiss bank account; moneys paid for asking questions in Parliament on behalf of businessmen; promoting various local industries and encouraging potential investments in South Yorkshire. Consultancy fees and speaking engagements had enabled him to raise a mortgage for a small flat in Pimlico. He had bought a couple of tailor-made suits, voted faithfully with his Party and put himself about a bit. In fact, it was that which was causing his brow to furrow at the moment.

As a result of toeing the party line he had been appointed to the Department for International Development as deputy chairman of the committee that approved British Government funding for overseas aid projects. It was the committee's job to decide which projects would get aid and which wouldn't. Naturally, there were many requests from poorer overseas countries for assistance. The list was long and the amount available limited, so a lot of research and investigation was required before decisions could be made.

Currently, one of the projects which had come before the committee was to provide the funding for a new port in the Comorantes Islands in the Indian Ocean. They were an ex-British colony that gained independence in 1985 and claimed they needed a deepwater port in order to develop their trade.

Nobby scratched his head as he read through the papers again. It was a large project, over $150 million was the estimate. The International Bank for Reconstruction and Development, known generally as The World Bank, could also be involved. The department would be in charge of managing the project and seeing the whole thing through. Any extra funding would go from the World Bank to the Department for International Development and from there to the Comorantes Government.

He noted that the department had appointed a British firm of consultants, CONDES, to carry out the initial studies which involved preparing an outline design and an estimate of cost. A report from civil servants confirmed that they were a very reputable firm based in London. *Hmm!* he thought, *there could be potential there for a tickle.* His problem was that all the money for the construction would go through the finance department of the DfID and thence to the Comorantes Government directly, without passing anywhere near his sticky fingers.

This was big money, and the problem that he was wrestling with was a simple one: how could he get his hands on even a small slice of the action? A slice of the consultant's fees would be nice, but a slice from the construction costs would be much more rewarding. That could really stiffen up his Swiss 'pension' fund.

Desmond Fitzpatrick, the chairman of the committee, was in favour of approving the funding for the Comorantes port. There was only that silly bitch Penelope Cattermole, a Liberal Democrat from some godforsaken Scottish island who rabbited on endlessly about poverty in 'The Horn of Africa', who was against it. She wanted to use the money to educate the fuzzie-wuzzies – give them clinics, clean water and schools.

Nobby resolved in his own mind that, of the several shortlisted projects, the Comorantes project was the most promising for bracing up the Garside coffers. It would be approved at the meeting next month. Cattermole would simply be sidelined as a dissenting vote. It was the big money that both excited and worried him at the same time. It was clear that the only place where he might be able to get his hands on some of it would be at the recipient's end, before the budget was frozen – and that, he concluded, meant going to the Comorantes in person if he was to get anywhere.

Back in his Westminster office later that day he returned to the subject. There were two possibilities: the Comorantes Government and/or the construction contractor who put in the successful bid. The latter would be tricky; he wouldn't know who that was until the bids had been opened and then it could well be too late to add on his slice. There was absolutely no chance that he could get round all the bidders before they put in their tenders – besides, he had no leverage there. No, the Comorantes Government must be the best bet; there must be somebody at the top of that who could be suborned. After all, he reasoned, everyone knew that everybody south of Dover was corruptible. Those foreign Johnnies thrived on it. He tapped his large teeth with his ballpoint. The only way to find out who it was and with what, was to go there and assess the situation personally and that would be an expensive trip if he had to finance it himself. He tapped his teeth again. Yes, there was a way. Perhaps, as a key member of the DfID Committee, it might be possible to swing the costs of a fact-finding mission to the Comorantes on to his expenses? He would have to clear it with the parliamentary watchdog first, but as deputy chairman of the DfID Committee he could present a compelling case. After all, if $150 million was going to be laid out for some godforsaken island, somebody from the British Government involved with the financing should go and assess the lie of the land.

Then he would sound out CONDES, the consultants for Port Mahon, to see if he could touch them for a few pounds for providing advice.

Nobby reviewed the situation. Yes, that was the way forward; to concentrate on the recipient of the funding – that was where the big money would be, and the only way to do that was face to face with the top people there. If he could swing it with the committee he would get Miss Harbottle to organise an all expenses paid fact-finding trip to the Comorantes to supposedly check whether or not they really needed a new port and whether the location proposed was suitable. She could fix him appointments with the

Prime Minister and other big cheeses, the guys who made the financial decisions. It was a good plan. He rubbed his hands together, CONDES momentarily forgotten.

Laetitia Harbottle was not a happy woman. Unmarried and pushing forty-five she was desperate for a mate. Over the three years she had worked for Nobby Garside and Bill Brown, a fellow MP with whom Nobby shared an office in Portcullis House, Westminster, she had developed a deep crush on Nobby and made her interest as plain as she felt was decent for somebody who lived in South Cheam within walking distance of the tennis club. Unfortunately for her he was a man with the subtle sensitivity of boiler plate. He had paid no attention to her timid advances and made coarse jokes to Brown about the size of her tits. When he laughed with Bill Brown she was convinced now that he was laughing at her behind her back. She felt slighted and scorned, but Nobby was oblivious to the signs. Her ample bosom heaved and her cheeks flushed. *Right you fat pig* she thought, *that was it!* In future she would just do her job. She would do exactly, and only, what she was asked to do, nothing more, nothing less.

'He can like it or lump it' she sobbed through her tears in her tiny bedsit on Montfort Road, as she poked a tofu salad round her plate and dabbed her eyes with a lace handkerchief that evening. So now the pig was planning some jolly to an island in the Indian Ocean and she was buggered if she was going to make life easy for him.

Thus, when Nobby got the nod from the Committee for his visit, she sent only the barest minimum of information about him to the Comorantes Government.

****

SEPTEMBER, 2008 – WESTMINSTER, LONDON

Nobby saw himself as an opportunist. *'The world is there to be grabbed lad; by the throat or by the balls. One or t'other, it don't matter which.'* That was what his constituency Party Chairman, had told him when he was first elected as an MP. It was a philosophy that had served him well to date.

After a satisfying lunch at Wilton's paid for by some little creep who wanted support for his application for a development grant to extend his meat pie business in Rotherham, Norbert Garside, Member of Parliament for Mexborough East, scratched his ample stomach, put his hands behind his head, stretched out his legs on his desk and blew out a blast of alcohol fumes for the air-conditioning to deal with. He supposed there could be a few quid in it for him if he supported the application, but was it worth the trouble? No, not really so fuck him – he was small beer! Norbert had bigger fish to fry these days than bother with a constituent's pathetic problems, and today was the day when the fat in the fryer could begin to heat up.

He savoured the moment with nervous anticipation. Today he was off to the Orient as the self-appointed official representative of Her Majesty's Government. He pictured the scene. He would be treated like royalty: the red carpet, the stretched limo, the excitement as the British Envoy arrived in the Big White Bird from The Great Queen across the sea to bestow favours on the natives – but only if the little buggers returned the favours, of course. A frisson of apprehension made him shiver; it was unknown territory for Norbert. He'd never been further than the Costa Brava before and, he recalled, even at just two hours flight from England the beer had been like gnat's piss, the chips had been soggy and he'd developed a nasty rash in the groin. However, this wasn't a beer-drinking trip, this was government business. He pulled himself together; a skilled negotiator like him would be more than a match for any little dark-skinned wallah on a small island somewhere in the Indian Ocean.

Miss Harbottle, had been instructed to notify the Comorantes Government of his imminent arrival. His air tickets – Business Class – and travel schedule had arrived yesterday and she confirmed that she had booked a taxi to take him to Gatwick Airport at 4.30pm later that day, so all was set. He checked the time on his chunky astronauts' watch – a flashy gift from The National Union of Metalworkers that told the phases of the moon and the time in Tokyo.

Swinging his feet round he stood up and stretched. It was time to go and make his fortune.

He carefully locked the drawers of his desk in the office and tested that each one was secure by giving it a little tug.

Office space in Portcullis House was scarce and those without a government job had to share. His companion Bill Brown, a fellow Labour MP, who also represented a northern constituency was out. Brown was a little ferret of a man with a nose like the saddle of a racing bike; Nobby suspected that Brown looked through all his papers and files whilst he was away. Not that there was anything suspicious in those drawers, or in the desk as a whole for that matter. Anything private that could be even slightly incriminating was all locked away in the safe concreted into the wall of the semi-detached house he shared with Tottie back in Yorkshire. There was only one key and that was safely kept amongst the bunch of keys on the ring chained to his belt. He touched it to make sure it was still there. It reminded him of something. He opened the office door and looked both ways down the long corridor. There wasn't a soul in sight. He walked swiftly across to Brown's desk and took out his bunch of keys. The key he had had made after Brown had carelessly left his keys lying on the desk one day when he slipped off to the lavatory, fitted the locked drawers perfectly. He always knew the piece of plasticine he kept on his desk would come in useful. A quick press and a perfect impression of the key had been made.

A shuffle through Brown's papers confirmed only what he knew about Brown already – that he was unimaginative voting fodder with a weird tendency towards girls in rubber suits. There was nothing else there of interest. No threat to Garside's ambitions – and Nobby had ambitions.

Disappointed, he gathered up his jacket, checked in his briefcase that his passport, ticket and wad of dollars was tucked safely in a pocket, picked up his suitcase and hit the door with hope in his heart and a firm intention to rip off as much as he could from the British taxpayer.

Nobby chuckled to himself in the taxi as he recalled Brown's reaction to his trip. The Comorantes Airways tickets and tube of sun cream had been lying on his desk, deliberately left in an obvious position where Bill Brown could see them.

'I don't know how you get away with it, Nobby!' Brown had whined, his long nose twitching like a mouse detecting a piece of ripe Cheddar. 'A bloody fact-finding mission to a paradise island? Pull the other one. The Parliamentary Watchdog'll have you over the coals for that matey.'

Nobby flashed his big teeth in a triumphant grin. 'I've already cleared it with the PW, Willy. It's for a potential DfID project – and, by the way, Laetetia doesn't think you've got another one. She doesn't actually believe you've got one in the first place!'

He knew Brown hated to be called Willy, and Brown's totally unsuccessful attempts to seduce Miss Harbottle rankled - particularly as she flirted openly with him. He chuckled again at the thought of Miss Harbottle fluttering her eyelashes and crying 'Oh Mr Garside, you are a one' when he told her one of his dirty jokes. She had no chance; to him she was as sexless as a cod fillet. He'd sooner give Brown one than her! Now young Charlotte Pennyfarthing with the big tits in Dennison's office – she was a different matter; he'd have to spend a bit more time working on her.

SEPTEMBER, 2008 – ST GEORGE'S,
THE COMORANTES ISLANDS

It had been agreed by the Parliamentary Watchdog that he could fly Business Class, but Business Class in one of Comorantes Airways tired old clapped-out Boeings on a twelve-hour night flight could not, by any stretch of the imagination, be said to be luxury travel. The advantage was the seats were cheap. They were also broken down. The webbing supporting Nobby's large backside had supported too many large backsides in the past and decided that enough was enough. As a result Nobby's rear-end was fifteen centimetres closer to the floor than his immediate neighbour in the adjacent seat, a large black lady dressed in some sort of flowing kaftan printed like Kew Gardens. The back of his seat could only be fixed in two positions; vertical or semi-reclining. When the meal came round Nobby's table was nearly level with his chin in the reclining position and rammed tight into his chest when the seat back was vertical. The food was inedible: king prawns that were still half frozen, stringy beef with congealed gravy, and melted ice-cream with jelly. Sleeping was fitful – 'Kew Gardens' ate all her meal, commandeered the central arm between their seats and then farted throughout the night.

It was a tired, sweaty, hungry and angry Norbert Garside who disembarked with relief into the enfolding heat of Eric de Verteuil Airport on Grande Rocques. He was intercepted on the tarmac by a young black man in a sharp cream linen suit with a shiny BMW official car. His passport and luggage were whipped away and he was ushered into the back seats.

'My name is Serge, I'm a personal assistant to Henri Coquelin, our President and Prime Minister. I trust you had a good flight, Mr Garside?' Serge had a soft Creole accent. His courtesy was wasted on Nobby.

'No, I fucking didn't! It was dreadful! I've never seen such a knackered old plane as that. It's the first time I've paid serious attention to the stewardesses' instructions about what to do if we bloody crash as it seemed more than likely that we would. I just want a good shower and a sound sleep.'

Serge was quite unperturbed. 'Ah well, we have ordered a new fleet of Airbus 330s, they should be delivered anytime soon.' He continued with a sharp look at Garside. 'You didn't give us much detail about your visit, Mr Garside. The Prime Minister is a very busy man, but he can squeeze you in for a few minutes at eleven prompt tomorrow morning at his office. I'll pick you up in the car.'

Nobby bridled at that. 'What do you mean "squeeze me in for a few minutes"? I'm an official representative of Her Majesty's Government come to do your government a big favour – or *not* as the case may be,' he added, nastily.

Serge smoothed things over hastily. 'Your office didn't make it absolutely clear about the purpose of your visit to us. No doubt when you have seen our Prime Minister all will be clarified. I have been delegated to make sure that you are comfortable and well looked after.'

This sounded a bit better; so, somewhat mollified, Nobby allowed himself to be escorted into the lobby of the Fisherman's Wharf Hotel where he was reunited with his passport and luggage, shown up to a comfortable room, given a complimentary bottle of Comorantes Chardonnay and left to his own devices. The view from his window encompassed the hotel swimming pool and the pool encompassed half a dozen attractive girls in skimpy swimsuits stretched out on sun beds. From their travel bags they were stewardesses from some eastern airline on lay over. Nobby felt his interest rising; Mrs Tottie Garside back in the cold and damp of 'Mineanders', 14 Scargill Avenue, Cadeby, didn't compare favourably with these young nymphs cavorting before his libidinous eyes.

Still that was for another day. He was dog tired and his back was as stiff as a board from the uncomfortable seat. All he wanted now was a hot shower and a good sleep.

Next morning he woke early, had another shower and then cursed when he realised that his suit was still unpacked in his suitcase. He tried unsuccessfully to sponge out some of the creases without much success so turned up for breakfast looking a rumpled figure. Serge left him kicking his heels in the hotel lobby, arriving twenty minutes later than the scheduled time. So it was an irritated, uncomfortable Nobby who was deposited at the Prime Minister's office at twenty past eleven. It was an even more irritated Nobby who was shown through into the Prime Minister's personal office at ten past twelve, having waited in an ornate anteroom with nothing to do for fifty minutes.

The Prime Minister half-rose from his chair behind a huge desk, stretched out a casual hand and gave Nobby's fingers a brief press as though flushing a lavatory on Tangiers railway station.

'Good day Mr Garside, I am Henri Coquelin, please take a seat and tell me what we can do for you.' Wiping his fingers on a starched white handkerchief and glancing significantly at a large gold Rolex on his thin wrist he indicated a chair round a small coffee table and took a similar chair himself. No refreshment was offered.

Coquelin was a small dark wiry man dressed in an immaculately cut cream linen suit, sharp shirt and striped tie. His mouth showed white, even teeth in a smile that didn't spread to his dark, glittering eyes. The rimless spectacles gave him a sinister look. His morning had not gone too well so he wasn't disposed to waste more than a few minutes on this scruffy slob. The Comorante riyal had been under pressure and he was late for a business lunch lined up with an important American investor whose eighty-metre yacht had just berthed in St George's Harbour. He didn't want to spend time on this nobody who was obviously here for a jolly. He didn't attempt to conceal his impatience. There was no apology for keeping Nobby waiting; a little small talk just to be polite. 'Did you have a good journey?' and 'I trust we have made you comfortable?' Then it was straight to the point.

'I understand from your office that you are a Member of the British Parliament, so what do you want with me? Your girl indicated something about Port Mahon, although what that has to do with a British Socialist MP escapes me for the present. No doubt you will enlighten me in due course?'

Nobby Garside was stunned by this off-hand treatment. Didn't this little wog realise who he was and why he was there? He barely managed to curb the surge of anger that swept through him. He cursed under his breath, as it dawned on him that his preparation in setting up this meeting had been negligently scanty. He didn't realise *how* scanty, but it was clear that Laetetia Harbottle had dropped him right in at the deep end. He really had imagined he would be treated like royalty, his way strewn with flowers, his brow wafted with palm fronds and his every command obeyed. It wasn't like that at all, and, from the way Coquelin kept looking at his watch and the door, he realised that if he didn't do or say something very quickly he'd find himself skating down the corridor on his ear to the open air.

'Money, Prime Minister!'

This got the PM's immediate attention. He frowned. 'Money? What do you mean money?' The dark eyes flickered angrily as he wondered if Garside was going to touch him up for the loan of a few riyals; he had that sleazy look about him.

Nobby seized the opening. 'You have applied to the British Government for financial aid to construct a new port.' Nobby put it as a statement of fact not a question.

He continued. 'I am deputy chairman of the Department for International Development's committee that decides whether or not we allocate funds to any specific overseas project based on a variety of considerations. We then advise the World Bank whether we consider the proposal is a good investment or not. I am here to gather information to enable the committee to evaluate the risk/return ratio regarding your request for funding.' *In other words sunshine*, he added under his breath, *to decide whether or not you get the fucking money.*

Coquelin's heart nearly stopped. He gulped and blinked. Oh shit! He had totally misread the situation. He was not slow on the uptake; this was the man who could potentially make him millions and he had treated him as if he was an irritating dirty postcard vendor promoting his sister's virtue in the stews of Khartoum.

Stick that in your snotty little pipe and smoke it, Nobby thought smugly at the look of horror on Coquelin's face. He eased his fat bottom more comfortably into his chair. *That's stopped the cocky little bleeder in his tracks.* The horror was rapidly replaced by a smooth blandness as the fact that he had committed a massive diplomatic *faux pas* sank in. The back pedalling that followed was worthy of a one-wheel trick cyclist trying to fend off a wasp.

'I'm terribly sorry, Mr Garside; you caught me at an unfortunate moment. We have had some serious problems with Somali pirates around our waters threatening our fishermen and I'm afraid that they have been on my mind. Your office didn't make it precisely clear what the purpose of your visit was otherwise I, myself, would have received you at the airport and accommodated you in Government House. Anything, but anything we can do to help we will provide, of course. I'll have your things brought over immediately.'

Nobby thought of the air stewardesses splashing about in the hotel pool and thought that, even though Government House might be able to lay on some classy crumpet, it would be too restricting and he would be beholden to them before he had tested the waters for his deal. Anyway, it wouldn't be a bad idea to keep this arrogant wog at arm's length and on the back foot – to mix a metaphor horribly – until he had sussed out the lie of the land.

He held up a restraining hand. 'No thank you Prime Minister, the Fisherman's Wharf is very comfortable and we wouldn't want any suggestions of collusion being made, would we? The UK Parliament has become very touchy about things like that these days.'

Disappointment showed on Coquelin's face as his hastily proffered olive branch was rejected. They were well versed in softening up foreign dignitaries. Anna Lemartine would have screwed this big loud Englishman into a state of pliable quivering jelly prior to the opening of negotiations about funds for the port. He threw in his next offer.

'I assume you're with us for a few days to assess the viability of our proposed new port? Why don't I give you a typical Comorantes meal this evening and then we can have tomorrow morning to go through any points you wish to raise? We have some wonderful Creole cooking and wine on the islands; you must sample it before you return.'

He attempted an encouraging smile which was wasted on Nobby. 'My personal chef is a wizard, I suggest we reconvene at Government House at 7.30 this evening, if that suits you, and I'll ask my Minister for Ports and Harbours to attend?'

Nobby set aside thoughts of wet capering crumpet temporarily – that could come later; but after money and sex, food loomed large in the Garside menu of pleasurable activities. If this little squirt thought he could drink Nobby under the table he was in for a surprise. Nobby was famous for sinking fifteen pints of John Smith's Best Bitter at the Dinnington Miner's Welfare one New Year's Eve and still being able to ride his bike four miles home.

He nodded acceptance. 'Aye, alright then.'

'My driver will collect you from the hotel.' Coquelin stood up and offered his whole hand this time, which Nobby shook, and the next minute he was in the car on his way back to his hotel.

To his dismay the stewardesses had gone from the swimming pool and been replaced by large shapeless women in large shapeless swimming kits accompanied by even larger men who looked as though they had been hewed from the Siberian permafrost. They barked at each other in a Slavic language and displayed AEROFLOT on their travel bags. Russians, he thought to himself – nothing doing there. Disappointed he wandered into the bar, found himself a quiet corner and ordered a double brandy to think.

The question was how could he get his hands on a chunk of the aid funds that would be allocated for this project? That was the reason for his being here, but there were problems. The first being that he was not familiar with the mechanisms by which aid money was paid to, and distributed by, recipient governments. It was very unlikely that the Department for International Development would just hand over a big cheque and then fade away into the sunset. Secondly, he knew that CONDES, the consultants his Ministry had appointed to design this port, were also doing a report on costs – but that was just an outline figure to give some idea of the magnitude for assessing the viability. He assumed that the final costs would only be determined after bids for the construction had been analysed and a contractor chosen. It slowly dawned on him that until he found out a lot more about the way these things were arranged he was not only not going to get anywhere, but was going to look foolish and naive if he tried. All he could do was dangle some bait and see if the big fish sniffed at it.

Funnily enough that was almost exactly what Henri Coquelin was thinking. Garside had caught him on the hop by turning up virtually unannounced as the man who made the big decision about Port Mahon. Maybe Garside was cleverer than he appeared and had done that deliberately. That was why he'd shot him out of the office quickly before he could start to ask awkward questions and show up Coquelin's ignorance – and maybe force answers from him that he didn't want to be committed to. All that could be done at this stage was to give reassurance to ensure the project proceeded and probe Garside's character and conscience to see what he was morally made of. Anna Lemartine was still a card to be held in reserve. That comment about the UK Parliament being touchy could be taken as a positive sign that Garside was not averse to a sweetener arrangement - provided it was discreet, otherwise why mention it? But care would have to be taken.

He pressed his fingertips together and leant back in his chair thinking. The idea for a new deep-water port had originated from Phillipe Rouget, the Minister for Ports and Harbours. The Cabinet had agreed that it would be of benefit to the Islands, and for approaches to be made to see if it could be financed. There was no possibility of the Comorantes Islands putting up the money themselves, but they could make a good case for foreign aid. At present all cargo and ship passengers entered and exited the Islands through the small harbour at St George's but this could only accommodate ships up to 16,000 tons. If they had a deep-water port, not only would they be able to bring in the larger container ships, but there would be a lucrative spin-off to the Islands' tourist industry by providing berths for the bigger cruise liners. There could be other benefits as well. He chewed a fingernail thoughtfully as he recalled his private discussions with Rouget. Garside's arrival in St George's, with his revelation that he would play a key role in the funding, had caught him out. If they were to achieve what they wanted very careful handling was required, and it would be fatal to get off on the wrong foot. He reached for the phone.

'Get me the Minister for Ports and Harbours on his private line.' He tapped his fingers impatiently on his desk whilst he awaited the connection.

'Phillipe, get yourself over here as soon as possible. I can't talk on the phone, but bring all the files on Port Mahon – and clear your diary for this evening.' He terminated the call before Rouget could raise objections.

Rouget scowled at the phone and the peremptory order but decided, from the tone of the President's voice, it couldn't be ignored so he offloaded Florence, pulled up his trousers and went into his private bathroom to smarten himself up.

****

'Right Phillipe, talk me through the Port Mahon deal again.'

Rouget took a sip of his Scotch and narrowed his eyes. 'Is this to do with that guy who's come over from London? I told Serge to look after him. He's lodged him in Fisherman's Wharf.'

'Yes I know; he came to see me this morning. We've made a fucking a cock-up there. He's not just a minor politician on a freebie, he's the guy who's going to decide whether or not we get financing for our port – or rather his committee is, but he says he's the deputy chairman. I apologised for not meeting him personally and gave him some flannel about Somali pirates being on my mind. The important thing is he's coming to dinner in Government House this evening and you and I have got to butter up the sod so he goes back and reports favourably.'

'What's he like?'

'Hard to tell. He seems a bit crude, but it could be an act. His suit looked as if it had been knocked up in Mombassa by a one-armed cane-cutter, and he'd slept in it. I got rid of him before he started asking questions with the promise that we'd meet this evening, so we'd better get our story straight before then.'

Rouget took another sip of his drink and flicked open the thick file he'd brought with him.

'Starting at the beginning, you will recall that I drew up a proposal for a new deep-water port for the Islands. The government approved the idea in principle but made it clear that we didn't have the funds to finance the whole thing ourselves. We commissioned Australian consultants to examine various sites and do a report recommending the most suitable. After hydrographic surveys they selected Beauregard Island and prepared a basic layout plan. We submitted this to the British Government and requested that the Department for International Development approve it in principle and appoint consultants to prepare a design and cost plan for the port and associated infrastructure. They appointed the British firm CONDES to do this work, but the costing for the infrastructure, access roads, housing, offices, power and water supply was kept separate from the actual port costs at our request. We said we would price that element using Island contractors and labour to give employment to our people.'

He glanced at Henri Coquelin whose dark eyes flashed knowingly behind his spectacles.

'So what is the current situation Phillipe?'

'We know that CONDES have priced the port at $119m. My department has priced the infrastructure at $25m – rounded up to, say $30m ...' He gave a knowing smirk. '.... And then there's administration and ancillaries – what do you think - another $3m? Nobody but us knows about our figures yet.'

Coquelin stroked his chin. 'Yes, that has a healthy margin built in.' He gave his thin smile and continued. 'Incidentally I had lunch with Kory Kronoff on his yacht today; he's hot for leasing Tern Island and building an exclusive holiday development. He says he's got investors queuing up to put money in; other Americans, Arabs and South Africans. You and I are getting a slice, naturally, but if we put in some cash as well we could end up with a fantastic investment, so we've got to convince Garside about Port Mahon.'

'Is he "persuadable"?'

Coquelin shrugged his thin shoulders. 'Don't know. It's tricky, but if I had to come down on one side or the other I would say he was bent. We can't afford to get it wrong though. It could blow the whole deal.'

'So what are you going to do?'

'Slowly slowly catchee monkey!'

'Probe him, eh?'

Coquelin nodded. 'Let's see if alcohol can loosen his tongue.'

CHAPTER THREE

SEPTEMBER, 2008 – ST GEORGE'S,
THE COMORANTES ISLANDS

'May I introduce His Excellency Phillipe Rouget, our Minister of Ports and Harbours. Phillipe please meet The Honourable Norbert Garside, Member of Parliament for Her Britannic Majesty's Government.'

They shook hands. Nobby eyed Rouget up as though he was inspecting a dubious fillet of monkfish on a fishmongers slab in Rotherham. Rouget was not an impressive figure on first acquaintance, being a small, narrow-shouldered man with a weak chin poorly disguised by a scrubby dark beard. His eyes flicked about without focussing on anything for very long. Nobby decided he could eat him for breakfast. Rouget's black wiry hair had a touch of grey, and brown liquid eyes momentarily returned his study and then returned to wandering over the room. There was a strong whiff of cheap scent about him; his hands were delicate with slender fingers, but his grip as he accepted Nobby's handshake was surprisingly strong. Nobby put him down as a ladies man but somebody to be careful about. Coquelin guided both of them to comfortable chairs on an open veranda with a magnificent view of the sun setting over the sea in a clear blue and indigo sky on the western horizon. A cooling breeze produced a gentle rustling from the leaves on the overhanging palm trees.

'Have you ever seen the green flash Mr Garside?'

Nobby shook his head – not only had he never seen it he'd never heard of it. Coquelin continued. 'It doesn't happen every time, the sky must be absolutely clear of clouds and when the last fragment of the sun drops down over the horizon the whole sky can flash bright green, just for an instant.'

'Really?' The only flash Nobby had seen recently had been a quick glimpse of Laetetia Harbottle's formidable underwear when she crouched down to pick up a dropped file. That had put him off flashes for a long time.

A white-jacketed steward eased up quietly and stood waiting.

'What would you like to drink Mr Garside?' enquired Coquelin raising an eyebrow.

'I don't suppose you've got John Smith's on draught here squire? Got a throat like a bill-poster's bucket, I could do a pint of that.'

The steward shook his head apologetically. 'We have a very good local beer sir, Comoro Special if you would like to try that?'

Nobby scratched his head; it was more than likely it would be another foreign fermentation that would taste like gnat's piss, but he didn't want to upset Coquelin so he nodded acceptance and said he'd try a small glass.

Coquelin ordered a mojito and Rouget a dry Martini.

Rouget drew Nobby's attention to the sun. 'Watch carefully, you could see the green flash any second now.'

47

Nobby stared hard at the brilliant orange ball as it slowly sank into the sea, but the strain of keeping his eyes open and fixed on the bright orb eventually caused him to blink.

'There!' cried Rouget. 'Did you see it? That was a good one.' But Nobby had had his eyes closed doing his blink and saw nothing.

'Yeah, brilliant,' he lied.

The steward eased up again with a silver salver holding the drinks. The mojito looked mouth-watering in a frosted glass with a sprig of mint: the Martini was also in a chilled glass with an olive on a stick. Beside them was a small plain glass half full of a pale liquid and half full of froth. The liquid had bubbles rising from the bottom. Nobby took it and waited for the froth to settle. It didn't. The other two sipped their drinks whilst Nobby continued waiting. Eventually he could wait no longer. It was either blow off the froth or end up with a nose full of it. He decided to blow and walked to the edge of the veranda. Night falls very quickly in the tropics and by now it was quite dark. At first he didn't notice the Prime Minister's shiny BMW parked beneath the veranda until the froth splattered all over its windscreen.

'Oh shit! Are those your wheels down there PM? I've just named it the good ship Coquelin. Ha! Ha! Ha!'

Nobody else laughed.

He slid back to his chair unabashed and took a tentative swig of the beer. He grimaced. It *was* gnat's piss, how could they drink this chemical muck? He was beginning to have doubts about Port Mahon. This overseas business wasn't what he'd expected at all. It was hot, humid, the beer was frothy crap, the people small and dark and they had no sense of humour. He was starting to sweat; he eased his collar and reviewed his situation. There were other countries and projects that needed grants. Perhaps they would be more amenable with better beer. He settled into a morose sulk.

Coquelin was a shrewd politician and he sensed the change in Garside's mood.

'Pierre!' he called. 'Get our guest another drink; a proper drink this time and take that stuff away. Comoro Special is only fit for coolies. What about a large ice-cold gin and tonic with freshly squeezed home grown lime Mr Garside?'

Nobby wished he'd thought of something like that before and nodded.

The drink arrived quickly in a tall frosted glass. Nobby took a long pull and it slid down his dry throat like liquid silk. Things began to look up.

'Right,' said Coquelin, 'do you have a plan Mr Garside? Is there anything specific you would like to see? Phillipe will show you our present port and you will realise why we need a new bigger one. He can take you to Beauregard Island, but quite frankly there's not much to see there at present. The best thing would be to fly there in my helicopter and you can get an overview from the air. We can go through the costings tomorrow morning - I expect you are personally interested in those.' He put a slight emphasis on 'personally' and gave Nobby a questioning look.

Nobby twitched. Was this a 'come-on' for some sort of deal? Nobby couldn't be sure so didn't respond, but a little surge of adrenalin went through his body.

Coquelin, slightly disappointed at the lack of response, changed tack and addressing Nobby said, 'Tell me about the workings of your government, it is of deep interest to us to learn how the Mother of Parliaments functions? Do you have consensus government or conflicting government? You have political parties, because as you yourself have told us, you are a socialist MP but, for example, if your party supports our proposal for Port Mahon would the other parties object to that?'

It never occurred to Nobby that he was being patronised; Coquelin knew perfectly well how the British Parliament worked. He was just building up Garside's ego.

Nobby shook his head. 'No that wouldn't happen. The Committee of which I'm deputy chairman is an all-party committee; whatever we agree is acceptable to Parliament as a whole.'

Coquelin affected surprise. 'You have a very responsible job then, a job that carries with it a lot of power if you can accept or reject projects costing millions and the whole government acts on your say so.'

Nobby tightened his jaw muscles and narrowed his eyes as he tried to look adamantine and inscrutable. 'Well, we have to make some tough decisions and it's not easy. There are many things I have to take into consideration.'

'Indeed! I'm sure there must be.'

There was a short silence whilst drinks were sipped and assessments made. Nobby felt quite pleased with himself that he had managed to re-emphasise to these guys the power he had to accept or reject their pet project. Perhaps that would promote an offer?

Impassively, Coquelin surveyed Garside over the top of his mojito. He took in Nobby's creased linen jacket, cheap trousers, tight shirt collar with its strained button and badly knotted tie, and was thinking that Garside was painting a picture of what he would like to be, not what he was. He had Garside pegged now as a vulgar ambitious pusher but the question was, was he bent? That was what he wanted to know. Clearly he was ambitious, but equally clearly from his dress and the manner of his arrival, he didn't have the means to promote his ambitions. In which case he was vulnerable. In Coquelin's view every man had his price; he wondered what Garside's was.

He glanced at Rouget for his take on the situation, but Rouget was away with the fairies at that moment, wondering if the purple underwired bra and thong with matching boots he had mail-ordered from Madame Giselle of Paris, would actually fit Florence's vast body, or should he increase the size to XXL?

He left all the negotiations over money to Coquelin. Henri didn't welcome third-party interruptions when he was trying to establish an 'arrangement' so his dreamy look was not much help.

Coquelin frowned and continued, 'Does every MP get the same basic salary? For instance do you get adequately rewarded for sitting on committees or chairing discussion groups and scrutinising draft legislation with all the additional responsibility?'

This caught Nobby in two minds; he had to convince them that he was politically powerful but that he was open to some assistance with his pension. He checked his reply, was this the right strategy? If they thought he was hard up they may only offer him a pittance on the grounds that he would be satisfied with anything. If they thought he was wealthy, then they would have to come up with something substantial to influence him. He cursed himself for taking a cheap flight out here and for not bringing his best suit. These two guys were immaculately turned out and there was no doubt that he was at a sartorial disadvantage. The thing to do was to play the part of a politically powerful, not very wealthy eccentric. Blowing the froth on Coquelin's car had been a shrewd, if opportune move in that direction.

Nobby explained that you did get extra income for carrying out additional duties. He added that he received a basic salary of about £60,000 per year. It was not much but 'covered the basics'. He also received expenses to run an office, pay for a small staff and cover his travel costs, 'but money was tight. Cabinet Ministers and Chairmen of Select Committees were paid extra in addition to their basic salary as an MP: this could add somewhere between £12,000 and £60,000 to their income.' He also added, as if it were an afterthought, that as deputy chairman of the Department for Overseas Investment he didn't get any extras other than increased travel expenses to cover his costs – like this visit to the Comorantes. He had to pay tax on his income and contribute towards a pension scheme, which he described as 'mediocre'.

'You would like a bigger pension scheme eh, Mr Garside?' It was asked with a smile that didn't reach Coquelin's dark eyes.

'Too right Prime Minister, wouldn't we all?'

'Henri, please, call me Henri. After all, this is an informal conversation between friends.'

The white-jacketed steward slid in to announce that dinner was served and put the remains of their drinks on a silver tray which he carried through to the dining room.

They sat at one end of a long table, Coquelin at the head with Nobby on his right and Rouget on his left. The dining room in Government House was a beautiful, high-ceilinged room with slowly rotating electric fans. The chandeliers were crystal, and round the light-coloured painted wood walls were portraits of old Governor Generals and the two Presidents who had preceded Coquelin. The silver gleamed on the table and the beautifully cut glassware glinted in the light from the candles.

Nobby sat back, this was more like it – he could get a taste for this sort of thing. It put the shepherd's pie dinners at Wath-on-Dearne Labour Club in the shade. They'd never in a month of Sundays believe that old Nobby Garside from Maltby was sitting down to dine in such luxury with a President and an Excellency.

Coquelin was saying, 'There's been some trouble about Members of Parliament claiming too much on their expenses, hasn't there? I seem to have read something about that. Did it affect you?'

Nobby blinked. He wasn't sure what the purpose of this question was. If he said yes, then it would demonstrate that he wasn't averse to a bit of fiddling on the side but, as he had managed to avoid being named in any of the wrongdoings and he said no, it might be taken that he was too honest to consider any offers that he hoped might come along.

He tapped his nose knowingly. 'What the eye don't see the heart don't grieve Henri.'

It was Coquelin's turn to blink at this pearl of wisdom. It left him none the wiser about Garside's flexibility in financial matters. He still had no idea whether Garside could be 'encouraged' to support the aid package and the nose-tapping threw him off balance completely. Was the nose-tapping a way of suggesting that a packet of the best Colombian cocaine was the way to cement Garside's agreement? If so that could be arranged; he supposed the police or customs would have a packet or two stashed away somewhere that he could get hold of. But again, if he'd read the signs incorrectly and Garside interpreted the gift as an indication that the politicians of the Comorantes were nothing but drug peddlers forever stuffing coke up their noses, it may harm the government's case for being granted financial aid. He examined Garside's face; his nose showed no signs of being ravaged by drugs. In fact it was a very large fleshy nose, complete in all respects. It crossed Coquelin's mind that with a nose that size, if it was cocaine he was after then two packets would have to be the minimum.

Conscious of Coquelin's piercing scrutiny of his face Nobby thought he must have developed a hanging bogey and surreptitiously rubbed his nose with the back of his hand. Nothing! He was now in an embarrassing quandary. He could hardly sit at the dining table in front of these two important people doing some nose-tunnelling to check if the problem was inside, so he dragged out a none-too-clean handkerchief and gave his nose a good blast. He took the gamble of not examining the result and pushed the handkerchief back into his pocket.

Coquelin was even more mystified by the rubbing of the nose with the back of the hand. What the hell did that signify? Did he want a noseful now so he could vacuum it up off the back his hand?

Nobby looked at the bewilderment on Coquelin's face and tried to think what else could be causing the problem. The thing to do was to go to the bathroom where he could check his face in a mirror.

He climbed to his feet. 'Sorry gents, got to go to the lav. Need to "point the prick". Which way is it?'

A white-jacketed servant guided him out of the room and down the corridor.

Coquelin reeled back. So it wasn't cocaine it was heroin he was into, and he'd just announced that he needed a needleful in the arm and gone out to give himself one in the Government House bathroom. He turned to Rouget.

'What do you make of that Phillipe?'

'What?'

'Garside! Do you think he's on drugs?'

Rouget's eyes widened in astonishment. 'Why? Do you think he is? He seems normal enough to me, just rather coarse.'

Coquelin nodded. 'Yes, I suppose so. Let's just play it cool.'

When Nobby returned, having satisfied himself that he was still the debonair Nobby he imagined himself to be, Coquelin resumed his probing without a flicker of a smile.

'As a prominent MP you must have a huge number of contacts. This must create opportunities for introducing politicians and business people to each other: a very useful ability and presumably rewarding?' Coquelin noted the flash of greed in Garside's eyes at the mention of 'rewarding'.

Nobby was relieved that Coquelin had changed the subject; this was something he could handle without any problems, and reward had now been mentioned. Maybe this opened the door.

'You're right there, Henri. A few outside consultancies covering that sort of thing are very welcome to stiffen up the old living expenses.'

'And the pension? We might be able to help...' Coquelin floated it out casually.

Nobby gulped. This could be it – and he couldn't see any harm in agreeing to that if it wasn't.

'Aye Henri, that always needs stiffening up – like summat else, eh Phillipe!' He gave a filthy grin towards Rouget. Rouget flushed, embarrassed because he thought that his face had betrayed his Florentine imaginations.

Coquelin nodded thoughtfully. We're nearly there, he reflected. One more little push and we've got him.

'Perhaps we can discuss how we can be of mutual assistance tomorrow morning Norbert. Now let us concentrate on this special dinner I've had prepared for you. The first course is our local *Pwason Sale*. It's a dry salty fish, a little like anchovies, a rare delicacy. After being dried in the sun it is marinated in brine.'

Nobby, adrenaline surging, surveyed the unappetising grey strips floating in brine put in front of him. The smell was powerful. He could detect it even when he leant back in his chair. He was conscious of two pairs of eyes watching him as he cut off a small piece and began to chew it. And chew it he did; he couldn't seem to break it down to enable him to swallow it. It was like shoe leather, the taste was very strong and very fishy. He managed to gulp it down whole without choking and pushed the rest away.

'A bit too strong for my taste Henri. I like my fish deep fried in batter with chips.'

Coquelin gave a thin smile. 'It is an acquired taste I agree, but never mind I'm sure you'll like the next course. It is our chef's speciality. It's a curry made with masala, hot chillies, spices and fresh coconut cream.'

The waiter removed the *Pwason Sale* and placed a pile of steaming rice in front of Nobby. He rubbed his hands together in anticipation. 'There's nowt better in my view than the good hot chicken masala you get down at the Mexborough Taj Mahal.'

The waiter ladled a healthy portion of a thick, deceptively light coloured curry with lumps in it over the rice. It smelt delicious and Nobby's mouth began to water.

'What is it? Chicken?'

Rouget laughed. 'No, you can only catch these creatures in the mountains on Bienvenue Island. It's the intestines of pregnant fruit bats.'

Nobby felt his gorge rise at the thought of eating curried foetuses and took a quick drink of his wine to steady himself.

'Bats? You mean those blood-sucking flying rats?'

'I assure you that they are very tasty if prepared properly, and my chef is an expert' Coquelin added, smoothly. 'Try it! It's a traditional, very hot, Comorantes recipe.'

Nobby overcame his repugnance and, determined to show that he was a man of the world, loaded a large forkful into his face. Unfortunately, he had overlooked one thing – amongst the ingredients Coquelin listed were hot chillies. No sooner had he begun to chew when the chillies struck with full force. It wouldn't have mattered whether he was eating roast swan or jellied sea slug, he wouldn't have tasted anything. He had never known such agony. His face turned bright red, his eyes bulged and sweat stood out on his large nose. He grabbed his wine glass and sank the lot in one go, then he snatched Rouget's glass and drank that as well, but the pain grew worse. He was torn between spitting out the mouthful or trying to swallow it. He went for the swallow. A big mistake; his throat felt as though he'd swallowed razor blades.

Coquelin ordered the steward to bring water fast whilst Nobby tried to suck as much cool air as he could into his mouth. Rouget was intrigued. He'd heard the expression "gasping like a fish" but had never seen anybody actually doing it before.

The water arrived and offered a few moments relief allowing Nobby to gasp out 'Blood and sand, Henri are you trying to kill me?' before the burning sensation returned.

Coquelin paled as he envisaged his new port and the other benefits high-tailing it over the horizon. He clicked his fingers. 'Bring those crushed bananas mixed with coconut milk quickly – that should relieve the pain.' The steward disappeared and returned with a bowl filled to the brim. Nobby shovelled it into his mouth as fast as he could.

Slowly his normal colour returned, the sweat ceased pouring down his face and he began to relax on his chair.

'Christ on a crutch, what the hell is that stuff?' he croaked glaring at both of them.

'Well you said you liked a hot curry and I did warn you.'

'Well I can't eat anymore of that, it's bloody torture,' he growled, pushing the plate to one side. 'Can't you just do me a steak?'

The steward nodded, shimmied out and Coquelin breathed a sigh of relief. The rest of the dinner passed with a sulky Nobby silently eating his steak and drinking frequent draughts of water whilst the two Comorantians ate the bat curry without any problems. Coquelin and Rouget needn't have worried about Nobby's reaction; there was no way Nobby was going to take his ball home now.

His eyes lit up and the sulks evaporated when a large bottle of Delamain cognac and a balloon glass were put in front of him. As the level in the bottle slowly dropped Coquelin watched for signs of weakness, but Nobby was much too hard-headed to let three quarters of a bottle of brandy affect him. Although Coquelin and Rouget accompanied him on the wine they ended up more smashed than Garside. So it was a friendly relaxed farewell at two in the morning when Nobby eventually loaded himself into Coquelin's BMW and Serge drove him back to the hotel.

CHAPTER FOUR

SEPTEMBER, 2008 – ST GEORGE'S,
THE COMORANTES ISLANDS

Next morning a lively, fully bacon-and-egged Nobby met with a hung-over Coquelin and a pasty-faced Rouget at the Prime Minister's office prior to Nobby being taken on his tour of the port. Over strong black coffee and dismayingly cheerful replies to polite enquiries about Nobby's health, Coquelin opened the proceedings.

He decided not to beat about the bush; Garside had confirmed last night that he was open to 'an arrangement for his pension' and so now it was time to hold his feet to the fire.

Swallowing down some bile he began. 'Our application is not complete yet is it Norbert? At the moment we have made an application in principle, your Department has approved it and asked consultants to do an outline design in association with Phillipe's Ports and Harbours. This part has now been priced.'

Nobby confirmed that was so.

'The next step is for a detailed cost plan to be produced which includes *all* anticipated costs and charges – including the Comorantes Government's costs for all the supporting infrastructure and ancillary expenses?' He raised a questioning eyebrow at Garside and looked him straight in the eye.

This was the crunch point. If Garside questioned the "ancillary expenses" it closed that particular door. If he didn't then these, as yet unrevealed expenses were obviously open for discussion and manipulation.

Nobby felt a surge of excitement; he wasn't stupid. He now knew in his bones where this was going. These guys were going to use "ancillary expenses" to rip off some of the funds by hiding them in the government costs. The problem was he didn't know yet how to get himself aboard this gravy train. He didn't want to be left waving in the station whilst these two disappeared with the loot down the tracks into a golden sunset.

He just nodded and fixing Coquelin with a riveting gaze said. 'The ancillary expenses will be agreed between the three of us I assume?'

Coquelin forced a thin smile and his eyes creased reassuringly behind his rimless spectacles. 'Of course: the whole idea is that we should help each other.'

Nobby remained impassive, but internally he heaved a huge sigh of relief. The way forward was now clear and the door opened without either side having given any damming commitments – and Coquelin knew he was going to get his aid funds.

The Prime Minister rose to his feet. 'Phillipe will give you a tour of our existing port facilities. I suggest you take the afternoon for recreation and we meet again here tomorrow to progress matters. In the mean time you will, of course, stay at Fisherman's Wharf as our guest. Anything you need, just tell Phillipe.' The implication was clear from the raised eyebrow and the faint smile that flickered across his face.

Nobby thanked him, said 'to tomorrow then,' and headed for the door. He didn't see Coquelin give Rouget the nod.

Nobby couldn't give a hoot about touring the port and listening to Rouget quoting endless statistics about imports and exports, tariffs and tax, but he put up with it, thinking all the while about nubile air stewardesses and overweight hairy Russian women round the hotel pool. The hint from Henri about 'anything' he wanted was clear. It would be better to ask Rouget to provide some classy crumpet – that might be the safest bet. He cut Rouget off in mid-drone from going on about demurrage.

'This afternoon Phillipe, I don't really feel like having a sleep, perhaps a bit of company who could show me some sights in Grandes Rocques and such? Can you recommend anyone?'

Rouget's irritation at being cut off was replaced by a glow of satisfaction as he contemplated what Anna Lemartine might do to this oaf.

'I think I could arrange that for you, Norbert. She's one of our best tourist guides – very accommodating, and a looker to boot. Her name's Anna. I'll ask her to call at the hotel – shall we say 2.30?'

Nobby leered acceptance, but before he could say anything his eye was caught by a large white vessel tied up at the quay. It was obviously a private yacht. There was a small green and blue helicopter sitting on a helipad at the stern.

Nobby pointed at it. 'Is that Henri's then?'

Rouget laughed. 'No such luck. It's American; it belongs to an investor. Henri's trying to talk him into doing a development here.'

He then clammed up and avoided answering any more of Nobby's questions about the American.

They took the presidential helicopter to Beauregard Island and Rouget pointed out the location of the proposed new port. The helicopter swooped and dived over the site whilst Rouget banged on about how important this new port would be for the prosperity of the Comorantes.

Nobby was beginning to feel the effects of three-quarters of a bottle of cognac mixed with three fried eggs and eight slices of bacon and decided he'd seen enough.

'Yes, yes, let's get back; I've seen all I need to see!'

In fact all he'd seen was a couple of rocky headlands with a carpet of palm trees between them, but at least he could say that he'd seen the site.

Rouget dropped him off at the Fisherman's Wharf. Nobby, feeling much better on *terra firma* called out 'don't forget Anna what's-her-name, will you?'

Rouget waved back, there was no way he was going to forget Anna! As soon as Garside had disappeared from view he was on his mobile to Coquelin.

'Henri, tell Anna it's all fixed for Garside – 2.30 this afternoon at his hotel? My guys fitted the camera whilst I took him in the helicopter. He's a big guy so she can give him the full treatment. He's gagging for it!' They both laughed.

'Well done Phillipe, that should help tomorrow's negotiations - if we run into difficulties.'

Anna Lemartine was a courtesan with a modern touch. In other words she only dealt with important people, but her repertoire was based on electrical devices that could start the heart of a dead elephant and then have it trumpeting with ecstasy in five minutes. She got the phone call from Coquelin just after lunch. You didn't ask how high when Monsieur le President said jump, so forsaking a large plate of banana fritters in honey, she dressed in her 'fuck me' outfit, collected her gear in a large holdall and hit the door running. This, for the normal spectator, would be a sight worth seeing, but for a potential customer was guaranteed to frighten the life out of them.

Well over six feet tall and tipping the scales at 250lbs, she was dressed in a tight-fitting, gold lamé top and purple hot-pants that only served to accentuate the crushing power of black thighs like tree trunks. She headed for her car.

Nobby was lying on his bed wearing a sports shirt and slacks and idly turning the pages of a tourist magazine when he heard the knock on his door. In his mind he had conjured up a picture of a shapely island girl, flowers in her hair, grass skirt and lovely smooth brown skin with sinuous fingers, sultry eyes and pouting lips. When he opened the door he almost had a heart attack. Anna sailed through into both him and the room like an aircraft carrier. She kicked the door closed with a neat back-heel and, big though he was she bore him straight backwards onto the large bed.

'Hello honey chile! I'm Anna. Feeling randy are we? Can't wait to get started? Well, we've got a bit of foreplay to do before we get down to the main event,' and with that she tore his shirt open with both hands. Buttons flew in all directions and there was a ripping sound as the material gave way somewhere. She cast a disparaging glance at Nobby's pasty-looking, flabby, hairy chest and then moved down to work on his slacks.

This had taken Nobby completely by surprise and as a result he had been overwhelmed by the first rush, but he had been around the block a few times and wasn't one to remain supine for long. Nobby heaved her to one side and wriggled round so he could get his feet on the floor.

'Aye up lass, what d'you think you're at here? Who are you and what the fuck d'you think you're doing?'

For one moment Anna looked shocked. 'You are Mr Norbert, aren't you?' The awful thought struck that she had attacked some innocent tourist who was just having an afternoon nap and ripped his shirt to shreds. Coquelin would have her guts for garters if that was so.

'Yes, I know who I am, but who the hell are you?'

She sighed with relief. 'I'm Anna, Anna Lemartine, didn't Phillipe tell you about me?'

'No he bloody didn't! Or at least he didn't tell me that you were...' he hesitated; she was frowning. The wrong choice of words here could result in severe physical injury, possibly painful death if she took offence. He swallowed hard '...that you would be so big as well as beautiful.'

'Ooo! Mr Norbert, so you're a gentleman. My friends told me that all Englishmen were gentleman, and you do say nice things to a girl.' She pouted coquettishly. 'I think we're going to get on fine.' She began to open her holdall.

Nobby's relaxation at her acceptance of the compliment was short lived as he watched what she was taking out of her case. Thick red and black cables with crocodile clips at one end were attached to a sinister-looking box with a numbered dial and a plug for a power socket; some odd shaped clamps, two of which had weights attached; a thing that looked like an electric cattle prod – no it *was* an electric cattle prod! He'd seen them in Maltby market used on calves and they didn't half make the little buggers jump. Finally some leather belts, straps and more wiring were revealed. It dawned on him that this stuff wasn't for use on her; it was for use on him.

He watched open-mouthed as she stripped off her meagre clothing and advanced upon him – a massive undulating figure, with bits of her wobbling in all directions and a determined look on her large face. He held up a restraining hand.

'Now steady on lass, I'm all for a bit of the old rumpy-pumpy, but I don't fancy the electric chair.'

Her big round face split into a grin like a ripe melon. 'Have you tried it?'

He shook his head, recalling that Gloria L'Amour at her massage parlour in Foundry Street, Maltby, had a vibrator, but no stuff like this.

'Well if you haven't tried it honey, how d'you know you don't like it? Most of my customers think it's the best thing since dried sea slug.'

As he'd never tried dried sea slug either, Nobby was not really in a position to make a judgement but eyed the pile of ominous-looking equipment apprehensively.

However, the afternoon turned out as Coquelin had predicted. Nobby had weights hung from parts of him he wouldn't have fancied. Clamps attached to other bits, wires attached to yet more. He writhed around in agony and ecstasy, vibrated like a jack-hammer and jumped about like a calf in Maltby market. He couldn't help himself, and after two hours he was a shattered wreck with a big smile across his face lying naked on the bed, his pale skin covered in red blotches.

Anna surveyed him with satisfaction: job done! Coquelin would be pleased. She packed away her gear, threw a duvet over the still twitching Nobby, collected the video from the laundry cupboard in the corridor and beat it back to finish off her banana fritters in honey.

By Christ, Nobby was thinking, that beats going down t'pit any day.

Next morning Serge was on time and whisked a remarkably fresh Nobby to Government House at nine o'clock. There was no waiting about this time; it was straight into the private office where Henri and Phillipe were awaiting him. The door was firmly closed with Serge posted outside to make sure that they were not disturbed. Coffee was already laid on and after a brief exchange of pleasantries it was down to business.

Coquelin was disappointed to see that Nobby showed no sign of yesterday afternoon's depredations with Anna. In fact, he looked alert and crafty; Anna must be losing her touch – maybe they'd have to get somebody else as a softener-up? Coquelin opened the discussion. 'So Norbert, now you have seen our tiny port and the proposed site for the new one, are you going to approve our application for aid?'

Nobby suddenly realised that he was back in control and that there was a hint of anxiety behind that question.

He stroked his chin and screwed up his eyes to build up tension. 'Well, Henri, as you said yesterday we haven't yet agreed your government's costs for the supporting infrastructure and ancillary expenses. I think we should deal with those first.'

Coquelin decided that it was time to take the plunge. The video they had of Garside's activities yesterday afternoon could be the clincher if he became difficult.

'Yes indeed. Phillipe will give you a copy of the supporting infrastructure breakdown of costs and, of course, we will submit these officially through the usual channels as well, but I don't think your consultants will have any problem justifying these. They are within the preliminary figures we gave you.'

He paused for effect. 'The ancillary costs we still have to agree.' He smiled at Nobby. 'But before we do that, let me put you in the picture about another project we are involved with, which could be of great benefit to you.'

'*Could be of great benefit to you!*' Those seven words stimulated everything that he desired in Nobby's heart. This was it; this was where he was going to make a killing. He could hardly wait for Coquelin to continue.

Coquelin saw the greed flare in Nobby's eyes and knew that he was on the hook. The question now was for how much? Had Anna softened him up sufficiently to slow down his thinking? They didn't want to give too much away. He and Phillipe had discussed this beforehand and Phillipe thought that a maximum of two million dollars would be more than enough.

'You noticed the big yacht in St George's harbour, with the green and blue trim? That belongs to a very wealthy American, Kory Z. Kronoff. He's an investor; he wants to build a high-class tourist development on one of our islands. He's put together a consortium and formed an offshore company to raise $80m. The Comorantes Government has agreed to lease this island to the consortium for 99 years in return for a 25% share of the deal. Certain other private investors can also put money in for a percentage. The lowest investment is one million dollars. The forecast returns are excellent. It would make a very good pension for any investor?'

The unasked question hung in the air like fly-paper.

Nobby's heart sank. 'But I haven't got anywhere near that sort of money!'

Coquelin gave his soft smile again. 'Perhaps we could help you there. Neither Phillipe nor I have that sort of money either, so what I propose is that we include a sum in the ancillary costs for Port Mahon that would cover our investments.'

'And this would go under the heading "Comorantes Government ancillary costs ..."?'

'... and you would approve it!'

Nobby considered this for a minute. He couldn't see a problem and nor could he see where he could be vulnerable. OK, that seemed fine, but exactly how much would be his share? They had mentioned a million dollars; he frowned. He felt that his contribution in approving the whole Port Mahon project was worth more than that – two million at least.

'What percentage of the project would I get for a million dollars?'

Phillipe replied rather too quickly, 'One per cent.'

Nobby didn't smile; in fact his face had a grim look. He shook his head. 'I want two million dollars put in for me, converted to two and a half percent'

Coquelin flushed angrily, not about the two million dollars – as long as Garside could get it through the Department of International Development's Committee he could have what he wanted – but there was no way that Kronoff and his investors were going to give away a further two and a half per cent. He knew the maths. The government was getting twenty-five per cent for the long lease: he and Rouget were getting five per cent each for setting the whole thing up plus a further five per cent for the five million dollars they were going to invest, which left Kronoff and his pals with sixty per cent. There was no way Kronoff would go lower than that. He knew that because he had tried hard and unsuccessfully to drive a better bargain for himself. He did a quick mental calculation. Garside's percentage would have to come out of his and Rouget's share.

He scowled at Garside. 'The American would never accept that! The best I could get you is one and a half per cent for one and a half million dollars.'

He held his breath, but Nobby was well and truly on the hook now so there was no way he was going to back out of this deal. He grumbled a bit and tried a few figures, but when it was clear that Coquelin wasn't going to budge, he reluctantly agreed and offered his hand for a binding confirmation.

Coquelin hid his satisfaction and shook Nobby's hand as did Rouget. They would have shaken anything to get Garside's agreement, a handshake meant nothing to them – they were politicians.

'Of course,' added Coquelin, 'your one and a half million and our three million will be included in the "ancillary costs".'

It was cleverly put, so Nobby believed that each of them was putting in the same amount for, he presumed, the same shareholding. The element of unfairness was removed from his thinking.

Now all this sounded very good, but there was one thing that was worrying Nobby. 'What exactly, would I get out of it?'

Coquelin laughed. 'A good question. There's no fooling you Norbert. The figures at the moment show a minimum of ten per cent return annually on investment so you, my dear Norbert, would get not less than $150,000 per year. Bear in mind that this is a minimum. When we have all put in our money Kronoff will be calling a meeting of all investors and everybody will be given a detailed prospectus setting out the company's policies for marketing and sales, with estimated returns based on up-to-date costs and projections.'

Nobby was still cautious; what he really wanted was a piece of paper setting these promises out clearly, but when he broached the subject Coquelin replied, 'But Norbert, you haven't done anything yet. We've put in our land, the other investors have put in some of their money, what have you done? We can hardly give you shares now if your government then refuses our aid package, can we?'

'No I suppose not, but I'll make sure it doesn't.'

'Yes yes, but can you guarantee that?'

He had to admit he couldn't.

Coquelin clapped him on the shoulder, 'Don't worry, this is a winner I promise you. Let's celebrate our agreement.'

Smiles all round and a bottle of Dom Perignon with three glasses appeared from behind Coquelin's desk.

They discussed the details to set up the deal. Coquelin said he would sort it out with Kronoff and Nobby would get his shares as soon as the money hit the Port Mahon account in the Comorantes Bank.

'By the way, Norbert, how did you get on with Miss Lemartine. Was she a good guide and did she show you things?' It was said without the trace of a smirk.

'By God, I'll tell thee summat Henri, Mrs Garside could learn a thing or two from that lady! Blood and sand, she left me in a right state, I can tell you.'

'Yes, we know,' Coquelin murmured, but Nobby was too excited for this to register.

Over a good lunch at Government House – they laid on prawn cocktail and a well-done fillet steak especially for him – Nobby tried to control his excitement. One and a half million dollars! Bloody hell, it was much more than he had dreamed of. Admittedly, he wasn't actually going to get his hands on one and a half million in cash – it was an investment with the Yanks – but that, plus $150,000 a year flowing into his Swiss bank account was breathtaking, and even that was a low estimate.

Coquelin suggested that Rouget could help him draft out his report to his committee, 'just so that you get the spelling of some of our local places correct,' and Nobby, whose report writing was not one of his best skills, was pleased to accept.

After lunch Coquelin said goodbye to Nobby, shook his hand warmly and said to leave everything to him – they'd be in touch.

Nobby departed with Rouget to his office at Ports and Harbours to draft his report.

****

Later that evening, after Serge had dropped Garside off at the airport, Coquelin and Rouget met over drinks at Government House.

'That went well,' observed Rouget. 'Do you know, he could hardly string two words together for his report...'

'... So you wrote it for him Phillipe,' finished off Coquelin with a grin.

Rouget frowned. 'Do you think he'll do it?'

Coquelin laughed. 'Of course he'll do it! Didn't you see the greed in his eyes when he realised that we were offering him an opportunity to get a slice of the action. This is a fortune to him.' He frowned. 'It all depends on how much influence he has with his committee, but I got the feeling that they were generally in favour of granting aid for our project already, otherwise why would we be having those discussions about the Royal Navy using it as a base. His report – or rather your report – should clinch that.'

Rouget pursed his lips. 'Yes, I see that, but we have another problem, don't we? You told Garside that we were adding three million to the ancillaries for us in addition to his one and a half million.'

Coquelin nodded.

'But we need five million to buy those extra shares. Where's the other two coming from?'

'Well there's no hurry is there? We're not going to get the money from London until we have a construction contract for Port Mahon, and Kronoff doesn't anticipate starting construction on Tern Island for eighteen months. It's going to take that long for us to move those people off

Tern and for him to get his planning, design and finances sorted out.'

'But we've still got to find that extra money!'

'I've thought of that. We always negotiate with whoever submits the lowest tender, right? Well part of the negotiations will be a kickback of two million to us if they want the Port Mahon job.'

'But what if they won't and threaten to expose our demand?'

Coquelin gave his thin simian smile. 'Then, my dear Phillipe, we'll just take Garside's share and tell him to fuck off.'

Alarm flashed across Rouget's face. 'You're not going to put it like that, are you?'

'No, of course not. I'll wrap it up in something about the Americans changing their minds and complications because he's a British MP etc, but that's what it'll mean!'

'He won't like that.'

'Of course he won't, but what can he do? He can't sue us, can he? And I don't suppose he'd like the contents of that video plastered all over the British newspapers – particularly the scene where Anna stuffs a cattle prod up his bottom and he jumps around like a dervish on speed.'

'You've got a good point there, Henri – or rather Garside did!' They both laughed.

****

Nobby had the same sagging seat going back on Comorantes Airways as he had coming, and it was a night flight. After another awful meal the cabin lights were dimmed, blankets unrolled and the passengers fell asleep – all except Nobby. He was too uncomfortable and too excited to sleep. He kept going over the deal with Henri Coquelin again and again. He was no fool; he realised that he would have to show his hand before they showed theirs, but there was no way round that. He'd just have to trust Henri to carry out his promises. If they screwed him he would make it his job to make life as difficult for them as possible, but he knew that there really wasn't much he could do because he wouldn't have any control over the money.

The first task, however, was to get the funds approved with the ancillary costs buried in the overall figure. That little puffy sod Rouget had done a good job with the report. Hidden amongst the costs of new roads, worker accommodation, water supply, drainage, power generation, and the myriad of stuff the government claimed that they needed to provide support and staff the new port as a full working facility was the four and a half million dollars for the 'investors'.

CHAPTER FIVE

OCTOBER, 2008 – WESTMINSTER, LONDON

The Department for International Development Aid Committee met two weeks after Garside's return. Nobby had submitted his report on Port Mahon to the civil servants who had included it on the long agenda to be discussed. He had also spoken to the other Labour members on the committee and received a favourable response. He had even talked to two of the Tory members who had previously been in favour of granting the funds and they were still for it.

Port Mahon was the third item on the list. The first two applications were first: funds for tube wells in Ethiopia, but because of instability in that country this was put on hold – much to the indignation of Penelope Cattermole – and second: a request for money to build a chain of clinics to help the people of Bhutan. This was approved.

Next was Port Mahon. Penelope Cattermole had prepared for this item carefully and, much to Nobby's dismay, presented a well thought-out case against putting up the money. She claimed that as the Chinese were expanding their fleet into the Indian Ocean, it was very likely that it would become a Chinese naval base. If not then the Indians would take it over as their base to prevent the

Chinese from using it. Her second point was that the Comorantes was, in effect, a right-wing dictatorship ruled by a despot called Coquelin who was notoriously corrupt. Nobby's heart sank even lower as these arguments hit home and he could see his 'pension' arrangements going up in smoke.

Desmond Fitzpatrick, the Chairman cut in. 'Do you have any evidence of this? After all, the Comorantes are a friend of Britain and a member of the Commonwealth.'

'Well no, not exactly – but everyone knows what is going on there.'

'Going on where Penelope?'

'In the Indian Ocean!'

Fitzpatrick smiled. 'Do they? Do they also know that Her Majesty's Government has come to an arrangement with the Comorantes Government that if this port is built it will be available for use by the Royal Navy? In fact, our consultants, CONDES, have been having discussions with the Admiralty about the navy's specific requirements.' He raised a warning finger. 'This is highly confidential information; we do not want to inflame relationships with other countries that abut the Indian Ocean.'

Cattermole collapsed in a heap muttering, 'Well I didn't know that, did I!'

Nobby's heart started beating normally again. He was slightly annoyed because neither Coquelin nor Rouget had mentioned this to him, but it looked as though the aid grant would sail through now – and it did.

'So what happens now?' Nobby asked Desmond Fitzpatrick after the committee meeting had ended.

Fitzpatrick gave him a pitying look. 'Not much! We wait whilst the civil servants push paper around to each other setting up systems. When they get tired of doing that, the consultants will be instructed to carry out the detailed design, draw up a bill of quantities and prepare tender documents. More paper is pushed about between them, the Comorantes Government and us and by this time next year we should be in a position to invite bids for the construction – or rather the Comorantians will.'

'But what about the money, the aid funds of $152 million? Where does that go?'

Fitzpatrick laughed. 'It doesn't go anywhere my dear Garside. It's just an allocation on paper. No money moves until we and the Comorantes Government have a signed construction contract, and that won't be for fifteen months at least. You don't think HMG is going to hand over a great wad of cash now to our newly emerged brethren in the Indian Ocean, do you? There's no knowing where it would end up if we did – in Switzerland attached to some sticky fingers more likely than not!'

Nobby's sphincter expanded alarmingly and he hastily sat down.

'Are you alright, you've gone very pale? I'll get you a glass of water.' Fitzpatrick poured out some water from one of the decanters on the table and put it in Nobby's hand. He drank it gratefully; he was feeling quite sick at this unforeseen turn of events. What the hell was he going to say to Coquelin? When they had their discussion Nobby had assumed that as soon as the funds were approved they would be paid to the Comorantes, he would make another visit, have the meeting with the Yanks and come away with a share certificate in his hot horny hand. He also assumed that that was what Coquelin and Rouget thought. Now, with no funds for at least fifteen months, the whole deal would be blown out of the water. All his hopes were dashed and his dreams of money and power evaporated into thin air because the stupid sodding British government didn't trust 'honest' Henri Coquelin not to steal it. And why did Fitzpatrick mention Switzerland? Was it a warning?

How could he possibly know about Nobby's secret account?

The sphincter expanded further. Muttering a brief 'call of nature' to Fitzpatrick, he brushed past him and headed out of the committee room hoping he could make it to the 'gents' in time.

Back in his office in Portcullis House he calmed down. Of course Fitzpatrick didn't know about his Swiss bank account; he was just using Switzerland as an illustration of where ill-gotten gains were stashed. The problem now would lie with Coquelin. Considered thought led him to realise that Coquelin must be fully aware that the British Government wouldn't just hand over the funds fifteen months before they were required, so the situation shouldn't come as an unpleasant surprise to him. But was Nobby's deal still on – that was the question? There was no secure way that he could contact Coquelin. Anything in writing, a letter, an email, a fax – they were all out of the question. He wasn't happy about a phone call either; these days journalists hacked phones and GCHQ at Cheltenham probably intercepted calls made to foreigners – particularly those to senior foreigners by government officials.

He chewed his fingernails and then decided that he had to know; he would risk a phone call but wrap it in an official call as deputy chairman of the Department's Foreign Aid Committee. He looked at his watch – there should just be time today if he was quick.

He pressed the key on his intercom. 'Laetetia, get me the Prime Minister of the Comorantes Islands on the phone now!'

'I don't have his number.'

Nobby blinked. Miss Harbottle hadn't been the same ever since he got back from the Comorantes. Initially he put it down to PMT, but when it continued he thought it might be some personal problem – the change or some women's thing. He had shrugged off her difficult behaviour, assuming that she would get over it sooner or later. This reply irritated him; she was wasting valuable time.

'Well get it for Christ's sake! This is the seat of the British Government here; we have information about everybody important all over the world so bloody well find it - and quick.'

Laetetia Harbottle bridled like the *maitre d'* at Claridge's on being tipped with luncheon vouchers. She gritted her teeth and weighed up again the idea of handing in her resignation. It was a good job she held in the parliamentary offices and it had taken a lot of hard work to get there. She decided that she was damned if she was going to throw it all away because of a pig like Garside. Any affection she might once have felt for him had gone, to be replaced by an implacable desire for revenge.

She obtained Henri Coquelin's office number and dialled it. She got a secretary who said she would see if the Prime Minister was available to speak to Mr Garside. It turned out that he wasn't, but, she told Miss Harbottle, the PM was coming to London soon to sign the aid agreement for Port Mahon and might be available to see him then.

Miss Harbottle decided to convey this news to Garside personally. With a cursory knock on his office door she marched in. 'The Prime Minister of the Comorantes is not available to speak to you, Mr Garside.' She didn't tell him the rest of the message.

Her toes curled with delight at the shock on his face. Whatever it was, it was obviously a bitter blow to him.

'What do you mean he's "not available"?'

'When I told his secretary that it was you who wanted to speak to him, he sent a message back telling her to tell you that he was not available.'

'Is that all?'

'That was the gist of the message.'

Nobby's spirits sank even lower; it looked ominously as if he had been cut out of the deal. He thought long and hard. He could fly to the Comorantes again, but this time he had no reason to go and it would look suspicious. The only thing that cheered him up was thought that they hadn't got the money yet; it would be at least fifteen months before that happened and he might be able to screw the whole thing up for them if they had given him the heave-ho.

Miss Harbottle eased out of the office hiding the satisfied grin on her thin lips and musing that Mr Garside had become very touchy these days whenever the Comorantes was mentioned. She resolved to work on this weak spot in his armour whenever possible.

A fortnight later a memo arrived from Desmond Fitzpatrick saying that a delegation from the Comorantes was coming over to sign the aid agreement and Garside was invited to the Prime Ministerial reception at Number 10 to welcome them, and also to attend the signing ceremony the following day. She slipped it into Nobby's in-tray near the bottom, amongst some stuff he hadn't touched for weeks.

Nobby was still brooding on his misfortune when Fitzpatrick stuck his head round Nobby's office door and said, 'Garside, are you or aren't you coming to this reception next week? The PM's office wants to finalise the numbers and fix the guest list?'

'What reception?'

'For Christ's sake man, I sent you a memo about it over three weeks ago.'

'I haven't seen any memo.' He buzzed Miss Harbottle. 'Have you seen a memo from the Chair of the Development Committee about a reception that came three weeks ago?'

'Yes,' she said sweetly, 'I put it in your in-tray the same day for you to read.'

He tipped out his in-tray over the top of his desk and there it was. He cursed under his breath.

Fitzpatrick growled, 'You'd better get your act together Garside and get a grip on things – if you want to stay on my committee that is! So are you coming or aren't you?'

Nobby saw the lifeline immediately; if the PM was holding a reception then it must mean that Coquelin would be coming.

'Sorry Desmond, been snowed under these last few days. Yes, of course I'll be there – for both events.'

'Well let the PM's office know *toute suite!*' Fitzpatrick shot him an irritated look and departed.

****

The day of the Comorantes reception duly arrived; Nobby could hardly wait. He put on his best suit – a somewhat loud check, and his Maltby Cricket Club tie – purple and orange stripes, dismissed the taxi at the entrance to Downing Street, showed the policeman his invitation and passed through the hallowed portals of Number 10. He met Fitzpatrick in the hallway; Fitzpatrick glanced at his suit and shuddered.

'Been racing your whippets, Garside old chap?'

Still reeling from Fitzpatrick's jibe, Nobby was put well down the receiving line between a bloke from the Foreign Office and a dark-skinned overweight Rasta who turned out to be the Comorantes ambassador's brother.

Henri Coquelin, as dapper and well turned-out as ever in a light linen suit made his way down the line, being introduced to each person and shaking hands. When he got to Nobby his expression didn't change.

'Mr Norbert Garside, deputy chairman of our Overseas Development Committee,' murmured Fitzpatrick.

'Hello Henri, nice to...' His remark faded away as Coquelin totally iced him with a look Medusa would have been proud of, and passed on to the next person.

Nobby was stunned. All his worst fears had been confirmed; they had not just screwed him, they had punched, bored and reamered him. He had done his not inconsiderable bit to get them the money and now Coquelin had cast him to one side like an old boot. Rage flared in the Garside bosom; they would not get away with this. He would do everything in his power to expose them – but then he realised that he couldn't without revealing that he had been a party to it. It was *he* who had pushed through the extra money with his glowing report.

The rest of the Comorantes delegation passed by him receiving only a cursory nod attached to a scowl. He then grabbed a glass of champagne and retired to a quiet corner to brood and plot. One or two people tried to make conversation but received no encouragement so rapidly moved on to brown-nose somebody else. The Prime Minister, ever the smooth host, eased Coquelin round the more important members of his government before an aide called him to one side for something or other. Coquelin glanced round and detected a cloud of gloom and despondency hanging over one corner of the room under which stood a fulminating figure. It wasn't difficult to distinguish Garside from a sunbeam. Coquelin brushed aside a sycophantic hand and headed across to that corner.

'Mr Garside, how nice to see you again – wonderful news about our new port. It will make all the difference to the Islands' prosperity and we are duly grateful.'

Nobby forced a smile on to his face as the small flame of hope was rekindled in his heart. Coquelin obviously detected uncertainty in Garside's manner and put a reassuring hand on his arm.

'When the funds are released you must come and visit us again – as my guest, of course, so you will better appreciate what this means to everyone. We'll be in touch.' Nobby thought that he was given a knowing glance.

'But...'

But Coquelin had turned away and was being ushered to meet somebody else on the other side of the room.

So now what? Was he still in the deal or not? Had they given him the heave-ho or was Coquelin just being cautious in public. Weighing up what Coquelin had said, it seemed more than likely that he was still in, so it would be stupid to rock the boat. However, what Coquelin had actually done was buy himself fifteen months of time before Nobby could think of throwing a spanner in the works.

'Sod me,' he said half to himself, 'this corruption business isn't as straightforward as I thought it would be.' He grabbed another glass of champagne from a passing waiter and, feeling much more cheerful, decided that if he was to promote his political career, he'd better get networking.

Hugo Elmes, the senior director of CONDES the consultants for the project, was a great people watcher and was very interested in the various interactions between the guests in the room. He had been invited as a guest but, not being a politician, was only included amongst the supernumeraries, thus hadn't been on the receiving line. Without knowing who he was he had noticed the bulky figure of Garside glowering in the corner and then noted the friendly gesture by Coquelin and Garside's consequent change of mood. He wondered what all that was about.

CHAPTER SIX

DECEMBER, 2008 – CONDES OFFICE, LONDON

Hugo intercepted me at the top of the stairs as I arrived at the office just before 9.30. He pretended to glance at his watch.

'Morning Marcus, good God, is it lunchtime already?' It was an old joke and as such didn't warrant more than a weary smile of acknowledgement. 'You're not scoring a point for that old chestnut Hugo, but how was your weekend with the in-laws?'

He beamed cheerily. 'Neither are you for that – nil all then?'

He was my friend, co-director and mentor at Consultant Design Services – known as CONDES to the civil engineering profession,

Totally unabashed he continued, 'I thought you'd like to know we've just had confirmation of our appointment to do the full design for that Port Mahon project in the Comorantes Islands for the Department for International Development. An old friend, Desmond Fitzpatrick, phoned me from the Ministry to tell me that they're sending us a letter of appointment. I've been invited to Number 10 to some reception they're giving the Comorantes Government prior to the big signing ceremony.'

I must have looked puzzled because he added, 'You remember we put in an initial study and cost plan about six months ago? Well the Ministry have decided to give them the grant! It's a decent-sized job, a brand new port, but it's on some scrubby god-foresaken island right out in the sticks.'

'Is it?'

His smile grew broader. 'This'll be the third job we've got from them. You remember the sinking airport in the Pacific on that atoll where we got them out of a real mess with some brilliant ground engineering work. Martin Bishop, our chief soil mechanics engineer, sorted out that problem, saved them millions – and a lot of red faces?'

I shook my head.

'No? Well it must have been in the old partnership days when Arbuthnot was senior partner. They were so grateful that they asked us to design all the groundworks for that nuclear power station in Rajasthan. Desmond Doubleday was the engineer running that team.'

'Yes I remember that. Des was the guy who helped me settle into the firm. I was a member of the old Civils Team Two when he ran that.

'He died you know?'

I was shocked and saddened by this news. 'No, I didn't know.'

'The booze and fags got him in the end.'

I sighed. 'I had liked Des Doubleday – lazy, clever and a real gentleman, always called me "Dear Boy".'

Hugo shook his head, 'Ah, the old days! Now where was I? Oh yes, the Department for International Development.

Yes, their chairman, Desmond Fitzpatrick, tells me that they are pleased with CONDES and has told me in confidence that we will be on the shortlist for any future decent projects that come up.'

He touched my arm. 'Let's have a celebratory lunch, how are you fixed?'

'Today? I'm OK. In fact, I wanted to have a talk with you about your old friend Mazin Al Jabril. We can do that over lunch.'

He snorted angrily. 'That crook! He's no friend of mine! What about him?'

'I'll tell you later, but I'm meeting him at his Edgware Mansions flat on Wednesday. He wants to know if we'll let him off our hook.'

Mazin Al Jabril was our one-time agent in Egypt – until he stole two million dollars from us. He'd turned up again with a proposal we couldn't refuse. It was a big steelworks design and supervision contract in Sharjah, where his brother just happened to be the Minister of Industry. However, I had devised a plan that not only enabled us to recover our money but put Mazin in a position where he couldn't do us any harm. Now the project was nearly complete so he wanted our grip on his wind-pipe released. Over coffee after a good lunch at Simpson's I told Hugo that Brian Mason, CONDES finance director, had photocopied all the records of Mazin's Swiss company. I would tell Mazin that if we relaxed our hold on his throat and he made trouble for us then we would publish these in the Gulf. There was quite a lot of stuff he wouldn't want widely known, particularly by his brother the Minister.

'Like what? asked Hugo.

'Like the money he ripped off Pantocrator's furnace contract without giving his brother his agreed share. He told his brother that The World Bank had tightened up the finances so much there wasn't any commission.'

Hugo wrinkled his nose in disgust. 'The man's a congenital liar, he just can't stop!'

'Well, I for one will be pleased to get him out of our hair for good.'

I changed the subject back to Port Mahon. Hugo had been a bit downbeat about it, which was unlike him. I wondered if I was being blindsided.

'Tell me about Port Mahon?' I said.

A flicker of alarm passed across his face. 'What d'you want to know?'

'Well, who's going to run the design team?'

He grinned with relief. 'Well you can't, you've got too much on at the moment so I suppose I'll have to do it.' He had that bland look fixed on his face of the martyr laying down his life for the company. I knew it well.

'Where is it again?' I asked, suspiciously.

He waved a hand airily. 'I told you, some god-forsaken spot in the Indian Ocean. The Australians have done a location study and a full survey of the chosen site, so for us it will just be all office work.'

'Will it really? That's a bit of a bugger then, isn't it? So there'll be no need for site visits?'

His look wobbled a bit. 'Well maybe one or two, just to get the feel of the place, of course.'

'Of course,' I said, sarcastically. But I knew Hugo too well; he was only comfortable in one environment – in London and the Home Counties surrounded by his wife Emily, his children, his gentlemen's clubs and his golf courses. A basic island in the middle of the ocean would not be his scene these days, no matter how much of a paradise he imagined it might be. I could see it in the dreamy look that passed across his sun-tanned face. He was already picturing white sand, waving palm trees and buxom girls in undulating grass skirts. A few lungfuls of the scorching air, the sweat from the high humidity, the insect bites and the dysentery and he'd be back on the plane to London before you could shake the Piz Buin Factor 20.

'Pete Ashman has nearly finished the Aire Bridge review. You can have him as senior engineer – he's good,' I told him.

He nodded his thanks, called for the bill and we took a taxi back to the office.

On Wednesday Brian and I went to see Mazin Al Jabril in his apartment in Edgware Mansions. It was at least six months since I had last seen him and like all the best con men he was still outwardly the same old Mazin – immaculately dressed in a Savile Row tailored suit, not a crease or a fold in sight. Turnbull and Asser shirt, Monte Carlo Yacht Club tie and Lobb shoes which gleamed in the sunlight. I estimated his age at around forty-five; his capped white teeth sparkled in his lamp-tanned face as he greeted us. His handshake was firm and dry, but there was a wary look in his dark eyes and a hint of nervousness about his movements. He ordered coffee for us from his manservant and showed us to comfortable chairs in his sitting room. It could have been easy to forget that this man had not only stolen two million dollars from us in the past, but also had sneakily tried to acquire our firm behind our backs for a knock-down price.

He was obviously anxious to know what his situation was. The Sharjah Steelworks was virtually complete and had been built on time and to a tight budget. He knew that from his brother, the Minister of Industry in Sharjah. He tapped his fingers nervously on the arm of his chair. I gave him a nice smile and decided to string him out a bit more before I gave him any news.

'So how are you these days, Mazin? Still ripping off your friends and screwing your contacts?'

He gave a sickly grin, but his eyes flashed angrily. I sipped my coffee and watched him.

'Still the same old joker, Marcus.'

Then he went into his hard-done-by act. His voice changed, his shoulders drooped, his mouth turned down at the corners. It was brilliant; you wouldn't think it was the same man who had greeted us. He oozed pathos and despair.

'Joking apart, times are very difficult Mr Marcus, you wouldn't believe the lies and deceit that permeates the business world these days...' Well, he was wrong about that – a classic case of the pot calling the kettle black. '... Alas business is terrible, but I try to make a living. You wouldn't have a nice consultancy in CONDES for a very well connected Arab by any chance?'

You had to admire his bare-faced cheek, but I ignored his question.

'Pantocrator paid $2,400,000 into Investment and Resource Holdings SA last month.'

He perked up considerably at that; that was part of what he wanted to hear, but a nervous tic twitched his left eye. Investment and Resource Holdings was his Swiss holding company, but his problem at the moment was that he didn't hold it – CONDES did. It was IRH that he wanted returning to him and that was what this meeting was all about.

I thought again about all the trouble he had caused us and the financial agonies we had been through as a result of his behaviour, but in the end we had promised to return to him what was rightfully his – provided he behaved himself as far as CONDES was concerned. He had kept to that. I gestured to Brian and he opened his brief case and took out the IRH bearer share certificate and bank statements. He laid them down on the coffee table in front of Mazin like a solitaire hand.

I had to admire Mazin's self control, he didn't move a muscle. The whole of his fortune and future lay before him in those pieces of paper and he just looked at them, then at me.

'You were very clever,' he murmured. 'You know we could have made a brilliant team! What now?'

'What now nothing. We go our separate ways, but we don't trust you Mazin, so to ensure that you don't do us damage in the Middle East, Brian has kept photocopies of the bank statements showing all the receipts and payments. These will be kept in our bank.'

He flared up at this. 'That wasn't part of our agreement. How do I know I can trust you?'

'Our agreement was to return to you that which is yours, that's all. We never said we wouldn't keep copies – and as for not trusting us, that's a bit rich coming from a lying crook like you – so tough shit!' I could feel my anger welling up again at this rogue who had caused us so much trouble. I took a deep breath, it was time to go. I stood up and Brian followed suit.

'Goodbye Mazin, I can't say I hope we'll meet again because I don't!'

With that we left his flat - but we were destined to meet again, in unexpected circumstances.

I suppose I did owe Mazin something indirectly, because it was through Mazin that I had met Zoe. When I got back home that evening I told her that I had met an old friend of hers – Mazin Al Jabril.

'Huh!' she snapped. 'He's no friend of mine. All I did was sell him his apartment when I was working for Johnson Jacques, that big West End firm of estate agents. He never paid our fees so I didn't get any commission.'

I steered her away from the subject. 'Well we've seen the back of him; he'll not be missed by CONDES either I can tell you!'

****

FEBRUARY, 2009 – WESTMINSTER, LONDON

Nobby was still worrying that Coquelin and Rouget might be cutting him out of the deal; he knew he was very vulnerable and didn't like it.

Then an idea came to him – CONDES, the consultants for the Port Mahon project would have some control over payments. His understanding of the way these contracts worked specified that money could only be paid out on their say-so. As the construction progressed they would issue certificates allowing funds to be drawn down from the bank to pay the contractor.

He pressed the switch on the intercom for Miss Harbottle.

'Laetetia, get me the senior partner of a firm of consulting engineers called CONDES on the blower and make it quick.'

His phoned bleeped within thirty seconds. 'I have a Mr Hugo Elmes from CONDES for you on line one.'

'Hello, are you the top man in CONDES, Elmes? I don't want to be talking to the monkey, I want the organ grinder!'

Hugo Elmes grimaced at the peremptory tone. 'I'm the senior director, who are *you* may I ask?'

'Garside's the name, Member of Parliament for Mexborough East, and I can do your outfit a bit of good, Elmes. Why don't you and me have a bite of lunch sometime?'

Hugo's immediate thought was to tell him he couldn't spare the time, but then, because he was an MP, it might be worth hearing what he had to say. There couldn't be much harm in a lunch.

'If you give me your secretary's number I'll get mine to contact her to fix a convenient date.'

'Portcullis House, Miss Harbottle – and make it soon,' rasped Nobby and replaced the receiver.

Hugo regretted accepting the lunch as soon as he put the phone down. He'd never heard of Garside and didn't like the sound of him.

'Janet, can you look up an MP on the Net for me please, a chap called Garside who represents Mexborough East?'

Janet was back in ten minutes with a print out of Garside's career. Hugo scanned it quickly; the only thing of note was that he was deputy chairman of the Department for International Development's Aid Committee. Hugo stroked his chin – CONDES were doing that port project in the Comorantes that the Royal Navy wanted to use as a warm-water port. In fact, it was one of his projects, but he'd never come across, or even heard of Norbert Garside. He'd always dealt with civil servants, sailors from the Admiralty or the chairman of the DfID Aid Committee, Desmond Fitzpatrick. So what could Garside want or do?

It hadn't taken Nobby long to suss out all the best and most expensive restaurants in the West End and Miss Harbottle was instructed to book a table at Le Gavroche for the lunch date with Elmes. It didn't matter to Garside that it was one of the more expensive places to lunch in London – Garside had no intention of paying. Hugo arrived first and asked for the table booked by Mr Garside. The Head Waiter scanned the bookings and with a puzzled look on his face told Hugo that there was no such booking.

'He's an MP. Is there a booking for an MP from Portcullis House?'

The HW looked again and shook his head. As a last effort Hugo said, 'Try Elmes.'

This time he struck pay dirt. 'Ah yes, a table for two, number sixteen.' He clicked hid fingers and a lower-ranking waiter came and showed Hugo to a table tucked into a quiet corner. Hugo ordered a mineral water and waited.

Garside was half an hour late and flung out a cursory apology about 'delayed by important business in the House'. Hugo was not impressed.

'The grub's good here Elmes, a bit froggie for my taste but the steak's OK if you like it burnt.'

Hugo murmured that he had eaten here before and ordered just a main course – grilled turbot with a lobster sauce. Garside ordered some grilled king prawns and a fillet steak. 'Well done, mind you, I don't want the bugger climbing to its feet halfway through the meal!'

Hugo studied him discreetly; he recognised him from the reception at No. 10 and remembered Garside's reaction when the Prime Minister of the Comorantes spoke to him.

'So what is it you want to talk to me about?' asked Hugo as the coffee arrived.

Garside wiped a dribble of something brown off his chin with his napkin and turned to look at Hugo.

'A consultancy,' he said without preamble. 'If you give me a consultancy contract for say ten years, I'll see what business I can push your way. Ten grand a year should cover it. What do you say?'

Hugo had great difficulty in saying anything even remotely polite. He fell back on questions.

'What sort of business do you think you could get for my firm?'

Garside dropped his voice and cast a furtive look round before replying. 'This is very confidential, but I am the deputy chairman of the Department for Industrial Development's Aid Committee.'

'Are you indeed' responded Hugo, cheerily. 'I know your chairman, Desmond Fitzpatrick – a very nice fellow.' He didn't add that they were members of the same club. 'But what exactly is it that you think you can put our way? I thought any consultancy appointment for the Department had to be competitive?'

'Look Elmes, I'm telling you this in confidence, but I'm the one who pushed for your outfit, CONDOM isn't it, to be given the Port Mahon job.'

Hugo raised an eyebrow. 'Really? Is that so? I thought we were in competition with three other consultants and we got that appointment because we had the best technical offer with a keen price.'

'Well, yes you did – but there was very little to choose between you and the next bidder. It was me who pushed you forward.'

'Was it? And who "pushed forward" that Yorkshire firm Whiting, Stabbit and Bach?'

Nobby gulped. He had pressed for Whiting Bach's appointment because he thought that being local for him they would be the easier to talk into granting him a consultancy.

'A bluff Elmes, I didn't want it to be to be obvious that I was trying to help you.'

'And why would you want to help us? We've never met and have no connection with you as far as I'm aware.'

Nobby eased his collar with a fat finger. 'Look Elmes, just forget about that and concentrate on what I can do for you in the future.'

'You haven't told me what it is that you can do for us yet.'

'Well, I'm a close friend of the President of the Comorantes. There's other things as well; being an MP gives me access to all kinds of investment and development schemes.'

'Such as?'

'Well as an MP I come across projects, things, you know, design work etcetera.'

'No, I don't know. I'm asking you to tell me what you can do for CONDES that's worth £10,000 a year for ten years.'

Garside coughed and spluttered – cutting a slice of the action wasn't going to be as easy as he thought if people were going to be as difficult as this weather-beaten old sod in front of him. He felt himself getting angry. He was an important person so why did this old fart think he had the right to question him.

Hugo took a sip of his coffee and sat there patiently waiting.

'Do you want my bloody help or not? I can always go to other firms of consultants, heaven knows there's more than enough of you buggers around leaching on the taxpayer.

You scratch my back and I'll scratch yours. If you don't want to do that, that's your pigeon.'

Hugo ignored the implied threat and replied, 'Why don't you drop me a line setting out your proposals so that we can give them serious consideration?'

Garside glared at him; he had been around long enough to recognise the 'bum's rush' when he was getting it, and that was certainly what he was getting now. There was no possible chance of him putting anything like that in writing, even if he had something – which he hadn't.

'Fuck you, Elmes!' he snarled. 'Be it on your own head then!' and he got up in a huff and stalked out.

Hugo watched him go with a feeling of relief. *I don't think we'll be hearing from Mr Garside again*, he mused as he dropped his credit card onto the salver holding the bill.

****

Over the next few weeks the more he thought about that lunch, the angrier Nobby became. Who the hell did that jumped up, upper-class twit think he was dealing with? He would show that guy that you didn't mess with Nobby Garside and get away with it. In his pique he quite forgot that he wanted CONDES to keep a close eye on the Port Mahon money on his behalf; he just wanted to blacken their name now.

'D'yer fancy a pint in the members' bar, George? First round's on me.'

George Hartley, MP for Bassetlaw Central, raised an eyebrow in mock shock and pretended to clear his ears. 'Bloody hell Nobby, how can I refuse? You puttin' your hand in your pocket and buyin' a drink – has t'world stopped revolvin'?'

Nobby brought over two pints of John Smith's and they settled down at a quiet table in one corner.

'You're on the Transport and Communications Committee, aren't you George?'

'Aye, we've got a fair few new road schemes to sort out now our budget has been slashed, everything's on t' table for review.'

'You use a lot of consultants, don't you?'

'No, not really, we have an approved list of about half a dozen, no more.'

'Does CONDES ring a bell?'

'Aye, why? They're finishing off a big bridge in the Black Country and we're shortlisting 'em for a bypass job.'

Nobby drew in a breath through his teeth. 'I'd be a bit careful if I were you George, you don't want 'em going bust halfway through the job, do you?'

Hartley's eyes narrowed. 'Why, is there a problem? Do you know summat I don't?'

Nobby pretended to look concerned. 'Far be it for me to say anything, but I had lunch with their senior bloke a couple of weeks ago and I wasn't impressed. I think they're in serious financial shit and could go to the wall if they're not very careful.'

Hartley looked alarmed and Nobby gave a secret smile. He knew that a government department wouldn't take the risk if there was even the faintest chance of things going wrong.

'Thanks for the tip-off Nobby, God knows we've had enough bad publicity of late without inviting more.'

Nothing more was said about CONDES and they went on to talk of the usual Whitehall gossip. Nobby waited until Hartley bought his round and having drunk it retired to his flat in Pimlico, pleased with his evening.

He repeated this kind of conversation with three more socialist colleagues over the next few months and as a result CONDES name slipped out of the reckoning for at least two good design contracts.

With the DfID Committee Garside had more difficulty. Desmond Fitzpatrick rejected out of hand any suggestion that CONDES were going bust. He said it was nonsense – they had been thoroughly checked out and were perfectly stable.

Garside's next move was to corner Penelope Cattermole, the Lib-Dem MP and put into her mind the idea that Fitzpatrick was in CONDES' pocket.

'There's no proof mind you, Penelope, but I happen to know that CONDES' senior man and our revered chairman know each other very well. Their guy admitted as much to me when he took me out for an expensive lunch at Le Gavroche. I think he was sounding me out to see if I would play ball with them as well and push them forward. A £10,000 retainer was mentioned, but I told him to stuff it. Just to be on the safe side we should spread our consultancy net a bit wider. Don't you agree?'

She did, as did the other socialist members of the committee when it was suggested to them.

CHAPTER SEVEN

DECEMBER, 2009 – ST GEORGE'S,
THE COMORANTES ISLANDS

Nobby sipped breakfast coffee on his balcony at Government House and pushed aside the demolished tray of fresh pawpaw with lime, fried eggs and bacon and toast and marmalade that lay on the table beside him. From the balcony he could see Kronoff's yacht with its green and blue trim tied up at the private wharf. Sailors were washing down the superstructure with brushes and hoses. Of Kronoff there was no sign as yet.

Nobby finished his coffee and went into his bedroom to dress. A valet had put the modest contents of his suitcase away, sponged and pressed his suit and laid out clean pants, a clean shirt, his Maltby Cricket Club tie and polished his shoes.

This is the life he thought to himself, *I could go for a bit more of this, Tottie Garside's future took a turn for the worse as 'multi-millionaire Lord Norbert Garside surveyed his tropical estate with the hordes of dusky maidens running around to do his every bidding.* He shook his head to rid his mind of the idea. *Not yet Nobby. Not yet.*

The meeting with Kronoff on his yacht wasn't until 10.30. He supposed he should take notes but for what purpose he couldn't decide so he left his briefcase on the bed.

Coquelin and Rouget were waiting for him in the hall; he hadn't seen either of them yesterday. His flight had been late and after Serge had taken him to Government House he had gone straight to bed. Serge had told him about the morning's meeting with Kronoff and that Coquelin and Rouget would meet him in the hall at 10.15. They greeted him effusively, smiles and handshakes all round. Fortunately for Nobby, Coquelin had just agreed his deal for the $2 million kickback from Mumbai Construction, otherwise all Nobby would be shaking would be his head in despair at the venality of his fellow men. On the short drive to Kronoff's yacht Coquelin emphasised how privileged they were to be invited to invest with the great Kronoff. 'He only invites selected persons of the highest calibre to deposit funds with him.'

Nobby swelled with pride at the thought that he was now considered a 'person of the highest calibre'.

An immaculately dressed sailor was waiting at the bottom of the gangway and escorted the three of them to a sumptuous midships saloon where there was a big round marble table surrounded by gilded chairs. On the table were piles of glossy company reports and kid-leather folders with each of their names embossed in gold on the flap. The sailor handed out the company reports to each of them. 'Mr Kronoff would like you to take a look at these before the meeting,' he said.

Nobby looked through his. Each company had a specific development for which it was responsible. One had a hotel and conference centre in the Bahamas; another, a chain of luxury spa hotels in Indonesia; a third, a casino in Macao, and so on. The figures were given and none of them showed an annual return of less than 20% and all were financed by subsidiaries of The International Trading Bank of St Croix.

Most of it Nobby didn't understand, but he did understand the profit margins. He looked at Coquelin and Rouget. They were transfixed.

Another servant brought in cold drinks. 'Mr Kronoff will be with you in seven minutes.'

Precisely seven minutes later Kronoff appeared accompanied by a tall, distinguished-looking sun-tanned man clad in an immaculate lightweight grey suit. Kronoff greeted Coquelin like an old friend, embracing him and slapping him on the shoulder. Rouget and Nobby received firm handshakes. The tall guy was introduced as Mazin Al Jabril, a financier who represented a consortium of Arab investors.

Kronoff was a slightly overweight smallish man with a fringe of obviously dyed black hair round a brown dome like a boiled egg. His face however was lean and his eyes dark and hooded. Nobby put him at about fifty to fifty-five.

His approach was brisk and businesslike; there was no small talk.

'Over the last two years I have reorganised my operations to be more efficient and give a better return to my investors. As you can see...' he waved at the company reports, '... it is proving to be a great success. The arrangements for the

107

development of Tern Island, therefore, will be carried out – as previously, by Tern Island Developments Inc. But this company will be one hundred per cent owned by The International Trading Bank of St Croix [Tern Island] Inc.'

He held up a hand to stop the startled interruption from Garside.

'The reason for this is to safeguard your investments. You will deposit your portion of the funding with ITBSC [Tern Island] and they will issue to you Certificates of Deposit for the amount each of you have invested. These certificates are tradable instruments and will have a guaranteed annual return of not less than 15%. This will be paid annually from the date of your deposit, and you will not have to wait until the development is complete to show a return. Obviously, we are all expecting that when it does make profits, the percentage will be higher – probably much higher – I'm anticipating at least 25%. Mr Al Jabril and his Arab colleagues are delighted with the prospectus, as are my South African investors. With your contributions the total funding is secure and the lease for Tern Island has been signed. It is all systems go!'

He sat back in his chair and gave them a smile all round. 'You must admit gentlemen, that this is a deal and a half!'

Nobby, who had been totally lost after the first few words looked at Coquelin and Rouget, but they were politicians not financiers and looked back at Nobby assuming that, as a British Member of Parliament, he might know more about international finance than they did. As a result none of them wanted to appear ignorant by asking what might appear to be a stupid question like 'how much money were each of the other parties, including Kronoff, putting in', so they simply nodded agreement. They looked across at the distinguished-looking Arab and saw reassurance in his manner.

Kronoff pointed to the gold-embossed folders. 'If you will each take your folder, all the information I have given you plus the financial forecasts for Tern Island are in there so all I need from you now are your cheques for your investments gentlemen.'

Coquelin said, 'The Minister will arrange the payment for all three of us' and nodded at Rouget. He took a National Bank of Comorantes cheque book out of his case and wrote out three cheques to The International Trading Bank of St Croix [Tern Island] Inc and wrote on the accompanying slips for his records: preliminary operations for the redevelopment of Tern.

Kronoff took from each of them the beautifully engraved and embossed Certificates of Deposit, signed them with flourish and sealed them with a large red seal that read International Trading Bank of St Croix [Tern Island] Inc.

A secretary was called in to add his signature as a witness.

'Well that concludes today's business gentlemen.' The certificates were replaced in the folders and handed back to each of them. Kronoff shook their hands, asked Coquelin to remain behind with him and Al Jabril, and Nobby and Rouget were ushered off the boat back down to the quay.

Nobby was almost beside himself. He had made it! At long last he had made it; he was going to be a rich man. He clutched his folder – he *was* a rich man!

'Why has Henri stayed behind?' he asked Rouget.

'Oh, it's probably something to do with the lease, that's all.'

'When do you think work will start Phillipe?'

Rouget laughed. 'It started about six months ago, clearing the jungle, building the air strip, building a jetty, forming a channel through the reef. Things like that.'

'Can I go and see it?'

'I'm afraid not. It's Kronoff's private island now and security is very tight. We don't want reports about it leaking to the media so no visitors are allowed near the place.'

All three of them then had lunch at Government House.

'That Arab man Al Jabril was pretty impressive. If the Arabs are backing this scheme it must be a good investment,' observed Coquelin.

Nobby's reassurance factor hit a hundred per cent. He was on a winner in the world of international finance; he couldn't lose.

As this was an unofficial visit to the Comorantes paid for by them, and nobody else knew where he was, Nobby didn't want to be away for too long so he caught the night flight on Comorantes Airways back to London.

Again it was an uncomfortable, restless flight and it was whilst trying to doze off that a disturbing thought struck him. Nobody, Coquelin, Rouget and especially Kronoff had asked him anything about himself. Kronoff could have no idea who he was apart from the fact that Coquelin may have told Kronoff he was a British MP. But nobody had asked him where he wanted his interest/dividend paid! He fumbled in his bag for the leather folder and read though the information again. *Returns to investors would be paid on an annual basis commencing one year after the deposit had been made.* He gave a sigh of relief. So there was plenty of time to sort that out, however it would be sensible to take some precautions, and an arrangement with CONDES would give him both the opportunity to keep an eye on the development of Tern Island, see what was happening to the money and keep him in touch with Coquelin. He resolved to make contact with that chap Elmes again and see if he could resurrect a deal.

That was going to be a bit tricky. He cursed himself. He had been too hasty in walking out on Elmes in Le Gavroche and sticking him with the bill. He was going to have to do some serious rectification of that situation to see if he could still get himself involved. He hoped to hell that his bad-mouthing of CONDES hadn't reached Elmes' ears.

*****

APRIL, 2010 – CONDES OFFICE, LONDON

It was a rare occasion when I beat Hugo into the office in the morning and this wasn't one of them, although I *thought* I was early. Feeling on top of the world after my fortnight skiing with Tony Scales in Austria I was ready for the fray. My co-director's BMW was already in its parking slot when I swung the old MG TF alongside it. It was a crisp spring morning in London; one of those days when the blood seemed to circulate at warp speed, the cool air tingled the cheeks, the blue eyes sparkled, the stride was brisk, the shoulders held back, and it felt as if it was going to be a 'be good to Marcus Moon' day.

There were two additional reasons for this: my beloved girlfriend Zoe was due back this afternoon after spending two weeks with her ailing mother in Church Stretton, which promised a night of unbridled ecstasy to make up for lost time; and the second was my office makeover.

Zoe Garrard and I had first met at one of Mazin Al Jabril's lavish, snobby but extremely dull cocktail parties. We caught each other sneaking out of the door as early as we decently could, sidling behind everybody's backs to avoid being noticed.

You know when you have one of those rare moments in life when the world seems to stop and everything pales into insignificance? Well I had one then. It was not that she was beautiful in the glossy magazine sense, but she radiated an aura. I quickened my step so we arrived at the exit at the same time and I threw out my carefully cultivated chat-up line, honed in the snug bar of the Frog and Nightgown over the years.

'Hello,' I said. For a moment I thought it was going to have the success it normally did with stunning girls – falling flat on its face; however, she smiled and said, 'You're Marcus Moon.'

It was me who was stunned. 'How on earth did you know that?' I'd gasped.

'Mazin Al Jabril was talking about you and I overheard him.'

Curiosity got the better of me. 'What did he say?'

Her smile broadened and the way her blue-grey eyes crinkled made my toes curl.

'He was pointing you out to a greasy-looking little fat chap and I think his exact words were, "You see that lanky son of a castrated camel over there, that is Marcus Moon, so get on with it!"'

Ah yes I remembered; the 'greasy-looking little fat chap' was Ahmed Marzouk, Mazin's lawyer and I'd commented that Mazin needed to brush up on his reproductive biology.

As a result of that we chatted all the way to the entrance to the flats.

It turned out that both of us were hungry and neither of us had anything else to do that evening. I tentatively suggested that we have dinner together at a little Italian restaurant in Holbein Place – and that, as they say, was that!

It was one of those evenings when time flew by without either of us noticing until the management decided that, as their broad hints for us to depart, like leaving the bill and hovering round the table clearing their throats and giving the bill an ineffective poke now and then, had been ignored, they would start clearing everything away round us and noisily stack the chairs on the tables. To our astonishment, on looking round we discovered that we were the only people left. We shared a taxi that dropped her off at her flat in Pimlico and took me on to Palmerston Mansions in Battersea. We arranged to meet again the following week.

Now we shared a terrace house in Chelsea and had been together for the past three blissful years.

My other reason for excitement was that whilst I was away skiing, my office had been given a makeover. New office furniture had been delivered and installed under the watchful eye of Major Margaret Braithwaite – my secretary. Brian Mason had told me that it was the first time he had seen delivery men actually break into a trot when carrying a desk, but with the Major barking instructions in their ears I wasn't surprised. I chuckled inwardly at the thought.

Belinda, my original long-term secretary, had given up waiting for a more permanent relationship with the Moon body than we had, and gone off and married a lawyer with a chin like a ploughshare.

She had left CONDES to produce an offspring which, after an anxious few months on my part, fortunately turned out to have no resemblance to me whatsoever, being chubby and brown-eyed. I noted that it didn't have much resemblance to him either, but that was not my concern. She had settled down to married life with the litigious chin and seemed content. Her departure had left a vacancy and, without my knowledge, my co-directors and alleged friends decided some time ago that I needed 'organising' and seized the opportunity. They had recruited Margaret Braithwaite, an ex-Women's Royal Army Corps Major for the task, and, after a few initial skirmishes to establish who was boss, we had settled down to a good working relationship. I know what you're thinking and, of course, you're right – it was her!

Her office, through which people had to pass to get to mine, was a model of military precision. Efficiency pulsated in the air from its shining white, precisely aligned furniture and humming computers to the pot plants, which appeared to be standing to attention. My office had been a tip, I admit it, but it was *my* tip and I felt comfortable amongst its homely mess.

Margaret had managed to persuade Brian Mason, our Finance Director, to allocate funds to smarten it up. This took some time because simultaneously I was secretly persuading him that the money could be better spent expanding the business. I was very fond of my tip! It was a sort of all-enfolding womb of familiarity.

This had all come about when the original partnership, Consultant Design Services, had been reconstituted as Consultant Design Services Limited – still known as CONDES – and most of the old partners retired. Hugo Elmes, the original senior partner who happened to be the youngest partner, took over as managing director. I was just an associate partner creeping my way up the ladder when Hugo had brought me in as a full director and shareholder to run the business with him.

After we had sorted out the major trauma caused by Mazin Al Jabril, supposedly our Egyptian agent who had nearly bankrupted us, we realised that these days we needed someone with financial acumen. So we had appointed Brian Mason, the accountant put in by the bank, as our Finance Director.

Hugo had the smart office, all green leather, Scandinavian wood and stainless steel, overlooking Battersea Park, and that was used for conferences and entertaining clients. My office was quite small but had a great view of the Thames between Albert and Battersea bridges. It was filled with battered furniture that was the pick of what was left from the old partners' offices – some of which must have been bought circa 1970.

When there was a meeting, my office was used for dumping visitors' coats. Now, thanks to Major Margaret, I had the uncomfortable feeling that I was being moved into the twenty-first century. No more coat dumping; the Major's first move had been to organise the construction of a proper cloakroom using some spare space next to Brian's office. That was when I knew I was fighting a losing battle, but, as they say, if you're going to be screwed lie back and enjoy it, so I was very interested to see what she had come up with.

A sunny smile from Amanda our receptionist, a brisk sprint up the stairs, a few "Good Mornings", "Hi's" and nods to passing engineers and I hit the lair of Margaret Braithwaite just before nine o'clock.

'Hi Margaret, is it all ready?' I nodded towards the door of my office which, unusually, was closed. Ah, so this was to be the big opening ceremony. We had spent a few hours discussing what I wanted and what she thought I would want if I knew about it – if you follow my meaning. I wasn't certain that she had taken everything I'd said on board, but I had concluded by saying that if I didn't like it, it could all go back from whence it came and we would start again.

She smiled expectantly. 'Did you have a good holiday Marcus? Was there plenty of snow? You look nice and brown. Thank you for the postcard, Innsbruck seems a pretty place although I've never been. My sister went there once...'

I grinned at her attempt to build up the tension.

'Just get the bloody door open and put me out of my misery!

I half expected her to stand up and throw open the door to my office with a grand flourish, but she was too canny for that. I also detected a satisfying gleam of uncertainty in her eyes. Satisfying because I didn't like being too predictable and obviously she wasn't sure what my reaction would be. I walked past her desk and opened the door myself, half expecting to be blinded by stainless steel, white plastic, blazing halogen lights and floor to ceiling electronic gadgetry. Instead, my gaze was met by mellow wood, soft tones, concealed lighting, a plain blue wool carpet and an air of comfortable efficiency.

My eyes widened in astonishment and I stood amazed. It was me! She had got it just right, the only thing missing were the normal piles of documents, plans, reports, studies etc. that littered my old room and made industrial espionage impossible because only I knew where everything was. Mrs O'Reilly, the cleaning lady, had been threatened with a very painful death involving her mop and bucket if she tried to tidy up.

'It's all labelled and filed away in those cabinets,' Margaret's voice at my elbow murmured as she pointed to a row of discreet filing cabinets, anticipating my question. I crossed the threshold and drifted across the soft carpet to the window. The view of the river and Chelsea Embankment opposite was still the same and the river sparkled in the morning sun. She followed me in and waited anxiously for my reaction.

'Brilliant Margaret, I love it. Thank you! And I thought you weren't listening to a word I'd said.'

She gave a strange smile part relief and part something else and just said, 'I'll get your coffee. The usual: hot, strong, sweet and black?'

As she turned to leave, the short spare figure of Hugo appeared in the doorway. He strolled in looking round. His face, still tanned from sailing and his regular Sunday golf creased into a smile. 'Very nice, not at all Moon-like.'

'I'm glad you like it!' I replied. 'But don't worry, I'll soon have it knocked into shape – *my* shape. Coffee?'

He accepted and plumped himself into one of the visitor's chairs.

'Good holiday?'

We chatted about that and what had events had taken place whilst I was away, then his kindly face took on a serious expression.

'There are a couple of things that are worrying me, Marcus. I don't know if you realise it, but since we designed the Wolverhampton three-level intersection we haven't had a single enquiry from the Department of Transport.' He continued. 'Nor have we had anything more from the DfID or the Department of Defence. I know the Government is cutting back on spending, but there are other consultants who are getting enquiries. If we don't pick up a decent-sized road job soon, we're going to have to reduce the size of our roads and bridges section.'

I frowned. 'Is there any reason?'

Hugo shrugged, 'Not as far as I can tell. The civil servants say it's just the cut-backs and the politicians seemed to be looking at a wider agenda.'

'What on earth does that mean?"

'I'm looking into it with my contacts.'

'What's the other thing – you said there were two?'

'Ah, yes! When are you going out to the Gulf again? Jack Fourie phoned me to say that there is a bit of a problem on Port Mahon. I know it's my project, but we could kill two birds with one stone if you could fly on from the Gulf to the Comorantes and help Fourie sort his problem out. It would save my time and the company money.'

Hugo Elmes was my co-director, friend and mentor. He was a clever, kindly man; a brilliant design engineer and as cunning as an old fox can be. He gave me a soft smile and I gave him one back. I had known Hugo too long to fall for that smooth line. Was there more to this than met the eye – or rather the ear? Further questioning was required.

'Put me in the picture about Port Mahon, Hugo. All I know is that it's an aid project and our fees are paid by DfID.'

His smile turned into a broad grin as he acknowledged that I hadn't walked into the trap.

'As you know, we have been appointed by the Department for International Development to design and supervise the construction of a small port on Beauregard Island in the Comorantes Group in the Indian Ocean. It's a $150-million project and it's mostly funded by the British Government and part-funded by the International Bank for Reconstruction and Development – The World Bank.'

I nodded, so far so good.

'We've designed the whole project and, on behalf of the Comorantes Government, bids were invited for the construction...'

Nothing tricky yet.

'...The tender list was drawn up by the Comorantes Government. We had no say in the matter...'

A slight feeling of unease.

'...The contract was won by Mumbai Construction of India, a reputable firm...'

The slight feeling grew stronger but I kept quiet.

'...We have appointed site supervision staff under a Resident Engineer – Jack Fourie, who's a South African – to supervise the construction. Work started on site five months ago...' He paused.

'Yes?'

'... and it is already two months behind programme.'

I whistled in astonishment. 'How come?'

'Well, according to Jack, Mumbai Construction hasn't been paid a dollar. The contract provides for a 20% down payment against a bank bond to cover all their setting up costs and they have provided the bond. Jack has authorised a further four monthly certificates – but so far not a bean has been paid. As a result Mumbai haven't been able to provide half the plant, equipment and labour necessary.'

I scratched my head; maybe it was just another international finance cock-up where every party is waiting for somebody else to make the first move. Nobody does, so the project freezes. Our coffee arrived and I sipped mine thoughtfully.

'What's the financial chain, Hugo?'

He tossed a piece of paper on to my shining new desk. For an instant I felt quite mortified that its pristine surface should be sullied by a grubby article of commerce, and then I started to laugh.

'What's so funny, I can't see anything funny in that?' he said, huffily.

I explained about getting all protective about my new furniture.

He raised his eyes heavenwards. 'Heaven forbid that you should become a normal person, Marcus and start to conform – it could be the ruin of our business!' He pretended to clutch his heart and then continued without pause. 'As you will see, all the funds are channelled through the Department for International Development here. They then go to the Government of the Comorantes' Port Mahon Account at The National Bank of Comorantes. The Comorantes Ports and Harbours Authority have drawing facilities on this account based on CONDES monthly certificates confirming that a certain amount of work has been carried out in that month. From there the payments should be made to Mumbai Construction in accordance with the terms of the contract. i.e. a down payment and then against our monthly certificates.'

I thought about what he had told me for a few moments. There didn't seem to be anything tricky or devious about this; it sounded like the usual bureaucratic balls-up that happens all the time with government projects. It was like a bath filling with water – it just needed somebody to find the plug and pull it out and all would flow satisfactorily thereafter. That was the theory!

'So you want me to go and loosen the blockage?'

'And have a general nose around. It's always good to see what is going on, with whom and why.'

I gave him a sharp look, but his kindly face remained expressionless. This was even more alarming.

'Are you suspicious then?'

'Well, I can tell *you* are,' he riposted. 'It was written all over your face when I told you who'd won the contract.'

I blinked. This was not good news either. Not that I was suspicious, but that my face had betrayed the fact. Being away from the office for two weeks skiing must have softened me up. The Moon face had been trained to be impassive when I wasn't sure whether I was having smoke blown in my ear or not. Some practice in front of the mirror was called for. Thinking about this I missed the point that Hugo hadn't answered my question but had merely returned the ball into my court.

Hugo coughed, gently. 'Are you alright? You seemed to drift away for a few moments there.'

I gave him the 'I was weighing up mighty matters' look and called through the open door to Margaret, knowing that it irritated her that I didn't use the intercom. 'When am I next due in the Gulf, Margaret?'

My intercom buzzed and I pressed the switch. She said primly, 'You're booked on Etihad next Thursday.'

Hugo shook his head in bewilderment at this exchange, but I wasn't going to yield my informal position. I called out for her to book me on from Abu Dhabi to The Comorantes on the Sunday and a local flight to Beauregard Island on Tuesday, leaving the return flights open; and to let Jack Fourie know.

As he was going out of the door Hugo turned back for a moment. 'Oh, by the way there's one more thing... I don't think it will affect your visit, but I've been contacted again by that MP chap – Garside.'

I blinked. 'What MP chap?'

'Didn't I mention it some time ago? This Garside bloke, who is apparently an MP for some northern constituency, invited me for lunch at Le Gavroche – wanted us to pay him ten grand a year as a consultant to advise us on political matters and said he had a very influential position as deputy chairman of the Department for International Development. I told him I knew his Chairman. That rocked him back, so I asked him what exactly he could do for us. He waffled on about nothing much so I told him to write to us, setting out his proposals and he hastily buggered off leaving me to pay the bill.'

I grinned. 'You don't often get caught like that Hugo – you'll have to start taking the tablets.'

'The point is, young Marcus, that Desmond Fitzpatrick – the Chairman – told me that Garside was the guy on his committee who knew all about Port Mahon and the Comorantes. He claimed to be a personal friend of both the President/Prime Minister and the Minister of Ports and Harbours.

'So?'

'So he's rung me recently to try to fix another lunch.'

'And have you?'

123

'No, I've made an excuse. I thought I'd mention it in case you come across him whilst you're there.'

CHAPTER EIGHT

2010 – CONDES OFFICE, LONDON

When Hugo had departed to return to his own office Margaret brought in all the mail that had accumulated for me whilst I was away and collected the coffee cups. I checked my emails first, but fortunately there was nothing momentous or disastrous amongst the lot.

I leant back in my new adjustable swivel chair to do some thinking, and was about to put my feet on the desk when there was a discreet cough from the door. I wasn't sure if it was a subtle reprimand or a call for attention, but I dropped them to the floor again and said, 'OK Margaret, come in and sit down. What's on your mind?'

'It's Richard.'

'Ah!' I said. Those two words "It's Richard" sent a shudder down my spine.

Since the unmarried Major Margaret first came to be my secretary/PA I had detected subtle shifts over time in both her appearance and attitude, which seemed to focus around me. She'd arrived wearing thick woollen jumpers and tweed suits. Her hair was cut in a severe bob and her make-up looked as though it had been applied by a colour-blind plasterer. Gradually this changed; her hair was styled, shaped skirts and blouses replaced the jumpers and tweed and the orange lipstick with heavy green eye shadow became a subtle pink with a touch of mascara. She also, and even more alarmingly, became more touchy/feely. When I discovered that the structural engineers were referring to us as "The Happy Couple" I decided feet must be put down and something be done – and quickly.

Richard had turned up quite fortuitously as a result of me advertising Margaret's availability as a companion in various contact magazines – without her knowledge, of course. These ranged from 'Bonk' and 'Crumpet' at one end of the scale to 'Gentlewoman's Musings' at the other.

She wasn't too pleased, to put it mildly, when she received a pile of letters, mostly from sex-starved perverts or braggarts, who thought their willies should be in *The Guinness Book of Records*. In fact she threatened to "*strangle with her bare hands the filthy joker who had set this up*" – if she ever found out their identity. I managed to filter into her mind that it could be one of the structural engineers and she went along with that – they fitted the bill! Now Major Margaret Braithwaite, ex-Women's Royal Army Corps, could probably stop an armoured column single-handed, so I was very relived when she found one sensible letter amongst this dross and decided to follow it up, dropping her interest in manual strangulation for the time being. The outcome was Richard. She hit gold on her first strike. She had brought him to various firm's functions and he seemed a very nice, charming man. Quiet not forceful, which fitted in with the Major's plans; about the same age as her and a widower, so he had had some experience with women. They seemed very happy together. The benefit of this, of course, was that she had dropped her suspected interest in me.

So "It's Richard" could mean many things, not all of which would induce tranquillity in the Moon bosom.

Had he given her the heave-ho? No, unlikely: she didn't seem unhappy or downcast. In, fact I'd heard her humming to herself in her office that morning so it couldn't be that.

Had he, as they say in "bodice ripper" novels, made unwelcome advances? For a few months I had been dying to know if they had got it together and he had given her one, so to speak. Perhaps they had and she was going to tell me she was pregnant? No, also unlikely; she was over fifty – but not impossible these days. IVF could work wonders.

He was moving to foreign parts and she was off with him to deepest Africa or Amazonia – also possible, and from my point of view, disastrous.

She wanted to form a threesome. Definitely a non-starter – at least if she was expecting *me* to make up the trio!

So what was it?

I refocused on her; she was gazing at me in total bewilderment.

'Are you alright, Marcus? You seemed to go into one of your trances. Shall I get you a glass of water? Did you hear what I said?

Bugger! I'd done it again. 'Oh yes, sorry Margaret, what about Richard?'

'He's asked me to marry him.'

'Fu ... Blow me, has he!? And what did you say?'

She actually blushed and replied, 'I said I'd think about it and let him know. I wanted to talk to you first.'

'Me?!' I was left speechless for a few seconds. Why would she want to talk to *me*? Was she looking for a counter offer? This was dangerous ground. A veritable quicksand and I wasn't sure how to extricate myself. Maybe a small joke...?

'About the birds and the bees? Well this bee gets this bird and pulls its pants down and—'

'No, you idiot, not that! It's my job. If I marry Richard, will I keep my job? It's the best job I've ever had and I don't want to lose it.'

I heaved a huge sigh of relief which produced a puzzled frown on her brow, but that disappeared when I followed it up with, 'Of course you can keep your job Margaret, there's no question about that. I'd be totally lost without you.'

'Oh thank you, thank you, Marcus. I can tell Richard yes now. I'm so happy,' and she plonked a big wet kiss on my cheek and shot off back into her office humming, *Oh What a Beautiful Morning*.

Slightly baffled, I watched her leave. She was a brilliant secretary; tough, efficient, friendly, and since Richard had entered her life, she had totally abandoned the military make-up and formidable clothes and looked pretty good for a fifty-year-old with the makeovers she'd taken. Why she thought she might lose her job defeated me – unless she thought that the idea of her tying the knot with another would have broken my heart and I would fire her in a fit of jealous rage.

'Strange creatures aren't they?' I said shaking my head. I must have spoken aloud because Janet, Hugo's secretary said, 'Who are?'

I had been so wrapped up in my thoughts that I hadn't heard her come in and she made me jump.

'You lot!' I said. 'The whole monstrous gamut of worldwide women.'

She grinned, 'So Zoe's been sorting you out, has she Marcus? It's about time somebody did.'

'What can I do for you Ms Granger?' I said, primly.

'Hugo asked me to give you Fourie's latest site reports from Beauregard Island.' She handed me a folder.

She looked round my office. 'Very nice,' she commented, 'the committee didn't do a bad job after all.'

I was flicking over the pages of Jack Fourie's reports and heard what she said with only half an ear so it didn't register then. It was only later. when I thought about it, that I realised Margaret must have chickened out of taking full responsibility for reorganising my office and roped in the other senior staff for advice. I had a quiet chuckle to myself – she wasn't so confident.

****

Zoe and I had pooled our financial resources and bought a terrace house in one of the less fashionable areas of Chelsea – at least that was its postcode, although the Fulham boundary was within a footballer's spitting distance. I wondered about that as I was driving home. Did footballers have practice spitting sessions during training?

'Right lads let's see who can project a glob of phlegm into "the box" from out wide. That's effin' useless van de Schnitzel - I want to see a nice curving arc not a dribble down your stubble. You've got to put in more work on those tongue muscles and propellant if you want to make the first team squad lad.'

The angry sound of horns being blown jerked me from my reverie and I noticed that the traffic lights had gone green. I gave an apologetic wave to those held up behind me and slipped the clutch on the MG.

The car was slotted in to a vacant residents' parking place within easy walk of the house and I quickened my pace as the thought of Zoe waiting and what would surely follow grew. I slid my key into the lock and opened the door. There was a delicious smell of cooking and the sound of her singing quietly to herself in the kitchen.

I slapped my forehead. Blast, I'd forgotten to buy some flowers. I eased out again and quietly closed the door. A quick sprint down the road to Exxon Filing Station on the corner rectified the problem and I was back at the house in five minutes. I went into the small hall calling out 'Hello'.

'Is that you Marcus?'

'It had better be! Who did you think it was? That big horny milkman from Express Daries who ogles you every time he sees you?'

She came running out of the kitchen, blue-grey eyes sparkling, her long chestnut hair tied back in a pony-tail and a huge smile across her face. She hurled herself into my arms and planted a very suggestive kiss on my receptive lips. She stepped back and noticed the flowers. 'Oh, you shouldn't have!'

I didn't tell her I nearly hadn't, and cursed under my breath that I might have wasted five quid, but there you are.

However, I had a feeling that they had actually served their purpose.

I grabbed hold of her again, but she wriggled free. 'Food first sunshine, I haven't slaved over a hot stove all afternoon for it to go cold whilst you have your wicked way with an innocent convent girl. Besides, my long thin streak of passion, you're going to need something to sustain you over the next few hours after we've eaten – we've two weeks to catch up on!'

This sounded even more promising than I'd anticipated so I allowed myself to be led through into the kitchen/dining area where she had set out two places with candles and soft music. A fizzing large gin and tonic was pushed into my hand and I studied her as she bustled about setting out our dinner.

Her eyes were too far apart, her mouth was too wide, her teeth were very white and slightly uneven, and her chin showed determination. She had a great figure and was nearly as tall as me. The whole effect, however, was stunning. She radiated an aura that turned heads when she entered a room.

I gave soft smile; you lucky sod, Marcus Moon.

This evening she was clearly determined that I wouldn't run out of energy later on, and the smoked salmon and fresh prawns followed by roast lamb with all the trimmings and finally, the pièce-de-résistance, treacle sponge with chap's custard – my favourite pudding – provided a surfeit of calories that just managed to last out until we both fell into an exhausted but dreamy sleep in each others arms. I don't know what there is about the air or water in Church

Stretton, but they should bottle it and export it to China. It would out-sell rhino horn.

****

Etihad Airlines had a daily flight from Abu Dhabi to the Comorantes Islands and so I had a late dinner with Dave Moran, our chief engineer in the Gulf, and he dropped me at the airport to catch the flight to Grande Rocques which was due to take off just after midnight. There was a technical fault and as a result the Airbus 320 didn't leave until 3.30, so I eventually arrived at Eric de Verteuil airport crumpled and tired, and just in time for breakfast. Having collected my duffle bag and passed through immigration I took a taxi to Fisherman's Wharf Hotel.

Hugo had spoken to his contact at the Department for International Development and been given the name of the guy in the Comorantes Government Ports and Harbours who was dealing with the financial side of the aid package. So after checking in, having a good refreshing shower, putting on some clean clothes and wrapping myself round fresh paw-paw with lime juice followed by bacon, egg, mushrooms and tomato, I felt fit enough to tackle Minister Philippe Rouget in his lair at the Comorantes Ports and Harbours office.

The taxi dropped me off outside a smart two-storey building painted yellow and cream, close to the harbour. A smiling dark girl with a lovely Creole accent told me, 'Please take a seat and I will notify the Minister that you are here.'

She dialled a number and spoke quietly on the phone for a couple of minutes.

So far so good. I thumbed through couple of brochures which took me about fifteen minutes and then resorted to looking round the reception area. That took about two minutes. The receptionist was doing her nails and listening to some local radio station.

'You did tell the Minister that I'm here and I've come all the way from London to see him?'

She smiled. 'Oh yes, he'll be with you shortly.'

"Shortly" in the Comorantes obviously meant something quite different to "shortly" in the rest of the world because half an hour later I was still sitting in the reception chewing my fingernails and waiting for the bugger to show up.

It was time for positive action. I picked up my folder and headed for the staircase where a sign with an arrow pointed upwards to "Director of Ports Office".

The girl reacted with alarm. 'Excuse me sir, you can't go up there'.

'I can and I am,' I replied, and sprinted up the stairs two at a time, leaving her wails fading behind me.

A long corridor faced me at the top of the stairs and I reasoned that the big cheese would have the smart office at the far end with the view over the harbour and not at the end where I was standing, which had a view over a scrapyard. I headed off along the corridor. It was very quiet except for the sound of a radio or radios playing the same music the girl in reception was listening to and a muted telephone conversation from an office marked "Administration".

The second door from the end had a sign which read "Florence Le Lievre – Secretary to the Director". I gave a brief knock and walked in. It was empty. There was another door which obviously led into the office of The Director himself.

I gave that a brief tap and walked in.

There are times in one's life when things don't turn out quite as you expect – this was one of them. The Director – I assumed it was him, and his secretary – I assume it was her, were both there. The problem arose because, whilst he was virtually invisible sitting in his chair, she was a big lady very visibly sitting astride him. One didn't need to be a Mensa member to work out what they were doing. Fortunately, she had her back to the door and she was blocking his view as well. They were at it so vigorously with lots of gasping and grunting that both my knock and entry had passed unnoticed.

Ah Moon, I thought to myself, we have here a very tricky situation. A German would probably have said, 'I'll call back in five minutes when you've finished whatever it is you're doing.' A Latino would have asked if he could be next – with whom it wouldn't matter. A Frenchman would have cried 'Magnifique!' and applauded. I, being English, felt I should have raised my hat, said 'Good morning, I see you're busy' and left quietly. Not wearing a hat I just slid back out into the secretary's office and closed the door gently.

M'sieur Rouget clearly wasn't going to be receiving visitors for some time so I beat it back along the corridor and down the stairs.

Trying to hide a big grin I called to the receptionist as I passed through her domain, 'I'll come back this afternoon at two o'clock when the Director has got his breath back' and handed her a visiting card.

At two o'clock I was back at Ports and Harbours and was directed straight upstairs where I was received at the top of the stairs by a large dark lady wearing a flowery kaftan and thick eye make-up. She was attractive, in a heavy sort of way, with a pleasant smiley face.

'Hello, Mr Moon, welcome to St Georges. My name is Florence.' She offered a heavily beringed hand the size of a small ham, which I shook warily.

I recognised her when she turned her back to me to lead me down the corridor. It was a back that would be difficult to forget.

'Minister, this is Mr Marcus Moon from London.'

I didn't recognise him though. He was a small, slight figure and all I'd seen of him this morning was the top of his head – and then only intermittently each time Florence reached the perigee of her oscillations. He didn't seem any the worse for wear so he must be a man of some stamina to withstand Florence's crushing weight.

'Welcome Mr Moon, did you have a good flight?'

We went through the customary routine platitudes and I was offered a cold drink, which I accepted. Then it was down to business. I opened the proceedings.

'Minister, we are somewhat concerned about the lack of progress on Port Mahon. As you are aware, we are the consultants and project managers and I have been asked to raise with you the problems Mumbai Construction are

135

experiencing with payments. They are claiming that they haven't been paid anything yet and are not able to continue financing the project any further. Also they say they cannot afford to provide the necessary plant, equipment and labour to do the job properly.'

The little man's eyebrows shot up to his hair line – but he deliberately avoided my gaze. So, this wasn't news to him.

'Are you sure Mr Moon? This is the first I've heard of it, that's very disturbing if it's true.' He called out, 'Florence, bring me the Port Mahon Finance Files.'

A prickle of unease entered my mind. So what's going on? It clearly wasn't the first he'd heard of it; both Jack Fourie and Mumbai had been pressing them for weeks for payment. Still, as a politician, if he wanted to plead ignorance that was understandable as most of them were ignorant in the first place.

Florence was certainly not overtaxed in carrying the files through. They consisted of one thin folder, which he opened holding it up as though he was reading a book so I couldn't see the contents. From the small glimpse I did get they looked like bank statements and copies of CONDES certificates. Not much else.

'Ah yes,' he said. 'Our accounts section hasn't finished checking these yet.'

Rubbish. I thought, but keeping calm I pointed out, 'The 20% down payment doesn't require any checking. They should have received it automatically on signing the contract as soon as their bond was in place. It's now six months since that date.'

He smiled, but it was a smile that didn't reach his eyes; in fact it gave him a cunning look. 'Is it really, well that does surprise me. We must attend to that immediately. Time does fly, doesn't it Mr Moon?'

My antenna twitched again. When people are nice to me about money I always get that feeling. If he had said 'Well we've been hanging on to it to make a bit of interest – business is business – but OK I'll sort it out.' I would have had no suspicions because that is what governments and organisations do. But to plead forgetfulness, that was nonsense.

'So will you make the transfer into Mumbai's account today?'

He hesitated for a second, but I held his gaze, and then he nodded and called out 'Florence, draft out the instruction to the bank to release the 20% down payment and I'll sign it.'

I hadn't finished with him yet. 'What about the four outstanding monthly certificates? Will you pay those as well?'

He didn't like that and became all ministerial with me.

'They will be paid when we're satisfied that they are correct.'

'I'm sorry Minister, but it is CONDES' responsibility to ensure that they are correct before we sign them off. The bank should pay them automatically on receipt. He liked that even less, closed the folder and threw it on his desk irritably. It slid across leaving one corner overhanging on my side.

'I'll look into it,' he snapped. 'Is that all? He turned to some other paperwork on his desk. The meeting was clearly over.

I was not happy about getting the heave-ho so quickly, but now wasn't the time to be confrontational – and he *was* a Minister after all. However, I sat tight.

'I'll be at Port Mahon for a few days and as soon as Mumbai confirm that they have got the money, I'll put pressure on them to increase their staff and equipment and draw up a programme to make up for the lost time – provided the other payments are made. I'd like to be able to confirm to the World Bank in Washington and DfID in London that all is going well when we submit our report next week.'

That brought him up short. 'What report?'

'As consultants, we have to report on progress and payment problems to Washington and London. The next one is due when I return to London. If nothing happens we will have to mention the lack of payment in our next report.' I sucked in some air. 'That will almost certainly trigger a high-level inquiry.'

I gave him a nod and stood up to leave. Brushing against the file I knocked it on to the floor. Some of the documents spilled out and by the time Rouget had rushed round his desk to pick them up I had gathered them together and replaced the file on his desk. 'Sorry about that Minister.'

I gave Florence a wink as I passed her. 'Keep it up,' I said, 'See you again.' She smiled back.

As I was going down the stairs a big, burly man with a red face was coming up. We were on a collision course so I stepped to one side but so did he. I stepped to the other side and so did he.

'For Christ's sake get out of my fuckin' way!' he snarled and pushed passed, stepping on my foot as he did so, and vanished down the corridor towards Rouget's office. The accent was familiar but not the cretin who spoke.

In the taxi back to the hotel I phoned Jack Fourie on my mobile and filled him in about my meeting. I told him I'd get the inter-island hopper flight to Beauregard at 10.00am the next day and go through everything in more detail with him and Mumbai's site manager.

I also wondered about the brief glimpse I had got of the bank statements for Port Mahon whilst I was picking up the papers from the file. There were three items listed in the debit column, but I didn't have time to see the details. As the only expenditure allowed on that account was for Port Mahon and no down payment or monthly certificates had been paid, what were they for?

CHAPTER NINE

2010 – BEAUREGARD ISLAND,
THE COMORANTES ISLANDS

The day was heating up when I boarded the inter-island Beechcraft King Air flight to Beauregard Island. As we climbed to 6,000 feet I had a bird's eye view of an enormous private yacht moored in St George's harbour. It had a helipad on the stern with a blue and green helicopter sitting on it. Midships there was a small swimming pool surrounded by a brightly coloured awning, also in blue and green, but I couldn't see anybody using it.

It was an interesting flight; the view from the cabin window showed the whole pattern of green-covered islands in lagoons surrounded by coral reefs spread out on the azure sea. Fifteen minutes later we banked steeply over the sea and the pilot lined us up to land on a concrete air strip. The plane taxied to a hard-standing beside the small, corrugated-iron-roofed building that served as Beauregard's air terminal. Jack was there to meet me and we shook hands. I hadn't met him before, only spoken on the phone. He was a big friendly sort of guy, fair haired, blue eyes, a rugged outdoor face and a strong South African accent.

'I've arranged for you to bunk with me in my bungalow, the small hotel here is pretty basic.'

On the short drive to the site I filled him in about the detail of my meeting with Rouget and assured him that Mumbai would get their down payment within the next few days. The monthly certificates might take longer, but I had threatened to mention poor payments in my report to the DfID and the World Bank.

'What report?' he said, puzzled.

'The one Rouget believes I'm going to write if he doesn't come through with the money.'

'Ah!' He chuckled.

'By the way, have we or Mumbai, or anybody else for that matter, had any payments at all from the Port Mahon account money?'

'No, not that I'm aware of, why?'

'It's just that the Ports and Harbours Finance file fell on the floor Rouget was round like a ferret up my trousers to pick it up, but before he could I caught a glimpse of a bank statement and I'm sure there were items in the 'payments' column. Three items. Mind you, it was only a glimpse so I couldn't be sure.'

'Well, no money has been paid here.'

He showed me round the site in the afternoon. It was hot now, *very* hot, and my clothes were wet with sweat after just ten minutes. Jack was right; there was absolutely no sense of urgency about any of the activities taking place. A few workers could be seen wandering around aimlessly, spending more time trying to find some shade rather than working; the excavator drivers were moving earth at about half speed and there were several lighters waiting to be unloaded at the temporary wharf that Mumbai

141

Construction had built. It was clearly both underequipped and understaffed.

'Bannerjee, their site agent, is due back from India tomorrow morning. I suspect he may have instructions to stop work altogether if no payments have been received by then.'

Port Mahon was being constructed round a small deep-water bay. It was intended to build a long wide concrete jetty out from the northerly headland, with warehousing, storage and cranes for handling large container ships. This would be protected from the prevailing south-westerly winds by a stone breakwater that curved out from the south headland. Additional wharfage for smaller vessels would be built closer inshore within the confines of the outer harbour.

At present, some concrete piles had been driven through the seabed down to rock for the jetty and the reinforced concrete frame started.

On the other side two cranes were there to place large boulders to form the breakwater, but only one appeared to be working. Some local children were using the rocks on the sea side of the breakwater to jump and dive into the sea with squeals and shouts of joy. I watched them for a few minutes, smiling at their freedom and uninhibited laughter.

Jack asked me if I'd like to have a look round the island. 'We can either drive or I've got a small sailboat and we could use that? The sea is nice and calm and there's good breeze.'

I was all for a sail so we walked round to the next bay where there were three boats pulled up on the sand. Jack's was the Wayfarer. It had a small outboard engine already fuelled up so we pushed it down the beach into the water, climbed aboard, hoisted the sails and he helmed the boat whilst I settled down on a cross bench to look at the passing scenery.

In most places the greenery came right down to the white sandy beaches, tall palm trees with a thick undergrowth of broad-leaved scafola forming an almost impenetrable barrier. There were couple of small villages with tin-roofed houses and fishing boats bobbing at moorings, and a small jetty that I assumed was currently used for importing Beauregard Island's basic requirements and exporting shellfish or whatever the villagers caught. The wind was staring to increase and the boat heeled over and fairly zipped along with the port gunwale just clear of the water. We rounded the headland to the windward side of the island where the breeze was much stronger, turning the waves into white caps. As soon as we rounded the headland I knew something was wrong. The children on the breakwater were no longer laughing and swimming but were shouting and crying, and pointing at something in the sea.

'Somebody's in trouble Jack, let's get over there fast.'

Jack reacted quickly, putting the helm over and tacking towards the breakwater, but the wind was too strong. It was obvious that it would take us a long time to get to where the children were pointing. He dropped the sails with the intention of starting the outboard but a halyard jammed in a block and the boat broached. If somebody was in trouble, it was going to take too long to get there in the boat.

Instinctively, I dived over the side and swam towards the breakwater. At first I couldn't see anything and my mind was thinking that maybe they'd seen a shark or something like that, but then I saw a patch of red in the water and a small black object close by. As a wave lifted it I realised it was a child floating face down. I swam to it and turned the child over on its back. It was a boy, he was very pale and lifeless, a large gash on his forehead was oozing blood. I held his head above the waves and swam on my back towards the boat. It seemed to take ages. Jack had managed to start the engine and I grabbed hold of the boat's gunwale. Between us we hauled the boy into the boat, his limbs were all loose and he flopped around like a rag doll.

'Get the water out of his lungs,' I said, so we turned him on his face and pressed hard on his back. There was a great gurgle and a torrent of seawater spewed out of his mouth. We turned him over, he still wasn't breathing. Jack said 'leave this to me, I've done a CPR course,' and began chest compressions. For a couple of minutes nothing happened then the boy gave a gasp and his chest started to heave. He was suddenly violently sick, his eyelids fluttered and he opened his eyes. We sat him up and I tied a none-too-clean handkerchief round his head to try to stop the bleeding of the deep cut. Jack opened the throttle and headed across the bay.

'Mumbai Construction has got a first-aid room in their compound with a doctor so let's get him over there.' I took over the steering whilst Jack called Mumbai Construction on his mobile and alerted them. They immediately sent one of their big work boats out to meet us. It was quicker for them to tow us in rather than try a tricky transfer in the rough sea

They took the boy to their first-aid room whilst I squelched about in my wet shoes and clothes. Somebody gave me a towel. The Indian doctor came out and reported that the boy seemed to be OK and none the worse for his ordeal. He was going to suture the wound and they would keep the boy in under observation for a couple of days to check there was no residual concussion. If there was any sign of a problem they would call the air ambulance from St George's and get him taken to the main hospital.

'Who is he by the way, and what happened?'

We shook our heads. 'We don't know. He was just one of those youngsters playing on the breakwater; he must have hit his head doing something there.'

The doctor frowned. 'We've told them often enough not to play on the site, it's dangerous, but you know kids...'

Jack phoned for one of our guys to come and pick us up. He left the boat at Mumbai's dock saying he'd collect it later. I changed out of my wet things and Jack's houseboy took them away to wash and dry.

That evening we sat outside in the warm air, watching the frigate birds wheeling and swooping in the darkening dusk sky. We were drinking a chilled South African Sauvignon Blanc and eating freshly barbequed red snapper with mangoes and papaya prepared by his Creole cook. The barbeque was fired by coconut husks to give the fish flavour.

Soon the sky was jet black, free of any light pollution; there was no moon and millions of stars blazed from horizon to horizon. The searing daytime temperatures had dropped to a comfortable level, the night creatures croaked and chattered and the palm fronds whispered together in the light off-shore breeze. It was as close to an earthly paradise as I could imagine.

'It's a good job you wanted to sail,' Jack observed, 'otherwise that kid would be dead.'

'That's life – or death, I suppose. I wonder who he is? Some mother somewhere must be mightily relieved.'

I decided to ask in the morning and turned to thinking about the project. If Rouget kept his promise and we can get this job back on track, I reckon I can talk Hugo into letting me take it over – as a big favour to him, of course! I developed the idea later on and with a smile on my face I drifted off to a sound sleep.

First thing next morning I called in at Mumbai Construction; the boy had had a good night, his name was Jacques Doublet and his father was actually a clerk in their administration office on the island. They told me that the father was very grateful and would be in touch.

After a breakfast of fruit, freshly baked rolls and coffee we waited for the arrival of the morning flight from Grande Rocques. Instead of the expected Beechcraft it was a larger, very ancient Comorantes Airways Fokker Friendship F27 that hit the concrete strip on Beauregard Island that morning. It contained a large number of people, mostly Indians, some in suits and others clearly labourers. The last man off the plane was a huge Indian with a grin like a split melon. He rushed up to Jack and embraced him heartily.

146

'Thank you Jack, thank you – ve are saved! The down payment arrived in our bank yesterday afternoon together with the first of the monthly certificates. Mumbai has told me "all systems go!"'

He seemed to notice me for the first time. Jack said, 'Don't thank me Raul, thank Mr Moon here, he's the man who got your money released.'

Bannerjee suddenly became serious. 'Are you *the* Marcus Moon? CONDES' director?'

I laughed, 'I am a Marcus Moon, there probably are others, but yes, I am a CONDES director. Mr Elmes asked me to help sort out the payment problems.'

'Vell, thank you Mr Moon...'

'Marcus,' I told him.

'Vell, thank you Marcus. Vat is the expression "*a stitch in time saves nine*". That vas certainly just in time. B K Menon, a man vid whom you don't mix trifles, had instructed me to close the site down yesterday morning. He damn well had to verk all evening getting this lot together on the night flight from Mumbai.' He waved towards the crowd milling about on the apron beside a decrepit pile of luggage chuckling to himself.

At that moment two battered buses drew up with Mumbai Construction painted on their sides and the mob climbed aboard with their kit. Bannerjee shook my hand and shouting 'see you later', rushed off to join them.

'God, that's a relief, I can start running a proper construction site now,' sighed Fourie. 'It was like trying to drive slave labour before.'

'Can you make up the time?'

He grinned. 'Oh yes, if they're getting paid those guys will work their socks off – that is, if ever they wear socks. Old trainers and flip-flops are the normal footwear.'

We piled into Jack's Land Rover and headed back to the site. The word had spread already and there was visibly more activity than yesterday. I phoned Hugo on the satellite phone and told him the financial logjam had been loosened. I also told him that I had managed to establish a friendly and personal relationship with Rouget, the Ports and Harbours Minister; that it was blisteringly hot with mosquitoes at night and only *'mad dogs and Englishmen would go out in the midday sun'*. I also said innocently, that the food was awful – mainly dried fish and some weird slimy things called sea cucumbers - and the beer warm.

I waited for a minute trying not to laugh; I could sense his mind working as he digested what I had told him.

'I've got an idea,' he floated out. 'As most of the design work has been done, the Port Mahon project is so close to your Gulf projects, don't you think it would be better if you took it over?'

Now the secret here was not to accept with alacrity, in fact not to accept at all, otherwise he'd smell a rat before I could blink.

'Oh no! Oh no, no, no! I'm only here to do you a favour Hugo, not to have one of your crappy jobs offloaded on to me. You can keep the heat and sweat and insect bites.'

I heard him chuckle over the crackling phone link and he smoothly backed off. 'We'll talk about it when you get back.'

Jack Fourie was looking at me with a puzzled expression on his face. 'I thought you liked it here?'

'Oh I do,' I grinned, 'but Hugo has only been to the Comorantes once and that was for two days in the middle of a tropical storm. All the power was cut off so there was no A/C and all he had to eat was cold curry. If he thought for one moment that it was as nice as it is, there's no way he would hand the job over to me. As it is, he thinks he's going to dump a crap job on me, and when I get back to England he's going to try to talk me round and then offer a substantial bribe for me to take it. So I get a double benefit. Port Mahon *and* a week's extra leave perhaps!'

Fourie looked at me with narrowed eyes. 'I'm going to have to watch my step very carefully with you around,' he murmured.

We went through a revised programme with Bannerjee and one of his planners and fixed a date four months ahead to get back to schedule. The important thing was to get the big breakwater finished before the windy season. We went outside to have another look at it; the children had gone and it was a scene of energetic activity now. Whereas yesterday nothing much seemed to be happening, both cranes were working and lorry-loads of stone kept arriving to be unloaded. Just as I was returning out of the sun into the relative cool of the CONDES office I stopped to watch a beautiful wooden two-masted boat sailing into the bay. Jack noticed my interest. 'That's *Nightwind of Karoo*, beautiful isn't she?'

'Who does she belong to, a wealthy Comorantian?'

'No, she's South African owned, but she's available for charter.'

'Lucky people,' I observed as one of the people on deck waved to us.

I caught the early morning flight back to Grande Rocques. My flight back to London via Abu Dhabi didn't leave until mid-afternoon, so after breakfast I called on Philippe Rouget both to thank him for his speedy response and to see if they would set up a regular system for checking and paying CONDES monthly certificates to Mumbai Construction.

Rouget was at a meeting at the Prime Minister's office so I had a long chat with Florence, his secretary. She told me that she was born on Beauregard Island and she had a sister, Evangeline, working in London as a nurse at St Thomas's Hospital. She told me that Evangeline was having problems with the British tax system and other employment rules and regulations. I gave Florence my card and suggested that her sister rang me and I would arrange for her to come to the office where Major Margaret would put her on the right track. She gave me a grateful smile.

I mentioned my idea about setting up a routine payment system for the Port Mahon project because, from my meeting with the Minister, it seemed a bit disorganised. She laughed, 'The Minister isn't very efficient, he tends to let things slide if he's not under pressure. Leave it with me Mr Moon and I'll set something up between this department and the bank along those lines.' She made a note on a pad.

'Great!' Then I remembered the three payments I'd noticed that we couldn't account for when I knocked the bank folder on to the floor in Rouget's office. 'Florence, can you do me a big favour? I can't remember whether Mumbai have been paid one or two of the monthly certificates. Could you just have a look and check that for me please?'

'Sure, no problem.'

She went to a sturdy metal filing cabinet, opened it with a key and riffled through some file dividers before extracting a folder that I recognised. She brought it to her desk and laid it flat before opening it. One of the first useful things you learn as a consultant is to read things that are upside down on somebody else's desk. Des Doubleday, my old colleague. claimed he could read the front page of *The Telegraph* upside down faster than if it was the right way up. It was not difficult for me to note three items in the debit column were marked 'PORT' before she closed the folder and said. 'Mumbai Construction have been paid their initial down payment and one certificate.' She put the file back in the cabinet and locked it.

'Thanks Florence, that's fine.'

Before I could say more a girl came in and handed her a message. She read it and her face fell and she clapped a hand to her mouth.

'Oh, I'm sorry Mr Moon, but I've got to go. Marie will see you out.' She grabbed her handbag and shot out of the door. I assumed Rouget had summoned her so I wandered back to Fisherman's Wharf, had a snack lunch and packed my kit.

****

Zoe collected me from Terminal Four at Heathrow in her company Toyota and we drove back to our little Chelsea house. She refused to drive my old MG TF anymore. She claimed it wasn't safe. 'There are no air bags, no crumple zone, the brakes are spongy and the hood lets in water! Why don't you get a better car? CONDES can afford one.'

I grinned. 'I'm very fond of it. It was my first car and I'm very attached to it. I like comfortable, old, spongy, familiar things round me, that's why I have you!'

She punched me on the shoulder. 'Don't be too sure about that sunshine, that bodybuilder two houses down has been eyeing me up. I like a man with muscles.'

'Yeah, he's even got a muscular brain. He chained his bike to his front gate last month and somebody rode off on his bike taking the gate with them.'

She burst out laughing. 'You've just made that up! You're jealous Marcus Moon! Uh-oh, so I've got you worried, have I? Well, we'd better keep it that way, keep you on your toes.'

'It would be a better idea if I kept you on your back I think,' and I reached out to grab her, but she easily avoided my grasp. 'Later!' she snapped with mock severity. 'I haven't spent all afternoon shopping and preparing a special dinner for us, to have it ruined by your insatiable lust.' Changing the subject she said, 'Tell me about your trip.'

So, over a cool Sauvignon Blanc in the kitchen, I told her about catching the Minister for Ports and Harbours *in flagrante* with big Florence, rescuing the little boy from the sea and loosening up the flow of money to get the job moving again. Over dinner she told me that she had managed to sell a big house in Hampstead to some Russian oligarch who had walked round the place with a couple of tarts on his arm. She said, 'I presume they were tarts, they were half his age and only spoke Essex English – I don't think marriage was at the forefront of his mind.'

Next morning, after a night of bliss, it was a toss-up whether to see Hugo or the Major first. In the event it was decided for me; I met Hugo in our reception. He looked at my unblemished brown face suspiciously. 'It doesn't look to me as if you've been plagued by insects?'

'Bed bugs Hugo – bites all over my body, or it could have been those black crawly things with bright red legs, they bite. Poor old Jack Fourie...' I shook my head sadly, '...I don't know how he sticks it.' I gave him the bland, 'but you know me, I'll do anything for the firm' look of the suffering martyr. This was a new Moon look based on the eastern 'crucified' expression of total tragedy as practised by souk carpet salesmen when offered a fraction of the amount they were asking. I'd practised it in front of the mirror, but this was its first public outing.

Fortunately, he was tied up with something else and, after a slight narrowing of the eyes, waved the piece of paper he was carrying at me and said. 'Give me ten minutes then come and join me for coffee.'

I could hear Major Margaret humming *I Feel Pretty* from *West Side Story* to herself as I approached my office. So Richard was still on the hook, I was pleased to note.

'Morning Margaret, lovely morning.'

'Morning Marcus, did you have a good time?'

I dropped my voice. 'Yes, but don't tell Hugo, I've still got to convince him to pass the job over to me – or rather allow him to convince me to take it over.'

She raised an eyebrow. 'It's that good, is it?'

I grinned. 'Tell you about it later after I've seen Hugo.'

'I've sorted out the mail; the urgent or important stuff is on your desk, the rest I've handed out to the design team leaders.'

I was really looking forward to settling in to my refurbished office, the shambles that it used to be quickly faded from memory as I sat down in my comfortable chair and glanced around at the warm furnishings. Then I had the doubts again. Was it *too* comfortable? Would it soften the brain, stultify the creative urge and take the cutting edge off design ideas? Had I finally and irreversibly crossed the dark chasm between the 'us' of the dynamic young engineers on one side and the 'them' of boring old management on the other? Well, time would tell.

I called out, 'Hold the coffee, Margaret, I'm seeing Hugo in five minutes and he's going to try and soften me up with some of Emily's flapjacks,' – because that's exactly what his invitation to join him for coffee implied.

Emily Elmes, Hugo's lovely wife, was a superb cook and although she kept Hugo on a strict diet he brought in her famous flapjacks for special occasions – of which trying to persuade me to take over the Port Mahon construction was going to be one – or so he thought.

I wandered along to his office where he waved me to a seat by the coffee table, on which Janet had placed two cups

154

and saucers, milk, sugar and a plate with three flapjacks on it. Three! So it really was going to be the hard sell.

To add a little veracity to the occasion I winced as I sat down and scratched vigorously at a few parts of my anatomy.

He poured me a cup of coffee but held the flapjacks back. We ran quickly through the activities of our Ajman and Dayah offices under Dave Moran. Ajman Steel was just starting to produce rolled steel sections and the Sheikh Qassim University project in Dayah was right on programme.

Then he said, 'OK fill me in about Port Mahon and the problems.' He refilled my coffee cup, but the flapjacks remained tantalisingly out of reach.

I explained about my meeting with the Minister for Ports and Harbours omitting my first encounter with just the top of his head over Florence's reciprocating back. 'I told the Minister that we would have to mention in our report to the World Bank and DfID that monies were not being released by the Comorantes Government and they would, no doubt, want an enquiry. He claimed it was just an oversight but, as a result, Mumbai Construction was paid by bank transfer that same afternoon! The site, which had been like a necropolis, was suddenly galvanised into action and became a scene of frantic activity. Mumbai should catch up on the programme within the next four months.'

'Hmm! You seem to have got on well with the Comorantians.' It wasn't a question I realised; it was his opening ploy to soften me up. I chuckled inwardly.

So with my face set in the Moon '*I am a mug ready to be taken for a ride*' look and totally free of guile, I walked into his trap.

'Well, I suppose I did. I think Phillipe Rouget, the Minister, and I hit it off quite well.'

The flapjacks were moved within reach, but I held back from taking one. Hugo frowned, the bait wasn't being accepted. More 'honey' needed to be poured over the situation.

'How about Mumbai Construction? Did you meet their site manager?'

I saved him the trouble. 'Yes, a very competent guy, Raul Bannerjee – he's a qualified civil engineer; we have a lot in common.'

I didn't know whether we had or not, but for Hugo to believe that we had would help further his 'cunning' plan.

He sat back in his chair and put his fingers together as if in deep thought, his face composed into '*the wise old patron dolling out wisdom to the younger generation*' look.

'You know Marcus; you've done a good job on Port Mahon in building up relationships and it really would save CONDES money if you took over the project from me now it's out of the design stage and on site. You seem to get on with everybody there – particularly the Minister, and as Ajman Steel is virtually finished and Dayah going well you won't have to spend as much time in the Gulf as before and could combine the visits.'

Then he made his decisive move.

He gave me a soft smile and cocked his head on one side as if to say checkmate. 'Have a flapjack.' He picked up the plate and proffered it to me as a clincher. I took one.

I feigned puzzlement, then shock. 'You cunning old dog, you've tricked me to taking on this tropical hell; this plague-ridden midden, haven't you?' I raised a finger. 'But it's not as easy as that, if I'm going look after this pestilential place I'll need some extra time off to compensate, and quite possibly recuperate from the infections, bites and diseases that are part and parcel of the place. I would think at least an extra week.'

He chuckled with relief at my reluctant acceptance and agreed with alacrity to the extra week.

Whilst he was doing this I ate the second flapjack.

Grinning, I told him, 'Emily doesn't allow you to have these, does she?' and then I reached out and took the third, stood up and, with it in my hand, headed back towards my office. The abject look of disappointment on his face as he realised the secret snack he had been anticipating was departing out of the door clutched in my grasp, more than compensated me for the stroke he had tried to pull.

****

Hugo admitted later that he'd watched my back disappearing down the corridor with a feeling of unease. He'd expected to feel smug satisfaction at having persuaded me to shoulder the white man's tropical burden, but somehow that feeling was absent – and it wasn't just the loss of the flapjack he'd been intending to snaffle.

Under strict instructions from Emily, Janet had been reluctant to put three flapjacks on the plate, but he had convinced her that it would need three to soften up me for the *coup de grâce* he was planning. Now he was left with a worm of doubt gnawing at him about something, but he didn't know what – and an empty stomach.

When I returned from lunch with Pete and Tony, a pub lunch at the Pontefract Castle in Soho, Margaret said that a Miss Evangeline Le Lievre had called and left a number. It took me a moment to work out who Evangeline Le Lievre was, then the penny dropped – it was Florence's sister. I rang her back; she had a lovely lilting voice with a delightful Creole accent. She was wasted as a nurse with that voice; she should have been on the radio. However, she explained that she was totally bemused by the British tax, social security and benefit system, and could I help?

'You're not the only one,' I told her, 'there's probably another twenty million people in Britain like you. However, if you come and see my secretary Margaret, she's a whizz at that sort of thing, she'll put you right. I'll transfer you to her.'

I called through the door. 'Margaret, can you help this girl out with her tax affairs? She's the sister of a friend in the Comorantes.' I transferred the call and heard Margaret arranging for Evangeline to come to the office and bring all her papers.

****

On Saturday Zoe and I caught the bus down the Kings Road, hopped off at Chelsea Town Hall and strolled down Oakley Street to the Frog and Nightgown. The strict drink-drive laws prohibited the use of the MG to go to the pub these days. Zoe insisted that I conform to them and two or three pints of Ruddle's Real Ale would put me over the limit. I wondered yet again if her refusal to drive the MG was so that she could have a glass of wine or two and not have to drive me home. Pete was there with Merrylees and waved to Jessie to set up drinks for us.

'Bob said he might be late, Joan has to go for a fitting for the new dress she's having made for her sister's wedding and he's bringing a friend along he thinks we'd like.'

Big Jessie came over with the drinks and set down two glasses of Sauvignon Blanc for the girls, a vodka and tonic for Pete and a pint of Ruddle's for me. I couldn't help thinking back to the old days when Jessie automatically brought over five or six pints of Ruddle's without being asked. Pete, of course, always had his in a glass with a handle. Bob Barclay claimed it was a habit instilled by his nanny who made him hold his Tommee Tippee mug by both handles to stop him playing with himself.

Just as I was thinking of Barclay, the door burst open and Barclay and Tony Scales sailed into the bar followed by Joan, an attractive brunette who I assumed was Tony Scales' new girlfriend, and a tall, good-looking chap of about our age.

'Three pints Jessie please and one of those things with a little umbrella in it for Joan. What'll you have Finola?' This was addressed to the brunette.

159

She glanced at our table, 'Oh a glass of the white wine will be fine.'

Tony pushed two tables together and dragged up some chairs whilst I gave Finola a surreptitious scan. She was not a typical Scales girlfriend; for a start she had intelligent light-brown eyes. She was casually but carefully dressed with a stunning figure but seemed quite at ease with our group of, to her, strangers. Scales' normal girls were dim, pneumatic blondes, usually with wide blue eyes, who did what Tony told them to do – but it was not diplomatic to go into that. Finola looked as though she had a mind of her own.

Bob made the introductions. 'This is Daniel, but he's generally known to his friends as Dan. He's also a Ruddle's drinker.'

Dan shook hands with everybody as we introduced ourselves, and Finola did the same.

I grinned to myself at Bob's clever way of telling us that Dan was a good bloke without going into a long spiel and embarrassing everybody.

We were seated round the tables in no particular order and Finola ended up between Tony and me. She told me she was an anaesthetist at Chelsea and Westminster Hospital and she had first met Tony when he came to A & E to have some infected scratches treated some months ago.

'Really? And how did he come by those?' I raised a questioning eyebrow ignoring Tony's sharp intake of breath and warning glare.

'Oh,' she said, airily, 'he'd being playing with what was supposed to be a tame lion cub when he went on safari in South Africa and it turned a bit fierce.'

Had he, I thought? Well if you're going to tell 'em make 'em big ones. To the best of my knowledge it was a sex-mad Swede called Ulla Hulten who had scarified his back in a fit of passion after I had set him up with her.

As Finola was sitting between us I could feel Scales' eyes burning through her head as he tried to catch my eye to warn me off that line of questioning, but he needn't have worried. I wasn't too keen on having my part in that episode broadcast to the world – well to the pub – either.

Tony gabbled, 'Marcus has just come back from some island paradise in the Indian Ocean, haven't you Marcus?'

It was a pathetic attempt to change the subject, but I was happy to go along with it. Finola turned to me and said, 'I thought you looked brown considering the rotten summer we're having this year. Was it a holiday?'

I shook my head. 'No it was work, but it's a very nice place to visit if you have to work.' And I explained about Port Mahon, the Comorantes and the financing. I told them about catching the Minister of Ports and Harbours doing naughties with his very large secretary and tiptoeing away leaving them to it.

'She was a big lady and he was pint-sized, but he didn't seem any the worse for wear when I returned in the afternoon.'

Bob asked, 'Is it a place to go for a holiday then?'

'Well I wouldn't go to Beauregard Island, it's a building site at present, but the other islands look fantastic. I should think the best way to see the place is to charter a boat and sail round. That could be brilliant; it really is a stunningly beautiful area.'

Joan Barclay grimaced. 'No way, I get seasick standing on a dewy lawn. The thought of living and sleeping on a boat that's being tossed around by the sea – ugh!'

I thought no more about this, but others remembered it. The subject switched to Dan, who had said very little up to now. In fact, apart from thanking Big Jessie for his pint, he hadn't uttered a word.

'So Dan,' Pete said, 'are you also a property man like Bob or do you plough a straight furrow in an honest job like Marcus and myself?'

Dan looked slightly uncomfortable at Pete's direct question, but the girls were obviously interested in what the good-looking Dan did. It turned out that Dan was a freelance journalist. Every week he wrote a society column for *The Times* using the pen name Icarus. He wrote the gossip column in *Private Eye* under the bitter byline 'Silver-plated Spoon', and articles for country magazines like *The Field* and *Country Life* under his own name – Dan Granchester. These provided him with a reasonable income. He told us he and Bob had first met on various shoots and got on well together. It wasn't difficult to see why.

More drinks arrived and the conversation as usual divided into boys – politics, sex and sport: and girls – houses, clothes and who knew whom and what were they doing now. Dan was an easy conversationalist and when eventually we split up to drift off for lunch he joined Bob, Joan, Zoe and I at La Terazza for an 'Italian'.

Something perplexed me about Dan and when Zoe and I got home I went straight to her collection of books. Being a junior partner in the smart West End firm of Galbraith, O'Neil, Davidson – known in the business as GOD – estate agents and property managers to the gentry, she had all the appropriate references books. I selected *Burke's Peerage*.

In fact, Dan had me puzzled about a few things. How could he write a gossip column for *The Times?* That required connections and insight into aristocratic social circles at a high level. Also, if he went shooting with Bob he couldn't be short of a few pounds. Finally, he said he wrote articles for country magazines under his own name, Dan Granchester.

I looked up Granchester.

'Ah-ha! There we are!' It transpired that Dan's full title was The Honourable Daniel de Carteret Granchester and he was in the 'inheritance business'. Dan was the eldest son of Viscount Granchester, an aristocrat who hung his hat in a stately home surrounded by leafy acres and rolling hills in the wilds of Northamptonshire. He also dossed down at the family's ten-bedroomed town house in Belgrave Square and seemingly lived an idyllic life of leisure as a lucky sod who happened to be born with a silver spoon in his mouth.

Prep school, Eton and Oxford had obviously been the plan, but strangely he actually went to Bristol University to read English. Hmm, I thought. That showed a degree of independence – as did working for a living as a journalist.

An interesting person was Dan Granchester, I decided I'd like to get to know him better.

CHAPTER TEN

2010 – LONDON, ENGLAND

On Monday morning the phone rang as I was going through the back files on Port Mahon. As it was buried under piles of drawings, letters and various cost analyses it took me a moment to find it. It was my private line so it must be either family or a friend. It turned out to be Bob Barclay with a question.

'You remember telling everybody in the Frog about the Comorantes? Well, can you tell me a bit more about the place – particularly about sailing round the islands?'

I was intrigued. 'There's not much more to tell, Robert. The main island Grande Rocques, has the capital St Georges and the airport. It's pretty flat, presumably mostly coral with some rocky hills in the south. It has a big reef around it forming a large lagoon with entrances for shipping; lush tropical vegetation with lots of beautiful flowers and trees; good roads, nice people and some fine restaurants. Apart from Beauregard, I've only seen other islands from the air. They vary from little more than coral atolls to much bigger islands, presumably granite, with quite high mountains. The beaches are white sand, the sea is turquoise, the jungle green. The whole scene is idyllic.'

'What about boat charter.'

'There are boats for charter, both 'bare boats' and with crew; I've only seen one and it was a beauty. Why, are you thinking of taking Joan there?'

He gave a snort of laughter. 'Are you kidding!? You heard what she said about boating. She'd sooner stuff chillies up her nose than sleep on a boat! No, I was thinking of a boys' trip.'

That stopped me in my tracks. All kinds of things flashed into my mind. On the face of it, it sounded like a brilliant idea, but these days were not like the old, single man/employee days when one could make instant decisions because then you were the only one to consider. To buy some time I asked him, 'With whom? Have you talked to anyone else yet?'

He chuckled, 'Well to tell you the truth I am sitting at my desk watching the rain pissing down from grey skies over Kensington, just as it was doing yesterday and the day before, and I thought to myself – what would I rather be doing at this moment? The answer came without effort. Floating in a tropical paradise surrounded by friends and sipping ice cold margaritas under blue skies wafted by gentle breezes scented with frangipani seemed, at that moment, to have the edge over London. So the answer is, I've only just thought of it, but I like the idea.'

And so did I! As my mind started to slot things into place I was beginning to see it working. From CONDES and Hugo's point of view it wouldn't be a problem. Hugo had already agreed that I could take an extra week's leave and I could combine the boat trip with a business visit to Port

Mahon. In fact, I could get there before anybody else and make sure the thing was set up properly.

'Is that a buzz saw I can detect or is it the Moon mind creaking into first gear?'

'Bob, you sound out the others, let's give it some thought and discuss it in the Frog on Saturday.'

After I had put the phone down I sat in contemplative mood for a few minutes. I would have to discuss it with Zoe well before then. To present it as a *fait accompli* was not the right approach in this case. It was going to need charm, tact, discretion, bread laid up in heaven, and all wrapped up in a cunning plan; all five of which I modestly prided myself I could produce! The problem was she had a mind like a scalpel and unless the cunning plan was very well disguised it would be filleted and slashed to ribbons, closely followed by my pride. I resolved to work on it and perfect it throughout the week. I forgot that once Bob Barclay got an idea in his head he was not somebody who let the grass grow under his feet, if you follow me.

Wednesday happened to be the anniversary of the day Zoe and I had met at Mazin's party. To celebrate Zoe said she'd grill me lamb cutlets for supper as a special treat, so when I parked the MG in a residents' parking slot, the saliva glands were beginning to work overtime.

She gave me a big welcoming kiss and pointed to the frosted glass fizzing on the coffee table. I watched the seven o'clock news on television until summoned to the feast.

I poured us both a glass of Burgundy, 'Rully' I think it was. The cutlets were served with little roast potatoes, green beans and peas. The pudding was apple flan with chap's custard. Over the coffee I was just settling down, wrapped up in smug self-complacency, thinking what a lucky guy I was to have met her and what a happy life we led – when she gave me the sweet smile.

'So are *you* thinking of going on Bob's sailing trip round the Comorantes in September then?'

Talk about an armour-piercing shell straight into the magazine, that's what it felt like. It was going to require all the tricky Moon fast footwork to get out of that and avoid sinking without trace. As it was only Wednesday I hadn't finished putting the final touches to the Moon cunning plan. In truth, I hadn't actually started!

'Er… ah, erm…' The brain was desperately trying to go into overdrive, but the gears were clogged up by lamb cutlets, apple flan and buckets of custard.

She was still smiling and looking into my eyes with her chin propped on one hand.

Very unconvincingly I managed to gabble, 'Nothing's fixed, angel. I was going to discuss it with you first and see what you thought. It was just an idea that Bob floated on Monday.'

Desperately trying to be nonchalant I enquired nervously, 'How did you hear about it?'

She appeared to ignore the higher pitch in my voice and without changing her expression, replied, 'Bob phoned earlier this evening just before you arrived, wanting to know if I was interested.'

I cursed Barclay under my breath and managed to put a brave face on it.

'So are you? It could be a lot of fun; very basic of course, catching and gutting our own fish, washing in sea-water and a bucket for a lavatory.'

I gritted my teeth. Bob had specifically said 'a boys' trip.' So what was he playing at?

Zoe continued, thoughtfully, 'He told me Joan doesn't want to go, Tony can't go, he has a dental conference to organise and Finola won't go without Tony; Merrylees can't go either so I would be the only girl.'

Hope flickered. 'Is that a yes or a no?'

Her smile broadened. 'I was thinking, why don't you take me shopping in Harrods next Saturday afternoon? We're not doing anything, are we?' she said, sweetly.

'No, no, we're not, that's true. What a good idea! It'll make a nice change from watching the boring old test match against the Australians on television.' I gritted my teeth even more, but I could smell a deal, particularly when it was shoved up my nose. 'I'll look forward to it with eager anticipation my angel.'

She refilled my wine glass and met my eyes with one of those looks that set you tearing off your clothes - so all was far from lost here, but it looked as though the 'pink ticket' was going to be expensive.

Later that night I turned over in bed because something had occurred to me. 'Zoe, if Tony isn't going, that only leaves Bob, Pete and me, and none of us can sail a boat.'

'Dan Granchester can, Bob has asked him to take Tony's place,' she replied, drowsily.

****

None of the girls came to the Frog the following Saturday; there were just five of us. Bob, Pete, Dan, Bob's co-director Martin Holmes and me. I was the last one to arrive.

'So the week commencing September 3rd is agreed then?' Bob looked at us.

I looked back at him puzzled. 'I don't remember a date being mentioned. It sounds OK to me, but I'll have to check with Hugo and Zoe. Where did you get that from?'

Bob beamed. 'When I phoned your house, Zoe told me that that it would be a good time for you to go. She said her mother's carer was taking two weeks holiday at the beginning of September so she'd arranged to go up to Church Stretton to look after her mother anyway. She also said she was worried about leaving you on your own for two weeks and the trip to the Comorantes would solve her problem.'

'Hold hard there, Robert! Do you mean to tell me that Zoe was quite happy for me to go off sailing with you lot because she couldn't come anyway and it got her out of a hole?'

'Didn't she tell you?'

I was virtually speechless, the cunning little minx. 'No she bloody didn't! What is more I spent over £400 on shoes and clothes and a whole afternoon plodding round fucking Harrods last Saturday to earn my 'pink ticket' to go!'

Pete fell about laughing. 'It looks like she's put a good one over you Marcus. Wait till I tell Tony about this.'

'Too right,' I said grimly, thinking just wait till I get home. I perked up at that, a sexy spanking to warm her up, followed by matters erotic and exciting; the afternoon might turn out to be brighter than I anticipated.

'Right, who's for another round?'

Bob waited until the drinks arrived and then continued. 'Right, now we've fixed a date the next thing is to find out what boats are available and how much. Marcus, can you get your guy out there to look into it and email you as much information as he can? I'll contact the Comorantes Tourist Office here – I presume they have one? They must have a website so leave that to me. Anything else?'

'What about flights?' asked Dan.

I cut in, 'One thing we must do is avoid Comorantes Airways. They fly very old aircraft and their reliability is questionable. The best way is to go via the Gulf like I do. Etihad or Qatar Airways are infinitely better and their Business Class is cheaper. It means changing planes at either Abu Dhabi or Doha. Avoid Emirates unless you want your baggage sent to Timbuktu.'

So it was fixed.

I rang Jack Fourie on Monday morning and explained the situation. 'Can you send me as much info about charter boats as you can, but I did like the look of that ketch we saw sailing into Port Mahon that day. What was it called?'

Oh, you mean *Nightwind of Karoo?* OK, I'll see what I can find out. Give me a couple of days.'

'I'll come to the Comorantes a few days earlier, go and see Rouget and anybody else and then come to Port Mahon.'

'Incidentally,' he said, 'do know anything about that boat's name?'

'*Nightwind of Karoo?* No,' I replied. 'Why does it have any significance? I just thought it was a nice name.'

He laughed. 'The Great Karoo is a desert in the Western Cape: a dry, barren plateau; a place of silence and stars. The night wind is a desert wind that allegedly stimulates weird thoughts. When that wind blows in the Karoo at night strange things happen to people. It has a hypnotic effect.'

'Do they and has it?' I said, testily. 'Well, we're not going to be sailing it in the bloody Karoo and most of the people on this trip are strange in the first place so it shouldn't make much difference!' I chuckled, and thought no more of it.

'How's the payment situation? Is Rouget still paying Mumbai Construction's monthly certificates?'

'Yes, but always two months in arrears. That's surprising in a way. I got Bannerjee pissed one evening and he hinted that somebody or bodies in the Government were getting a kickback from Mumbai. When I pressed him he claimed he didn't know who, but it was an arrangement sorted out by their Chief Executive B K Menon and whoever it was in the Government, after tenders had been submitted.'

I pricked up my ears at that. It wasn't surprising – east of Suez it was generally accepted that the receipt of tenders just opened the start of negotiations, but normally this was to get a lower figure for the contract. In this case it seemed that the contract figure must have remained the same or even increased and the 'saving' was going into someone's pocket. CONDES had had no say in who was included on the tender list – that was the Comorantes Government's decision; all we had to do was check the calculations from the priced Bills of Quantities, and if the arithmetic was correct that ended our responsibility. Hugo had handed all the files over to me, and Margaret had removed them from the corner where I had stacked them and filed them away somewhere. I'd check to see if Mumbai's tender figure was the same as the contract figure.

My office door was open as usual so I called out, 'Margaret, can you bring me all the finance files on Port Mahon please?'

My intercom buzzed. 'They're in the top drawer of that filing cabinet right beside your desk. They're filed under the ingenious heading "Port Mahon Finance Files". They're not very heavy!'

'Margaret, have we had a role reversal here? I thought it was me who did the funnies and you did the fetching and carrying.'

She laughed. 'Your coffee's coming in a minute.'

I found the files with the calculations for the estimates we had given, the DfID approval for the aid package and the thick file containing our tender reports. We had estimated $119 million to construct the new port with a proviso that the supporting infrastructure and ancillary design costs were the responsibility of the Comorantes Government and should be added to make up the total package. There was a side letter from Hugo to DfID saying that, in our opinion, these should not be more than $25 million.

The finally agreed package prepared by DfID amounted to $152 million broken down into $119m for the port $30m for supporting infrastructure and $3m for Comorantes Government's design costs and administration fees.

I then turned to the tenders file. Eight tenders had been received from international firms from various countries. They ranged from $173m from an American company to $145.12m from Mumbai Construction of India.

Apparently, after negotiations between Mumbai and the Comorantes Government, the contract had been signed for $147.78m to include all the infrastructure. When the $3m Comorantes design and administration costs were added to that figure the total was still below the aid package estimate so everybody was happy.

I looked through the figures again. The only suspicious element was that after negotiations the price went up a little whereas normally I would have expected it to come down. Still it was no skin off CONDES' nose as they say, so I put the files back and turned to something else.

Two days later a long email arrived from Jack with details of three boat charter firms, a list with descriptions and charter rates for their boats, and dates giving their availability. *Nightwind of Karoo* was available, with skipper and cook for the week commencing 3rd September. In addition to the crew's quarters it had four cabins which would suit our group. There was only one other boat of a similar size and that was a luxury racing-cruiser which looked as though it would be far too fancy for our taste. We wanted a fun boat where we could do things like actually sail it, as well as some fishing, scuba diving, the odd barbecue. We wanted it to be totally relaxed and informal. From its description, *Nightwind* fitted the bill perfectly. Also it was half the price!

I asked Zoe if it would be alright if I invited the other three to the house for supper one evening and she said she'd cook us a steak and kidney pie with all the trimmings. Next morning I phoned Bob and Pete without difficulty. I mention that because, although Bob's office knew me well, Pete's Harley Street practice had the formidable Miss Shorter as his gatekeeper, and if she thought you would waste Pete's time she didn't take prisoners. Fortunately, she seemed to like me and we always exchanged a little banter before she put me through to Pete.

'Oh Mr Moon. It's not one of your naughty Moon plans again, is it? Will Dr Smallwood's trousers be quite safe?"

'No Miss Shorter not this time, it's to do with Dr Smallwood's sailing holiday and his trousers are not in danger this time!'

'What a pity,' she chuckled, 'I love your wicked plans; they keep Dr Smallwood on his toes! I'll put you straight through.'

So Pete must have told her about a Moon plan or two including the one where his trousers were accidentally thrown out of the window of Bob Barclay's car and ended up on the front of a lorry going to Newcastle.

Pete confirmed he could come, and Bob spoke to Dan, so next Thursday evening was fixed in the diary.

****

After it was confirmed that the trip was on, Dan Granchester went to the library in his house in Belgrave Square and took out the big world atlas. The Comorantes

Islands were a group of islands just north of the Equator in the middle of the Indian Ocean. There was a brief statement about them which told him that they consisted of both volcanic and coral islands and had a variety of wildlife and vegetation that was unique. The excitement began to build up inside him.

It was only recently, when he realised that his father's health was deteriorating, that the enormity of his future began to loom over him. Until then he had been as laid-back and happy as anybody, without a care in the world.

He had told his younger brother Henry about the proposed trip and Henry had been very excited.

'Of course you should go, Dan you lucky sod! Just think of all those dusky maidens on sun-kissed beaches waiting for a young aristocrat to come along and give them one – or more than one!'

Dan gave a fond sigh. 'Is that all you think about, Henry? Is that the limit of your imagination?'

Henry looked puzzled. 'Yes! Why, what else is there?'

What else indeed, thought Dan? There must be something and maybe this trip, this break, this change of environment would bring it out.

****

It was an informal supper; I provided some decent booze and Zoe produced her promised steak and kidney pie. Bob had brought a bottle of old Armagnac so after eating we all retired to the sitting room for coffee.

I spread out the information from Jack Fourie and we all agreed that *Nightwind of Karoo* was just what we wanted. Bob produced information from the tourist office and Admiralty Charts of the waters round the islands. There was a whole variety of islands we could visit, some coral, some granite, most with unique wildlife.

Pete said we should order a suckling pig so we could have a barbecue on the beach one evening. As Bob had a PA and a secretary it was left that he would deal with it all. Book the boat, book the flights on Etihad Airways and make a list of all the things we might need including drinks.

'Any more special requests like Pete's pig?' he asked. Well, if you think of anything let Felicity know.'

Zoe said, 'It looks like you boys are going to have a good time. If it all works, next time us girls must come with you – or maybe we'll go on our own. Nice handsome young Comorantian sailors sound attractive.'

'All talk,' Pete commented, 'and no do – typical of you women.' Zoe smiled, sweetly.

I kicked him savagely under the table. That was not the way to handle it! You didn't throw out those sort of challenges to her because what was originally a carefully floated remark to test the water then turned into just that – a challenge; and she didn't shirk a challenge.

I quickly changed the subject whilst Pete rubbed his sore shin. 'I'm going out there next week and I'll be going out three or four days before our trip, so if Felicity gives me copies of everything I'll check that the skipper is doing it or has done it.'

Dan asked, 'what sort of kit do we need – anything special?'

'Hats with big brims, high-factor suncream and the usual blockers and blasters for any tummy troubles. Pete always carries an emergency medical kit so we don't have to take too much. It says in the bumph that they provide fishing gear, snorkelling and scuba-diving equipment for anybody who can use it. Bob has a satellite phone and, of course, CONDES has people there in an emergency.'

Then something we hadn't anticipated came to the fore: the journalist in Dan.

'Would any of you have any objections if I did an article about the trip, one of the travel magazines would jump at it?'

There was a long pregnant pause and Zoe burst out laughing. 'If you could see the looks on your faces! Talk about a bunch of naughty boys!'

'Ah! Now hang on for a minute. We don't know what exactly is going to arise or happen. Some might feel sensitive about having some of their activities plastered across a front page.' I glanced at Pete.

Pete said, huffily, 'Why are you looking at me? I would have no objection, but as a respected Harley Street professional, I would like to have editorial control over what it says about me.'

Bob frowned. 'Can't you make it anonymous; write it in the third person without mentioning names? That would be OK with me.'

It obviously made people feel slightly uncomfortable and there was nothing any of us could do if Dan came on the trip and chose to write whatever he wanted. Only Bob, who knew him, could advise on that.

'Let's leave that for later, I'm sure we can sort something out,' I said. 'You never know, it might be useful to have a bit of gentle publicity.'

Little did I imagine then what the consequences of having Dan along would prove to be...

****

Hugo stuck his head round my office door, saw that I wasn't busy – I was *thinking*... Well, that's my story! – and came in.

He sat down and with a defensive cough began, 'I was at the Gold and Silver Wire Drawer's Company Dinner last night and happened to sit next to Desmond Fitzpatrick. You know, the Chairman of the Department for International Development's Aid Committee.'

I nodded.

'I mentioned that, having been told that we would be on the shortlist of consultants for their projects, we hadn't had any new enquiries from them for nearly fifteen months now, was there a problem?'

'He looked a bit shamefaced and told me that, for some reason or other, he didn't know what, we seemed to have got on the wrong side of the deputy chairman – a fellow called Garside – and he thought Garside had persuaded his fellow Socialist members on the Committee, plus a Lib-Dem woman, that CONDES was getting too much work and it should be spread out more. Although Desmond pointed out that we had seriously saved their bacon on one occasion and never let them down, he was outvoted. He also said that he had heard on the grapevine that Garside had told other people that we were flaky.'

I raised a questioning eyebrow. '*Have* we got on the wrong side of this bloke Garside?'

He shrugged. 'You remember I had a lunch with him last year, which didn't go too well, but it never occurred to me that he would take umbrage. He's been trying to phone me again recently, but I don't see the point of meeting him. I think he's a waste of time.'

I thought about this; it could be much more serious than it first sounded. If we were, in effect, being blacklisted by one government department, it didn't really matter what the reason was – rumours about CONDES could spread to other departments, and we depended to a large extent on government design contracts. If Garside was the source of these rumours, I didn't know what we could do about it at the moment.

CHAPTER ELEVEN

2010 – CONDES OFFICE, LONDON

Margaret brought me my coffee and carefully put it down so that the third finger of her left hand was turned up in my direction. I was impressed that she managed to do this without spilling a drop in the saucer. She left it there a split second longer than normal and hesitated before standing upright.

'Hold on there, Margaret,' I cried theatrically. 'Steady up! Was that a glimpse of true love I spotted on your finger, glinting in the morning sun?'

She pulled her hand away quickly, 'Well if you're going to be like that!'

'Just teasing you, Margaret, come on let's have a good look at it.'

It was a beautiful ring, a solitaire diamond with two sapphires supporting it mounted in white gold. It must have cost a pound or two.

She smiled when she saw the admiration on my face. 'We chose the design some time ago and Richard had it made specially.'

'All I can say, Margaret, is that he's a very lucky man. For a ring like that lots of ladies would lay down...' On the spur of the moment I couldn't think of the right words and unfortunately, left the sentence hanging there, unfinished. This produced some vivid blushing from her, a loud 'Pah! and a hurried exit during which I heard her mutter, 'You men are all the same – one-track minds!'

My day was saved by my phone ringing.

'Hi Amanda?'

'Oh Marcus, I've got some woman on the line who says she's the secretary of an MP called Garside. She wanted to connect him to Hugo, but Hugo told me that you were dealing with it now, so he should speak to you.'

I did a quick change of mental gear; this must be the Garside Hugo had told me about – the one who was blocking our appointments with the DfID. So what the hell did he want? The only way to find out quickly was to speak to him, and I needed a time lag to allow things to settle down with the Major.

'OK, put her through.'

'Hello, Marcus Moon speaking.'

'I'll put you through to Mr Garside.'

A voice with a northern accent said, 'Is that you, Elmes?'

'No,' I replied. 'My name is Marcus Moon, I'm Hugo Elmes co-director.'

'I wanted to speak to Elmes, I've spoken to him before.' Irritation had crept into the voice.

'If you tell me what it is about perhaps I can help?'

'Look Moon, I don't want to waste my time again, can you make big decisions or can't you?'

'Big decisions about what?'

'The Comorantes port project that your company is doing and other consultancies.'

I grew wary at this. I couldn't immediately recall exactly who or what this guy was, what his involvement with Port Mahon was or what he might want. I compromised by saying, 'I have taken over the running of Port Mahon from Mr Elmes if that is what you want to know. Why?'

There was a long pause as if he was making up his mind about something, then he said, 'I'm a busy man Moon, but I can spare you half an hour. I'll be at your office at 11.00am tomorrow.' And with that he cut the call.

I scratched my head in bewilderment. Amanda had said he was an MP so I supposed it was something to do with the government and Port Mahon, but for the life of me I couldn't think what.

The brain eventually kicked in. 'Margaret,' I called through the open door, 'can you find out all you can about an MP called Garside? That's all I can tell you I'm afraid. Oh, and am I doing anything at 11.00am tomorrow?'

The next thing was to talk to Hugo. Garside claimed he had done so, so maybe Hugo could tell me what it was all about.

I set off for Hugo's office; I knew he was in because Amanda had mentioned that he wouldn't take Garside's call.

Janet told me he was going through our management accounts and would probably appreciate a diversion.

'Ah!' he exclaimed when he saw me. 'I thought you'd be along. It's about Garside, isn't it? Have a seat and I'll fill you in. I didn't mention this to you before because I assumed it was a dead duck months ago. So now he's reared his ugly head with us again. What are you doing with him – if anything?'

'He's invited himself here tomorrow morning.'

'Has he, by Jove, well let me tell you all I know about our friend Garside, apart from the fact that he's anti-CONDES. He's an MP for some northern constituency. He's also the deputy chairman of the Department for International Development's Aid Committee. As you are aware my friend Desmond Fitzpatrick is the chairman. Garside obviously knew we had been appointed by them for the Port Mahon project – in fact, he claimed it was him who got us the appointment.'

'Did he? But I thought you negotiated that with your contact, what's-his-name – Fitz-somebody, and that Undersecretary guy?'

Hugo grinned, 'I thought I did. However, Garside invited me to lunch at Le Gavroche. When I got there I found he had booked the table in my name. We had an uncomfortable meal and over coffee he got to the point of the meeting. He suggested that we might like to appoint him as a consultant to advise us on politics and the weird and wonderful ways of the workings of Westminster.'

'Nice alliteration Hugo, you've been reading books again, haven't you?'

He grinned, ruefully. 'One – nil to you Marcus, but seriously, I thought he was just another chancer. He suggested that ten grand a year for the next five years was the sort of thing he had in mind.'

'And what did you say?'

'I told him I'd have to discuss it with you. Personally, I thought he was a total waste of time.'

I whistled at that.

'When I pressed him about what he could do for us he waffled and couldn't come up with anything concrete. I told him to write in with his proposals, but he took off in a huff and left me to pay the bill.'

'Did he!'

'I assumed that would be the last we'd here from him so I didn't mention it then. However, do you remember when I went to that reception for the Comoratians at Number 10 prior to the signing of the aid agreement? Garside was there looking as miserable as sin. The Comorantes Prime Minister, a guy called Coquelin – in whose honour the reception was being given – obviously knew Garside quite well and had a private chat with him. After the chat Garside brightened up considerably.'

'So, after blocking our appointments, why do you think he's got in touch with us again?'

'I suspect that he's going to bring up the consultancy again and point out that he could either do us good with the Comorantians for more work or do us damage. I don't suppose he knows that we know he's been doing that already.'

'What's he like?'

'I suppose "crude bully" would be a kind description. He has a certain bluff charm but it's only skin deep.'

'Great!' I said. 'So you've stuck me with this gentle loving soul who loves kiddies and tickles kittens' tummies.'

Hugo gave me one of his disarming smiles. 'Well, you're the one who took over my project on this "mosquito-infested swamp" where, what was it you quoted? Oh yes Noel Coward's *"Only mad dogs and Englishmen go out in the midday sun"*, so you've got to take the rough with the rough!'

I gave him a penetrating look.

'Yes,' he said, still smiling, 'Zoe was telling Emily all about The Comorantes and your sailing trip to that "white man's grave" when she came over for coffee last week.'

I mustered a weak grin. 'Well, it's not as good as all that,.' was the best I could do.

Hugo raised an acknowledging finger, 'I think that's two – one to me.'

Margaret confirmed I was clear for 11.00am tomorrow and gave me some information she had printed out about Garside. It didn't tell me anything enlightening. I gave her the gist of what Hugo had told me.

'He sounds an extremely unpleasant man,' she opined.

'Well, he's no friend of ours or likely to be,' I replied

The next day eleven o'clock came and went with no sign of Garside. At 11.30 Amanda phoned to say that Garside was in reception. 'Send him up,' I told her. Margaret went to meet him at the top of the stairs and left her door open. I could hear their voices from my office.

'My name is Garside, where's this bloke Moon?'

'If you'll come this way Mr Garside, I'll see if Mr Moon is available.'

'Available! He'd better be bloody available. I've come all the way from the House of Commons to see him and we have an appointment.'

'*Had* an appointment, Mr Garside! Your appointment was for 11.00am, it is now 11.33am.'

'Do you know who I am?'

'No I'm afraid I don't. You claim to be a Mr Garside, but if you're not sure who you are then I regret I am not able to help you. When you've found out who you are please let me know and I'll see if I can be of assistance. You may use the telephone in my office if you can remember the telephone number of who it is you need to ask. In the meantime, please take a seat.'

He must have noticed my door ajar. 'Is that Moon's office through there?' and started in my direction.

'SIT DOWN Mr Garside!'

I grinned; thirty years in the Women's Royal Army Corps had certainly given her the power of command. I think the whole of CONDES must have sat down at that moment, whatever they were doing, in case she was talking to them. Garside stopped in his tracks as if he'd been sledgehammered and sat down where she indicated.

'I'll see if Mr Moon is free.'

She knocked on my door for show and came in, closing it behind her.

'Garside's outside, do you want to see him?'

I couldn't stop smiling. 'Now you've softened him up Margaret, you'd better send him in.'

'You won't like him.'

'No, perhaps not, but I'd better hear what he has to say.'

She was right, I didn't like him. I recognised him instantly. He was the rude bastard who had told me 'to get out of his effing way' on the stairs at Comorantes Ports and Harbours office. He clearly didn't recognise me because he advanced with a smarmy smile and an outstretched hand.

'Mr Moon, how nice to meet you. By 'eck lad, that's a tough old bird you got out there as your secretary!' The door was still ajar and I heard the small explosion from Margaret's office.

'You're right there Mr Garside, Ex-Special Forces Major Braithwaite was trained to kill with one blow of her hand, it's a habit that's hard to break, you know.' There was another explosion from Margaret's office.

I shook his hand and pointed to one of my new guest chairs.

'So what can I do for you? I asked.

'Nowt!' He said with a smirk, 'It's what *I* can do for *you*.'

'Oh, and what is that? You've already met my co-director and we never heard from you again.'

He brushed that aside. 'Well, for a start I'm like that...' he held up two crossed fingers, '...with the President of the Comorantes and the Director of Ports, as well as being deputy chair of the Government's Aid Committee.'

'So?'

He scowled, 'What d'yer mean "so"?'

I wasn't smiling now. 'So what can you do for us? Claiming to know people is all very well, but what can you do? What work can you bring in? You know as well as I do the British Government work is competitive, and what other big civil engineering projects do the Comorantians have that they can pay for and you can get for us?'

His face grew redder. 'That's not the point! The point is I can introduce you to these top people.'

'But do they appoint consultants for civil engineering work? *That* is the point. I've already met Minister Rouget and I doubt if they have any more large projects in the pipeline.'

I had had enough of this; the guy was just a chancer as Hugo had said. It was time to call his bluff.

'However, if you want to recommend CONDES to your many and varied contacts please feel free to do so. It's been very kind of you to come in and we look forward to hearing from you.'

I stood up, didn't offer my hand and called 'Margaret, please show Mr Garside the way out.'

He flushed angrily and casting a wary eye on the door to Margaret's office, said, 'Now hold on a minute. If I do that, what's in it for me?'

I feigned surprise. 'What's in it for you? You mean that as a highly paid Member of Parliament, if you promote British firms to the outside world to aid our export market, help us fight off foreign competition and bring new jobs to your constituents to raise their standards of living, you expect something? Well the answer, Mr Garside, is job satisfaction. The pleasure you will feel in doing a job well.' I smiled benevolently at him – he didn't smile back.

'Are you taking the piss, Moon? I can do your firm a lot of damage, particularly with the Comorantians.' He bared his large teeth in a savage grin. 'Do not monkey about with me, you young puppy, or it'll be the worse for you!'

'Mr Garside, one other thing...' I gave him what I hoped was the Moon Medusa look, although when I tried it out on The Reverend McCavity, the next-door neighbour's cat, it began to lick its balls. I trusted that it wouldn't have the same effect on Garside, '...we understand that certain malicious rumours have been spread about CONDES in the corridors of Westminster so, to put your mind at rest, I confirm that we are nowhere near going broke – as a glance at our accounts would tell you.' I sharpened the look to a double-eye whammy and added pointedly, 'Slander can result in massive damages, bear that in mind. I take it that that is the end of our discussion? We're doing a good job with Port Mahon and if you try to foul it up then everybody will know at whom to point the finger.'

Margaret came in on cue and Garside with a final glare allowed himself to be ushered out of the door.

'Phew! Where do these people come from?' I said to her when she returned. 'Do they imagine we're soft in the head?'

She looked serious. 'He's a nasty piece of work, but do you think he can do us any harm?'

I shook my head. 'Well, he has so far, but I think that Hugo's friend Firzpatrick is on to him. I don't think the DfID Committee would let a bully like Garside influence them.'

She nodded agreement. 'Changing the subject, I've got all your tickets and bookings for your sailing trip and visit to Port Mahon next week, and I've liaised with Bob Barclay's secretary about Mr Barclay and Mr Granchester. Miss

Shorter in Doctor Smallwood practice has done the same thing so everything is set up.'

'Thanks Margaret, you're a gem – and I was only joking about you being Special Forces and trained to kill.'

She gave me a sweet smile and said, 'But I was!' and strolled out.

****

THE COMORANTES ISLANDS – 2010

I was met outside 'Arrivals' at Eric de Verteuil Airport on Grande Rocques by a cheerful, stocky weather-beaten chap of about thirty summers, holding up a board that read MARCUS MOON in big letters.

'Cap'n Jim,' he announced himself in a broad South African accent, 'at your service mate! Is that your gear?' he said with a raised eyebrow as he pointed at my battered holdall and the large Fortnum & Mason hamper that Barclay had insisted I bring.

I shrugged with a slight embarrassment. 'Wait till you meet Bob Barclay,' I told him and he seemed to accept that as a reason.

'Your email said the other three arrive on Wednesday on the same flight at the same time.'

'They do. I'm the advance guard, but I've got to nip across to Beauregard Island for two days. We've designed a new port there for the government.

He picked up my bag and between us we carried the hamper to a pick-up truck. On the way to the boat I explained who everybody was; Pete's a doctor; Bob's into property; Dan is a journalist and I'm a civil engineer. Only Dan could call himself a sailor but we were all willing and we wanted to see everything and do everything.

'Your email gave me a list of drinks to stock up and also asked for a suckling pig to roast – is that right?'

I smiled, 'that's Pete's idea – he wants to lay on a big beach barbecue for some of the islanders on one of the remote islands.'

'Oh does he! Well with all the booze Mr Barclay's ordered on top of yours I doubt if any of you will be sober enough to organise a banana sandwich let alone a barbecue.'

I blinked. 'What booze?'

'Yeh, Barclay sent me an email saying that you were a tight-fisted teetotaller and would never order enough so I was to add the contents of his list to yours.' He grinned, 'I've had to stack it in one of the cabins.'

The pick-up stopped alongside some stone steps leading down to where a big Zodiac inflatable was tied to a cleat. I noted that it had a 200 horsepower Evinrude engine. We humped the hamper into the boat, locked my gear in the truck and Cap'n Jim fired up the outboard and took me out to where *Nightwind of Karoo* was tugging at a mooring.

Standing on deck ready to catch a line was a very tall, very pretty black girl wearing a bikini, the material of which she must have cut from an eye-patch.

'That's Eve; she does all the cooking and housework on the boat.'

'Does she?' I replied, thinking of Tony Scales joke about the best aid to sailing ever invented – 'You screw it on a bunk and it does all the chores!'

'She's also my girlfriend.'

Ah, so that was setting out the rules of engagement – or not as the case may be. As far as I was concerned I was out of the running, but Cap'n Jim would have to fight his own corner with Bob, Pete and Dan.

I had a good feeling about *Nightwind*; it was immaculate but it felt a fun boat. The cabins were bright and cheerful, the saloon welcoming in a tidy but casual way. I felt that I wouldn't upset anybody if I did my own thing there.

'D'you want me to plan out a programme? Is there anything special that you want to do?'

'No, not really. We'd like to go to some of the uninhabited islands, see some of the wildlife, do a bit of snorkelling, Bob wants to fish and Dan and Pete want to do some diving. The idea is to get away from civilisation and chill out.'

He nodded, 'OK I'll draft something out.'

He took me back to the airport to catch the flight to Beauregard.

The plane flew in over the site of Port Mahon, and I could see the improvement and the activity which confirmed Jack Fourie's last report. He was all smiles when he collected me from the airstrip. 'Bannerjee has really got them running around now; I reckon we'll beat that programme for getting back on schedule.'

'Payments OK?'

192

'Yes, they're paying our certificates two months late, but Mumbai are now getting monthly payments. Anyway, they seem happy with that.'

So Florence must have done her stuff. I decided to call in and thank her when I got back to Grandes Rocques.

'Anything else?'

He frowned. 'Well, about a week ago Rouget turned up in a private plane with half a dozen Chinese – at least I presumed they were Chinese, the plane had a red flag with the stars on the tail fin. They didn't talk to me but went straight to Mumbai's compound. Bannerjee showed them round and they took photographs. He said they told him they were merchant navy people checking the new port for trading ships. They were all in civilian clothes, but there was something military about them.'

I shrugged, 'I suppose all kinds of people will be interested in a new port in the Indian Ocean – particularly the Indians, Japanese and Chinese. By the way how's that lad we saved from drowning? What was his name, Jacques something?'

'Jacques Doublet, oh he's fine, no ill effects. His father came over with a load of fresh pawpaw and lobster as a thank-you gift.'

My eyes lit up, I liked fresh pawpaw with squeezed lime. He noticed the look on my face. 'You're too late mate, I've eaten them!'

I gave him a look of disgust and he laughed.

We had a walk round the site and I exchanged a few words with Raul Bannerjee. He showed me his speeded up programme and thanked me again for sorting out their payments. Next morning I flew back to Grandes Rocques to get ready for our sailing trip, but first I had to call at Ports and Harbours.

****

Florence was a good Catholic woman with a cheerful nature and healthy appetites, but sitting at her desk she was worried. Things were happening around her that she was not happy about. First, she was away from her husband who worked on Beauregard Island but to compensate for that her broad Comorantian views allowed her to have occasional sex with somebody else - and in her case that somebody was Phillipe Rouget. She didn't particularly like him, but he was very willing and, most of all, convenient. Unfortunately, he had become more and more demanding and when she started to demur, he threatened her with losing her job. Good jobs were not easy to get on Grandes Rocques so she had little option but to accede to his demands.

She also knew that he had been stealing money from the Port Mahon account. She didn't know exactly where or to whom it had gone; all she had been given were the slips that said 'Preliminary Operations for the Redevelopment of Tern' so she recorded this long name under the acronym of PORT.

Finally, she had not been there when her son had nearly drowned and had been rescued and revived by the two CONDES men, Moon and Fourie. Apparently Moon had risked his life by diving, fully clothed, into the rough sea and had thus been quick enough to prevent Jacques from going under for the last time. Her husband had thanked Fourie, but she hadn't seen Moon since he had had that long talk with her a couple of months ago.

Today, Rouget was out at a meeting and Florence was just shedding a quiet tear thinking about her problems when she heard strange footsteps coming along the corridor.

****

'Good morning Florence, just a little thank-you for sorting out the Port Mahon payments problem,' and I put the box of sugared almonds on her desk.

This produced a reaction that positively astounded me. She shot round the desk, seized me in her meaty arms and pulled my head down into a bosom so vast and deep I thought I was being swallowed by a black hole. She began patting my head.

'Oh, thank you, thank you Mr Moon. Oh, thank you again,' and she burst into tears. Fuck me, I thought, if a measly box of sugared almonds produces a reaction like this I was glad I hadn't gone the whole hog and brought chocolates and flowers. I managed to detach myself before asphyxiation took hold, and gulped down a couple of deep breaths.

'Florence,' I gasped, 'for Christ's sake, it's only a box of almonds!'

She dabbed at her eyes with a tissue, 'No Mr Moon, it's for saving my son's life.'

The penny didn't drop. 'Saving your son's life – when?'

She gave a half smile. 'Three months ago on Beauregard.'

'But he's called Doublet and you are Mrs Le Lievre,' I pointed at her name on the door.

'My married name is Doublet, I use my maiden name for work.'

'Ah,' I said, as everything became clear. That message she received when we last met must have been telling her the bad news.

'Well, I'm so pleased he's not showing any ill effects. I was asking Mr Fourie about him this morning.'

She smiled gratefully and went and sat down behind her desk again.

'So what can I do for you Mr Moon?'

'Marcus,' I told her. 'Nothing really, I just called in to say thank you, tell you that my secretary has sorted out your sister's tax affairs – and also to pay a courtesy call on the Minister.'

'My sister was so grateful, she said your secretary is a lovely lady and very efficient. The Minister's at a meeting, but he should be back in a minute or two. Can I get you a coffee or a cold drink?'

I chose the cold drink. She told me again her sister was very grateful for what the Major had done and I told her that I and 'the boys' were off on a sailing trip for a week on *Nightwind of Karoo*.

I added, 'Who does that big yacht in the harbour belong to, the President?'

She laughed, 'No it belongs to an American gentleman, a Mr Kory Kronoff. He's doing an investment here on Tern Island.'

'Holiday homes?'

'I don't know, it's all very secret.'

On a hunch I asked her casually. 'What do the initials PORT stand for?'

'Oh that's something to do with it, but I—'

Before she could say more we heard footsteps in the corridor. 'The Minister,' she said and clammed up.

Rouget walked through the door and checked his stride when he saw me. A look of suspicion flashed across his face and he looked from me to Florence and back.

'Mr Moon, what brings you here?' His eyes were wary.

'It's a courtesy call, Minister, I was combining business with pleasure, visiting the Port Mahon site and arranging a sailing holiday for some friends.'

He visibly relaxed. 'Come through,' and he ushered me into his office. 'So no more problems then?' He gave a thin smile.

'No Minister, not at the moment. The project is rapidly catching up to its original programme and the standard of work by Mumbai is excellent.'

'Good, good. I was there myself a week ago showing some people round who might be interested in using our cargo facilities there. They were impressed as well.'

'The Chinese?'

He waved a nonchalant hand. 'They're just one of many countries who may use our new port, being located, as we are, in the middle of the Indian Ocean.'

We exchanged a few more platitudes and then I said, 'Well, I'll leave you in peace sir, I'm sure you've plenty to do running your department,' and I got up, shook the proffered hand, gave Florence a nice smile, got a bigger one in return and left. I didn't hurry down the corridor but bent down to fiddle with a shoe, out of sight but within earshot.

I heard Rouget come back into Florence's office. 'What did he really want?' He snapped at Florence.

She explained about her son and he seemed to accept this, but he finished by telling her, 'Don't you dare breathe a word about Tern Island and the money. That's top secret...' I was unable to hear any more, a door opened up the corridor and a man came out so I stood up hastily and walked on.

So what the hell was all that about? I didn't think it had anything to do with me or CONDES so it may just have to remain a mystery.

****

Cap'n Jim and I waited in the arrivals building for the Etihad passengers to filter through customs. The 'boys' were instantly recognisable. Pete Smallwood was out first. He was dressed up like a rotund Sir Thomas Lipton in 1936 skippering his Americas Cup yacht round the Isle of Wight. Yachting cap with an anchor badge, blue blazer with a large sculptured badge made from gold wire on the pocket and brass buttons, white trousers, white canvas shoes and a coloured cravat which turned out to be the colours of the Royal Thames Yacht Club. The only thing he didn't have was a telescope under his arm.

Cap'n Jim was speechless, his chin near the floor – as were most of the other scruffy looking meeters and greeters waiting for friends or relatives. A hush fell over the crowd as this vision parted them and headed for us. I heard a voice say, 'Christ, it's a Japanese admiral!'

I wanted to hide, but I was too late. 'Marcus!' he called, waving at me and then I noticed a porter behind him pushing a trolley holding a large brown cabin trunk fastened by leather straps.

'Oh my God! I said wearily, 'I hope the other two aren't like this.'

Cap'n Jim recovered enough to pretend that he was only at the airport for the ambience and strolled off to one side leaving me to cope with Pete. Forunately, Dan Granchester was the next one through customs and he was dressed normally in a white cotton open-necked shirt, rust-coloured chinos and deck shoes. A camera slung over his shoulder. His luggage consisted of a middle-sized holdall. I ignored Pete and greeted Dan, pointing out Cap'n Jim who had perked up a bit at the sight of Dan.

Barclay strolled out carrying nothing, but he was followed by a retinue of porters each carrying something. The first was staggering under the load of a large holdall; the second had his video camera; the third a small wicker basket and the forth a bundle of tubes which I assumed contained fishing rods. The crowd parted once more, this time with reverence, to let this large figure in the Panama hat, cream linen jacket, MCC tie and bright red trousers pass by with his train. Cap'n Jim's face fell again.

'Is that the lot mate?' he muttered to me.

Bob seized his hand and shook it vigorously. 'Well my good captain I hope your lugger is shipshape and seaworthy? I have to tell you that swimming is not my forte so I am relying on you to keep us afloat.'

I button-holed Pete. 'What's with the cabin trunk?'

He gave me a sniffy look. 'Changes of clothes, of course. Casual dress for the mornings, I shall breakfast in my dressing gown. Something a little smarter for luncheon, a change for the afternoon, particularly if we go ashore, and evening dress for dinner – a couple of white jackets, stiff-collared shirts, dark trousers and black ties. I assume it won't be too formal?'

'You could be right there Pete,' I told him.

'Cap'Jim!' I called, 'you've got fishing tackle on the boat haven't you, and Eve will do some washing for us?'

'Sure thing, Marcus.'

'Right let's all go into a quiet corner and sort out the luggage. If everybody takes three shirts, a pair of shorts, swimming kit, washing kit, nightwear, sun cream and a cap, plus what we are going to travel in now, the rest can be shoved in Pete's cabin trunk and deposited at the left luggage office here at the airport.'

Pete looked downcast. 'Now hang on a minute!'

'It's not the bloody Royal Yacht Pete, it's a boys sailing trip where everybody mucks in.'

Much to Cap'n Jim's obvious relief we managed to pack everything we needed into three big holdalls. Bob carried his camera and we made Pete change out of his silly outfit into a polo shirt, long trousers and his canvas shoes.

We crammed into the pick-up and carried the kit down the steps to the Zodiac. We had to move Bob around with the luggage to trim the boat and even then we had very little freeboard so it was a slow journey out to *Nightwind*. The boys' eyes lit up at the sight of Eve waiting to welcome us. I thought I'd give Capn' Jim a helping hand so I told them Eve was his girlfriend.

We stowed our gear in our cabins and went up on deck where Eve had four large frosted Planter's Punches waiting on a table surrounded by four comfy deck chairs. It felt as if the boat was welcoming us. There were huge sighs of contentment all round – the holiday had really started.

****

After a superb cold lunch of lobster mayonnaise, fresh pawpaw and chilled South African Chardonnay we helped Cap'n Jim put up the sails and cast off for one of the outer islands. *Nightwind of Karoo* creamed along in a brisk south-easterly breeze and we all stretched out on deck to catch a few rays. As dusk fell Cap'n Jim piloted us into a sheltered bay on the leeward side of a small island. We dropped anchor and Eve began to prepare the evening meal whilst Bob poured out the drinks.

'Is it safe to swim?' Dan asked and was assured that it was so we all dived over the side and swam round the boat a couple of times to freshen up.

Dried off, and with drinks in our hands I said, 'Jack Fourie told me the origin of the boat's name. The Great Karoo is a desert in the Western Cape: a dry, barren place of silence and stars. The night wind is a desert wind that allegedly stimulates weird thoughts. When that wind blows in the Karoo at night strange things can happen to people.

In your case Pete, that's already happened so we won't expect any changes there!'

To distract us from beginning to specify a long list of things about him that we thought might be considered strange, Pete turned to Dan.

'Obviously Bob knows you very well, but Marcus and I have only met you a few times down at the Frog so can you fill us in a little about the long history of the Granchesters. I, being a distinguished Harley Street physician, am used to rubbing shoulders with the aristocracy but Marcus here is from Yorkshire and gets embarrassed when he is confronted by anybody with a loftier title than Mister.'

Dan gave a weak grin. He said apart from what we knew there wasn't much more to tell. He didn't want his whole life spent amongst long-nosed, stiff-necked men who did nothing but hunt, shoot and fish in the winter and 'The Season' in the summer – and twirly girls who did likewise, but with a Harrods' card and the voracity of a black widow spider for wealthy males.

He told us that he had been sitting in the drawing room of the house in Belgrave Square and gloomily surveying the worn Savonnerie carpets, the tattered Aubusson rugs and the rotting drapes so fragile that it was impossible to draw them across the windows for fear they would disintegrate, when Bob phoned him and invited him to the Frog and Nightgown.

But, as Bob explained, Dan had a serious problem. It may seem strange to the average person living in a house or a flat and with a daily job but the future, to Dan, looked like living death. He was the heir to that vast estate in

Northamptonshire, and all that went with it. His father, the sixteenth Viscount was in poor health, brought to that situation by the cares and vicissitudes of maintaining the estate. To preserve this treasure for the nation and avoid having it broken up to pay death duties and inheritance tax, the land and buildings had been put into trust years ago, and the contents and treasures of the houses likewise some years later. Hence, his father could neither sell anything nor buy anything for the estate without the approval of all the Trustees – and they were reluctant to give it to say the least. The old Viscount was thus merely a resident curator, a custodian allowed to live in part of the East Wing, who was obliged to maintain this vast edifice with whatever income he could scrape together from the use of the house and estate. The local planners refused to consider using some of the land for building. They even refused permission for some of the grassland to be converted to farming which would have provided extra rental income. For a modest charge the public were encouraged to tramp through the principal rooms of the house six days a week exhaling carbon dioxide and other noxious vapours, and then spend their hard-earned money in the garden centre and the estate shop. The income from this barely made a dent in the maintenance costs for the leaking roof, the rising damp, the dry rot, the flaking stonework and the heating and humidifying costs necessary to preserve the pictures and furniture inside the house from the vapours. The stress had worn the old man down, and at the relatively young age of sixty-six he was just a shell of the man he used to be. Dan couldn't have had his future mapped out more clearly or devastatingly.

He had two brothers, both younger. Giles, the next one down, had taken holy orders and gone into the church. He eked out a fragile existence as the rector of a collection of country churches in Norfolk. Henry, the youngest, worked for a West End public relations company, liked fast cars and even faster women, was always broke and looking for a sub from Dan – who uttered dire threats and lectures but always obliged because Henry was a good source of gossip from the younger elements of the West End for his newspaper columns.

Dan's ambition was to make it big in journalism before his father died.

I looked at Dan in a different light after Bob had explained that. It was not a situation that I envied and I could see that even Pete, who would have given his eye teeth for a title, was thanking his lucky stars that he didn't have his life constrained to that extent.

Next morning, after a refreshing swim and a hearty breakfast of fresh fruit, eggs and bacon and fresh bread, we hauled up the anchor and creamed along with the port gunwale barely above water. We took it in turns to man the wheel and made good time. As evening approached we dropped anchor in a sheltered bay and watched the sun go down over the top of freshly made margaritas.

Eve laid on a delicious meal of grilled grouper and turtle stew then the four of us stretched out on the deck whilst Cap'n Jim poured out generous measures of Armagnac. He handed glasses to each of us and kept one for himself. Eve was down in the galley singing quietly to herself in Swahili as she tidied up.

I took a contemplative sip of my Armagnac and opened up the now traditional evening discussion.

'Do you think that there is just one person in the world who is your ideal mate or do you think that there are many, maybe thousands, with whom you could happily spend the rest of your days?'

I had been thinking about that for some time and wondered what the other three thought.

After a moment's thought Pete was the first to reply. 'It must be the latter. There are six billion people in the world; the chances of you finding your perfect soulmate amongst that lot are so remote as to be untenable.'

'Ah, but maybe most people don't find their perfect soulmate. They remain forever undiscovered whilst people make do with second, third or fourth best without realising that that is what they are.'

Dan chipped in, 'Yes, but you can rule out a lot of people can't you? All the Chinese and Indians; the Africans and non-English speakers; the peasants and poorly educated. That would get the number of potential soulmates down considerably.' He smiled artlessly at us.

I egged him on. 'Do you mean that as far as you're concerned only the white English upper classes are available for your consideration?'

Dan kept digging his hole. 'No, of course not. There's the French, the Norwegian and Swedish – although they are a bit frigid, I suppose. But the Danes would be OK.'

Pete spluttered, 'Well that's a relief, for one moment I thought that only British royal princesses had a chance with you.' He was having difficulty believing what he was hearing 'You are taking the piss Dan, aren't you? If you aren't you want to get out a lot more. Thousands, even millions of disparate people mate with each other in this world. Europeans pair up with Chinese, Africans marry Europeans, Indians cohabit with Americans. The rich marry the thick and stupid and vice versa – provided they're beautiful – so you should be alright there Dan. For heaven's sake you can't just exclude someone because of their race, religion or social status.'

I cut in, 'We're getting off the point I made. How many people find their "perfect soulmate" as you put it? Don't you think that people just settle for somebody with whom they can rub along without finding perfection? What the hell is perfection anyway?'

Bob raised a forefinger. 'Ah, there you have it. We don't know what perfection is, nobody does – except Dan. Some people, usually those with a limited imagination, think they have found the perfect mate because they don't know any better.'

'That's a very cynical view.'

'No, it's a realistic one. How often have you seen the old Darby and Joan couple, who've been together for seventy years and never had a cross word, put forward as the ideal example of married life? They must be as boring as hell. They live a cow-like existence, a life of mental grazing and intellectual cud chewing. You can see Dan drifting along that path if he doesn't get hit by something to move him on to a more challenging track.'

I put my hands behind my head and stretched lazily like a cat. 'I think that there is more than one ideal soulmate for each of us. Not many, they are few and far between. There is some instant chemistry which draws you together, which doesn't have a logical explanation, but both people know it immediately. If you're lucky just two or three times in a lifetime you'll meet somebody who will knock your socks off. It might be just a look across a room, but when your eyes meet, the spark flashes into fire. The people round you and your surroundings fade into insignificance; you are bewitched. Such feelings are so powerful that they have started wars, relinquished thrones, lost countries and established cultures. They blind you to everything else. Common sense goes out the widow. They transcend everything; you simply know that you have got to spend the rest of your life together. They are all consuming; you are in paradise when you are together and desolated when you are apart. It is as if you are a part of them and they of you... It's called 'love' Dan – and it does happen.'

'I didn't have you down as a romantic Marcus, surprising for an engineer.'

I grinned. 'You just wait Granchester, one day lightning will strike that lump of stone you call a heart.'

'What about you Marcus, you seem well set up? You and Zoe seem to be very well matched.'

I stretched out languidly in my chair again and smiled a quiet smile. 'Oh I am, I am indeed.'

'Well, is that it?'

'What more is there to say?'

'You could tell us how you managed to get a girl like that.'

I smiled again. 'I suppose it's character and strength of personality combined with good looks and a warm heart.'

'No, you misunderstand me. I meant how did you manage to get a girl like that!'

I gave him a sharp look, but there was no guile on his face. There had not been a stress on the word 'you', I saw only a rather sad wistful look. For the first time I began to appreciate the pressures that must be on Dan Granchester.

CHAPTER TWELVE

SEPTEMBER 2010 – THE COMORANTES ISLANDS

Cap'n Jim broke the spell by producing a chart of the Comorantes, which he spread out on the deck. 'Is there anywhere special any of you would like to go?'

I pointed to a small island that was remote from the others and was marked "Oiseau" on the chart. 'What's that island?

Cap'n Jim shook his head. 'That's a private island; some American multimillionaire is building an exclusive development on it. Nobody knows much about it; it's very hush-hush and nobody is allowed on it without special permission. It's name has been changed, it's now called Tern Island.'

Is it, I thought? Rouget had said something to Florence about Tern Island and 'the money' when he was giving her a roasting for talking to me. I had a hunch.

'I'd like to go there, if possible.'

Cap'n Jim frowned. 'There's not much to see and you won't be allowed ashore. If we do go there we'll be wasting a day.'

The other three looked at me puzzled. 'Something of interest to you, Marcus?' Bob asked.

'Could be, it's an itch that I'd like to scratch.'

The three of them looked at each other and shrugged. 'OK, it's no skin of our noses, we can do some fishing on the way, let's go.'

It was half a day's sailing across open water to get there. Like the other coral islands in the Comorantes Group, Tern was surrounded by a reef with the waves breaking on it. We approached staying well clear of the reef; it looked as though an impressive development was taking place on the south-east side of the island. We could see villas, flats and larger buildings, which were probably shops and restaurants. Some appeared finished, others were in various stages of construction. An inflatable with a big outboard containing two tough-looking men shot out from a small jetty and, after negotiating a passage through the reef, came alongside.

One hailed us. 'Hey you! This is private property and nobody is allowed here without a permit so push off.'

'Who says?' called back Pete.

'Security,' said the man and flashed some sort of badge. 'This is a government project and your captain could lose his licence if you trespass.'

I had beckoned Bob round to the opposite side of *Nightwind* so we were out of sight of the men in the boat. I handed the binoculars to Bob. 'You're a property man Robert, have a look at that and see if you can see anything unusual?'

There was a landing craft tied to the other side of the jetty which had "Kronoff Construction" in large letters painted on its side. Two men were rolling some barrels down its ramp on to the jetty.

Bob scanned the partly constructed buildings carefully.

'Well?'

He turned and looked at me. 'If it was one of my sites I'd fire the lot of them.'

I nodded. There were perhaps a dozen men all milling about opposite where our boat was lying off shore, but no other workers could be seen. Apart from the sound of a generator there was no other indication of activity. I had been on many building sites in my time, but I'd never seen one as lifeless as this. The development appeared quite large, which made it even more peculiar.

'We'd better go chaps,' called Cap'n Jim. 'The security men are getting a bit fretful.'

He started the engine and we moved away from the island and away from the setting sun into the dusk.

'OK, where now?' asked Cap'n Jim.

'How big is Tern Island,' I said.

'Not very big, I suppose it's about a mile across.'

'And is there a landing beach on the far side?'

'Yes, but I can't take *Nightwind* through the reef if that's what you're thinking.'

'But at high tide we could get the Zodiac over the reef, couldn't we? When's high tide?'

Pete and Dan were looking puzzled; Cap'n Jim totally mystified; only Bob seemed interested.

'You think there's something funny going on, don't you Marcus, so why don't you fill us in?'

I scratched my head. 'It could be a load of nonsense, but there are three things that puzzle me about Tern Island. As you know, we are the consultants for Port Mahon on Beauregard Island. We prepared all the cost estimates except for work that the Comorantians would do themselves – although we did an estimate for that to make sure the Department for International Development wasn't being ripped off too blatantly. When the final figure for the aid package was agreed there was $5,000,000 that was only vaguely accounted for. We couldn't explain it, only the Comorantes authorities could do that – but it wasn't CONDES' problem.

'Next, when I got a glimpse of the Port Mahon bank statements in the Minister's office, there were three payments that the Minister's secretary had marked "PORT" that CONDES couldn't account for. We hadn't certified any such payments and this only came to light because of the Minister's inefficiency in dealing with the Port Mahon contractor's payments.

'Finally, the Minister's secretary, a nice lady called Florence, owed me a favour. She was just telling me that PORT was to do with Tern Island and not Port Mahon as I thought, when the Minister cut her off and gave her a bollocking for even thinking of mentioning Tern Island.

'Now we've seen the development – admittedly from a distance – both Bob and I think that there's something dodgy about it.'

I looked at Dan. 'There could be a story in this for you, Dan.'

Little did I know how prescient that remark would be.

Cap'n Jim filled in the rest for me. 'So you want to go ashore tonight and have a look round? Is that your plan?'

'In a nutshell, yes!'

'Well forget it! No way José! I'm not risking my charter licence for some hair-brained scheme you've thought up, Marcus. There is no way I'm taking my boat anywhere near Tern Island, and that's final.'

I looked at Bob, the most persuasive man I knew. A man who could talk saints into sin and vice versa. It was time to put the world champion into bat.

'Bob, perhaps you and Jim should have a little chat whilst we pour ourselves a bracer or two?'

Fifteen minutes later Cap'n Jim was saying, 'Well as long as you take all the responsibility if you get caught, it's nothing to do with me.'

It was a beautiful night. A three-quarter moon shimmered across a calm sea. Bob, Dan and I had no trouble manoeuvring the Zodiac over the reef; we had two hours before the tide would fall. Dan ran the inflatable up on to the beach and we tied the painter to a palm tree. We found a track through the jungle that headed across the island. The throb of the generator guided us and there were lights in the builder's compound but none on the site. We waited and watched for fifteen minutes, but there was no sign of any security or watchman; they must have assumed that they were secure by their remoteness.

By the light of the moon we wandered round the development becoming more astonished at every turn.

'It's like a Hollywood film set,' Dan murmured, the houses and flats facing the sea were just false fronts built with concrete blocks painted over to look substantial. The roofs were corrugated tin sheets painted red and supported on scaffolding. Even the larger buildings with concrete frames and false fronts had no internal floors. The roads were just packed sand and there was no sign of any services. No drainage, no water or electricity supplies – nothing. Areas that could be seen from the sea were screened with trees and colourful shrubs.

'Bloody hell!' exclaimed Bob. 'Somebody's conning somebody in a big way here.'

Dan was all excited. 'You were right, Marcus, there could be a story here, but I'd need some photographs to back it up.' He held up his camera.' I could try for some moonlight shots, but I doubt if they'd be much use and we daren't risk using the flash. Look,' he said, 'I know this is presumptuous, but would you mind if I hid on the island and you picked me up tomorrow night? I've heard of this guy Kronoff – he's supposed to be a financial wizard, a lot of people are investing with him. If this is the sort of thing he's doing then the sooner it is brought to light the better.'

Bob frowned. 'Do you think that's wise? Those two security guys looked like hard men; if they catch you they'll smash your camera and beat the shit out of you – if you're lucky. If this is part of a big swindle it could be much worse.'

'I'll take my chances; I have my mobile phone. At least you lot know where I am and if I don't appear then you can call the authorities.'

It occurred to me that maybe the 'authorities' already knew about it and were party to it, whatever it was, but I kept quiet.

We plunged into the deep brush and using broken palm fronds helped Dan create a make-shift hiding place/shelter. I went back and got a couple of bottles of water from the

Zodiac and some boiled sweets. He'd have to survive on those for a day. We said we'd pick him up from the same beach at 11.00 the following night.

'I'll phone you,' he said. 'For Christ's sake don't try to phone me. I'll switch off my phone, my ringtone would wake the dead!'

We sailed until we were out of sight of the island and anchored in shallow water for the day. Bob fished and Pete and I did some scuba diving. The fish were spectacular, there were some large sharks cruising around, we identified them as lemon, reef and black-tipped, but they showed no interest in us. As dusk fell we sailed back to Tern Island arriving off the reef in the moonlight.

Bob and I picked Dan up at the pre-arranged place without a problem. He was thirsty, hot, hungry, badly bitten, sweaty and as chuffed as a pig in shit – and smelt about the same.

'Hey guys, I've got some cracking photos! Nobody saw me, most of 'em spent all day planting shrubs and trees to hide the buildings – if you can call them that. It's a farce. It isn't a real construction site – it's a theatrical prop for some massive swindle. Boy oh boy, I can't wait to write this up. We need to find out more about this guy Kronoff and why he's being allowed to do this in the Comorantes.'

We got him back to *Nightwind* and pushed him in the shower. Eve made him a special meal, but he was so excited he could hardly eat it.

'Slow down Dan,' Bob told him. 'Marcus knows more about this than you do so let's not rush into anything. It won't go away and we've come here for a holiday.'

'Yes, I suppose you're right, but I know there's a big story here.'

'What's the journalist's code?' Bob asked.

'Make it short, make it snappy and make it up,' Pete chuckled.

Bob ignored him. 'Collect all the facts, do the research, fit it all together and write it up.'

Much as I sympathised with Dan I had to talk to Hugo about this; not so much about what was happening on Tern Island but the diversion of British aid funds to a private project – and a dodgy one at that. They were coming out of an account for which we had some responsibility and that worried me. We had done the budget, checked the costs and the tenders, so how had somebody – who I didn't know – managed to fiddle out a chunk of money – how much I didn't know – to spend on Tern Island?

As I fell asleep on my mattress on the deck I resolved to sweet-talk Florence into letting me examine the bank statements for Port Mahon.

A leisurely day's sailing, swimming, diving and fishing took us to a larger inhabited island. We anchored in a sheltered bay. Cap'n Jim told us that this island was the home to wild gigantic tortoises a metre and a half long and about three quarters of a metre high. They seemed amiable enough and Pete even managed to have a ride on one. When he tried to reward it by offering it some leaves its jaws snapped shut with a clang and nearly took his fingers off. After that we treated them with caution.

Pete decided that we had had enough of the serious stuff and that evening he would hold his big roast suckling pig barbecue party on the beach and invite some of the locals to join us. Cap'n Jim and Eve loaded the Zodiac with beer and wine, bread, salads, potatoes and all the kit for the barbecue and set it up on the beach. We collected wood for the fire and soon there was a good blaze going. All four of us decided to go back to *Nightwind* for a shower and a bracer or two whilst the piglet roasted on its spit. In the firelight we could see a few people in loose shirts and ragged shorts drifting up and Eve handing out drinks. Bob waved the gin bottle and said, 'We'd better finish this off before we go ashore, so we all had another large gin and tonic. By the time that had been drunk the fire on the beach had reduced to glowing ashes and we thought that the suckling pig would be done to a turn, so we climbed into the Zodiac and headed for the shore only to be met on the beach by a worried looking Cap'n Jim waving his arms and pointing to the spit.

'I couldn't stop them,' he cried. 'Once they'd got into the beer they started on the food.'

Pete examined the skeletal bones of his piglet hanging forlornly from the barbecue, a few shreds of gristle left on the carcase. The beer, wine and food had all been consumed and a dozen or so happy locals were stretched out on the sand. Those that were sober were chatting away.

'Great party squire,' called one waving a half empty bottle of Bob's favourite *Cos d' Estournel,* 'You must do it again sometime!'

Apart from that we had a brilliant week sailing round the islands and the four of us slipped Cap'n Jim and Eve a good tip. The 'boys' went off to the airport whilst I checked in for one night at Fisherman's Wharf. I told Dan I would see if I could find out any more about the financing for Tern Island.

I decided not to phone Hugo on an open Comortel line but to wait till I got back to London. I did phone Florence, however, and asked her if she was free to talk. She said she wasn't, the Minister was in his office. I said, 'How about lunch somewhere?' and she agreed, suggesting a little bar out of St George's where it would be quiet.

A taxi took me there and she was already waiting. We ordered beer and sandwiches and found a table in the corner. There were only two other people in the place and they took no notice of us.

Before I could say much she told me, 'The Minister was furious when he learned that you had been to Tern Island.'

'Was he? We didn't go ashore; security wouldn't let us even go inside the reef. What is going on there, Florence?'

She shrugged her massive shoulders. 'I dunno... It's all very secret. All I do know is that some American called Kronoff has leased the Island from our government and is building an exclusive resort there.'

'But what about the money? What is this PORT money you mentioned?'

She glanced round nervously but was reassured when she realised that there was no chance of being overheard.

'It's just an abbreviation I used for "Preliminary Operations for the Redevelopment of Tern". I don't know. I don't like it Marcus – it's stealing!'

She was clearly torn between her job and her conscience.

'Look Florence, this money – the aid money is British taxpayers money, people like me have paid taxes to provide it for the benefit of the people of the Comorantes. My firm CONDES is responsible for it. If somebody is stealing it I'd like to know because it could be me who will be held to account, and I don't fancy spending time in prison for something I haven't done.'

She looked shocked. 'It won't come to that, will it?'

'It might!'

She looked at me horrified. 'I wouldn't want that on my conscience, not after what you did for Jacques.' She paused for a moment. 'All I know is that the Minister signed three cheques for $1.5m each, all made payable to some bank in the West Indies.'

'Can you remember the name of the bank – it's important.'

'I think so. It was the International Trading Bank of St Croix.'

'...and three cheques?'

'Yes.'

'You've no idea who or why there were three cheques?'

She gave a small smile, 'I suppose they would be for three persons.'

'Yes, I suppose so, but why not just one cheque to cover all three? Probably they are separate investments?'

I thought about this for a minute. Rouget had signed the cheques so obviously he was involved. If he was then the PM must be as well – that was two of them. Who was the third person?

******

CONDES OFFICE – LONDON, 2010

I flew back to London the next morning. Zoe wasn't due back from her mother's until Thursday so that gave me a couple of days to get the house straight. She left a note pinned to the pillow. 'Hope you had a great trip and are not too shagged out by those dusky maidens that must have swarmed around you to do your duty to a lonely girl who is missing you very much'.

I laughed, I should be so lucky.

After a good night's sleep I was up early, grabbed a quick breakfast and beat the rush hour traffic to the office, which judging from the open mouths and dropped jaws when I strolled in, caught everybody on the hop. I was even earlier than Hugo, which surprised both of us. When he arrived I was waiting for him in his office with a pot of coffee Janet had made for us.

'You look astonishingly healthy for a man who has just returned from ten days in a hellhole of pestilence and disease. I expect you'd like another extra two weeks holiday to recover?' He gave me his disarming smile again. Now there are two ways of responding to Hugo when he's in his '*taking the piss*' mode. The first is to ignore it – pretend you haven't noticed. The second is to take it at face value as though you believe it to be genuine. Now I'm not one to turn down a good offer if it's made, so...!

'That's very generous of you Hugo, thanks. Another two weeks holiday will be fine – you can't stretch it to three, can you? At this rate I'll soon not need to come into the office at all, I'll be on permanent holiday and you can just send my share of the profits straight to the bank.'

'Ha, bloody ha! No chance! Who'd have to do all the work then – me! So how was the trip and how's Port Mahon getting along? Desmond Fitzpatrick was asking me about it at the Merchant Taylor's dinner last night.'

I took a sip of my coffee to give me time to get my thoughts in order. You might think that that was just a normal question, the sort that any engineer might ask his colleague when he had been away. Well it wasn't. There was something hidden here. Why would Fitzpatrick ask Hugo about Port Mahon at a livery company dinner? They were social occasions when the great and the good of The City of London put the world to rights through a haze created by gallons of superb port. The thing to do was to play it straight until you had sussed out what the real point was behind it.

'The trip was great; I'll tell you more about that when you and Emily come round for dinner on Friday. As for Port Mahon, the job itself is going well. They've caught up to the original programme and Jack's got a tight grip over the quality, so no worries there. Is there any special reason you ask?' I raised a quizzical eyebrow.

Hugo chewed his lip, a sure sign that he wasn't happy. 'Fitzpatrick told me that he had heard we were not performing well and we were letting the programme get out of control.'

I blinked with surprise. 'That's nonsense! Who told him that?'

'He said that chap Garside had heard stories to that extent from the Comorantians.'

'Oh Garside! That explains it. He threatened to do us damage when we turned him down as a consultant. This must be his way of getting revenge.'

I looked him in the eye. 'However, there is something odd going on, not with Port Mahon itself but with the funds allocated for it. You wouldn't know anything about that perchance?'

It was his turn to look perplexed. 'Not that I'm aware of. What sort of thing?'

I told him everything I had learned. I told him about three lots of money being taken out of the Port Mahon account, the Tern Island fiasco and the little I had discovered about Kory Kronoff.

'We could be held responsible for that money,' I pointed out.

Hugo frowned and chewed a bit more lip. At this rate Emily Elmes wouldn't need to prepare supper that evening. Hugo could well have eaten himself. I was wondering if such a thing was possible in humans. I'd seen pictures of a snake that had tried to eat itself and just ended in a tight ring but it had started off with its tail – starting with a lip would be very tricky.

There was a loud noise as Hugo cleared his throat. 'Are you still with me, you seemed to lose yourself there?'

'Sorry Hugo, I was wondering about that money.'

'Really,' he said, sceptically. 'Well, I don't think we can do much about Tern Island, it's not part of our remit. However, I'll definitely speak to Desmond Fitzpatrick about the missing money and also put his mind at rest about Port Mahon.'

Zoe was due back later today. I could hardly wait for the afternoon to pass by so I left the office early and drove to Paddington Station. Parking the old MG illegally behind some large wheelie bins I slipped through into the concourse. Zoe's train was right on time and, as I waited at the barrier half concealed by a pillar, I spotted her long before she saw me. I studied her as she approached. Her long chestnut hair shone in the gloom of Paddington Station. Her blue-grey eyes scanned the awaiting crowd: she had a presence and many envious looks were cast in her direction. When she saw me studying her she broke into a run and hurled herself into my arms, planting a breathtaking kiss on my lips, to the applause of some of the other meeters and greeters.

We linked arms and I carried her holdall to the car.

'You were watching me, weren't you, pretending to hide behind that pillar? I saw you.'

'And a very pleasant sight it was for a sex-starved, salt-encrusted, civil engineer.'

She grinned mischievously and gave me the full benefit of those blue-grey eyes. 'Two of those I can cure in the shower, but alas there's nothing I can do about the engineer bit. That, I'm afraid, is a lost cause.'

Heaving her case into the back of the car I asked her mischievously, 'Do you want to do some shopping on the way home?'

She punched my arm. 'Are you feeling ill lad? No? Then just get in the car, Moon and press the pedal to the metal. Sex first, shopping later!'

I cut through the late afternoon traffic back to Chelsea like Jenson Button on 'uppers'!

Two days later Hugo intercepted me just as I was going out to a meeting with Bob Barclay. 'You and I have been asked to attend a meeting in Whitehall on Wednesday. It seems that your news about the diversion of funds has thrown them into a real tizz-wazz. They stressed it was important so can you cancel anything you may have got on for that morning?'

We took a taxi to one of those anonymous tall-glazed, stone-faced buildings that front Whitehall filled with similar tall-glazed, stone-faced occupants who looked through their spectacles and down their noses at the world. Our credentials were checked, we passed through security and were led up to a conference room on the first floor.

There were eight people waiting there drinking coffee and munching biscuits. Hugo and I were offered the same. I glanced around: three people were in uniform, a vice-admiral and a captain in British naval uniform and a commander in American naval uniform; the others were in dark civilian suits. Desmond Fitzpatrick introduced us, but I didn't catch any of their names except that the admiral was Sir somebody or other and James White was the tall, thin, distinguished white-haired patrician who called the meeting to order. We took our places round the table. Hugo and I were at the bottom facing the chairman.

The chairman gave a summary of what had transpired to date with Port Mahon, starting with the Comorantes application for aid funds to build their new port and concluding with progress to date. He spent some time explaining that negotiations had taken place, and were continuing to take place, regarding the availability and use by the Royal Navy and the US Navy of the facility when it was completed. He said that the consulting engineers – with a nod at us – had been in several discussions with the Navy and incorporated certain requirements into the design. Part of the reason for granting aid to the Comorantes had been the use of this facility.

He explained as to how the total sum of aid had been arrived at, stressing the fact that a large chunk was a requirement of the Comorantes Government to cover their own costs.

'However, we understand from our consultants that some funds have been diverted from the Port Mahon project, possibly to something else. Mr Moon, a director of CONDES, discovered this just recently and will fill in the details.'

It's strange isn't it, I had been quite relaxed up to that point, but suddenly the mouth felt dry and the throat muscles tightened. My first words were nothing more than a croak. Hugo quickly passed me a glass of water whilst the others waited impatiently.

The vocal chords were loosened up with a clearing hawk and I explained what I had discovered as briefly as I could, omitting any reference to what we had found on Tern Island but concluding that it was likely that both the President and the Minister of Ports were involved.

A sharp-suited guy with gelled hair cut in. 'You said that there were three payments made from the account? Who is the third person?'

I shrugged, 'I don't know, and in any case, I was speculating. I don't know for certain that the President and Director of Ports are involved except that the latter signed the cheques so presumably they must be.'

'Why would the Director of Ports and Harbour's secretary give you this information? It seems a big breach of trust.' The question came from a long-nosed, pale-faced man with burning eyes. It was a good question.

If I said it was because I'd done her a favour, that could be interpreted in embarrassing ways – and no doubt would. It was better to come clean.

'Our resident engineer and I saved her son from drowning a few months ago so she felt she owed me a favour. In addition, she is a good Christian woman and thought that CONDES could be blamed for stealing this money and that would not be right,'

The other people round the table had a short discussion and seemed to reach some agreement.

The chairman resumed. 'We have a serious problem, gentlemen. You are aware that our discussions with the

Comorantians about using Port Mahon as a naval base are strictly confidential?' We nodded. 'Well, I have to tell you that the Comorantians are being a wee bit difficult at present.' He sucked in his breath through his teeth.

'If this other thing came to light publicly it could scupper the whole thing. So I must demand of you that you do not breathe a word of this to anyone, and remind you that this comes under The Official Secrets Act.'

He addressed Hugo and I. 'We would like you to keep your ear to the ground and if you learn anything further please contact Captain Drysdale at the Admiralty.' He nodded at the captain.

With that the meeting broke up, Drysdale handed me his card with a wry smile and said, 'Normal office hours, Mr Bond!'

In the taxi back to the office I speculated to Hugo that it was all very well for 'patrician' to swear us all to secrecy, but what about Dan Granchester? If the Government didn't get their secret deal signed up with the Comorantians very soon, they might find their cunning little wheeze spread all over the front page of *The Times* in 72 point bold capitals!

On Saturday morning Zoe and I caught the bus down the King's Road and got off at Chelsea Old Town Hall. She wanted to do the shopping we didn't manage to do last Thursday and said she'd meet me later in the pub. I made my way down Oakley Street and turned off into the little square that sheltered the Frog and Nightgown. Bob, Dan and Pete were already there sitting at a table in the

227

courtyard with Tony Scales, back from his dental conference and accompanied by Finola. Robin Fullerton was there with Fleur keeping a watchful eye on him. Zoe arrived twenty minutes later to admiring glances from the regulars round the bar. As usual people soon got tired of talking across each other so the group gradually split up between the boys and the girls. This was probably just as well because Robin had been ogling Finola and Fleur sizing up Dan. I think she fancied being Lady Granchester. I could feel the friction building up in the Fullerton family – a not uncommon event.

I wanted a quiet word with Dan so I took him off to one side out of Fleur's range. I told him what I had learned from Florence, omitting my speculation that the Prime Minister and Director of Ports were involved. He excitedly told me that he had taken the outline of his story and the photographs to his editor and *The Times* had gone for it like a rat up a drainpipe. Apparently, there had been a stories floating around about Kory Kronoff and his financial affairs for some time, but so far, nobody had been able to pin anything on him. He said that *The Times* were proposing to infiltrate a reporter into his business and see if they could pull off a sting operation.

Tony Scales eased alongside us, having overheard part of the conversation. 'It sounds like I missed a great trip.

'You did – apart from the disaster with Pete's suckling pig!' I told him the story about the locals eating it all before we had chance. 'And, of course, we think we might have discovered a scam of the first water, that's what I was talking to Dan about.'

Dan explained what we had done and that he was hoping that this might turn out to be the scoop that would launch him into the world as a star reporter and not just the writer of a social column.

'I've heard of Kronoff, a lot of celebrities have invested money with him for fantastic returns,' Tony observed.

I laughed, scornfully. 'Not if Tern Island is an example of what he's selling!'

****

Norbert Garside was feeling full of himself; he was also full of three large scotches, a bottle of claret and half a bottle of Warre's finest port on top of smoked eel, roast beef with all the trimmings and a large treacle tart and custard. He'd just been entertained to a huge lunch at Simpson's and agreed a nice little consultancy contract with the general secretary of the National Union of Sheet-metal Workers. He would tell them what the Labour Party was thinking and they would pay him £5,000 a year. It was a sweet deal for him and he was just lurching cheerfully along the corridor of Portcullis House, making for the haven of his office to sleep it off when Desmond Fitzpatrick buttonholed him.

'Ah Garside! Been meaning to have a word with you old chap. It appears we've run into a little difficulty with one of our aid projects.'

Nobby struggled to get both eyes focussed on the speaker. 'Not now Desmond, can't it wait?' He leant against the wall for support and belched.

Fitzpatrick glared at him and recoiled hastily as a blast of gravy-flavoured alcohol fumes enveloped him.

'No it can't wait! It's one of the projects you pushed through – Port Mahon in the Comorantes.'

A small spurt of alarm shot through Nobby's befuddled brain.

'What about it then?'

'Apparently, some of your little dark oriental chums have been filtering off cash that doesn't belong to them. HMG is not in the business of doling out swathes of aid so that tricky little sods can stash it in their personal Swiss bank accounts, you know.'

Nobby staggered and blanched. Fortunately, Fitzpatrick put it down to the drink. 'How do you know this?' he managed to gargle out.

'Our consultants saw the bank statements.'

'So what will happen?'

'Nothing – yet. We're keeping it under review.' He looked at Nobby carefully. 'If I were you I'd take a Resolve tablet or something, you look quite ill.' And he strolled off, leaving Nobby heading for the 'gents', not sure which of his ends was going to evacuate first.

He sat in a cubicle, his head between his knees as waves of nausea and terror swept over him alternately. *Oh God, if this gets out I'm finished. Everything I've bloody worked for – gone!* Castigation, humiliation, incarceration and degradation seemed to sum up his future prospects. He finished what he was doing and cleaned himself up in front of a mirror. He looked dreadful, his head ached, his mouth tasted of bile, his bloodshot eyes watered and his suit was a crumpled mess.

Worse was to follow: when he reached his office both Bill Brown and Miss Harbottle were there thumbing through some pages in a magazine. They quickly closed it and Brown hid it behind his back but not before Nobby had caught a glimpse of the title – *Rubber News*. He felt too ill to comment as he staggered through the door and collapsed into his chair. Their initial embarrassment changed to knowing grins as they took in his dishevelled appearance and bloodshot eyes.

'Had a good lunch, Norbert?' chuckled Brown. 'Where did you go – Salvation Army kitchen?'

'Up yours, Brown!' Nobby snarled and then ignored them.

Christ, he needed to think and the brain wouldn't concentrate on the problem. All he could think of was that he must contact Coquelin and warn him. Maybe getting him to scrub the whole deal, or at least keep Nobby's name out of it. Coquelin owed him that much at least. He was alert enough to know he must not phone from the office; a call box well away from Westminster would be the place to make the call. He'd wait until he'd sobered up enough to get a taxi back to his flat, there was a call box at Pimlico underground station.

****

2010 – GOVERNMENT HOUSE, THE COMORANTES ISLANDS

Coquelin phoned Rouget. 'Phillipe, something has come up about Tern Island that we should discuss. Come round to Government House for a drink this evening and bring the finance files on Port Mahon with you.' There was no alarm in Coquelin's voice so Rouget was not worried. He ordered Florence to pack what few files there were on the finance side into his briefcase and strolled round from his house at 7.00pm.

A servant brought each of them a drink, a mojito for Coquelin and a martini for Rouget and when he left them and closed the door Coquelin began. 'I got a panic-stricken phone call from that idiot Garside late this afternoon. The fool phoned me from a call box and ran out of money before he could finish his story, but I got the gist of it. Apparently that consultant chap Moon has seen your finance files and told the Brits that some money has gone missing.'

Rouget gasped. 'He can't have! Those files are in a locked cabinet. It's impossible!'

'Well he has! Have you ever had them on your desk when he's been in your office?'

Rouget went pale. 'Yes, but I always hold them up so he can't read them even upside down – but he did knock a file on the floor once and by the time I got round my desk he'd picked the loose sheets up and put them back. I suppose he could have seen something then. Oh God, this sounds serious, what's going to happen?'

Coquelin smiled; it wasn't a nice smile. 'You're an idiot Phillipe, but I don't think there's any harm done. We haven't finished negotiating that deal with the British to allow their navy and the Yanks to use Port Mahon for bunkering and supplies. I don't think they'll want to rock the boat over the odd million or two, do you?' He answered his own question. 'No, they won't want to make a fuss over that.'

He stroked his chin. 'The problem, Phillipe, is that we don't want something like that to happen again, do we?'

Rouget gulped and started to sweat. 'No Henri, we don't. I'll make sure it doesn't.'

'Of course you will, Phillipe, but we must be prudent. What you will also do is arrange for Moon to have a visit from Anna the next time he stays at the Fisherman's Wharf, and that we have some nice video of the event.'

Rouget shuffled his feet uncomfortably. 'Er, but how will I know when he's going to stay there?'

Coquelin lost his cool and snapped, 'Jesus Christ man, you're a Minister of the Government! Just tell the hotel to send you a list of all their bookings or we will put the inspectors in to check their books. That'll frighten them. Wilbert Janvier, the owner, has been fiddling his taxes for years! For fuck's sake, have I got to do everything?'

Rouget blanched and hastily said he would arrange that.

'Now, let's have a look at the Port Mahon finance files.'

Rouget got them from his briefcase and spread them on the table.

'Is that the lot? Coquelin asked.

Rouget nodded.

'And which file do you think Moon saw?'

Rouget pointed out the one containing the bank statements.

'That's all?'

Rouget muttered, 'Yes.'

'You're sure? And that's Florence's writing.'

'Yes.'

'Then my dear Phillipe, we have nothing to worry about! We are entitled to take some of the money allocated for Comorantes Government administration costs, and PORT means Port Mahon!'

CHAPTER THIRTEEN

2011 – CONDES OFFICE, LONDON

Amanda on reception phoned me. 'I've got Jack Fourie on the line from Beauregard Island, shall I put him through?'

I was puzzled, I had spoken to Jack two days ago and things were going well so what could this be about?

'OK Amanda.'

'I'm glad I've caught you Marcus – something strange came up this morning. You remember I told you that Rouget had shown some Chinese guys round the site but didn't contact us? Well, a guy from Comorantes Ports and Harbours turned up at our offices and wanted two full sets of our drawings. He had a letter of authority from Rouget and wanted to know how much they would cost. I told him I would have to get permission from London to do that and it would take at least a day to print them out.'

'Did he say why they wanted them?'

'He said that as the client they may want to make some minor changes and add a few things.'

'You told him that Mumbai Construction are working to a fixed price?'

'Sure, but he replied that they were quite minor, and the Comorantes Government would cover any extra cost.'

'Well, if that is what they want and they pay for it, they are the ultimate client so we'd better give them two sets. Charge them at cost. You think this has something to do with the Chinese, Jack?'

'It could just be a coincidence, but I thought I should let you know.'

'OK keep us informed. We'll just have to wait and see what they come up with.'

'When are you coming out here next?'

I called Margaret to check my diary. 'I think it's in a couple of weeks...'

Margaret called out the fourteenth.

'...The fourteenth Jack, I'll come to the Comorantes first and go back through the Gulf.'

Jack said, 'OK I'll let Rouget know. Will you overnight at Fisherman's Wharf?'

'Yes, I'll pay him a courtesy visit.' As I put the phone down I was thinking I'll also see if Florence has any more information.

****

THE COMORANTES ISLANDS – 2010

Coquelin had been singularly unimpressed by Nobby's frantic call. He'd kept telling him to calm down, take it slowly, think it through, but all Nobby could think of was Bert Grindle MP, former occupant of the next flat to him in Pimlico, now currently a guest of Her Majesty in Wormwood Scrubs Prison. All he had fiddled on his expenses was a few thousand quid for his mistress's rent. The thought of what sentence he'd get for stealing $1.5m was brown-trousering. The other worrying thing was that he'd run out of money for the coin box before he could emphasise to Coquelin that his name must be kept out of it. He couldn't phone again because Coquelin had blasted his ears off for phoning in the first place and said he wouldn't take any more calls from him.

Tern Island preyed upon his mind continuously; he had sleepless nights and even when he did manage to drop off he had nightmares about red-robed judges pointing down to the cells with the words 'for life' ringing in his ears.

He stopped going both to The Houses of Parliament and his office in Portcullis House because he found himself interpreting every look or glance in his direction as knowing. When he took refuge in 'Mineanders' in Cadeby he couldn't shake off the feeling of persecution. Tottie gave up trying to cheer him up and went out to bingo or round to her mothers. Even George, the ticket collector on the 'Master Cutler' back down to London, noticed the aura of gloom and despondency and only added to it with his quip. 'Cheer up Mr Garside, tha looks as if tha's lost a million and found a sixpence.'

However, when after two weeks no axe had fallen, he began to relax and poke his head above the parapet. Life seemed to go on as normal around him, people still cracked jokes, pushed paper around and Laetitia Harbottle and Bill Brown seemed to be getting on well. Laetitia was still cool towards him but had dropped that air of open hostility.

Bill Brown noticed the resurgent Garside and clapped him on the shoulder. 'What's been up with thee Nobby, tha seems to have had the moon coin on thi shoulders for the past two weeks.'

Nobby passed it off with, 'Not felt too well, Willie. The doc says it could be overwork.'

He wondered about CONDES and whether they had done any more snooping around, but at least Coquelin had assured him that he would take care of that problem.

****

It so happened that at that very moment 'that problem' was boarding an Etihad flight to the Middle East. I relaxed into my Business Class seat and ordered a Buck's Fizz – and Phillipe Rouget, having learned from Jack Fourie of the date of my arrival on Grandes Rocques and checked with the Fisherman's Wharf that I had a reservation, was phoning Anna Lemartine with precise instructions.

At Eric De Verteuil International Airport on Grandes Rocques there was some muttering and tapping of computer keys when I presented my passport, but after a short delay I heard the admission stamp being whacked on to a page and I was waved through with a 28-day visa. Customs also waved me past and I took a taxi to the hotel. My room, number 110, overlooked the swimming pool where some air crew from an Asian airline were splashing about happily. I phoned Jack Fourie to let him know I had arrived and told him I would fly to Beauregard tomorrow morning. He said he had something to show me, but it would keep till then. I then phoned Florence and asked her to fix me an appointment with Rouget in the afternoon – nothing important, just a courtesy call. She was very chatty and told me Jacques was now fully recovered from his ordeal and back to normal.

After a shower and a change of clothes I drifted down to the bar, sank a cold beer, had some lunch, and took a cab to Ports and Harbours.

The meeting with Rouget was strange. He was overwhelmingly welcoming – very effusive, offered me a cold drink, sat me down, told me that the next certificate had been paid and they were pleased with the progress of the job, and finally that he hoped I would have a good stay in St George's. As he said that, there was a suppressed smirk on his thin face and his eyes watched my face like a hungry cat lining up a robin hopping about for crumbs in the snow.

Back at the Fisherman's Wharf I decided that as the flight to Beauregard was at 6.00am I would have an early night. I had just returned to my room when my doorbell rang. I opened the door to behold an enormous black woman in some sort of red top and hot pants carrying a large holdall from which protruded some black and red electrical wires.

She looked slightly taken aback when she saw me.

'Are you an electrician?' I asked very puzzled, because anybody less like an electrician it would be hard to imagine.

She seemed to recover and advanced irresistibly into the room like a bulldozer moving a small copse.

'What's your name dearie?' she said, dropping her bag on the floor with a thump.

239

'For what it's worth it's Marcus Moon, but what's that got to do with you? Who the hell are you anyway?'

I could get a better view of her now and although not unattractive she was huge. Well over six feet tall. I'm tall, but she topped me by two inches. She had on a tight red tank-top which showed off a pair of massive breasts, a skimpy pair of denim shorts revealing thighs like redwood trees and a smile that reminded me of one of those machines than turns tree trunks into wood pulp.

The smile slowly dissolved to be replaced by a puzzled frown. 'Did you say Marcus Moon?'

'Yes.'

'Are you the guy that saved young Jacques Doublet from drowning?'

I frowned; I couldn't see where this was going.

'Yes, well two of us did.' Uncertainty and indecision flittered across her face.

'Bloody hell!' she exclaimed and then put a finger to her lips to indicate silence. She grabbed one of my arms and proceeded to drag me back out of my room into the corridor. I followed – well, I didn't exactly have any choice; it was either that or end up short of an arm. By now I was totally mystified. She found an empty room on the other side of the corridor and pulled me inside, closing the door behind us.

'Sorry about that,' she said, 'I'm Anna Lemartine. Florence is a good friend of mine and told me all about it.'

I was still none the wiser and it must have showed on my face. The circumstances prevented the Moon blank look from being concealed on this occasion.

240

'You don't know what the fuck I'm talking about, do you?'

I shook my head awaiting the explanation, without a clue as to what it might be.

She took a deep breath. *Steady on* I thought, *with a chest that size any more of those and she'll extract all the oxygen from the room and we could die of asphyxiation. Well I didn't fancy giving her the kiss of life and I sure as hell didn't want her giving it to me. One blow and she'd inflate me like a hot-air balloon. I'd explode with a bang and be splattered all over the furniture. Not a pretty thought!*

Her forehead wrinkled and she looked at me with some concern. 'Are you all right, Marcus? You seemed to drift away for a minute.'

I shook my head apologetically. 'Yes, sorry, carry on.'

'I'll start at the beginning. You know M'sieur Rouget, our Minister?' I nodded. 'Well, he asked me to get the man in number 110 into a... er... compromising situation and video the whole event.'

Things became a little clearer but still quite hazy.

'You mean he asked you to... er... not to put too fine a point on it... screw me and you would video it?'

She grinned, sheepishly. 'Not just that, much more than that. I have a whole bag of tricks – vibrators, electrical stimulators, cattle prods, etc. You were to be given the full treatment and it would be recorded by the secret camera fixed in your room. The recorder is in the closet outside your door, I switched it on before I pressed the bell. I did the same for that guy Garside.'

'Garside!?' I raised an eyebrow in surprise. There was a lot of information to be analysed here but first things first.

'Why would Rouget do that?'

'I don't know but obviously they want some hold over you for something, but I couldn't do that to somebody who saved my godson's life.'

'Jacques is your godson?'

'Yes, I told you Florence is a good friend of mine.'

'You said "they". Who's "they"?'

She hesitated for a moment and obviously decided that as she'd gone so far she might as well give me the whole nine yards. 'Rouget and our President, M'sieur Coquelin. He's the one who asked me to fuck Garside.'

This was going to require some considerable thought, but the present situation needed resolving first.

'So I take it that all bets are off now?'

Slightly crestfallen, she nodded.

'So what do we do now? If the video recorder is still running it will have picked up your entry into my room and our subsequent disappearance. That will have to be explained or deleted. The best thing would be to delete it and claim the recorder jammed. Can you do that?'

She said she could and opened the door a crack. The corridor was still empty, the rest of the guests were down in the bar judging by the noise. We went across to a laundry cupboard and sure enough, on the top shelf was a DVD recorder spinning away. She switched it off. 'I don't know how to erase a disc,' she admitted, so I did it and gave her the now blank disc.

We heard the lift moving so hastily went back into my room and closed the door. I eyed up the mysterious holdall wondering just what had happened to Garside.

She gave me a lop-sided smile and put a hand the size of a small ham on my arm. 'I like you, Marcus, you don't fancy having a free go with my services, do you? They're very good, you know. Your Mr Garside went into ecstasy when I gave him the cattle prod up the bottom?'

I pricked up my ears at that. 'Did he now?' But I wanted time to work this out. 'It's a good offer Anna, but I must say thanks but no thanks. Why don't you get a drink from the mini-bar whilst I have a think?'

She looked disappointed but, after giving her bag a reluctant kick, went over to the mini-bar and opened a half-bottle of champagne.

I sat on the bed trying to make some sense out of all this. Why would the President of a sovereign state and his sidekick, want to set me up so that they had some hold over me? I was missing something. Then a thought struck me. 'Anna, you don't happen to have a copy of the Garside video, do you?'

She nodded, 'I always keep a copy of my clients' reactions.'

My heart missed a beat. 'Is it possible that you could make me a copy of it?' I crossed my fingers.

'I don't see why not, the President has a copy.'

So the President wanted a hold over Garside too. Why? And then I had another idea.

'What we have to do now is fake the DVD to allay any suspicions that you didn't follow instructions. Give me the disc.' She handed it over. She pointed where the camera was cunningly concealed on top of a cupboard behind a false architrave, so I directed it at the ceiling. We replaced the disc in the recorder and switched it back on for a few minutes. I wobbled the camera about and then blacked out the lens for a few seconds until she switched the recorder off. She removed the disc and I told her to give it to Rouget telling him that she'd given me the full treatment. She also said she'd drop a copy of the Garside video off at hotel reception for me.

One other thing puzzled me.

'Anna, does Florence know that you are here?

'Lordy me no! We always keep business and pleasure separate.'

'You're a nice lady, Anna.'

She gave me a sad little smile. 'Nobody has ever called me a lady before.' Then she picked up her bag, gave me a peck on the cheek that felt like having a blocked sink cleared with a rubber plunger and left.

I sank into a chair; there were many things to resolve here. I returned to the first problem. Why would Rouget and the President want to set me up? It could only be because I knew something they didn't want me to pass on. It wouldn't be the Tern Island scam because they couldn't know I knew about that. The only other thing I could think of was the money taken out of the Port Mahon account. I had told our Government about that, but we had all been sworn to secrecy because of the Royal Navy deal, so why would our Government tell the Comorantians? The answer was they wouldn't. No, there was more to it than that. I was still missing something.

And Garside – Garside must have been to the Comorantes again. That was the first I knew about that. The Comorantians had obviously set up Garside for a reason, otherwise why would the President want a video of the event? The answer came suddenly. They needed a hold over him. Why? Because he knew about the Port Mahon account and the money taken from it – and if he knew about it, then he must be a party to it.

Garside was the third person!

Bloody hell, a British MP ripping off $1.5m from the aid package! Christ, that coupled with the video of Garside with a cattle prod stuffed up him would really make a story for Dan Granchester.

The snag was, I had no proof; it was just speculation.

But it provided a possible link to what Rouget had tried to do to me. Somebody in our government had told Garside about the missing money and who had discovered it, and he had told the Comorantians.

Uh-oh! When they discovered the video was blank they might try something else to fix on me instead. These were powerful people in the Comorantes, they could do anything. They must have been on the lookout for me this time, hence the hang-up at the airport; I'd have to keep on my toes now.

True to her word, Anna dropped off the Garside video that evening and I caught the morning flight to Beauregard Island. The first thing I did was arrange for Jack to courier the video to me in London with his monthly reports. I didn't want anything incriminating found if they searched me at the airport. We watched the video with incredulity and helpless laughter. 'Blood and sand...' I observed, '...that's what they had lined up for me!'

'You might have enjoyed it!' Jack ventured.

'Oh yeah! I'll give you Anna's phone number for the next time you're in Grandes Rocques and you can give her a try!'

I changed the subject. 'What is this thing you wanted to show me?'

He pulled out a set of the port drawings. 'This is one of the two sets that Rouget asked for some time ago. The additions and alterations he wants us to make I've marked in red. I've asked Bannerjee to price them, but I reckon they won't cost more than a couple of million dollars. Rouget says he will confirm that the Government will pay the extra.'

I looked through the drawings; there wasn't much – some extra bollards, an additional bunkering point, a small dropped section that could accommodate small boats, a secure warehouse and a separate residential block for fifty people in pretty basic accommodation.

'So?' I said.

'Just look at the drawings from a flat angle. You can see where some notes have been written and then erased.'

I bent down and looked as he had said. I could see the indentations where the notes had been, but I couldn't read what they said because they were in Chinese.

We looked at each other. 'Small fast patrol boats based here for the Chinese Navy. Fifty Chinese marines on shore – easy to take over the whole base if necessary?'

Jack nodded. 'That's what I thought.'

'Can I take these back to London? Have you made copies?' He nodded.

I scratched my head. 'It's not up to us to make decisions about this; we must do what our client wants, and the Comorantes Government is our client to all intents and purposes. So we must incorporate these items. You say Mumbai are pricing them, when will they give us a figure?

'Bannerjee says in a week.'

'In that case we do nothing until Ports and Harbours have confirmed, *in writing*, that they accept the extra cost and then we'll add them to the design.'

****

I was a bit apprehensive about passing through immigration at Eric de Verteuil airport on my way to Abu Dhabi, but nothing untoward happened and I went through into the Business Lounge with a feeling of relief.

The feeling lasted precisely thirty seconds because that was the time it took for me to look round and see Mazin Al Jabril sitting with his legs crossed and a smirk on his handsome face watching me.

My first thought was *Christ, how the hell has Mazin managed to get his sticky fingers on the Port Mahon project?* Then I realised that he couldn't have, unless he was involved with Mumbai Construction. If that was the case then that was their problem not mine.

'Long time, no see, Marcus!' He stood up and held out his hand. 'No hard feelings?'

'Not long enough,' I replied, but shook the proffered hand tentatively and pretended to count my fingers.

I sat down next to him. 'What on earth are you doing here, Mazin? It's way off your area of criminality.'

He shrugged, nonchalantly. 'Looking at potential investments for my Arab clients.'

I chuckled. 'Isn't that a bit dangerous? I mean if you bugger off with their money they're not going to take that without some severe retribution.'

He forced a weak smile. 'It's not like that these days. I'm advising clients where to invest their money. It's a legitimate business and I'm trusted to give sound, well-researched advice.' He glanced around and then leant towards me. 'This is a big one, Marcus. This is really big money.'

He couldn't resist showing off, and told me all about this huge investment he had made for important Arab clients with a world-class investor called Kory Kronoff. 'You must have heard of him, he only deals with top-class people.'

Does he?' I responded. 'And what is this investment?'

He just smiled and wouldn't be drawn any further except to say that he had already invested tens of millions of dollars of Arab money in it.

I kept a dead straight face thinking, is it that massive con on Tern Island? Nobody had mentioned any other big scheme going on for Kronoff in the Comorantes.

For the first time I felt the faintest twinge of sympathy for Mazin. If what we believed to be happening with Tern was true, he was in for a massive shock and some serious explanations. Before I could decide what to do, if anything, his flight to Bahrain was called, and with a casual, 'See you around' tossed over his shoulder, he disappeared to the gate.

So was I correct in my reasoning? The thing to do was not to start with Mazin but to start where the big money was floating around. Where the honey is that'll also be where the bear is. The big money in the Comorantes was in only three places as far as I could tell. Port Mahon – and I was pretty certain he wasn't involved there; then there was the big chunk of American aid money to develop businesses in the Islands – possibly, but that was scattered about and the locals will be pillaging that pot. Besides that wouldn't show big enough returns. Finally, Tern Island. It *must* be Tern Island! He wasn't the third man – that was small money, and Garside was still in the frame for that. No, but was he putting a large slice of Arab money into the Tern Island scam? Now the other question was, was he a scammer or a scammee? Scammer would normally be his scene but, representing investors as he had claimed, he could just be on the receiving end. I cheered up at the thought of Mazin getting some of his own medicine and having to hide from a band of unforgiving, vengeful Bedouins seeking his blood. It was another angle for Dan to consider.

****

I was feeling a bit knackered by the time I got through Heathrow customs, braved the M4 traffic and Fulham Broadway. It was dark when I reached our house in Chelsea; I could hear Zoe singing in the kitchen as I opened the door and my spirits rose. She didn't hear me so I listened for a

249

few minutes. There was pure happiness in her voice and it made me feel cleansed from all the grubby politics and chicanery I had left behind in the Comorantes. I took a few moments to look round at our house. It was a happy house, warm and cheerful and she had made it that way. As you will have appreciated from my choice of office furniture and décor - before I was taken in hand by the Major – my taste embraced the tatty, scruffy and macabre!

'Hello,' I called. 'I'm back.'

She ran out of the kitchen and threw herself into my arms. Anna Lemartine, eat your heart out – this was the real thing!

A couple of days later the courier arrived with the package from Jack Fourie. I put the video in a drawer in my desk.

I had mentioned to Hugo that I had bumped into Mazin at Grandes Rocques airport, but I thought it was purely coincidental and he was busy ripping off some other poor sod. I didn't mention Tern Island. We went through the 'Chinese drawings' together and he came to the same conclusion I had – that the Chinese were horning in on the Port Mahon deal in a serious way.

'As this is political I suggest that we don't go through Captain Drysdale, but as you know Fitzpatrick, we go direct to him.' He gave me Fitzpatrick's number and extension. I rang him there and then.

'Hello Mr Fitzpatrick, it's Marcus Moon from CONDES, we met at the Ministry to discuss some stolen money a few weeks ago.'

'Ah yes, I remember. So what can I do for you Mr Moon?'

'I've just returned from the Comorantes and something has come up that I think you should know about. I don't want to explain over the phone, but if you could spare me a few minutes I'll come to Westminster.' I tried to inject some urgency into my voice.

There was a short pause and then he said, 'How about ten o'clock on Wednesday? My personal office is in Portcullis House; just ask for me at the Reception.'

I wondered whether to take the Garside video as well but decided against. Last time they thought the stealing of a few million dollars was small beer compared to the Royal Navy contract. Anyway, what did it prove apart from the fact that Garside could jump two feet up in the air with the right stimulation. The remainder was speculation – something the media revelled in, not serious government departments.

I was shown up to Desmond Fitzpatrick's office where he greeted me in a friendly fashion.

'Now, what is the latest on Port Mahon then?'

I unrolled the set of drawings I had brought back, explained about the Comortantes Government's request to incorporate certain items in the design and showed him the Chinese markings on the drawings with my interpretation of them.

He sat back in his chair and scowled. 'No wonder they're dragging their heels, the bastards are negotiating a separate deal with our yellow brethren.' He looked at me. 'So what are you going to do?'

'Well, strictly speaking they are our clients. They've said they'll pay for these extra works – although I suspect that the Chinese are actually paying – so we have little alternative but to incorporate them as they request.'

'Hmm! I suppose so. What about timing?'

'Putting them on the drawings is no problem, a few days' work at the most, but the state of the construction programme at the moment is that if we do incorporate these, Mumbai Construction won't be able to start work on them for three months.'

He stroked his chin; it was the same gesture Hugo used when he had a problem. As they were both members of the same club it occurred to me that it might be a secret sign and trigger off some sort of chaps' action so I stroked mine to see what would happen. Nothing did, except that he asked me if I was all right because I'd seemed to lose focus on the subject. Still giving me a strange look he said, 'I'll have to talk to the Secretary of State and the Prime Minister about this, particularly as the Americans are involved with Port Mahon. This could be serious; can you leave these drawings with me?'

I nodded.

'Thank you Mr Moon, somebody from the Department will be in touch with you in due course.' And I was ushered out.

Fitzpatrick didn't waste any time. Whilst I was on my way back to the office he was on the phone to The Right Honourable Herbert Jones, Secretary of State for Defence.

'Bert, we have a problem with our Naval Base in the Comorantes. It's serious and I think you should have a look at it and see if we should take it to the PM.'

Bert Jones was not a decisive man; he preferred to have a mob around him and get a consensus, and so far he had been lucky to come down on the right side. Fitzpatrick's call worried him. It looked as if it might call for a decision from him. Not just any decision but one involving the Prime Minister, and the last time he had taken a minor military problem to the PM he been told in no uncertain terms that he was the Minister who was there to make decisions about defence, and if he *couldn't bloody well do so then somebody else would be found who could*.

So it was with some trepidation that he awaited Fitzpatrick's visit.

After Fitzpatrick had explained the situation Bert Jones relaxed. As this involved the Americans it would definitely have to go to the PM.

'So it will be up to the PM to decide what to do about it then?' He smiled.

Fitzpatrick frowned at Jones obvious relief. Although they were in different political parties, Fitzpatrick was conscious that an element of national security was involved here and he despised Jones' weakness. A more positive approach was necessary.

'Bert, you've got to give the PM *some* idea of what he should do. He doesn't have time to analyse the whole position, he's relying on you – his Minister – to do that and give him a situation report.'

Jones' face fell. 'But what shall I say?'

'Look, why don't you take me with you and I'll explain the position to the PM. You can tell him that you asked me to do a report, but as it was urgent you thought it better if we didn't wait for that.'

Jones thought about that for a minute, trying to see if there were any political angles that might damage his position. He was reluctant to take Fitzpatrick with him to the PM's office but was terrified that he might get the whole thing wrong if he went on his own. In the event he told Fitzpatrick that he'd think about it. Fitzpatrick told him not to think about it for too long because the Comorantians might well sign up with the Chinese at any time and then there'd be hell to pay, and somebody would be held responsible...'

****

CONDES OFFICE, LONDON – 2011

I was drafting out a summary of information for Dan Granchester when Margaret appeared and hovered in the office doorway. It was the sort of significant hover that you just know is going to be followed by a request. She looked very secretarial today: neat hair, white blouse with its collar showing above a dark blue sweater. Her spectacles were hanging on a cord around her neck and rested on what was quite an impressive bosom. A quick scan of her face didn't reveal trouble afoot so I relaxed. Richard must still be on course for his voyage down the aisle and thence up the Amazon so to speak. I grinned at the thought, so I waited patiently for whatever question she was going to pose.

'Do you think I might have a word?'

'Well, it hasn't stopped you in the past so why not?' I murmured, gesturing for her to come in.

She sat in one of my visitors chairs. 'You know that my father was badly wounded in Korea and has great difficulty walking...' I nodded. '...and I haven't got any male relatives that I am particularly close to.' She hesitated for a moment then continued with a nervous smile. 'So I wondered if you would 'give me away' on my wedding day?'

'Margaret, if that's all right with your father, I will be delighted to. It will be an honour and a pleasure.'

She hesitated. 'You don't think it will look a bit odd, do you?'

'Odd?'

'Yes. A fift... middle-aged woman being given away by a younger man?'

A *much* younger man, I thought, but confined myself to, 'No, I don't think so.' I smiled. 'People will just think I was your toyboy and you're dumping me now that some rich old man has heaved up over the horizon.'

She looked horrified at that. 'Oh my God, they won't, will they!?'

'Only if I tell 'em!'

I couldn't keep a straight face, all the years of practising Moon faces in front of the mirror crumpled in the face of her obvious concern. I reassured her hastily, 'No Margaret they won't, it was just a joke.'

'Well, I didn't think it was funny,' she sniffed.

I switched the conversation to happier things. 'Have you actually fixed a date and a venue?'

She told me that they were thinking of a Saturday in the spring and that they both wanted the full works, so St Peter's in Kingscastle – her home town – was being lined up to fire the starting pistol.

'White wedding?' I couldn't keep the questioning smile off my face.

'Wait and see!' she snapped, still nettled at my 'toyboy' remark.

'And will you still be Ms Braithwaite in the office or Mrs Hewetson?

She smiled. 'I'll keep my maiden name for work otherwise you might get confused.'

'Touché!'

She went back to her office whilst I contemplated how the mysterious wheels of the world turned. She would never know that she could thank me for Richard and I wasn't going to risk a painful death telling her why!

Still I thought, there was no way Richard was going to slip out of her clutches now so I'd better start getting measured up to hire a morning suit.

CHAPTER FOURTEEN

2011 – CONDES OFFICE, LONDON

I started drafting out something for Dan again. Tern Island was nothing to do with CONDES and I shouldn't be wasting time on it. However, there was the matter of the stolen money from the Port Mahon account and if that came to light I was worried that we might get loaded with some, if not all the blame. Politicians are devious people.

To get it clear in my mind I took out a pad and jotted down a summary of what was known about Tern Island under two headings: *'Fact'* and *'Speculation'*.

Under 'Fact' I wrote:

[1] The British Government allocated $152m of aid to the Comorantes Government to build a new port. This money has been placed in the Port Mahon account and should only be released on production of building certificates signed off by CONDES. Included in that sum is $3m for Comorantes administration costs. We hadn't been asked to sign off any of that yet.

[2] $4.5m has been taken from the Port Mahon account in three tranches of $1.5m each without CONDES' knowledge.

[3] This money has been allocated to 'Preliminary Operations for the Redevelopment of Tern', which the Minister's secretary told me she had shortened to PORT. The

cheques had been signed by Minister Phillipe Rouget and made payable to the International Trading Bank of St Croix.

I frowned and crossed out *'the Minister's secretary told me she had shortened'* and replaced it with *'had been shortened.'* I didn't want Florence's cooperation to leak out.

[4] Tern Island has been leased by the Comorantes Government to an American wealth-management investor called Kory Kronoff to enable him to build an expensive resort scheme. This resort scheme is just a front; apart from façades there was nothing there – the whole thing was faked. I jotted after this: *Dan has photographs to prove it.*

[5] The Prime Minister of Comorantes set up Norbert Garside [a British Member of Parliament and deputy chairman of the committee who had allocated the aid funds] with Anna Lemartine and now has a very compromising video tape of the proceedings.

I frowned again. I wasn't supposed to know that. Anna Lemartine had given me a copy of that tape in confidence following similar circumstances. Besides which, I felt in my bones that my activities – or lack of them – with Miss Lemartine were better kept secret at the moment, particularly from the penetrating wit of the boys in the Frog, so I deleted that item.

[6] Mazin Al Jabril claimed to have invested 'tens of millions of Arab dollars' in a scheme promoted by Kory Kronoff.

I tapped my teeth with my pen, then wrote *'Speculation'.*

It is likely that included in the $152m allocated for Port Mahon there is an amount that Garside and the top Comorantian politicians intended to steal for their own purpose. They have used these funds to make an investment in Kronoff's Tern Island scheme. Following on from that, the three separate cheques indicate three people are involved. They are likely to be the Prime Minister Coquelin, the Minister of Ports Rouget, both almost certainly; and from his connections to Coquelin and Rouget, plus Anna Lemartine's video, the third person involved was likely to be Garside. In addition, this was not a spur of the moment theft; it must have been pre-planned at the time the budget was prepared.

I paused thinking, until our Government had got the Navy deal signed, sealed and delivered Dan couldn't involve Garside. I'd have to leave Garside out of the script for the time being.

I thought about Mazin. It was likely that the scheme Mazin was boasting about investing his Arabs' money in was the same Kronoff scheme.

It was also possible – although this was stretching it a bit – that as Kory Kronoff is scamming people with Tern Island he is doing the same elsewhere and I would lay a pound to a penny that he was not putting any of his own money into any of these schemes.

This didn't seem to make sense though. Surely people would realise pretty quickly that they had put money in but nothing was coming back in return. Mazin certainly would, he was as sharp as a pin. There must be more to it than that.

I started to laugh. There was a third story, of course. *The Sun, The Mirror, The Daily Sport etc* would have a beanfeast with Garside's video. This could be considered separately from the Port Mahon money. I set that idea to one side for the moment. I typed up my amended notes on my desktop leaving out the 'Speculation' item and printed out a couple of copies.

Putting the handwritten notes in a desk drawer together with the Garside video I phoned Dan Granchester. I got his answerphone so I left a message to ring me as soon as he could.

****

As Port Mahon was a Department for International Development project and not specifically a Defence project the Right Honourable Herbert Jones MP and Secretary of State for Defence eventually decided that he wouldn't lose any political face if he took the Chairman of the DfID Committee along with him to see the Prime Minister. They all met in the Cabinet Room where Fitzpatrick spread the drawings of the new port showing the additions required by the Chinese on the table, and gave a summary of the situation.

The Prime Minister frowned. 'Are you handling the negotiations on behalf of the Navy with the Comorantes, Bert?' This was addressed to the Minister.

He confirmed that it was his department that was doing that.

The PM frowned at this noncommittal reply. 'Why are they taking so long? From what Desmond says, this should have been tied up at the time the aid grant was made.'

'The Comorantians are deliberately dragging their feet, Prime Minister. My staff tell me that every time things appear to be agreed they come back with changes. They want more rent, they want more locals employed, they want a month's notice before one of our or an American ship docks there, and so on. Now it appears that they are negotiating with other parties, certainly the Chinese.'

The PM stroked his chin. 'The problem is that we don't have the political clout with these places that we used to. If we put pressure on them they shout 'colonialists' and turn to the Indians or Chinese for handouts.'

He thought for a minute and turned to Fitzpatrick. 'You said that there is an American naval officer here liaising with the Royal Navy about this.'

Fitzpatrick confirmed that there was.

'Give him all the information you've given me and ask him to pass it to Washington and I'll mention this to President Williamson when I talk to him next week. Uncle Sam may be able to lean more heavily on the Comorantians than we can.' He gave a thin smile, 'We tend to be too diplomatic these days whereas the Americans don't give a shit who they upset as long as they do as they're told.'

As they stood up to leave the Cabinet Room the PM leant across the table and eyeballed Jones. 'Bert, get a grip of this fucking thing for Christ's sake. Don't just leave it to your staff, do it yourself and I want a positive result!'

****

I took my notes along to the Frog and Nightgown on Saturday. Normally discussing business was taboo on Saturday lunchtimes, but this wasn't really proper business; it was a follow up from our sailing trip. As I had arranged, Dan was early and had come with Bob so we could get the heavy stuff out of the way before the others arrived.

Big Jessie set up three pints of Ruddles and we got down to the purpose of the meeting. Dan was fizzing with excitement.

I gave both of them a copy of the notes. I hadn't asked Margaret to type them – the fewer people who knew about Tern Island and Anna Lemartine the better, and Margaret may be involved with a bit of pre-marital pillow talk with Richard. I'd caught her yawning a couple of times in the office recently and I didn't know what his business interests were.

They read through the notes and then Dan said, 'Let me fill you in with the current situation at *The Times*. We've got a team working on this now. They have collected some of Kronoff's glossy brochures and financial projections for half a dozen of Kronoff's other projects and visited them, together with two other alleged developments. They vary from three completed schemes, two of which are mainly occupied and presumably income-producing and the third, a block of apartments in Dubai – which was empty and neglected – to four partly finished schemes at various stages that look good from a distance but are really nothing but basic shells and are definitely not income-producing, of which Tern Island is the worst. *The Times* chartered a light plane and one of their staff photographers flew over it and took some very revealing aerial shots. There are also some empty sites with a few desultory labourers pushing rubbish about where construction hasn't even started. The point is, he is taking stacks of money from investors and giving fantastic returns, yet has very little income. It looks as though he's using the money from more recent investors to pay out and keep happy the earlier ones instead of using it to build the promised developments. As they say, all he's doing is kicking the can down the road. I suppose he can keep doing this until he's rumbled.'

Bob had listened with interest. 'Do you know what that's called? It's a 'Ponzi' scheme and it's illegal. So, what's *The Times* going to do about it?'

I was puzzled. 'What exactly is a 'Ponzi' scheme, Bob?'

'It's named after a chap called Charles Ponzi who used it in the 1920s. It develops when an over-confident, highly optimistic, egotistical businessman, who thinks he's cleverer than everybody round him, persuades folk to invest through him in various complicated financial instruments. In Kronoff's case he has picked property. That's clever, because he can physically show a successful development to entice more investors. It starts off when he identifies a potentially good site somewhere – preferably owned by a small country's government whom he can manipulate. He offers to spend a lot of money developing the site, for instance for tourism, and produces a scheme and financial plan which shows that he can guarantee very attractive returns. He takes this to the government and persuades them to lease him the site for say 99 years, in return for which he offers them an attractive stake in the development. Thus, the site costs him nothing. He then goes to investors with his scheme, showing them the lease on the site and his guaranteed returns, and persuades them to invest all the money to carry out the development. He doesn't put in a penny of his own money. As part of the deal he undertakes to pay them an abnormally high return on their investment from day one. To do this he uses part of their investment money to pay their returns and with the balance starts to build the development. He then sets up a similar scheme somewhere else with different investors. But after they have coughed up for their development, he takes a slice of that and uses the remainder to finish building the first scheme and continue to pay the returns to everybody. He then does a third scheme and hopes that by this time the first development is completed and sold or let and shows a much higher return than he has originally forecast. So naturally the first investors are very happy and wax lyrical about this financial genius. He uses this to attract more investors to invest in yet more schemes – and so on. He hopes to keep this going *ad infinitum*. "Using Peter to pay Paul" and each time taking a healthy slice for himself.'

Bob scowled. 'If you think about it, this is bound to fail eventually because it requires a constantly increasing stream of investment. He just runs out of investors at some point. If the market takes a down turn then this accelerates the failure.

'I think Kronoff's problem has arisen because the property market slumped and the punters stopped buying property or spending money shopping or gambling so the returns on his developments began to show losses. He's riding the tiger; he can't get off or it will eat him, so he has to cheat. That's what is happening with Tern Island. He has to use the money he raised for that scheme to keep paying previous investors their guaranteed returns so they don't smell a rat and he hasn't enough money left to finish it. He just hopes the market will pick up.

'Eventually the money runs out and everybody loses. However you look at it, it's fraud on a grand scale.'

'It sounds just like the Government's pension scheme,' I murmured.

Dan grinned, happily. 'We're going to run a series of articles in the next couple of weeks ripping the whole thing wide open and gradually exposing the Ponzi fraud. I'll write some of the articles using my photos of Tern Island plus photos of his other developments and empty sites. They've promised me a byline and I've been asked to join the Inquiry Team.'

I frowned; this was heavy stuff.

'You look serious, Marcus,' observed Bob, and indeed I felt serious.

'Too right there Robert. The investors aren't going to take this lying down, are they?'

I turned to Dan. 'There are going to be a lot of very unhappy people when this comes out, Dan. Kronoff only takes investments from the rich and powerful and it is those chickens whose feathers are not just going to be ruffled but plucked, drawn and hung out to dry for public scorn and derision. They are not going to be happy at being exposed as mugs – on top of losing all their investments. Also Kronoff himself is rich and powerful so I should watch your step if I were you.'

He waved an airy hand, 'There's always some risk in investigative journalism.'

'So when is this revelation going to start?'

'Our inside man is just collecting the final evidence so we expect to launch the story in two weeks' time.'

I put forward another point that had been worrying me. 'Are you going to mention Garside?'

'Oh, you mean the MP that you think might be the third man? No, I don't think so. As you said it's speculation, and if we get it wrong he could sue for thousands.' Then he added, cheerfully, 'We could mention the money the Comorantians stole from your Port Mahon account, that's factual.'

No you can't, I thought, and chewed a lip pensively. I couldn't tell Dan about the current sensitivity of the relationship between the UK Government and the Comorantians with respect to the Navy deal unless I wanted to be prosecuted under the Official Secrets Act. A long stretch looking over Dartmoor through a barred window wasn't part of my holiday plans. I just hoped to hell that they got that deal signed up before the shit hit the fan.

Then there was the Garside DVD? Only Jack Fourie and I knew about that, but I couldn't see much use for it. It was in an unmarked case so I had tossed it into a drawer with some other blank DVDs. That seemed to wrap that up for the moment.

I drained the last of my pint.

Our timing was spot on. The bar door crashed open and Tony Scales, Finola, Martin Holmes and Pete with his arms round both Merrylees and Zoe, burst in.

'Hello hello, what's all this? A plot to take over the country? Is it going to be King Daniel, Prime Minister Barclay and Court Jester and Pimp to the Bedchamber Moon,' grinned Pete, wincing when Zoe punched him non-too-gently in the kidneys.

'Dry white wine for the girls Jessie, Ruddles for the men and one of those poncy alcopops for Doctor Smallwood,' I called to the bar. 'And stick a cherry in it, I suspect he lost his last night.' It was my turn to wince as Merrylees punched me.

****

2011 – GOVERNMENT HOUSE, THE COMORANTES ISLANDS

Coquelin's phone rang and the telephonist in State House said, 'I have the American ambassador on line one sir, shall I put him through?'

Coquelin frowned. What was this in aid of? Normally the Americans kept a low profile unless they wanted something.

'Yes, put him through.' There was a short pause then a mid-western voice rasped, 'Prime Minister, how ya doin' today?'

'Very well Mr Ambassador, thank you. What can I do for you?'

'Well, Prime Minister, we have a problem. I don't want to go into details over the phone, it's better that things are handled *mano a mano*, but my President wants it sorted out lickety-spit so he's sending an official envoy over to the Comorantes to help you come to a decision.'

Coquelin frowned. Why would he need to be helped to make a decision? He was the President and Prime Minister of a sovereign state and he didn't need the damned Americans to help him do anything whatever it was.

'That won't be necessary, Mr Ambassador,' he replied, coldly.

'It's Deputy Secretary of State Mitchinson, he's arriving tomorrow on Air Force Two. He'll stay at the Embassy and will see you at your office at 11.00am. Have a nice day.' The call was terminated.

It was as though Coquelin hadn't spoken.

Coquelin was livid; what the hell was that about, cocky bastard? He was very tempted to go off on a visit to one of the outer islands just to show the bastards that he wasn't going to be pushed around by anybody, particularly the Americans. However, he had other things arranged for tomorrow so decided to stay. There wasn't much he could do about it anyway, you can't stop a diplomatic plane from landing, but he was buggered if he was going to meet this envoy at the airport. He told Rouget to go and do the honours and keep them low-key. He also told his secretary to rearrange appointments and keep 11.00am to 12.00 noon free.

The special Boeing 747[400] touched down at Eric de Verteuil airport at precisely 10.30am to be met by a vast

Cadillac from the US Embassy with the Stars and Stripes fluttering on the bonnet. Serge driving Rouget in the BMW, lurked in its lee. Hands were shaken briefly, Rouget and Mitchinson climbed into the Cadillac and they set off for Coquelin's office.

The American just walked straight in with Rouget trailing behind, ignoring gasps from a couple of aides in the outer office.

Mitchinson was a big man, six foot six and 260 pounds of muscle. His face looked as if it had been hewn out of Mount Rushmore and his grey eyes squinted at Coquelin as though he was surveying ten thousand head of cattle three miles away across the prairie. When they shook hands his hand totally enveloped Coquelin's. Rouget was asked to leave and, when his dudgeon had come down a notch or two from its heights and he departed, the American got down to business. There was no wasting time or smooth platitudes.

'I'm James Mitchinson, Deputy Secretary of State for Foreign Affairs, you can call me James.' The gravelly voice rasped with confidence. He helped himself to a chair and sat down. He still towered over Coquelin who remained at his desk.

'I've been asked by the President to have a word with you about a little problem that seems to have arisen, Henri. You don't mind me callin' you Henri, do you?' He took it for granted that the answer would be in the affirmative and continued.

'You see we Americans have some very funny customs, when we agree things with our friends – we have this ridiculous habit of expectin' them to stick to their side of the deal. You followin' me?'

Coquelin blinked and was puzzled about where this was going. As far as he was aware they had stuck pretty close to the American aid package deal agreed some years ago and there had never been a hint of trouble there. OK, so he and his cronies had filtered off a few dollars here and there, but it was nothing that would warrant the President of the United States sending over his personal representative in an Air Force Boeing 747[400].

'But we have stuck to the aid deal! You can see our new sugar mill, the fertiliser plant and the fish meal factory, all bought and paid for with your aid money.'

Mitchinson sucked in air through his teeth and shook his large head.

'It's not the fuckin' aid package, Henri. I'm not here about that. It's our Brit friends.'

A spurt of alarm went through Coquelin, although he couldn't imagine why the Americans would be interested in a few million dollars being siphoned out of a British development aid package. The British knew about it and they didn't seem to care.

'What you've got to understand, Henri, is that the Brits and us – well, we're like friends – particularly in matters of defence against potential evildoers, ne'er-do-wells and malefactors who might wish to harm our two nations. Are you with me yet, Henri?'

Coquelin shook his head. He wished Mitchinson would stop calling him Henri as though they were old friends.

'OK, let me lay it on the line for you, Henri as you don't seem too fuckin' smart. We have a deal with the Brits that in areas of mutual interest we share things. It saves a duplication of items and saves the US taxpayer a few dollars, thus helpin' our President project the image of a prudent man. Capeesh?'

Coquelin was totally lost now, but he had a very nasty feeling that something was coming out of this that was not good news.

Mitchinson took his silence for acquiescence. 'So let's take Port Mahon, for instance. The Brits give you the money to build it, but part of the deal is that it will be available for use by the Royal Navy – which, because of our close association, means that it will also be available for the US Navy. But, of course, you knew that!'

His voice took on a grimmer inflexion. 'However, we understand that, in spite of the agreement, the deal is not signed up yet because you're draggin' your feet.' His narrow eyes bored into Coquelin. 'What also concerns us is that word has it you are talkin' to other parties who, shall we say, do not have the interests of the US of A at the forefront of their hearts and minds.'

Coquelin bridled at this. Who the hell did this guy think he was, interfering in Comorantes business?

'I think I should remind you, Mr Mitchinson, that we are an independent nation. We can talk to whom we like. It's up to me to get the best deal for the Comorantes that I can. I refuse to be dictated to by some ex-colonial power who thinks that they can decide what we do!'

271

Mitchinson sighed, 'I had hoped it wouldn't come to this, Henri, but OK, you don't want it the easy way so you can have it the hard way.' He cracked his knuckles; the sound was like a gun shot to Coquelin.

'You do a deal on this new port with the fuckin' Chinese, the Indians or men from Mars, in fact anybody else other than the Brits and us, and the Comorantes is dead! You got that, motherfucker? We'll cut off all your aid, stop your credit, encourage the opposition – by whatever means necessary – and bring your hickey little islands to their fuckin' knees. Then we'll put in a government that does what it's told. You got that as well? Nobody will want to touch you; you can starve in the sun for all we care. Ok, you can crawl to the Chinese, but what will they do? Nothin'. They just want a base – you have nothin' else they want. No minerals, no oil, no money. You're fucked. They'll eat you up and spit out the pips.'

Coquelin blanched. Mitchinson's slate-grey eyes continued to bore into him. He wasn't smiling now; this was hard ball with a rock. There was no doubt he meant exactly what he said. Coquelin suddenly felt his bowels turn to water, and muttering some excuse, made a rush for the door. Mitchinson watched him go; a sardonic smile flickering on his lips. He knew that Coquelin would climb down.

In the bathroom Coquelin couldn't stop shaking, after he'd evacuated his watery bowels he splashed cold water on his face and tried to pull himself together. He'd just experienced power at its most raw and terrible; it terrified him. He realised that he now had no choice but to sign the lease with the British or die politically, and maybe physically if the threat about supporting the opposition materialised. He straightened up and returned to his office. Mitchinson was nonchalantly picking his teeth with a silver toothpick.

Coquelin tried to pass the incident off, but his voice came out an octave too high. 'Sorry about that, must have been some raw fish I ate for breakfast.'

He returned to his desk, and trying hard to keep the quaver out of his voice, continued, 'You were talking about your President's concern over the Royal Navy's lease on Port Mahon? I think he's been misinformed. I can assure you there's no problem there; we've just had one or two administrative hiccups, but I understand the lease will be signed this week.'

Mitchinson smiled. It was not a kindly smile designed to fill Coquelin's life with sunshine and song; it was a smile as cutting as the icy wind sweeping across the Badlands of South Dakota in winter.

'That's fine Henri, good decision. I'll phone the President from our Embassy today and tell him that it's all sorted out and will be concluded without fail by twelve noon Brit time on Friday this week. Why don't you phone the British Ambassador now and tell him.' It wasn't a question.

He waited. Coquelin eyed the phone and then looked back at Mitchinson's implacable face. There was no way out. He picked up the phone and told the girl to connect him to the British Ambassador.

****

Through my open office door I heard Hugo say, 'Morning Margaret, you look nice this morning. How are the wedding plans going?'

'So far smoothly; we're just praying for a nice day.'

'I'll second that.'

He strolled through the door and said, 'I've just heard from Fitzpatrick that the Navy's lease has been signed. It looks as though the Chinese are out.'

'Yup, I got an email this morning from Jack saying that they had been told to stop work on the design changes so I assumed something had happened.'

'Fitzpatrick wants us to go to an emergency meeting about the stolen funds. They're going to pursue that matter now.'

The emergency meeting at the Department for International Development was fixed for Wednesday. However, on the Monday *The Times* ran Dan's first long article about the Tern Island scam, together with photographs showing the false construction and pointed speculation about Kory Kronoff's other developments. It created a sensation, the media went mad. Reporters and television crews were dispatched round the world to check out Kronoff's other alleged developments. On Tuesday *The Times* kept its lead on the scoop and the follow-up article listed Kronoff's developments in detail and the progress, or lack thereof, on each one. By Wednesday other papers had taken up the story and the American media were sinking their teeth into

Kronoff's leg. *The Times* published details of his spurious prospectus forecasts set against their estimates of the actual returns. The wealthy and powerful investors were beginning to demand some serious answers to serious questions like 'Where's my money?'

As an American citizen, a large section of his investors were American, and when the first doubts surfaced, they had no hesitation in putting political pressure on the US Government to do something.

Alarmed by the reports, the United States Securities and Exchange Commission put in a financial analyst to examine Kronoff's wealth management schemes. It didn't take him half a day to come up with the shocking revelation that it was both legally and mathematically impossible for Kronoff to continue to achieve the returns he had promised. The FBI was asked to investigate Kronoff, but when they went to look for him he was nowhere to be found.

Panic ensued. The early investors had made money but these were relatively few compared to the increasing number Kronoff had needed to keep paying out, and they went bananas. Hugo and I read all about it with interest.

****

Nobby Garside received a phone call from Fitzpatrick at home on Sunday evening after staggering home half-pissed from a long day at the Wath Labour Club bar.

'Where the hell have you been, Garside? We've been trying to get hold of you for two days!'

'Er, I've been holding constituency surgeries, Desmond. Why what's the panic?'

'There's an emergency meeting of the DfID Committee on Wednesday afternoon and I want you there!'

A spurt of alarm went through Nobby's fuddled brain. 'What's it about?'

'Can't tell you over the phone, just be there!' And the call was terminated.

Nobby took stock; there was no real cause for alarm. It could be some problem with any of the DfID projects so he dismissed it from his mind.

It was when he switched on the BBC News on Monday evening and saw the report about Kory Kronoff and Tern Island that it hit him right between the eyes. He went through the whole gamut of emotions: stunned incredulity, steaming rage, abject disappointment and finally terrifying fear. First thing Tuesday morning he was down at the newsagents buying *The Times*. He read and reread the lengthy article, but there was no mistaking its message. Kronoff was a crook and there was no substance to his empire. It looked as though billions of dollars had been lost by investors in his schemes. He sat in his front room white as a sheet and shaking as the implications slowly began to dawn on him. His investment, his prize nest egg had gone, and in the ensuing furore would he be exposed as a thief and a crook? He thought long and hard about that and decided that there was no reason why his name need come out. There were no documents in Kronoff's records with his name on them. Only Coquelin and Rouget knew he was an investor – and, as it appeared, a very minor one in the vast scale of Kronoff's activities. No, he was reasonably safe from exposure.

Nobby read more about the Kronoff revelations in Wednesday morning's *Sheffield Telegraph* on the train to London – it only increased his fury and gloom. The cheerful ticket collector passed by oblivious to the smoking bomb in seat 24A. 'Morning Mr Garside, going to show those Southerners how to run the country, eh?'

'Fuck off, George, can't you see I'm busy!'

'Ooh! Bit touchy this morning, are we?' George walked on, oblivious to the fact that he had come very close to a painful death involving his hat and ticket punch.

For the rest of the journey Nobby tried to analyse his emotions. They were mixed; rage and disappointment that his anticipated fortune had almost certainly disappeared, but also a sense of relief that now there was nothing incriminating about him that could come to light with the collapse of Kronoff's empire. The Government had dropped any enquiry into the alleged missing aid money some time ago so he was in the clear – or so he thought.

The DfID meeting was due to take place that afternoon but nobody had sent him an agenda. However, he didn't have any concerns about that. DfID had many projects on the go; as he'd already told himself, it was probably just a minor hiccup in one of those.

****

By Wednesday afternoon we had all had a chance to read the latest revelations about Kronoff in that morning's papers. The meeting was chaired by the same tall white-haired patrician as the previous meeting we had attended, but this time there were no Navy personnel present. Instead, we were introduced to two guys from the Treasury, one a laid-back, drooping eye-lidded cove with an off-putting drawl; the other, younger with spiky hair, and very sharp eyes like twin lasers. The three remaining members were the chairman and deputy chairman of the Aid Committee – Desmond Fitzpatrick, none other than our 'old friend' Norbert Garside, and a woman politician introduced as Penelope Cattermole. Garside looked surprised and his eyes narrowed when he saw Hugo and me, his handshake was cursory. When we took our places he was seated next me so I couldn't see him full face, but he was clearly nervous. This seating arrangement made things rather tricky. I decided to play it straight down the middle with just the facts. No speculation – the meeting could draw its own conclusions.

The chairman opened up with confirmation that the deal with the Navy and US Navy had been signed thanks to a little help from the US side that had loosened the log-jam. He spread his hands on the table.

'Now we can return to the matter of the alleged missing aid funds. Perhaps Mr Moon for our consultants can give us a resumé of the facts as they appeared to him.' His voice oozed scepticism.

I twitched at this so I didn't appreciate the significance of Garside's muffled exclamation. This wasn't going quite the way I had expected to be introduced to the discussion. So the missing funds were now 'alleged', and the facts were 'as they appeared' to me.

Garside stood up and muttered, 'Excuse me for a minute, it must have been something I ate,' and hurried out of the room.

'Well sir,' I started, 'the facts, as they appeared to me, are that three cheques each for $1.5m have been withdrawn from the Port Mahon account on the signature of Phillipe Rouget, the Minister for Ports and Harbours. The side note on the bank statement for these items appeared to me to read PORT. On enquiring what PORT was an acronym for, I was told it stood for Preliminary Operations for the Redevelopment of Tern. Tern, I believe, refers to Tern Island. As you are all aware from this week's newspapers, Tern Island is a Kory Kronoff development in association with the Comorantes Government.'

The door opened and Garside returned wiping his mouth with a handkerchief. Everyone looked at him irritably, so he issued a muttered apology.

'Did you actually see the cheques?' This was asked by the spiky haired, sharp-eyed treasury man.

'No, I did not.'

'You said three cheques, each for $1.5m?'

'Yes!'

'Have you any idea why there were three cheques?'

'No, I have not. One reason could be that they were for three people; another that they might be for three separate payments to the same person or intended for three different things.'

'Eagle Eyes' turned to Desmond Fitzpatrick. 'Mr Fitzpatrick, have you any idea what these alleged cheques are or could be for?'

Desmond shook his head. 'Nothing that I'm aware of.'

Desmond looked at Garside. 'Do you know anything about this, Norbert?'

I felt Garside tense up. 'No I don't,' he snapped, and turned to look at me. 'Anyway, how do we know that this feller's telling the truth? He said he only had a glimpse of something. There's no concrete evidence that such cheques exist or that money has been taken from the account. But I should point out that if money has been taken then only CONDES can authorise payment. If funds have gone missing perhaps we should look more closely at them?' He glared at Hugo. 'Wouldn't the best thing be to ask the Comorantes Prime Minister to investigate this before we do anything based on such flimsy, hearsay evidence? After all, we don't want to upset a friendly government unnecessarily, do we?'

I saw Hugo's face blacken, but before he could speak I cut in quickly. 'What Mr Garside said could be quite true and from our point of view, we wouldn't want there to be any doubts as to our integrity, so why doesn't the Treasury put in a forensic accountant to go through all the Port Mahon bank statements, cheque books etc in the Comorantes to find out the truth? If what I've seen is correct then it is possible that the Prime Minister himself might be involved.'

Nobby's jaw went slack as he realised that he'd dropped himself right in it. He hastily tried to back pedal. 'No, no, I don't think that's necessary, Mr Chairman. I don't think we should go to all that trouble, I'm quite 'appy to take the young feller's word.'

I looked squarely at him. He wasn't going to slide out of this that easily now he'd brought it up. 'I'm sorry Mr Garside, but it's important for CONDES' reputation to establish the facts, if British taxpayers' money has been misused. I think we'd all like to get to the bottom of this.'

The chairman nodded. 'Yes, I think so. In fact, Mr Philips here is a forensic accountant...' He indicated 'Eagle Eyes', '... and we're fully entitled to carry out checks on the way our aid is being spent, so he can carry out an analysis without troubling their Prime Minister. Perhaps Mr Moon could have a word with Mr Philips afterwards and give him the names of the people to contact. Are we're all agreed?'

There were nods all round, except from Garside who slumped in his chair and wiped his face with a handkerchief that he dragged out of his trouser pocket.

The meeting also agreed that the Comorantes Government would just be notified that this was going to happen as a normal follow-up to the granting of aid packages. No other reason would be given.

When the meeting broke up I tried to move away from Garside, but he grabbed my arm and gave me a look so full of venom that it would have curdled milk. I thought he was going to say something but he didn't; there were people within earshot but his meaning was clear. He was going to fix CONDES if he could.

That Wednesday was not the best day in Nobby's life and it got worse.

The fact that Hugo and Moon were present meant that the meeting was about Port Mahon and that rang alarm

281

bells in his mind. The chairman's opening remark seemed harmless enough and he began to relax, but when the chairman turned to the question of the missing aid money, Nobby's innards turned to jelly. He had assumed, quite wrongly, that this matter had been regarded as trivial – the sort of thing that went on all the time with aid money – and had been dropped some time ago. Now it was being resurrected with full force and that snooping shit Moon was stirring it all up again. The only comfort he could extract from the discussion was that they seemed sceptical about what exactly Moon claimed to have seen. He had decided to play on that as a way of nullifying the whole thing, but that had backfired spectacularly and now they were putting in a bloody ferret to find out if and where this money had gone. Christ, he had to get hold of Coquelin and warn him, but more importantly Coquelin had to keep his name out of it at all costs. He would pay back his portion of the money – then he realised he couldn't. Kronoff had exploded spectacularly and disappeared – there wasn't any money. With a sinking feeling he realised his only hope was that Coquelin would not reveal his involvement. God, it was so unfair. He was sweating profusely and mopped his brow. It was all that nosy bastard Moon's fault – what was he going to tell Philips? He'd bloody well make sure that his firm never got any more DfID work if it was the last thing he did. When the meeting broke up he glared at Moon but could do no more than that, and after brief goodbyes he shot off back to his office to work out how to contact Coquelin.

This time with a pocket full of change, he rang Coquelin from the call box at Pimlico Underground station. For the first three calls Coquelin refused to speak to him, but eventually his patience snapped and told the girl to put Nobby through. He snarled, 'What do you want Garside?'

'Jesus Christ Henri, the shit has hit the fan over here. They're putting in a forensic accountant from the Treasury to examine the Port Mahon account!'

'So?'

'So he'll find out about the Tern Island money,' he cried desperately.

'I don't know what you're talking about, Garside.'

Nobby recoiled at this blunt denial and then realised that he was being less than discreet over an open phone line. He took a deep breath.

'Look Henri, if questions are asked for Christ's sake keep my name out of it. Tell him that all that money was used for Comorantes Government expenses. That's what you've got to say; he'll believe you.'

Coquelin's voice became more soothing. 'Don't panic Norbert, we've got everything under control here, don't worry, just relax.' And the line went dead.

'Oh God, I hope they have,' Nobby moaned to himself as he replaced the receiver and staggered out of the phone box.

CHAPTER FIFTEEN

2011 – THE PRESIDENT'S HOUSE, THE COMORANTES ISLANDS

As soon as *The Times* articles about Kronoff and Tern Island began appear, the Comorantes ambassador in London reported their content immediately to St George's. Coquelin and Rouget met urgently in the privacy of Coquelin's house to consider the implications.

Coquelin blamed Rouget, his cold, dark eyes glared at Rouget through his rimless spectacles.

'What a disaster, what a cock-up! Bloody hell, Phillipe, you were supposed to be keeping an eye on Tern Island. How the hell can something like this happen if you're watching what's going on?'

He scowled at Rouget. 'What the hell is going on anyway? You're supposed to know! If what it says in these articles is true it looks as though we've all been screwed and Tern Island is a sham, a fake and we've been ripped off by this bastard Kronoff. I suggest you get the police over there now, take everybody on the island into custody and seize whatever assets there are. Don't let anybody else near the place until we've decided what to do – if anything.'

Rouget threw up his hands defensively and shot back. 'I did keep an eye on it but, as you are well aware, Kronoff wouldn't allow anybody other than his own people inside the lagoon. He said it was for security reasons. He had guards and fast boats to stop trespassers. From outside the reef everything looked normal and his weekly reports said it was all on programme, so I had no reason to be suspicious. Anyway he was *your* friend. *You* were the one who brought him to the Comorantes; *you* were the one who granted him a free lease and *you* were the one who said we should invest our money with him.'

Coquelin grimaced. 'If there's any minor consolation to be extracted from this, it is that it wasn't our money. We personally haven't lost anything; the money that looks as though it's gone down the tube is Brit money, don't forget that.'

'What about Garside?'

'What about Garside! Fuck Garside! We don't have to worry about him, what can he do? He can't do or say anything without revealing that he's as twisted as a corkscrew, can he? No, we don't have to bother about him. What does concern me is that our ambassador told me that *The Times* are going to reveal more. My secretary has been instructed to get copies of the paper off the web early so we'll know what's going on. God knows what else is going to come out.'

He slammed his hand down on the table. 'How did *The Times* get hold of this stuff in the first place if Kronoff had this project bottled up as tightly as you say, that's what I want to know?' He glared at Rouget again.

Rouget hastily picked up the phone. 'I'll tell Commissioner Prevost to send two boatloads of armed officers to Tern immediately.'

Coquelin slumped back in his chair and sighed heavily. 'God, I hate Americans!' He shook his head and sighed again. 'There's not much more we can do until we get the rest of the story. Bastard Kronoff! I should have sniffed out that he was a crook when I saw how flash he was. I don't suppose his other investors are going to take this lying down either.'

On Saturday morning, after Garside's panic call to Coquelin, he and Rouget met again in private at Coquelin's house.

'So that's it then Phillipe; the whole of Kronoff's empire has imploded, people have lost billions of dollars. The US Government has appointed a court trustee to try to begin recovering some of the money, but they don't hold out much hope. I spoke to one of their partners and he said the only thing about Tern that was worth anything was the lease and we could buy it back when he had done a valuation. I told him, in no uncertain terms, that he could forget that. The terms of the lease specified that a development would be built and if it wasn't, the lease was forfeited. So either they got on and finished the development or we took the lease back for nothing.'

He put the tips of his fingers together. 'However, now we have another problem to sort out. The Brits are going to put in a forensic accountant to examine the Port Mahon account. Garside phoned me on Wednesday night shitting bricks. He wants his name kept out of it and suggested that we claim that the money we took out of the account for Tern Island was the money allocated for our government expenses.'

Rouget bit his lip. 'But we told them to allow $3 million in the aid package for that. How do we account for the $4.5 million that actually went?'

Coquelin didn't feel like smiling: his Chinese deal with its 'backhanders' had gone down in flames; his hopes of a fortune from Kronoff looked as though it was going the same way, and now exposure and diplomatic embarrassment lurked in the person of a forensic accountant sent by the British Treasury – but he smiled, nonetheless. It was the smile he had learned from Mitchinson, the American envoy. Coquelin wasn't very good at it; he didn't have the same craggy features as Mitchinson or the narrow Marlboro cigarette eyes. His thin screwed-up face gave Rouget the impression that Coquelin was going to throw up any minute so he hastily moved out of Technicolor-yawn range.

'Don't worry about that Phillipe, thanks to Monsieur Garside, I have a plan.'

He changed the subject; it wasn't necessary for Rouget to know the details of the plan, principally because he was going to be set up in it as the local fall guy.

'That smooth Arab fellow, what was his name – Mazin Al something? He won't be a happy man.'

'Neither will his investors, they put in millions,' Rouget replied with a cynical smile.

****

That was the understatement of the year.

Mazin didn't learn about Kronoff's alleged evildoings and Tern until they hit the airwaves on Wednesday: it was the lead story on Al Jazeera Television. He watched with increasing horror as the pictures of the fake development on Tern flashed across the screen and the reporter outlined the spectacular collapse of Kronoff's businesses.

Then he went ballistic. His long-suffering servant at his house in Cairo was accustomed to Mazin's towering bouts of rage and knew that the moment the first scream of fury echoed round the apartment, the thing to do was to drop everything and run for the hills. He was out of the door and down the street like a scalded cat seconds before the television was hurled through the window. By the time Mazin cooled down from volcanic eruption to merely sulphurous bubbling, the curtains had been torn to shreds, all the ornaments smashed or hurled through the other windows, the desk lamp lay embedded in the computer screen and the rug torn from the floor and chewed in his rage. Fortunately for it, it was a very well made Isfahan carpet fully resistant to Mazin's teeth and nails so all that resulted, apart from caps from his teeth being scattered round the room, were a few loose threads left hanging off each end.

He gradually got a grip of himself and surveyed the enormity of what was happening. Not the wreckage of his office, that was the least of his concerns, but the fact that he had invested a huge amount of time and his own money to persuade Kronoff just to deal with him and not to take any more investors for Tern Island. He had arranged for his Arab contacts in the Gulf, including his brother the Minister, to put up all the rest of the money to construct the development for a 51% share. They were a suspicious lot, his Arab investors, and they wouldn't be above working out, based on previous experience, that all this might well be a clever con so that Mazin could pocket their money for himself. He shivered at the thought of their wrath and the consequences. A quick disappearing act was called for until things became clearer. He called for his servant but in vain. The servant was still going like an express train and, at that moment, was crossing the Nile heading up Al Saraya Street. He was just beginning to run out of steam.

Mazin picked up one of the overturned chairs and set it back on its feet; he slumped into it whilst his brain raced at high speed round all his alternatives. He could stay in Cairo and try and talk his way out of it; he could fly to the Comorantes and see if anything could be salvaged from what had been constructed on Tern Island; he could hide in London for a few weeks until the Kronoff thing became clearer; he could go to all his investors in the Gulf and explain that it wasn't his fault – or he could blow his brains out. The latter seemed the most likely and attractive solution at the moment, before somebody else did it for him.

He decided that going to the Comorantes was the best bet, and then, if there wasn't anything worth salvaging, he would go and hide in London.

But first he had to get his teeth fixed, his split and torn fingernails treated and a few self-inflicted cuts and bruises attended to.

****

Coquelin sat at his office desk thinking. It was vital that the letter got to Downing Street well before this Treasury snoop started his investigation. It would require very careful drafting. He tapped on his desk with his fingers and picked up a pen. The letter would be marked HIGHLY CONFIDENTIAL.

After several fruitless attempts he eventually hit on a formula.

Dear Prime Minister.

That was no problem. Then perhaps a little flattery...

I commend you on your speech on terrorism to the United Nations General Assembly last week. I think you covered all the points succinctly and admirably.

On behalf of the people of the Comorantes Islands I would also like to thank you, your Government and the people of Great Britain for the magnificent donation of financial aid which is enabling us to construct Port Mahon. This will revitalise our trade and help to increase the overall prosperity and welfare of the citizens of these Islands. We are extremely grateful.

Finally to the essence of the letter...

However, I regret to have to inform you that, much as it distresses me, I must report certain circumstances in connection with this aid money which give my government very grave concern.

When we first applied to the Department for International Development for financial support you sent Norbert Garside MP, the Deputy Chairman of the Committee to evaluate and assess our application. He informed us that the final decision about who was granted aid and who was not lay with him. We endeavoured to satisfy him of our needs and answer all his questions.

When it came down to the quantum, however, to our astonishment the tone of the discussion changed. It was made very clear to us that unless a sum of money for Mr Garside personally was included in the aid package, our application would be rejected. He demanded $3 million be included and hidden in the costings. My colleagues and I were totally shocked and dismayed by this, but after serious consideration we decided that for the benefit of our country we had no option but to accept. We managed to negotiate him down to $1.5 million.

You will appreciate the difficult position we were in; we were not sure if Mr Garside was serious about this so decided not to follow this up with an official complaint at the time. However, when the money was transferred into the Port Mahon account here in St Georges some fifteen months later, he demanded immediate payment of the $1.5 million and regrettably my Minister of Ports and Harbours, who had befriended him, paid him – foolishly and without my knowledge. An internal investigation into this matter is ongoing.

We believe he invested the money in one of the infamous Kory Kronoff schemes and thus it has probably disappeared.

This sort of blackmail is not what we expected from a British Government Minister and I am conveying my disappointment to you that such a thing should have happened in a transaction between two friendly countries. We expect you to take action to prevent this sort of thing happening again.

Yours Very Sincerely

Henri Coquelin
President and Prime Minister.

He read it through again, it was a bit thin, but the fact that it came from a country's President and Prime Minister should make up for the lack of substantiating detail.

He added an instruction saying that the letter was to be sent on his private notepaper as President of the Comorantes Islands, and, when he had signed it, it was to be put in the urgent diplomatic bag for delivery to the Comorantes Ambassador in London for immediate onward hand delivery to the British Prime Minister's Office at 10 Downing Street.

He gave his mirthless smile as he put in the last full stop. That should ensure that if any shit was going to be shovelled, it wasn't going to be shovelled on Henri Coquelin.

Coquelin's secretary ran the letter off on her word processor, took it in for signature and arranged for it to go in the diplomatic bag. Then she went for lunch with Florence le Lievre and two other senior secretaries. Hence, by evening that day, most of Grandes Rocques knew that Garside was a blackmailing crook and by lunchtime the following day the news reached Beauregard Island, and from there was relayed to me via Jack Fourie's satellite phone.

****

At roughly the same time as I took Jack's phone call, Alan Ritchie, Prime Minister and First Lord of the Treasury of Great Britain and Northern Island tossed the letter across the Cabinet Table to Sir Oliver White, Cabinet Secretary.

'What do you make of that, Oliver?'

Sir Oliver read it through, absorbing the contents rapidly. He put it back on the table and looked at the PM. 'It's an odd sort of letter; it has a whiff of CYA about it.'

'CYA?'

'Cover Your Arse. It's the sort of letter somebody might write if they were trying to hide some misdeed by going on the attack. But if it's true, Prime Minister, it could be another one of those scandals that you are anxious to avoid.'

'Yes, yes, I realise that,' the PM said, testily. 'But what the hell do I do about it?'

The Cabinet Secretary thought for a few seconds. 'I don't know this man Garside, I presume he's one of yours? What do you know about him?'

'Not much. Some northern constituency, I believe. He's deputy chairman of Fitzpatrick's committee – and tells dirty jokes.'

'Not a lot to go on then,' the Cabinet Secretary commented, dryly. 'Perhaps we shouldn't do anything until I've looked into it. Leave it to me.'

'Just what I didn't need at this time, with a narrow majority and a bloody by-election coming up in that marginal seat in Wolverhampton,' observed the PM, gloomily.

'Quite so.' Sir Oliver slid out of the room leaving the PM to contemplate Coquelin's missive as though it was an unexploded bomb.

He was back within an hour.

'Right, Prime Minister, I think we have to take that letter at face value. Garside is the deputy chairman of the Aid Committee; he did go out to the Comorantes on a fact-finding mission, but at his suggestion not the Government's. Money has allegedly been taken incorrectly from the Port Mahon account. I say allegedly because a small select committee under the Permanent Secretary, James White – no relation...' he added with a smile, '... has been looking into this following a report we had from our consultants. They first brought it to light some time ago, but the committee agreed then that as the negotiations for our naval base were at a delicate stage they didn't want to rock the boat.' He smiled at the typical civil service pun, but the PM was not amused.

'Get on with it man!' he snapped.

'Sorry, Prime Minister. The committee has now decided to send Mr Philips, a forensic accountant from the Treasury, to the Comorantes to examine the books. It does rather look as if it is all true, but I suggest we wait and see what Mr Philips' report says.'

The PM saw the danger immediately. 'Oliver, I don't want this report flying about all over the place. It's to go only to me, to you and the senior members of the Government, and civil servants on James White's investigation committee, no one else. And I don't want Philips told about Garside's alleged involvement. Let him do his report and see what he comes up with. I don't want this thing leaking out before we have had chance to fully assess the situation and decide on a course of action. Is that absolutely clear?'

The Cabinet Secretary nodded. 'I'll contact Philips immediately; he's not due to leave until Thursday.'

****

Dan's articles had not mentioned the missing Port Mahon money; they had only hinted that Kronoff's activities embraced not just private investors but politicians and governments of various persuasions.

When we all met as usual on Saturday morning in the Frog, I mentioned to Dan that there was a rumour going round the Comorantes that their Prime Minister had written to our Prime Minister complaining that a British MP called Garside had blackmailed them into handing over to him a huge chunk of money from the British aid package set up for Port Mahon. Ten million dollars was the figure being bandied about on the islands.'

Dan got very excited about this. I was just reporting a rumour so I didn't tell him it was, in all probability, the PORT money. I knew the facts about that, and if it was, then ten million was a gross exaggeration.

I held up a staying hand. 'What're you going to do Dan; you can't print a rumour like that!'

He chortled, 'No, but I'll get my editor to ring Downing Street and say we've heard a rumour that a British MP has blackmailed a foreign government into paying him a large sum of money – in the millions – out of an aid package, and is there any truth in it? They've got to say something, even if it's "no comment". It's vague enough to be difficult to deny because they'll be worried that we know much more than we've told them.'

Fleur Fullerton, who was into things like hugging trees and cuddling bunnies, observed, 'I feel sorry for this man Garside, to have rumours like that floating about. He's a British MP for heaven's sake; they just don't do that sort of thing.'

'Fleur,' I said, 'I've met this man. He's a bully and a braggart; he tried to screw CONDES into paying him ten grand a year for nothing, and when we refused he's told lies about us to a Government department that was a major client of ours. As a result, we haven't had any work from them for two years – and maybe other departments as well. I think there's no doubt he's taken money from British aid; the problem is how much and from what – and proving it.'

'How can you be so sure?'

Care was needed here, Fleur was a notorious gossip and I didn't want the details of the Garside story leaked to the coffee mornings and flower-arranging soirées of Chelsea before there had been some official movement, so I headed her off by telling the gathering the story of Garside's encounter with the Major and how she'd wiped the floor with him.

'It was like listening to that famous dog trainer Barbara Woodhouse. She told him to "SIT!" in her best parade-ground voice and boy did he sit fast. I told him afterwards that it was a good job he did because she was ex-Special Forces, trained to kill with one blow of her hand. It was credible because Margaret, when really ruffled, made Pete's Miss Shorter – a well-known dragon who ate timewasters for breakfast – seem positively benevolent.'

Pete pursed his lips. 'Hard to believe, she's always so nice to me, but you can tell she's a strong personality. That's why Marcus is so crushed and cowed.'

'Not crushed and cowed enough to point out that it's your round, Doctor Smallwood.'

****

Margaret's marriage was coming up in ten days' time. She had invited all the senior staff, both girls and boys, and the girls were buzzing about trying to forecast the weather to decide on dresses. The boys weren't bothered; they would just turn up in lounge suits. Hugo had his own morning suit, but I went to Austin Reed to be measured up for a hire job. Margaret was taking the week off before the wedding to finalise all the arrangements. Stuff such as the usual final fitting for the dress and the bridesmaid's dresses; organising the reception at Great Fanling Hall – a country hotel near Kingsbridge; ordering the flowers for the church, the buttonholes for the bridegroom, best man and ushers; planning the music for the organist and choir and the other myriad of details that needed to be sorted out. One thing I was certain about was that she would have it brilliantly organised, whatever the weather, whatever the circumstances and whoever did or didn't turn up – provided it wasn't Richard. I joked about that thoughtlessly, for which I received a brittle smile in return. This made me feel about ten centimetres high. I knew that this wedding meant so much to her so I swore to myself I wouldn't tease her anymore about it, or make unfunny jokes.

Friday afternoon was to be a full rehearsal, so on Friday morning I drove down in the MG TF to Kingsbridge with Zoe by my side and lodged us in the Royal Oak Hotel just across the market place from the church. It was a dry sunny day with those big puffy white clouds that you can imagine form shapes – an elephant, Brazil or a big willy. The forecast for tomorrow was similar – Margaret could be lucky!

Zoe checked us in and as we were going up to our room the main door burst open and about twenty very fit-looking, mostly very attractive women came in, all carrying similar holdalls and all talking at once.

'It's a good job I'm here,' whispered Zoe, 'I wouldn't trust you an inch with that lot in the hotel.'

'What makes you think that you being here makes any difference?' I asked with a twinkle.

'You dare, Marcus Moon, and you'll be singing a high treble before you can plead insanity.'

We had a quick freshen up and strolled across to St Peter Within-the-Walls. Margaret and a chap in a clerical collar, who I assumed was to be the conductor of the ceremony, were talking in the sunshine outside the main door. She gave us a warm smile and introduced us to the Reverend Kevin. I focussed on him with interest. He was unusual to say the least. He looked as if a small explosion had taken place inside his head. His hair stood straight up, his ears stuck out, his eyes bulged like a duchess goosed in Harrods, and his mouth resembled Boot Hill after a hurricane. I noticed that he had spots and a cross tattooed on the side of his neck.

'Kevin, this is my boss, he's going to give me away. Zoe is his girlfriend.'

The ragged teeth were revealed again as he offered a limp handshake and gave me a disinterested smile before turning to ogle Zoe's cleavage.

'So vicar, are you all geared up for tomorrow? Got your kit blancoed, brasses polished and your shoes bulled up to a brilliant shine?' I looked down at the scuffed brown leather sandals sticking out from under his cassock. 'Well, perhaps not!'

Zoe chatted away to Margaret whilst the vicar and I maintained an uncomfortable silence. He sucked his teeth and I pretended to examine the flaking stonework surrounding the church door. I thought of asking him if he actually believed in God, but then more people began to arrive so I missed the opportunity. A car drew up at the gate

299

disgorging Richard and three other men of a similar age. He gave Margaret a kiss on the lips, shook my hand and kissed Zoe on the cheek.

'Yo bro and praise the Lord!' cried Kevin. 'A cool dude man!' and with that seized Richard in an all-embracing bear hug. They wrestled around locked together for two minutes, with Richard trying to free himself and Kevin hanging in there like a punch-drunk boxer buying time to clear his head. Margaret looked embarrassed.

'Kevin's new,' she muttered to me. 'The Reverend Philpot, who was supposed to take the service, came down with laryngitis on Thursday and the bishop sent Kevin. He's been telling me he plays the guitar.'

'So is he going to play it at the wedding?'

She snapped, 'No he bloody isn't! I've only just met him and we haven't had a word yet!'

Turning to the gathering she said, 'Would you excuse us for a couple of minutes' and led Richard and the Reverend Kevin off to one side out of earshot, but the finger wagging was clearly visible.

'What's that all about?' asked one of the ushers.

'Oh,' I told him, 'that's the Reverend Kevin getting his lumps. He's apparently under the impression that he's running this wedding and he's just finding out that he isn't!'

They were back after five minutes, the Rev Kev with a hangdog look on his acne-decorated face and Margaret briskly giving instructions.

'For the rehearsal we'll only need Richard and me, Marcus, Selwyn, and the four bridesmaids. The rest of you are very welcome to stay and watch, or you can repair to the Royal Oak and we'll join you in half an hour.'

There was a muffled exclamation from the vicar. 'Oh yes,' smiled the Major turning to him, 'and Kevin, of course, we'll need him.'

We did a run through, with me taking Margaret slowly down the aisle followed by the four bridesmaids, who turned out to be four of her old friends from the Women's Royal Army Corps. The other sixteen were to form a guard of honour outside the church. I dropped her off at Richard's side. The Rev Kev gave a long-winded run-through of the order of service; Selwyn, the Best Man stepped forward fumbling in his pocket for the ring; there were pauses to indicate various musical items and readings; they mocked up the signing of the register and then arm in arm, and obviously very happy, the future Mr and Mrs Richard Hewetson trooped back down the aisle to the open air, leaving me to wonder if they were going to practise anything else later. The Rev Kev was taken to one side again and told to sharpen up his act, and then we pushed off to the Royal Oak to join the others in the Highwayman Bar.

By then more people had come so there was a jolly crowd milling around and chatting. A lot of them seemed to know each other. Under the watchful eye of Zoe I ended up talking to two very attractive WRAC captains who had been trained by Margaret. It was obvious that she was very popular and highly respected by the WRAC, which didn't surprise me, and they were intrigued that I was her boss.

'She actually takes orders from you, does she?'

I glanced modestly at my fingernails and was just going to launch into a long dissertation about the chain of command and the strength of personality required for leadership when Zoe cut in and said, 'Marcus wouldn't know what to do without her, he'd be totally lost!'

'Aah!' they both said knowingly, and giving me a dismissive look, turned to talk to Zoe.

Suitably chastened, I wandered off to join Richard and Selwyn in an all-male group where we could explore our fantasies without being diverted by the facts.

The next day dawned bright and sunny, the sounds of the country drifted through our open bedroom window. Animals making... well animal noises, and birds twittering and chirping in the trees. I think it must have been the birds because when I turned over in bed to ask Zoe if she wanted breakfast sent up to our room, it didn't come out at all like that.

Some time later, out of breath and flushed, we had a long shower and got togged up for the second exciting event of the day. Zoe looked stunning in a bluey-grey dress that matched her eyes perfectly and one of those little fascinator hats that sit on the side of your head.

Hugo, Emily and the rest of the CONDES team had driven down that morning and were chatting outside the church to an elderly couple with a very military bearing. The man was leaning heavily on a stick. It turned out that they were Brigadier and Mrs Braithwaite, Margaret's parents. The Brigadier gave me a tight smile. 'Thanks for standing in for me, old chap, gammy leg you know, caught one on the Imjin.' He tapped his artificial leg with his stick.

'No problem, sir, I'm delighted to help out. She's a great lady.'

He brushed his white moustache with the back of his hand. 'Hmm, good show what. Never thought she'd get hitched. Do her good; always got her own way; teach her a damn lesson!'

I gave a feeble grin at his optimism, and leaving Zoe with them, went to collect Margaret from her sister's house in the hired Rolls with the white ribbons.

As she walked to the car with one of the bridesmaids holding the train of her white wedding dress, I must say she did look in good shape and I told her so.

'Richard doesn't realise yet what a treasure he's getting. You look stunning.'

It was a huge change from the day when she first turned up to be my secretary straight from the army. All mixed make-up, severe shingle haircut, thick woollen jumper and heavy tweed skirt. Understandably, she was nervous. To relax her I recited the humorous words to Mendelssohn's *Wedding March* for the entry of the bride:

'Here comes the bride
All fat and wide
See how she wobbles
From side to side.'

Strangely, that didn't go down too well!

The wedding went off without a hitch. They trooped back down the aisle both as happy as Larry. Margaret looked radiant and Richard had a grin on his face like the Cheshire cat – so perhaps tonight was the night! Outside, a guard of honour of WRACs of all ranks in dress uniforms held up an arch of swords; cameras clicked, videos whirred, dried rose petals were thrown and a horse-drawn landau waited to take the newlyweds off to Great Fanling Hall for more photographs and the reception. The WRACs sheathed their swords and climbed into their own bus.

The rest of the crowd milled around aimlessly with the ushers seemingly helpless, not sure what to do. Zoe grabbed a couple and suggested that they went and helped people get out of the car park and told two others to guide people without cars to the coach that was parked just outside the gate. The Rev Kev was wandering about like a spare whatsit at a wedding – which I suppose he was – so I suggested he headed for the coach sharpish otherwise he would have to cling on to the spare wheel of the MG for the ride to Great Fanling Hall.

CHAPTER SIXTEEN

ST GEORGE'S, THE COMORANTES

Mr Philips, ignorant of Garside's alleged involvement, wasn't sure what sort of reception he was going to get as the UK Treasury's auditor for the Port Mahon account. Being an accountant he was accustomed to the odd sling-shot and arrow fired in his direction, but the behaviour of foreigners, particularly in hot climates, was unpredictable. He needn't have worried. When he deplaned stiff, sweaty, tired and apprehensive, from the Air Comorantes clapped-out old Boeing into the scorching sun of Eric de Verteuil airport, he was welcomed on the ramp by the State of Comorantes Treasurer with the usual highly polished BMW and Serge at the wheel. An ice-cold towel was clapped on to his forehead, a green coconut containing cool coconut milk was thrust into his hand and he was whipped off to Government House, avoiding any formalities at customs and immigration. The conversation on the short journey was confined to the weather and the lush scenery.

Henri Coquelin was a bit surprised at Philips' appearance; although he was travel-stained and weary, his sharp eyes missed nothing. Henri was determined that Philips would return to London bearing the 'correct' report, absolving any Comorantian officials, especially him, from any wrongdoing and, at the same time, nail Garside's feet firmly to the floor. The 'correct' information would have to be carefully presented. He would brief Rouget that evening

'Welcome, welcome, my dear Mr Philips,' he cried effusively, shaking Philips' hand and waving to a servant to take Philips' bag up to the guest suite.

'Anything we can do to make your stay more pleasant you have only to ask.' Coquelin caught a whiff of stale sweat wafting from Philips hidden crevices and hastily added, 'I suggest that you freshen up with a good shower and then meet Minister Rouget and I down here for a refreshing drink in, say, one hour? No doubt you wish to start your audit as soon as possible so Minister Rouget will escort you to his office tomorrow morning where we have made a private room with full communications available for you. Ask anything you want of anybody, we are as anxious to get to the bottom of this unfortunate affair as much as your Prime Minister.'

Philips was puzzled by this. What *'unfortunate affair'* he thought, and then the attraction of a cool shower and a change of clothes drove the thought from his mind and he followed the servant up to his luxury suite.

After a good Government House breakfast Rouget deposited him at his assigned office at the Ministry of Ports and Harbours. Florence had collected all the relevant files and statements and put them on his desk. It only took him fifteen minutes to discover the missing four and a half million dollars.

Florence was called in to explain it but told him she was acting on instructions from her Minister, but that the letters PORT referred to Preliminary Operations for the Redevelopment of Tern. Philips took the bank statements and cheque stubs through to Rouget.

'Minister, I wonder if you would be kind enough to enlighten me about these three cheques which apparently were made payable to the International Trading Bank of St Croix [Tern Island] Inc.?'

Rouget's brown liquid eyes narrowed and his weak face took on a concerned expression.

'I'm glad you've asked me about that. It is a matter which is causing our President and Prime Minister some considerable concern.'

He shook his head and pursed his lips.

'A very unfortunate event indeed; we did not expect this sort of behaviour from a senior member of your government. No, Mr Philips, a regrettable event on both sides. We were put in the unfortunate position of having to comply with it for the good of our country, but we should never have been put in such a position to start with!'

Philips' was taken aback by these remarks; he didn't know what on earth Rouget was talking about. What *event*? All he knew was that it had been alleged that some money had been taken out of the Port Mahon account using three cheques and he was expected to find out what it was for.

'Perhaps, Minister, if you could explain to what event you are referring, it might help.'

Rouget stared at him.

'You mean you don't know? We thought that was why you had been sent – to gather evidence.'

Alarm bells started to ring in Philips' mind. Evidence? Evidence for what? Evidence meant wrongdoing. That meant trouble, and Philips' civil-service training had taught him to avoid trouble whenever possible. But to avoid it you had to know what it was you were trying to avoid, and that meant asking – which, in itself was dangerous because by asking you automatically became involved. A catch-22 situation. He decided not to ask.

'Can we return to my original question – will you explain what the three cheques to that Caribbean bank were for?'

It was Rouget's turn to look puzzled.

'That's what I was telling you. Two of them totalling three million dollars were for the ancillary expenses on Port Mahon expended by the Comorantes Government in accordance with the aid agreement, and the third, of one and a half million dollars, was the blackmail money paid to your man Garside.'

Philips blinked. 'Let me get this straight. You're saying that although all three cheques were made out to the International Trading Bank of St Croix, two were legitimate payments and one of them was blackmail money paid out on behalf of a British Government representative called Garside?'

'Exactly!'

'Why did all three cheques go to the same bank then and what was this fellow Garside blackmailing you about?'

Rouget frowned. 'It's a long story,' and he launched into a tale of how Garside had told them he was the man who would decide if the Comorantes would get the aid money for their new port and how he would veto it if they didn't sweeten the deal for him. Naturally, they were horrified that such a demand should be made, but in the interests of their country they had no option but to go along with it. When Garside demanded his cut he also found out that the Comorantes Government was negotiating a huge potentially profitable deal with an American investment banker called Kory Kronoff and were going to invest their three million dollars in that. He then demanded that his money be included in the Comorantes package. He received a Certificate of Deposit from the bank confirming his interest. Unfortunately, as Mr Philips and most of the world now knew, Kronoff turned out to be a crook and they lost all their money.

Philips listened in amazement; he was not a man ignorant of the wicked ways of the world, but if what Rouget was telling was true, then this could be a serious political scandal.

He returned to his temporary office to consider what he had heard. There was no evidence in the books or financial records of the Port Mahon account to support Rouget's allegations, and the fact that three identical cheques had been drawn on the Port Mahon account could be interpreted in many ways, of which Rouget's allegation seemed the least likely. However, it wasn't his brief to make a judgement, only to report the facts.

Philips was a meticulous man and his report to Sir Oliver White included everything that he had uncovered or been told. The Port Mahon account had been dealt with in an efficient and accurate manner apart from two things: the initial late payments and the three cheques.

As instructed, Sir Oliver told his secretary to send copies only to the senior members of James White's committee. She made five copies, in addition to the one for the PM: one for Philips' files, one for James White the Permanent Secretary, and one each for the three politicians on the committee. Philips hesitated for a moment about sending Garside his copy, but as he had decided earlier, it wasn't his job to make judgements. However, a worm of doubt nagged him so he decided him to hold Garside's copy back for a day. Thus Garside's copy, marked STRICTLY PRIVATE and CONFIDENTIAL, was delivered by messenger to the office Garside shared with Brown in Portcullis House twenty-four hours after the others had received theirs.

Sir Oliver re-read the report carefully and took it through to the Prime Minister.

'There is now no doubt that money has been taken illegally from the Port Mahon account, Prime Minister. The Comorantians claim that the three million dollars they took they were entitled to, to cover their ancillary costs on Port Mahon. That could well be true – dodgy but possible. We cannot prove otherwise. It appears that that money, plus an additional one and a half million dollars taken from the account, was invested in a bank run by that Ponzi chap Kronoff, but Philips says there is no tangible proof that Garside was involved.'

The PM read it through again. 'What about this Certificate of Deposit with Kronoff's bank, Oliver? If

Garside has taken this money then he'll have the certificate somewhere. That would be hard evidence.'

'But how could we find out?'

The PM thought for a minute. 'The letter from Coquelin is sufficient for us to initiate a police investigation, but it will have to be handled very carefully. We've already had a fishing phone call from *The Times* hinting that something is going on. My private secretary fobbed them off, but this sort of rumour spreads pretty quickly as you well know. Call a meeting here this afternoon with the Commissioner of the Metropolitan Police, the commander who heads the Fraud Squad, and the Speaker of the House of Commons.'

Sir Oliver raised a questioning eyebrow.

'We'll have to search Garside's office and that requires the Speaker's permission for the police to enter parliamentary premises.'

The five of them plus a secretary met in the Cabinet Room at 2.30pm. They were given copies of Coquelin's letter and Philips' report.

The Commissioner was asked to contact the Chief Constable of South Yorkshire Police, explain the situation and coordinate a search of Garside's house in Cadeby with the search of his office and flat in Westminster. The Met Police would obtain the necessary search warrants.

Commander Neil [Nadger] Badger of the Fraud Squad said he would have all the necessary paperwork and a team of expert searchers ready by tomorrow morning. They would arrest Garside and hold him for questioning long enough for both his London and Yorkshire premises to be searched.

'There is one thing...' he said, '... as the alleged theft took place in the Comorantes, shouldn't it be the responsibility of their police for initiating action?'

Consternation reigned for a few moments as this sank in, until the PM said, 'Well it was *our* money.'

The Cabinet Secretary interrupted, 'Strictly speaking it wasn't. It was their money; we had given it to them.'

Whilst the others sat there looking glumly at each other Sir Oliver picked up Coquelin's letter. 'However, their Prime Minister does say at the end of his letter that they expect us to take action. I think we may take that as confirmation that they have officially transferred the responsibility for taking action to the United Kingdom.'

There were relieved sighs all round and the people departed to deal with their respective parts in the drama.

The Prime Minister looked at the Cabinet Secretary. 'I hope to hell that they find that damned Certificate of Deposit or we'll be stuffed – unless he confesses.'

****

Next morning Nobby Garside was not in his office when his copy of the report arrived, so Bill Brown signed for it. His curiosity was aroused by the STRICTLY PRIVATE and CONFIDENTIAL on the packet, but he locked it away in his desk for safety to await Garside's return. However, other events rapidly overtook matters and he forgot all about the packet.

Brown was at meeting when Nobby arrived. Since his last phone call to Coquelin, Nobby had heard nothing. *No news is good news* he contented himself by repeating, and the longer there was no news the more he began to relax. He put his feet on the desk and shouted for Miss Harbottle to bring him a cup of coffee.

What arrived was not what he expected. Six large men, two in police uniform, barged into his office, flashed their warrant cards and pinned him at his desk in one corner.

'What the fu—' He was cut off by Commander 'Nadger' Badger.

'I am Commander Badger from New Scotland Yard. Norbert Arthur Garside, I am arresting you on suspicion of theft, mis-use of government funds, blackmail and involvement in corrupt practices. You do not have to say anything, but it may harm your defence if you do not mention when questioned something that you may later rely on in court. Anything you do say may be given in evidence. Do you understand?'

Nobby was speechless, his brain numb with shock. He could only nod.

Nadger continued, 'I have authority from the Speaker of the House of Commons and a warrant to search these premises.' He waved two sheets of paper, but Nobby was too stunned to take notice.

Two policemen seized him by the arms and escorted him down to a police car whilst the other four donned protective suits and gloves and began to go systematically through everything in the office.

313

Laetitia Harbottle, who had been watching Nobby's discomfiture with astonished glee, suddenly realised to her alarm, that the police were searching Bill Brown's stuff as well as Garside's. Booklets about latex rubber wear and photos of her and Bill Brown doing extraordinary things in tight black shiny garments were being laid out for examination by grinning policemen. She flushed with embarrassment and went and hid in the ladies lavatory. The police found Garside's packet locked in a drawer in Brown's desk, opened it, read the contents, decided they were not of any significance to their search and threw it back in the drawer.

Nobby was taken to Belgravia Police Station and lodged in an interview room. He was offered a cup of tea, which he declined. Apart from that they left him there to stew under the gaze of a watchful uniformed constable.

He had no idea what was coming – was it the Comorantes? Was it his Swiss bank account? Was it something else? Whatever it was, he was going to deny it and then say nothing. He thought about a lawyer, but the only ones he knew were local solicitors in South Yorkshire. His brain began to function slowly. He resolved to sit it out. He would wait and see what they had arrested him for, say nothing until he knew what it was and then ask for a lawyer.

Whilst this was going on the police searching his office reported in that so far they had turned up nothing incriminating. The South Yorkshire Police had sent a similar team to search his house. Tottie Garside had taken exception to great beefy policemen clumping about her pristine house, and when a horny-handed copper began to

314

investigate her knicker drawer a little too closely, she lost her temper and laid about him vigorously with the first thing that came to hand, which happened to be a wok. With very satisfying *BONGS* she managed to put two of the searchers in hospital with concussion before they could subdue her and cart her off to the local police station. This delayed the search so it was couple of hours before they found the safe that Nobby had concreted into the wall and hidden behind shelves that looked as though they were fixed. A local locksmith was called to open it and there they found Nobby's Certificate of Deposit.

They also found details of his Swiss bank account. These were packaged up and sent down to New Scotland Yard by motorcycle courier.

In the meantime, Nobby had been interviewed by a Detective Chief Inspector and a Detective Sergeant. He had been told that the charges related to the theft of money from the Port Mahon account. By then he had worked out that there was no physical evidence that could connect him with the Port Mahon money, even if Coquelin had snitched on him. He hadn't written anything, he hadn't signed anything, he hadn't touched anything. The cheque to Kronoff was signed by Rouget. The Certificate of Deposit was very well hidden and he was confident that they'd never find that, in the unlikely event that they discovered such a thing existed, so he denied any wrongdoing whatsoever.

'I have done nothing wrong. I know nothing about any money being taken from the Port Mahon account. I have not demanded anything from the Comorantes Government. The only people who could take money from that account were the Consulting Engineers – CONDES. Why don't you arrest them?' was the mantra he kept repeating.

When he realised that they weren't going to give up and release him, he asked for a lawyer.

Nobby's luck took a turn for the better, although he didn't realise it. The usual police station hacks were at lunch or too busy to make themselves available so the job of duty solicitor was allocated to a very bright young lawyer who was looking to make his way in the world. He arrived at Belgravia Police Station at the same time as the package from South Yorkshire Police was forwarded on from New Scotland Yard.

The same DCI and DS resumed Nobby's interview and explained to the lawyer what the charges were. 'So far your client has repeated that he has done nothing wrong, he knows nothing about money taken from the Port Mahon account and he hasn't demanded anything from the Comorantes Government.'

'Is that so? The lawyer asked Nobby. 'That's all you've said?'

He agreed it was.

The DCI then opened a file and took out a plastic folder containing a gold embossed Certificate of Deposit from the International Trading Bank of St Croix [Tern Island] Inc., with Norbert Arthur Garside inscribed on it in copperplate writing, and laid it on the table in front of Nobby.

The beauty of the calligraphy was not the first thing that crossed Nobby's mind at that moment; the location of the nearest lavatory preceded it by aeons.

When asked to explain the Certificate of Deposit the lawyer quickly told the stupefied Nobby not to say anything more and asked for time to consult his client privately.

'Not here,' said the lawyer. He knew the interview room was overlooked and bugged so he demanded a private office.

A now shattered and trembling Garside was taken to a private office and closeted with his lawyer for two hours. Cups of tea were brought in, but they didn't improve Nobby's situation.

'You now say that the President of the Comorantes offered you an investment in Tern Island worth one and a half million dollars because they were grateful for your assistance in helping them secure this aid package for Port Mahon? You also say that you had no idea that they had taken money for this from the Port Mahon account?'

'Yes, er no,' he cried. 'I just thought it came from the Government of the Comorantes as a gift for my help.'

'So the allegation that you asked for this, shall we say, 'present', is totally without foundation?'

'It came as a complete surprise to me, right out of the blue.

'Really,' said the lawyer, dryly. 'And you never thought to mention it to anybody? Well, we'll have to do our best with that.'

They returned to the interview room.

'My client would like to make a statement,' the lawyer said, and then carried on not trusting Nobby not to make a balls of it.

'My client says that the Certificate of Deposit records an investment in a project to develop Tern Island. It was an unsolicited gift from the Government of the Comorantes for all the help and assistance my client had given to them over the years to enable them to construct a lifeline new port on Beuaregard Island. My client assumed that the money for this investment came out of the Comorantes Government account. He has no knowledge of any funds being taken from the Port Mahon account whatsoever.'

In spite of intensive questioning Nobby stuck to this line and wouldn't be budged. The statement was typed out, Nobby signed it; the lawyer said, 'I presume my client is free to go now?' The police said that on surrendering his passport he would be released on police bail whilst they pursued their enquiries. The papers would then be passed to the Crown Prosecution Service.

****

My phone rang, it was Amanda – she sounded curious. 'I've got the American Embassy on the phone. They want to talk to you, they asked for you specifically.'

I was curious as well. Why would the Americans want to talk to me? How had they got my name? As far as I was aware I didn't have any dealings with them either in business or privately.

'OK put them through Amanda.'

'Marcus Moon speaking, what can I do for you?'

'Hi Marcus, FYI my name's Burtt with two tees Rogers. I'm a Dep AUSA from the DoJ attached to the SEC INVESTDIV in DC.'

He'd got me on the back foot here. What the hell was he talking about? For a start was he an American golfer bragging about his equipment, wanting to take me on over eighteen holes at The Wisley? And what was a Dep AUSA attached to the something or other?

'Hello, hello, are you still there Marcus?'

'Yes, sorry, so what can I do for you Burtt?'

'Kory Kronoff.'

'What about Kronoff?'

'The USAO on behalf of the SEC is FU-ing several alleged federal felonies against him. As he is a US citizen, the FBI, with the help of INTERPOL, has arrested him in the AVI and handed him over to the FBoP whilst the DoJ gathers evidence,'

'Really, well there you are. But where do I fit in?' Somewhere between BEWILDERED and TOTALLY LOST I would've thought.

'You've hit the nail on the head, Marcus. You're a STAT 1 KEYWIT, re Tern Island to be precise, that is our PSE and you have intel in that connection. We want a face-to-face with you, *mano e mano* for a Q & A session. I suggest we interact at your POW today PM or tomorrow AM?'

I was starting to lose the will to live and, KEYWIT or not, was very tempted to tell him to either PO, or more firmly, FO. Instead, I tried to divert him.

'Dan Granchester of *The Times* knows more than me, why don't you interact with him?'

'We have, it was him who, on advice, GUI about you and the money. Get hold of the Dep CEO at CONDES and he'll PIOU.'

I was sure Dan said no such thing, but I cursed him for dropping me in it. I supposed I'd better talk, sorry

INTERFACE, with Burtt with two tees, so I agreed to meet him at CONDES tomorrow AM.

Margaret was still away on honeymoon, and as Hugo was having a week off golfing with his friends in Brittany, Janet was looking after me. She showed the Burtt through into my office.

Twenty-five-ish, crew cut, well scrubbed fresh face, Brooks Brothers' suit, shirt with a buttoned-down collar, New York Athletic Club tie and a shiny briefcase with 'US Attorneys Office' stamped in gold on the flap. They obviously didn't go in for apostrophes in the New York Attorney's office.

He handed me his card. 'Burtt' with two tees 'Rogers', I'd guessed right; 'Deputy Assistant US Attorney'. All was made clear now – more or less.

'Coffee, tea, fruit juice or water?'

He went for the water. I didn't tell him it came out of the Thames and not a crystal spring in the Highlands, and that he was probably the fourth or fifth person to drink it between its source and London. Janet brought his water in together with my coffee.

He started off. 'As I expounded to you over the wire yesterday I'm a Dep. AUSA and I'm on the Kronoff case. I'll continue from there, shall I?'

'Well, if you wouldn't mind running through it again, just so I get things clear in my mind.'

He gave a slight frown. 'OK. Well, I'm a Deputy Assistant US Attorney working out of the DoJ in Washington...'

'Hold hard there, the DoJ?'

'Department of Justice. We're acting on behalf of the SEC INVESTDIV...'

He stopped when he saw my raised eyebrow. 'Securities and Exchange Commission, Investigation Division.'

I nodded for him to continue.

'Kronoff has been arrested and is being held by the FBoP – Federal Bureau of Prisons – whilst we collect evidence under several headings. Securities fraud, investment advice fraud, money laundering, false statements and theft.'

Explaining things clearly obviously worried him and he couldn't contain himself any longer.

'There are many US agencies involved in this: the BoT, the BEA, the CIA, CFIUS, The DoC; the IRS and the FCSC. It's very complicated.'

'I'm sure it is, but what do you want from me?

He produced a pocket tape recorder and set it on my desk. I picked it up and put a table mat under it – still office proud you see!

I just gave him the facts, no speculation, and I refused to speculate when he pressed me about who or what I thought the three payments were for. I told him what I'd seen on Tern Island and what, in my opinion as an engineer, was going on – or rather not going on there. That was all.

He asked a few questions about the security, access to the island and the 'Hollywood' set that Kronoff was constructing. I told him how we had been warned off but had sneaked ashore. I didn't mention Dan spending the day there.

He seemed satisfied, switched off his tape recorder, thanked me and turned to leave. I stopped him.

'Incidentally, just to satisfy my curiosity what is the FCSC?' I wanted to make sure that the bastard hadn't been winding me up.

'The Foreign Claims Settlement Commission,' he replied easily.

'Ah!' I said, so I was still no wiser about all the rest of the alphabet.

After he'd gone Janet said, 'What was all that about?'

I shrugged. 'Don't ask me; just consider what life will be like when we all speak in text-speak and acronyms. Dep AUSA can C U at FCSC in DoJ on 3/7 at 11.45AM. Will U W8 4 him? It's going to make report writing a bit of a bugger.'

Zoe and I strolled into the Frog and Nightgown on Saturday morning. It was a lovely summer's day, the kind of day when the heat of the sun lays heavy on the thick green leaves of the plane trees and the air was still. We had walked, hand in hand, from our house, me looking at all the girls in their summer dresses as they promenaded along the Kings Road, and Zoe nudging me warningly in the ribs.

Tony, Finola, Bob, Pete, Merrylees and Dan were sitting in the courtyard round a large table holding a champagne bucket with two bottles of Laurent Perrier sticking out of it.

'Bob's horse won yesterday at Kempton,' explained Tony, 'and he was there to see it.'

I raised an eyebrow. 'Is that the same horse that came last at Lingfield a couple of months ago and you were going to turn it into carpaccio and sausages?'

Bob grinned. 'Ah yes, but I wasn't there then.'

'What difference does that make?'

'Well, you see before this race I went round to the stables to talk to the jockey and see the horse. I was just giving the horse a lump of sugar when the Duke of Norfolk heaved into sight around the corner. He's a former Steward of the Jockey Club, you know. He looked at me suspiciously so I ate one of my sugar lumps and gave him one just to show there was nothing wrong with them. Later, when he had gone I was giving my jockey his instructions. "Hold him back in the middle of the field..." I told him, "... then when you get to the last bend let him have his head – and don't worry, because if anything overtakes you then, it will either be me or the Duke of Norfolk."'

We all laughed at his joke, but I wasn't so sure – you never knew with Bob.

'What's new on the Comorantes/Kronoff front?' asked Pete, changing the subject.

Dan told us the *The Times* had been given the stonewall treatment by Downing Street, but one of their sources in the Met. Police had told them that Garside had been arrested and taken to Belgravia Police Station. He didn't know if he had been charged or was just 'helping the police with their enquiries'. However, he had walked out of there later apparently a free man. All he would say to the reporters waiting outside was 'No Comment'. He had been driven away in a car to an unknown destination.

The Times Inquiry Team had also discovered that his office in Portcullis House, his Pimlico flat and his house in Yorkshire had been searched by the police. Apparently, Mrs Tottie Garside took exception to her drawers being searched, felled two coppers with a wok, and damaged another. She was being held at Wath Police Station.

'It looks as though they're having difficulty proving anything,' Bob observed. 'They wouldn't have let him go if they had rock-solid evidence against him.'

I said I hadn't heard anything more except that I had been interviewed by Burtt with two tees Rogers, who was a Deputy Assistant US Attorney acting for the American Securities and Exchange Commission. They had arrested Kronoff on his yacht in Charlotte Amelie in the American Virgin Islands and were going to throw the book at him. Burtt thought he might get as much as 150 years in jail. They seemed to think that Tern Island was a key plank in their case or, as he put it, their PSE.'

'PSE?'

'Yeah, they talk in acronyms; I assume it means something like Prime Subject for Examination.'

CHAPTER SEVENTEEN

WHITEHALL, LONDON

Sir Oliver White tapped on the Prime Minister's door and came in.

'I just thought you'd like to know that the police found the Certificate of Deposit made out in Garside's name. It was in a concealed safe in his Yorkshire house. However, they have released Garside on police bail. The duty solicitor turned out to be a very bright young man who advised Garside to admit everything, with the vital exception that he claims this investment in Kronoff's scheme was an unsolicited gift from the Comorantes Government, which came out of the blue in recognition of the help and support he had given them over the past eighteen months.'

The PM frowned. 'That's not what Coquelin's letter said!'

'But will Coquelin be prepared to come over and give evidence to that effect in person? If it goes to court then that is almost certainly what will be required to stand any chance of a conviction.'

The PM thought for a couple of minutes. 'This is starting to get a bit smelly, Oliver. I don't like it. I think it could well be time to move it out of my office and on to the Foreign Secretary and the Attorney General. Will you brief them?

The Foreign Secretary can phone Coquelin to find out if he is prepared to come over, but quite frankly I don't hold out much hope. The Attorney General can speak to the Commissioner at New Scotland Yard and the Director of Public Prosecutions and advise me on what he thinks the chances of a conviction are with and without Coquelin's appearance in court. We've also got to work out a fallback position in the event that it doesn't go to court. I'll think about that.'

The Cabinet Secretary said he'd get on with it immediately and eased out leaving the PM scratching his head as he weighed up the political fallout whatever course was followed. There was no way that this could be swept under the carpet; it was going to leak out one way or another. The rumours were spreading and hints of a government scandal were building up. *The Times* was linking the rumours with the Kronoff affair, which was not good. The best thing would be to issue an official statement as soon as possible - but saying what?

****

THE PRESIDENT'S OFFICE, ST. GEORGE'S

Henri Coquelin was sitting at his desk wondering, amongst other things, why he hadn't had even a flicker of interest from London following his explosive letter. It was one of those occasions when the thought seems to trigger off a response because just then the phone rang and his secretary said, 'I have the British Foreign Secretary on the phone for you, sir.'

Coquelin's heart missed a beat. Powerful foreigners caused that sort of reaction these days; his nerves were still jangling after Mitchinson had shredded his self-confidence.

He gingerly told her to put the Foreign Secretary through.

'Good morning to you, Mr President.' The fact that it was afternoon in the Comorantes was not the sort of trivial detail that the British Foreign and Commonwealth Office bothered itself about. If it was morning in Whitehall then it was morning in the rest of the world. The FS continued, 'The Prime Minister wishes me to thank you for your letter and for bringing this very regrettable affair to our notice. He has asked me to apologise wholeheartedly on behalf of the British Government and to assure you that we are taking action against the perpetrator and that such an event will not happen again.'

Coquelin breathed a sigh of relief; the Brits appeared to have swallowed the story that $3m taken from the Port Mahon account was legitimate and were only concentrating on the $1.5m laid at Garside's door.

The Foreign Secretary added, 'Mr Garside has been arrested and it is very likely that he will be charged with theft, corrupt practices, tax evasion and a whole host of offences against the Crown.'

Coquelin's stony heart was unmoved; he didn't see what was coming.

'And rightly so,' he spluttered, indignantly. 'That sort of behaviour is reprehensible. It put me and my Government

327

in an untenable position and we took very great exception to it. I trust that you are taking drastic action?'

'Quite so,' said the Foreign Secretary, dryly. 'It is in that connection that I am telephoning you. You must realise that politically, this is a highly sensitive matter. We can't afford a miscalculation here, so to ensure that the evidence against Garside is rock solid it will be necessary for your vital evidence to be given in person.'

This statement was left hanging in the air whilst Coquelin grasped the full implications of what he had just been told.

'Are you still there, Mr President?'

Desperately scratching about for an answer Coquelin managed to gasp out that he would be prepared to swear an affidavit regarding Garside's involvement and confirm the contents of his letter, but the Foreign Secretary rejected that idea out of hand.

'Regrettably Mr President, and I know that this is imposing on your valuable time, but if we are to get to the bottom of this, the evidence must be in person. All you would have to do is confirm to the court that the information in your letter to our PM is correct.'

The turn of events set Coquelin back on his heels; he hadn't anticipated this. There was no way he was going to help the Brits to 'get to the bottom' of anything to do with the Port Mahon money – that was the last thing he wanted. However, just confirming his letter was true didn't sound unreasonable.

'And that would be all that would be required of me?'

'I assure you that that would be all – with perhaps a few clarifying questions under cross-examination,' the Foreign Secretary said, soothingly.

Coquelin shied away like a startled horse. Cross-examination! No fucking way was he going to be cross-examined. You never knew what might be dragged into the sunlight. That sealed matters in his mind forever. A close shave there, he had nearly fallen for it. To buy some time he excused making a decision by saying that he'd have to examine his schedule for the year and would get back to the Foreign Secretary in due course.

He sat back in a cold sweat. The Foreign Secretary had been just too smooth, too persuasive. There was no way now that he was going to set foot in England and risk being arrested, the whole thing could be a trap. That bastard Garside had probably given the British authorities the whole nine yards about him already; Rouget; the Port Mahon money, and Kronoff. And the very thought of being cross-examined by a sharp barrister with a mind like a stiletto – and in open court – gave him watery bowels.

He waited for a couple of days and then told his secretary to phone the British Foreign Office, get hold of senior official there and tell him or her to tell the Foreign Secretary that unfortunately the President's schedule didn't allow him to visit England for the next twelve months at least.

He also warned Rouget that if he got a call to do the same.

Sir Oliver gathered up the memos from the Foreign and Commonwealth Office and the Attorney General's Office, slipped them into a plastic folder and headed off to see the PM.

'Garside, Prime Minister. It's no go, I'm afraid. The Foreign Secretary spoke to Coquelin and told him that if we were to get a conviction then his personally giving evidence in court was absolutely vital. Coquelin said he'd think about it after consulting his appointments schedule. The Foreign Secretary then received a message a few days later saying that Coquelin was unable to visit England for at least twelve months. It's an excuse, of course; he doesn't want to get involved for some reason.'

The PM scowled. 'I bet he doesn't. I bet the little shit is worried that all sorts of nefarious activities might come out if he showed up in court. Jesus Christ, we can't keep this under our hat that long! What does the Attorney General think?'

Sir Oliver pursed his lips. 'He thinks it would be far too risky to go to trial based solely on Coquelin's unsupported letter, the Certificate of Deposit and Garside's testimony.'

The PM thought for a few seconds then brightened. 'This could work to our advantage you know, Oliver. We can't avoid some scandal, but a court case about corruption in government – for that is how it would be seen – would make national headlines. The media would hammer us, "Who else is at it?" they would cry and we would be pasted by the opposition in Parliament. We'll have to handle it differently. That bugger Garside will escape incarceration, but better that than a full-blown scandal that would damage the Government and the Party. No, I have another idea.' He pointed a long finger at the Cabinet Secretary to emphasise what he was going to say.

'The Crown Prosecution Service must defer any charges and let Garside off the legal hook. However, the Chief Whip has got to haul Garside in and point out to him, in no uncertain terms, that charges have only been deferred. To save his face and the probability of a long jail sentence, he must admit his misjudgement in accepting that 'gift', humbly apologise, and resign his seat in Parliament, together with all that goes with it. That must be done immediately to staunch any speculation. Would you be so kind as to ask the Chief Whip to come and see me as soon as he can – like now?'

The Chief Whip was a small insignificant man who would be lost in a crowd – until you looked at his face. Tight thin lips, eyes like flints and an implacable expression that revealed experience of many knotty conflicts – ninety-nine per cent of them won. An interview with him frightened the life out of MPs.

The PM laid out the whole Garside saga in front of him.

'What d'you think of that, Dennis?

'Bloody hell, is it true?'

'Oh yes it's all true – except Garside's explanation. The swine must have asked for something right at the beginning of this job and managed to filter his slice into the estimates somehow. He was the one who pushed the whole thing through the DfID Committee, but the proof that he's been deliberately corrupt is a bit too weak to guarantee a conviction. He admits that he benefited from the Comorantes but claims it was an unsolicited gift rewarding him for his assistance, and he didn't realise that he should have either refused it or disclosed it. I don't believe a word of it and we can certainly nail him for that but I think that's all. However, we can't let him get away with it – he's got to go. So I suggest you haul him in, give him the hard word and kick his backside all the way back up to Mexborough. We'll release a statement on his behalf that covers his resignation but minimises damage to the Party and the Government.'

****

Following his release on police bail Nobby didn't know what to do. To minimise publicity he had been held in Belgravia Police Station and it had taken some time for the news to filter out that an unmamed MP was 'helping police with their enquiries'. As a result there were only a few reporters outside the police station when he was released. However, instead of boldly walking out with a smile and brushing off any shouted questions he made the big mistake of skulking out hidden under a blanket, refusing to say anything which made the reporters very suspicious so they followed him and discovered his identity.

His first inclination was to bolt back up to Yorkshire and hide himself away from everybody in 'Mineanders' with Tottie, who was also out on police bail. However, he'd been told not to leave town without notifying the police.

He didn't fancy going into his office and facing the jeers and sneers of Brown and Miss Harbottle so he hid in his flat in Pimlico with the curtains drawn and the door bolted.

The now eager newshounds gathered outside and waited in vain in the pouring rain for some sign of life, but the curtains didn't even twitch.

After two days one of them had a bright idea and phoned the police saying that there had been no sign of Garside, but they thought they'd heard a gunshot.

This sent the police scurrying round at high speed with forced-entry equipment. Having hammered on the door for five minutes with no result they smashed the door in and followed by an enterprising cameraman rushed into the bedsit. All they discovered was an unshaven, bloodshot-eyed Nobby in the semi-dark, sitting in front of a flickering television eating a can of cold baked beans with a thee-quarter empty bottle of Scotch beside him.

The inspector in charge grasped the position immediately and told his men to eject the cameraman from the room. The camera flashed but fortunately for Nobby only took a picture of a constable's hairy ear.

'Are you all right sir?' the inspector asked with some concern.

'Of course I'm not all right, you stupid sod! Would you be all right if you were besieged by the wolves from the bloody media day and night? Knocking on the windows and hammering on the door. Ringing up at all hours, I've had to leave the phone off the hook. I'm an MP you know and it's your bloody job to give me protection. I'm going to complain personally to the Home Secretary about this!'

'I'm terribly sorry sir for the intrusion, but we did have concerns about your personal safety. A senior official in your party has been trying to contact you without success.' He glanced at a piece of paper, 'A Mr Dennis Straker. He would like you to phone him, I'll leave you the number,' and he put the piece of paper on the table.

He added, 'We'll send some people to repair you door, but in the meantime I'll leave a couple of officers outside to make sure you're not disturbed.'

He ushered the police back out of the front door and left two burly constables standing on the step.

Nobby eyed the piece of paper warily. He knew Dennis Straker was the Chief Whip and, if he had a choice, he'd sooner pull out his own teeth than have a heart-to-heart with Dennis.

Ever since he was released without charge, he had been wondering what the fallout was going to be. He wasn't naïve enough to imagine there wasn't going to be any and this could be it. Well, he'd just stick to the story he'd given the police and humbly apologise for failing to declare the gift, saying he didn't realise that it was obligatory. They wouldn't want a scandal so they'd probably remove him as deputy chair of the DfID Aid Committee and he'd be consigned to the back benches. Humiliating but better than ten years incarcerated in Wormwood Scrubs.

After giving a few minutes thought to his tactics, he decided that if the bullet was to be bitten he'd better get on and bite it. He reached for the phone.

****

What Nobby didn't know was that when Bill Brown and Miss Harbottle were allowed back into their searched offices Bill Brown had found the now opened packet marked STRICTLY PRIVATE and CONFIDENTIAL and addressed to Garside still lying in a drawer of his desk. He slid out the copy of Philips' report and read it.

'Bloody hell!' he murmured to himself, 'so that's what all the police raiding and arresting is all about. Old Nobby has been caught with his sticky fingers in the till – and in a big way by the look of it. $1.5 million is one hell of a lot of bread to nick! Christ, he'll be sent down for years if this gets to court.'

He was interrupted by a flustered and flushed Laetitia Harbottle who began frantically collecting up all the kinky magazines and photographs.

'I should never have let you talk me into this Brown, you filthy deviant,' she wailed. 'Oh God, please pray it never gets out. I'll never be able to show my face at the Tennis Club again if it does.'

Bill Brown, nettled by her loading the responsibility on to him, snapped back, and what might one day have turned into a beautiful friendship was terminated on the spot.

'Well it was your idea you oversexed, fat, kinky bitch. Bugger your Tennis Club, bugger Balham and bugger whatever else ails you! What worries me is that Mrs Brown will hear about it. The bloody police leak things to the press at the drop of a hat. Here let me check those!' He snatched the photographs out of her hands, looked through them, then stuffed them into his briefcase.

'At least they didn't take any,' he said, more to reassure himself than Miss Harbottle.

He glanced down again at Philips' report and, on impulse pushed it back into the envelope and slipped that into his briefcase as well. You never knew when something like that might come in handy.

****

Shaved, showered and suited, with a red rose in his buttonhole and a red tie – both of which matched his bloodshot eyes, Nobby knocked tentatively on Straker's office door, half hoping that he would be out.

He wasn't, and a voice shouted, 'Come.'

Nobby pushed the door open and, trying to conceal his shaking knees behind a cool front, strolled in. He knew at once that all was not sweetness and light. Straker's visitors' chairs had been moved from their usual place in front of his desk to the side walls, so Nobby had no option but to stand like a naughty schoolboy in front of the headmaster. Nobby looked at Straker's face and then wished he hadn't. The unblinking eyes that glared back at him were as cold and penetrating as the winter wind whistling across the Siberian Steppes.

'I think there's been a bit of a misunderstanding here Dennis—' he ventured. He was cut off sharply. The rat-trap mouth moved slightly, the eyes never wavered.

'Shut the fuck up Garside and just listen – and thank your lucky stars that the PM is not a nasty, malevolent bastard like me! I would have thrown the book at you and hung you out to dry. If I had my way, you'd be locked up and the key thrown away so you could rot, but the PM decided that he doesn't want a big scandal and has asked me to deal with you more discreetly.' Straker's eyes bored into his; there was no trace of mercy in them.

Nobby shivered, wondering if ten years in jail might be the better of the two options. He felt he had to put up some form of defence so he tried again.

'Look Dennis, it's not like that.'

'Like what?' Straker's voice was suddenly disarmingly gentle.

'Well you know—'

He was cut off again. Dennis resumed his thin smile, which resembled the rictus grin of a three-day corpse.

'What I know and what the PM knows, and also what the Director of Public Prosecutions knows, is that you've stolen money from the Port Mahon Aid Package – effectively the British taxpayer – blackmailed a foreign government and involved yourself with that master confidence trickster Kory Kronoff. You are a lying, cheating, thieving, corrupt swine who isn't fit to be alongside even the current batch of lying, cheating misfits who make up our government. So what you're going to do, Garside, is resign your seat in the House forthwith, fuck off back North, keeping the low profile of the miserable worm that you are, and your trap firmly shut.'

Straker paused for breath, anger suffusing his face. 'There will be no compensations, and if you refuse or embarrass the Party in any way then you will go to jail. Remember one thing – the charges against you are not cancelled, just deferred.'

A spark of resistance flickered in Nobby's subconscious. 'You can't do that! There's absolutely no concrete evidence that I have done anything seriously wrong!'

Straker decided to stamp out that spark ruthlessly with a small lie. 'Oh, yes we can. The consultants on Port Mahon have told us that they have seen positive proof that you have stolen money from the Port Mahon account so think yourself bloody lucky you're not facing a long stretch in Dartmoor.'

That set Nobby right back on his heels; as far as he was aware there wasn't anything anyone could see that directly implicated him. They must have lied to the committee when he went out to be sick.

Straker continued, 'We'll draft out your resignation statement and the appropriate press releases. As an MP cannot resign you'll be stripped of your seat. You'll be appointed as Steward and Bailiff of the Manor of Dinnington, a paid office of the Crown – which disqualifies you from membership of the Commons – the salary is one penny per year. Now you can go and sit in your office and play with yourself until the security guards come to clear you out. Get out of my sight!'

Nobby stood for a moment white-faced, shocked down to his boots. It was much worse than he'd feared. They obviously knew a lot more than he expected, so either Coquelin had dropped him right in the shit or that nosy sod Moon had found out more than he'd originally told the committee. He couldn't think straight; Straker had resumed reading a document so Nobby had no option but to turn round and find the door.

Trembling, he stood in the corridor; his main concern at the moment was to avoid being spoken to or even seen. He crept along the corridors and up the emergency stairs avoiding looking at anybody until he reached his office. Both Bill Brown and Laetitia Harbottle were there, Brown looking angry and sheepish and Miss Harbottle with a tear-stained face, snotty nose and a damp handkerchief. He was too preoccupied with himself and his problems to bother much about either of them and when Miss Harbottle slid out of the room after giving him a Medusan glare, he was just left with Brown.

Brown perked up at Nobby's appearance and studied him with interest; it was payback time!

'Nah then Norbert, what's tha bin up to then? It must be summat tasty. Laetitia tells me it took two big bobbies to cart thee off to the nick.'

Garside flushed but ignored him. He looked at his desk with the splintered drawers, his files and papers spread neatly on the desk and surrounding floor and his photograph of Tottie in a silver frame with the back torn off.

Brown wasn't finished yet; he stood up and walked round his desk.

'They made a right bloody mess when they turned this place over, caused me a lot of aggro. So what have you been doing, Norbert? Got caught with your sticky fingers in the till? Performed homosexual acts on the Cabinet table? Fiddled your expenses again? It must be something serious.'

Nobby lost it; he turned on Brown savagely.

'One more fuckin' word out of you, you rubber-lovin' pervert and I'll kick your bollocks through your spine – that is, if you have a spine or any bollocks!'

Funnily enough that, roughly, was what Miss Harbottle had been expounding before Garside walked in, and Brown was very sensitive about it.

But that also was the moment that consolidated Brown's hatred of Garside in his mind. He bit his lip, turned round, and without another word went back to his desk and sat down.

'Jellyfish,' snarled Nobby, and began to collect all his personal stuff. He wasn't going to give Brown the satisfaction of telling him he'd been kicked out.

Two security men turned up and helped Nobby load his gear into a taxi and then, without a backward glance, Nobby shook the dust of Parliament from his feet and headed for his Pimlico flat. The next morning he bought all the daily newspapers in a local shop and skimmed through them in a taxi on the way to Kings Cross Station where he boarded the train for Doncaster.

****

Of course, I'd read Dan's articles in *The Times* and all the other stuff about Kronoff, but it came as a surprise when I read that an MP was helping the police with their enquiries and had left Belgravia Police Station yesterday hidden under a blanket. There was a blurred shot of a blanket-covered figure being hurried into a car. The article continued, '*It is thought that the MP is Norbert Garside, Member for*

Mexborough East, and he appears to have gone to ground at his flat in Pimlico. It has not been possible to contact him for comment. A Downing Street spokesperson said that they were unable to comment as it was a police matter.'

The article continued to say that there were unsubstantiated rumours that a large sum of money had been taken unofficially from an overseas aid package given to a foreign government, but there was no evidence that the two events were connected.

Well, well, so it looked as though Garside was being investigated, but I wondered how they had got on to him. I resolved to ask Dan if he knew the next time I saw him – which came sooner than I thought.

Over supper that evening Zoe said, 'Oh by the way Dan Granchester has asked us round for dinner on Friday. I looked in our diary and we've nothing on so I gave him a provisional "yes", subject to you agreeing?'

'Yes, fine by me, I want to talk to him anyway.'

She gave a mock groan. 'It's not going to be your boring old business talk all evening, is it? That stuff about Kory Kornflakes or whatever he's called?'

I laughed. 'No, I promise you it isn't, it'll not take more than five minutes. I just want to find out if he knows anymore about that MP bloke, Garside, that I told you about.'

Then a thought struck me. 'Is it a posh dinner and do you know who else is going?'

She chuckled. 'No, it isn't, so I won't get the chance to wear that new evening outfit you would love to buy me. He said it's casual; he wants us to meet his new girlfriend and

Pete and Merrylees will be coming. There will just be eight of us round the table.'

I wondered who the couple would be to make up the eight.

To some degree events overtook us because Thursday's newspapers, TV and radio programmes all carried the news of Garside's resignation. *The Times* printed the resignation statement in full with a pithy comment from the Prime Minister. It read:

Norbert Arthur Garside has relinquished his seat as Member of Parliament for Mexborough East following his admission that, whilst acting as Deputy Chairman of the Department for International Development's Aid Committee, he accepted, and failed to declare to the authorities, an unsolicited gift from a foreign government. He accepts that this could be construed as a matter that might be seen to influence his decisions on that Committee.

Accordingly Mr Garside apologises to the Committee and to Parliament for his error of judgement and feels that it is only right and proper that he should step down immediately.

The Prime Minister thanks Mr Garside for his previous services but wishes to make it clear that this kind of behaviour is not acceptable and he will ensure drastic action is taken against any elected member or official who transgresses in future.

So that's it, is it? I thought. It looks as though Garside has got away with only a slap on the wrist – relatively. Well, that's the end of him; he won't trouble CONDES anymore.

I stuck my head round Hugo's door. 'Did you see that stuff about Garside resigning?'

He nodded with a smile. 'No tears shed here then. He's out of our hair for good.'

On Friday evening Zoe and I took a taxi to Belgrave Square and were admitted to Dan's house by a rather pretty girl dressed in black with a white apron. 'The Honourable Dan is in the drawing room,' she said and directed us to a lofty room with a blazing fire and soft lighting. The first impression was of luxury and comfort, but then the musty smell, the damp patches on the walls and the rotting fabrics caught the senses. Without the fire the room must have been a dump.

Dan caught the expression on our faces. 'You're right, it is a dump. Normally I live in two small rooms on the first floor – the damp doesn't rise that far. The drawing room was only used for entertaining but there's very little of that these days.'

I nodded towards the maid questioningly.

'Oh, she's from the catering company. I can't afford a cook. A Latvian girl comes in two days a week to keep the dust down, that's all.'

We turned to the tall elegant girl standing beside him in front of the fire. 'This is Poppy, we met a couple of weeks ago at a friend's wedding. Don't you think she's gorgeous?'

Poppy had the grace to blush but offered a warm natural smile and a firm handshake. She had short blond hair, dark blue eyes, a very good skin and a slim figure that was shown of to advantage by a well-fitted blouse and tight jeans. Her jewellery was Catherine Best, expensive but tasteful. I thought Dan could have fallen on his feet with her. I could have fallen on my back with her any day – that is until Zoe gave me a sharp poke in the ribs and whispered, 'You're staring!'

Fortunately, the doorbell rang and Pete and Merrylees were shown in, together with the other couple, a tousled-haired, pinked-cheeked chap with twinkling eyes and a rather plain woman with a severe look. It turned out that 'Biffo' MacEwan had been at school with Dan, and his wife Jenny, was the leader of *The Times* Insight Team that was doing such a good demolition job on Kory Kronoff.

It was therefore inevitable that the conversation should start off with Kronoff and Tern Island. Zoe gave me a wry grin and murmured, 'Told you so'.

As she knew almost as much about it as me, she was not left out of the conversation.

After rehashing some of the funnier moments Jenny said, 'I had a very peculiar phone call today from a man who wouldn't give his name but said he had some hot information about that Labour MP Garside who resigned this week. It is rumoured that he nicked $10 million from one of our aid projects but, of course, we daren't print that. I asked for some details, but he said he wanted £50,000 for it.'

I pricked up my ears. 'Not $10m,' I murmured. 'So what are you going to do?'

She frowned, 'See what he's got and beat him down to ten grand if it's any good; kick him out on his arse if it isn't!'

That was interesting: her face didn't have any laugh lines and there wasn't a trace of humour in her eyes. I wondered how she and the cheerful Biffo got it together in the bedroom. It can't have been all that exciting – unless, beneath that cold, hard exterior lurked a smouldering passion like a dormant volcano, just waiting to be released. The idea painted an interesting picture. I suddenly noticed that the room had gone quiet and everybody was looking at me waiting for a follow-up to my question.

'Oh sorry, I got lost there.'

I explained what I had seen in the Port Mahon accounts but pointed out that although it appeared that $1.5 million dollars had disappeared, there was no proof that Garside had taken it.

'Maybe this guy, whoever he is, has got proof,' observed Pete.

Jenny frowned again. 'If we could just get positive proof that money had been stolen, that would be sufficient. We could run a story along the lines of: "*x million dollars have been taken illegally from an aid package funded by the hard-working British taxpayer. Those dollars were meant to help a poor nation to raise the standard of living of all the wretched people living in poverty below the bread line, and some corrupt rich fat cat has abused his position and deprived these people of that benefit. It is believed that the stolen money was put into one of Kory Kronoff's Ponzi schemes and is therefore lost.*

Norbert Garside, the disgraced MP for Mexborough East, was the deputy chairman of the Department for International Development at the time and responsible for this aid package. He has been helping the police with their enquiries." Etc., etc., blah, blah.

'But we need positive proof not just hearsay, and we'd have to get our lawyers to check it out carefully.'

CHAPTER EIGHTEEN

LONDON, 2011

On the train Nobby reread 'his' resignation statement. Straker – no it wouldn't be that ruthless bastard – he suspected it would have been the PM, had let him off relatively lightly, obviously to avoid the Party being damaged by a major scandal. For the first hour, as Potter's Bar, Hatfield and Peterborough flashed past the window, Nobby alternated between heartfelt relief that he'd got off the hook without a long jail sentence and fury that he had been so badly treated when there wasn't a shred of concrete evidence against him. It was all circumstantial he raged, and his clever story about the Tern Island thing being a gift was a plausible explanation. But the fact remained that he was now jobless, his hopes of a big injection into his Swiss bank account had been shattered, and Her Majesty's Revenue and Customs must, by now, be aware of that account and would demand some explanation.

However, on the positive side, from the resignation statement it could be interpreted that, although he had been foolish, he had done the honourable thing by resigning so all was not lost there. He would contact his mates in the unions and in the local authorities. There were jobs going for an astute operator in Health Service Trusts and local government; he might even wangle a chairmanship. He began to plan life after Parliament.

****

Bill Brown was leaning on the stained and chipped mahogany bar of the Blind Pew pub, sipping a glass of John Smith's Taddy Ale with half an eye on the television and the other half watching the entrance from Bentinck Street. Each time it was pushed open letting in a swirl of cold air he started forward, only to lean back again with disappointment. He glanced at his watch for the sixth time and the heavy hand of frustration gripped his heart even harder. The bitch wasn't going to show up; his thoughts of an expensive piece of jewellery to win back Laetitia Harbottle's favours began to shrivel. He was about to drain the dregs of his glass and hit the night air when his heart gave a leap. He had missed her entrance but a hard-faced woman was standing just inside the door holding a copy of *The Times* in clear view. Her eyes swept round the occupants coming to rest on him. He forced a smile and she came forward.

'Can I get you a drink?' he asked, tentatively.

'Large gin and tonic, Bombay gin, no ice and a slice of orange.' There was no apology for lateness. Brown ordered another beer.

She fixed him with a questioning glare. 'I hope you're not going to waste my time, so what have you got that may be of interest to us?'

'Er, hadn't we better agree terms first?' ventured Brown.

'Good God, man!' she snapped. 'I'm not buying a pig in a poke. Do you think I was born yesterday? Let's see what you've got and then I'll decide if it's worth anything.'

The drinks arrived and she took a long pull at hers without taking her eyes off Brown's. It was a stand-off and he lost. He bent down and took the copy of Philips' report from his briefcase and slid it along the bar towards her.

She didn't touch it. 'What is it?'

'It's a Treasury report confirming that money was stolen from a British aid package to the Comorantes Islands.'

'How did you manage to get hold of it?' she asked, suspiciously. She flicked it round with one finger so she could read the addressee. Her face didn't betray the spark of interest that shot through her when she read the name Norbert Garside MP.

Bill Brown hesitated. He wondered whether to reveal all or try and bluff his way through. The hard-faced woman opposite didn't look the bluffable type.

'I trust that you keep your sources of information confidential?' he ventured, nervously.

'Unless it breaches the Official Secrets Act. If it does, I don't want to touch it.' She raised a questioning eyebrow.

Brown shook his head. 'No, it's nothing like that. I shared an office with Garside and he left it behind.'

'And you are...?'

Brown started to sweat; it wasn't at all what he expected this meeting to be like. He thought *The Times* would bite his hand off to get this information. Instead, he was being grilled about himself.

'One of the conditions of me handing this over is that my name does not appear in any article arising from it, otherwise no deal.'

Jenny MacEwan gave a thin smile. 'Of course, I understand.'

She picked up the packet and slid out the copy of Philips' report. She speed-read it and concentrated on the conclusions. 'But this doesn't positively implicate Garside in the theft of money.'

'No, but it does confirm that money was taken and by three people. The Prime Minister of the Comorantes and Minister of Ports have both confirmed that they were two of the people and the Prime Minister told Philips that the third person was Garside.'

'But this was only a verbal confirmation; he didn't put anything in writing?'

Brown shrugged. 'That's all I've got,' he said, pointing to the report.

Jenny thought about it. There was certainly a good story here and this chap was obviously a fellow MP – he said he shared an office with Garside so it shouldn't be difficult to find out who he was, if necessary.

She had to have a copy of the report to back up her story otherwise *The Times'* lawyers would never allow the story she had outlined to be printed.

She pushed the report back along the bar towards Brown. 'It doesn't nail Garside so it's not much use to us. It's certainly not worth £50,000.'

Brown's heart sank; his hopes of instant riches at Garside's expense were in serious danger of disappearing up his own orifice.

'It must be worth *something*, there's a story there about money being stolen from the British Government,' he pleaded. 'That, in itself, is newsworthy!'

Jenny pretended to make a decision; Brown wasn't so stupid after all. 'OK,' she said, 'we'll pay you ten grand, but you'll have to sign an exclusivity agreement not to reveal any of this to any other media outlet.'

Brown accepted the offer with relief that he was going to make *some* money.

Five days later any sense of relief that Brown had was dispersed in a trice when he opened his copy of *The Times* on the tube that morning. The Port Mahon–Garside story was spread across two pages with 72 point banner headlines. He realised that he had been conned rotten by Jenny MacEwan. The copy of Philips report was worth far more than the measly £10,000 he had been paid; extracts from it were splashed all over the pages, the whole story was based on the evidence that the Philips' report confirmed. The only thing missing was the direct link between the stolen money and Garside, but it didn't take a particle physicist at CERN to put two and two together and make the connection. Jenny had got the positive proof that she needed that money had been stolen and she and Dan had gone to town with photos of Garside, photos of Tern Island, photos of Kronoff, photos of alleged Comorantian citizens living in leaky huts with buckets for latrines – and made it hot news.

Brown wasn't the only one to have conniptions that day. Nobby Garside was having a lunchtime beer in the Wath Labour Club. Nobody in the club took *The Times* and as Bill Brown had signed his exclusivity deal no other paper such as *The Sun, The Daily Sport or The Mirror* reported the story. As Nobby was taking the first pull at his pint Councillor Herbert Heptonstall bustled through the door, his face grim, his manner eager.

'Ah thowt ah'd catch thee suppin' ale here Nobby, hast tha seen *The Times* this mornin'? Tha's made t' headlines.'

Nobby gulped and slopped beer all down his shirt. 'Why? What's it say?'

'It says tha's nicked one and a half million dollars from t'aid fund.'

'Never! I've dealt wi' that, it were a gift. That's watter under t'bridge,' he said, scornfully.

'Not now it isn't. They reckon you blackmailed 'em into paying it. They reckon it were a set up from t' start!'

'That's bullshit, somebody's just trying to make trouble for me and I think I know who it is.'

'Well, tha'd better get it sorted because with that hangin' ower thy head nobody will touch thee wi' a barge pole.'

Nobby finished his beer, trying hard to affect an air of indifference. Nobody offered to buy him another. It was as if he'd suddenly contracted leprosy, so he strolled out of the club as nonchalantly as he could muster. When he was out of sight he sprinted across the road to the newsagent and bought a copy of *The Times*.

At first glance it didn't seem too bad; the photo of him was blurred and grainy, separate from the main article. He read it carefully and then went through it again. It didn't actually say that he had been paid the money, only that somebody very closely connected with the project must have set the whole fraud up from the beginning and taken the money. But the implication unequivocally pointed in his direction. He tried to persuade himself that it could equally well be interpreted that it was another Comorantian politician who was the third man – except for one damming fact: the article also mentioned that he had admitted receiving a gift of an identical amount.

Over the next few days it became abundantly clear that people believed that he had planned the theft and that he was as guilty as hell. Doors that had always been open were closed, people avoided him wherever possible, and when avoidance was not possible they cut him dead. Any thoughts he may have had about taking important local positions were extinguished like candles in a storm.

It was all so unfair! He repeated to himself again, there was no positive evidence that he had deliberately set out to steal money from the Port Mahon account – there couldn't be because it never existed. In any case, his story about the investment in Tern Island being an unsolicited gift covered all the other eventualities. He brooded over it and eventually came to one conclusion. All this must be down to Moon telling the committee that he had seen evidence that positively implicated him during the time he was out of the room. Moon had lied. He must have; that was why they had all given him strange looks when he returned.

As a result of Moon's lies Nobby was now stigmatised for life as a person who, put into a position of trust, had betrayed that trust and become a thief. He'd never get another job in politics and probably not with the unions either. He had to clear his name. He almost wept with self-pity, blithely ignoring the fact that he *was* a thief – such an admission was irrelevant to his thinking.

There was only one way to do this – in the courts. He would sue. He would sue CONDES generally, and Moon personally, to force him to admit that there was no concrete evidence that he, Nobby Garside – man of the people – had both planned to steal and had stolen money, thus blackening his name.

He thought long and hard; the only persons who could confirm the truth of this were Coquelin and Rouget, but by doing so they would have to admit that they also connived in the setting up and stealing. He gave a grim smile. No, there was no chance of them giving evidence in favour of CONDES and thus admitting to the world that they too were thieves. There would be absolutely no benefit to them to do this so they wouldn't do it. Anyway, Moon couldn't possibly know for certain what took place in his discussions with those two.

On the positive side, Dennis Straker had admitted that CONDES had told members of the DfID committee that concrete evidence existed, and Straker must have got that information from somebody on the committee. He'd get his lawyer to contact all of them. If they refused to help him, he would subpoena the lot of 'em. They would confirm what Moon had told them and it would be up to Moon to produce his evidence. As no such evidence existed, he would be unable to do that; Moon and CONDES would lose and he would be awarded huge damages for the indignities he was being forced to suffer, and his name cleared.

He felt better after that; now all he needed was a good lawyer. Anybody local was out of the question; all they did were wills and property sales. He wanted somebody with teeth who, when they sank these into an opponent's leg, didn't let go.

He scratched his head thinking back to all those drinks parties and receptions he'd attended and the people he'd met. He vaguely recalled a fleshy, big-nosed chap at a Law Society do he'd attended as a guest a few months ago. He'd sat next to this bloke but hadn't paid much attention to him as it didn't appear, after the first acquaintance, he could help further Nobby's career. He was a lawyer and he'd given Nobby his card.

He ran up the stairs to where his dinner jacket was hanging in the wardrobe and felt in the top pocket. There were four or five cards but there was one that read:

Jacob Abramowitz
ABRAMOWITZ, FEINSTEIN and GOLDBERG.
SOLICITORS.
Experts in litigation

With an address in the City and phone numbers.

Just what he needed; a firm of tough Jewish lawyers to handle his case.

Next morning he phoned Abramowitz, Feinstein and Goldberg and asked to speak to Mr Abramowitz. After he'd explained to the girl that he was a potential new client he was put straight through.

'Mr Abramowitz, my name is Garside. You may remember me; we sat next to each other at a Law Society function a few months ago?'

Jacob Abramowitz hadn't a clue who Garside was but, if he had attended a Law Society dinner, he must be worth a few pounds so he smoothly replied, 'Of course Mr Garside, so what can I do for you?'

Nobby said, 'You may have heard about me in the news recently. I was the Member of Parliament for Mexborough East and was forced to resign.'

'Ah!' murmured Abramowitz, his interest stirred. 'You're *that* Mr Garside. So how can I help you?'

'I have been the victim of the most vicious and vile slander, Mr Abramowitz, and I want you to seek full restitution and compensation on my behalf. A company and/or a person has spread lies about me to the Government, which have blackened my name and forced me to relinquish my position as an MP without any compensation. I want to take action against them to clear my name and I am prepared to pursue them to the ends of the earth, if necessary, to do it!'

Abramowitz brightened up at this and immediately suggested that Nobby come and see him at his office, bringing all the information he had. An appointment was fixed for two days hence.

As soon as he put the phone down Abramowitz rubbed his hands together and looked across the office at his partner Goldberg.

'A new client Hymie, someone who is prepared to go to the ends of the earth to prove his point.'

Goldberg smiled. 'Well he's come to the right man with you Jacob, because I'm sure you'll take him there.' They both laughed at the double entendre.

****

Nobby felt quite pleased with himself on the train back north. Mr Abramowitz had listened carefully to everything he had to say, tut-tutted a few times, made careful notes, asked some not very penetrating questions – mainly about Nobby's financial affairs – and finally assured Nobby that, if what he had said could be verified, he had a very strong case for substantial damages.

There was the small matter of a cheque for £10,000 as a retainer – non refundable, of course, and Nobby departed the doors of Abramowitz, Feinstein and Goldberg with hope in his heart and £10,000 less in his meagre bank account.

One thing worried him slightly; Abramowitz had emphasised that litigation through the courts could be a long, drawn-out expensive business. QCs would have to be briefed, retainers paid, accruing legal costs settled monthly, the witnesses made available etc. It would be vastly expensive if CONDES and Moon defended his claims, as surely they would. It would be better to notify them about potential litigation, but indicate that he would be prepared to settle out of court for say £500,000, plus a public apology.

Nobby had been thinking in the millions and for instant judgement, and this was giving him pause for thought. Even throwing in his Swiss money would stretch him to the limit. He'd agreed to go away and think it over.

Jacob Abramowitz and Hymie Goldberg met for lunch in Mishkin's in Covent Garden. Jacob had booked a quiet table in one corner and they ordered one course from the hovering waiter.

'By the way Jacob, how did you fare with that MP fellow Garside?'

'Not good Hymie, not good.'

'No money or a poor case?'

'Both Hymie, both.'

Retainer?'

'Hymie my boy! Do you think I'm losing my touch? Of course a retainer, £10,000 – cheque cashed. The problem is he's *gornisht*, he has very little money and he wants to run the case. There are just too many loopholes and unknowns. It could last until his funds are used up and he went bankrupt. It's not worth it, we could lose money.'

'Oy vey!'

'I'm trying to head him off into a quick settlement on the old "No win, no fee" basis. That way it only costs us a couple of standard letters off the computer. If the other side pay up something, either because they think they might lose or just to get us off their backs, we pocket 25% of the winnings.'

Hymie returned to his salt beef on soda bread with gusto, Jacob was still on the ball. It was a good job there were two different locks on the office safe and each of them had a key to only one.

Margaret laid the thick, white, linen-laid paper envelope in front of me on my desk. 'Private and Confidential' was typed at the top left-hand above my full name and the company's address.

An unexploded bomb doesn't necessarily have fins and a detonating cap in its nose; it can just be a round cylinder with a few wires or something as simple as a good quality paper envelope, but all three can emit a certain aura of menace that makes one want to stand back and give it a wide berth.

I gave the envelope a poke with a letter opener and turned it over. Printed on the back was the name *Abramowitz, Feinstein & Goldberg. Solicitors.*

A shadow fell across the desk, I looked up. Hugo was standing there clutching a sheaf of letterhead that looked as if it was made of the same paper as my envelope. He was wearing his usual tweed suit and an angry frown. He waved his pieces of paper.

'That fellow Garside is suing us for half a million quid for libelling him, causing him to lose his job as an MP and his name to be blackened in public. You have obviously got the same letter.'

But I hadn't. I slit open my envelope to find that Garside was suing me *personally* for £500,000 for the same reasons.

'What the hell is he on about?' I said with astonishment.

'Read on.'

I read on. He was claiming that I, or CONDES, or both had told the DfID committee that the third person in the

359

three-cheque scandal was definitely Garside, that he had planned the whole thing from start to finish, blackmailed the government of the Comorantes into going along with it and we had claimed to have concrete evidence of all that. As a result, the British Government had forced him to resign from his seat as Member of Parliament for Mexborough East without any compensation. Members of the Committee and the Labour Party Chief Whip had confirmed all this and would give evidence in court to that effect, if called upon to do so. A government report about the matter had been leaked to the press and the public had drawn the implication from it that those were the true facts. As a result, he had been unable to find employment elsewhere and his reputation was ruined.

If I/CONDES didn't pay him damages of £500,000 and issue a public apology to confirm that there were no grounds whatsoever to implicate Mr Garside in such an outrageous suggestion, he would sue through the courts for maximum damages which could amount to millions.

They awaited our response.

'Jesus Christ!' I breathed. 'That's absolute rubbish.' I have never told anyone that Garside was the third man. In fact, I have always gone to great pains to point out that there was no evidence linking Garside with the third cheque. Garside himself suggested to the committee that they put in a forensic accountant to look into the matter and I supported that – that was all. He has admitted he received a gift from the Comorantes – it was in his resignation statement, but what that was I don't know.'

Hugo tugged at his ear. 'That article in *The Times* said it was one and a half million dollars. But Abramowitz etc are claiming that committee members will confirm that you linked Garside to the third cheque.'

'For God's sake Hugo, you were at the meeting!'

He frowned. 'Yes, I must say I can't remember you saying anything like that.' He brightened up. 'But we've got a copy of the minutes. That should settle it once and for all.'

I sighed with relief and called through to Margaret to ask if she and Janet could look through our files and find those minutes.

My relief was short-lived. When they were dug out they just recorded the decisions made at the meeting not who said what to whom. I wasn't mentioned.

Hugo and I looked at each other as the implications sank in.

'You know what folk's memories are like for recalling conversations accurately – terrible. They either remember only what they wanted to hear or recall their thoughts about what was said rather than what was actually said. We could be in difficulty here,' Hugo opined. 'I can just imagine that bunch of politicians and civil servants in the witness box waffling on about what they thought you said. It would just be our word against that waffle and the judge would have to decide who was telling the truth. It would be a gamble and a very expensive one if we lost.'

He was right; my heart sank. 'What do you suppose we should do, make them an offer?'

'That's obviously what they want and they've pitched in at half a million for openers. We could offer fifty thousand?'

'Let's sleep on it and talk again tomorrow.'

As we sat eating our supper that evening Zoe said, 'You seem down in the dumps, what's happened to my normally perky Marcus?'

'Oh, just the usual "trouble at t' mill". It's that bloke Garside – you know the disgraced MP who was in the papers recently – he claims we've slandered him and cost him his job. We haven't, but it's very difficult to prove a negative and fighting it in court would be very expensive and too big a gamble.'

'It must be for him as well.'

'Yes, but if we lose it could wipe us out, but if he loses he can just go bankrupt and we'd still have to pay all our costs. It's a lose/lose situation.'

'So what are you going to do?' she asked with a worried frown.

'Hugo and I are going to discuss it tomorrow; we may have to offer to settle out of court. It's outrageous, but at least it keeps CONDES alive.'

I tried a smile. 'What are you doing tomorrow?'

Zoe pursed her lips, 'Anna and I are going to measure up this flat in Edgware Mansions that's just come on the market. We've been appointed sole agents.' She continued about this new commission they'd got, but she'd lost me after the first word. My mind was now focussed totally on the contents of a drawer in my office desk.

Anna? Of course! Anna Lemartine, I still had the DVD! That could be the solution to our Garside problem.

'Whoopee!' I grabbed Zoe, planted a big kiss on her lips and told her what a clever girl she was. They say that if you get a last-minute reprieve it makes you feel all horny. Well, it was either that, or the expression of absolute bemusement on her face as she totally failed to connect my change of mood with her rendition about a flat in Edgware Mansions, that made me want to embrace her, drag her up stairs, rip off all her clothes and give her a right seeing to. She, on the other hand, thought that I had cracked under the strain and was nervously backing away and reaching out for a blunt instrument.

The impasse was broken by the ring of the telephone. It was Hugo.

'I thought you'd like to know that I've spoken to Desmond Fitzpatrick. He knew nothing of Garside's claim against us. Garside hasn't spoken to him since he resigned his seat. I asked him if he could recall what was said at the DfID committee meeting about Garside. He said that as far as he could remember nothing was said about Garside, but Garside had suggested putting in someone to examine the books of Port Mahon. I asked him if there was any suggestion at that meeting that Garside might be involved and he told me that it did cross his mind, but he wanted to see the results of the forensic accountant's analysis before he came to any conclusion.'

'So Abramowitz and Co. are bluffing?'

'Not necessarily, we don't know what the other members of that committee will say, but in any case, even if they won't give evidence against us it's still our word against his.'

'Hmm!' This needed some thought. Hugo hadn't seen the Anna Lemartine video, I hadn't even told him it existed and I was not sure how he would react to the plan that was forming in my mind.

'Hugo,' I said, 'sleep soundly tonight, I think I have the solution to our problem.' I wouldn't say any more and we agreed to meet in the morning as before.

Fortunately, I was still feeling horny, but my conversation with Hugo must have convinced Zoe that I hadn't gone batty after all and so, as they say, a good night was had by all.

Next morning, feeling on top of the world, I slid the MG into its parking slot, breezed through reception greeting everyone with a cheerful 'Good morning' and a smile, bounded up the stairs leaving behind a few mystified faces, and caught Hugo practising putting across his carpet into a glass jar. He looked up sheepishly.

'I'm playing in the monthly medal on Sunday,' he offered, weakly. 'Thought I'd get in a few minutes' practice.'

'No problem, venerable partner, but I thought I'd put your mind at ease regarding our Garside trouble.'

'Yes, you said as much on the phone. How do you propose to do that?'

I had had time to think the whole thing through on the drive to the office. Revealing that I had the Garside video would provoke a lot of questions, revealing what was on it would provoke more and potentially very embarrassing questions, coupled with unmitigated hilarity and false assumptions in certain quarters.

Hugo was waiting expectantly, 'Well?'

'You don't want to know Hugo.'

He frowned. 'I definitely *do* want to know!'

'No, you don't!'

He winced. 'Oh God, it's not another of your Moon plans, is it?'

I breathed a sigh of relief; this gave me a way out. My Moon plans usually involved skating on thin ice, sailing close to the wind and teetering on the edge of disaster – and Hugo liked to keep well clear of that sort of thing. It wouldn't go down very well either at the golf club or in the City Livery Company world he frequented.

'Well sort of,' I told him. 'I'll give it a bit more thought,' and I shot down the corridor to my office.

I wondered whether to ring Garside there and then but decided not to be hasty and think it through a little more thoroughly. I opened the drawer in my desk to get the DVD.

It wasn't there; neither were the other blank DVD's. I checked all the other drawers in my desk – nothing. Did I give it to Dan? No, definitely not. Did I take it home? And risk Zoe finding it – no way! So where the hell was it? Panic started to set in. I glanced round my office to see if any other hidey-hole sprang to mind. None did.

With a touch of desperation in my voice I called out, 'Margaret, you haven't seen some blank DVDs that were in my desk by any chance?'

'Oh yes, I'm sorry Marcus I meant to replace them, but it slipped my mind.'

I could feel a massive "Oh shit!" situation coming on. A cold hand gripped my heart. 'What did you do with them?'

She came through into my office looking shamefaced. 'You were away and Richard wanted a couple of blank DVDs for his video recorder so he could send a copy of our wedding video to my parents.'

It was getting worse. I shuddered at the thought of the stiff old Brigadier and prudish Mrs Braithwaite inviting the local vicar and some elderly friends round to see Margaret and Richard united in harmony and blissfully walking down the aisle, when it suddenly cut to an enormous black Anna Lemartine in brief hot pants ramming an electric cattle prod up the revolting Norbert Garside's arse.

I took a deep breath; a lot depended on the answer to the next question – and not just Brigadier and Mrs Braithwaite's social standing in the community.

'Has Richard sent them off?' Everything I had was clenched tightly as I waited for her reply.

'No, not yet, he's going to do that tomorrow.'

Thank you God, thank you! I'll try to live a pure life hereafter.

'Margaret, I want you to go now and get a taxi, go to your house and bring back every one of those DVDs. You can buy replacements on the way there. Don't ask questions just do it!'

She looked puzzled. 'You're serious, aren't you?'

'Too right I am!'

I chewed my nails for an hour and a half until she returned with a carrier bag containing all the DVDs. I checked that Anna's was there – it was.

I wasn't going to let it out of my possession again so I slipped it into my jacket pocket, told Margaret I was going out for an hour or so and drove back to our house. The house was unoccupied; Zoe was at work and it wasn't the day for Mrs Marinkowicz, our once-a-week cleaning lady, to come and scatter fag ash over the furniture.

I slid the DVD into the player and switched on the television.

Blood and sand, it was ten times worse than I remembered from the quick play in Jack Fourie's office. God knows what would have happened if Richard had sent it out!

I made a note of two items, the cattle prod and some sort of electrical generator with clamps, then switched it off and put the DVD back in its plastic case.

Back at the office I slipped it between the pages of a textbook and pushed it amongst the other books in my bookshelves. Breaking the habit of a lifetime I called Margaret on the intercom and asked her to obtain Norbert Garside's home telephone number.

CHAPTER NINETEEN

CONDES OFFICE, LONDON

'Mr Garside, it's Marcus Moon from CONDES—' That was as far as I got.

'Speak to my solicitor!' he snapped and put the phone down.

This was not an unanticipated reaction to the opening shot in the Moon cunning plan. I gave him five minutes and then rang again.

When he answered the phone I said, 'Anna Lemartine' and I put the phone down.

I called Amanda on reception. 'In a minute or two a man called Garside is going to phone and ask for me. Tell him I'm not available, but I've left a message for him. The message is "cattle prod".'

'Is that it?' she said, obviously puzzled.

'That's it. If he persists tell him you don't know any more.'

'Well I don't!' she replied with some asperity.

'You're too young,' I chuckled.

Nobby was in two minds. He felt pleased with himself that he had cut that arrogant bastard Moon off before he could start pleading for mercy over the demands in Abramowitz's letter, but the second phone call, and just the name Anna Lemartine, had stopped him in his tracks. Was it a bluff? How could Moon possibly know about his er… 'activities' with Anna Lemartine? What did he know? The Fisherman's Wharf could have told him her name but not any details of his encounter with her.

He shuddered at the thought of anybody knowing what had happened to him under her ministrations. No, it must be a bluff, it had to be. It nagged at him; he had to be sure so more information was required – reluctantly he picked up the phone.

Those two words 'cattle prod', from a fool of a girl who told him that Moon was 'not available'; that was the message and that was all she knew, had frozen him to the spot. The hotel might know her name, but they certainly couldn't know what she had done. His confidence drained away. What the hell was he to do now? Phoning again was out – he'd just get the brush-off. He could go to CONDES' offices but the last time he did that, that beefy secretary had been clenching her jaw muscles and eyeing up his arm like a dog teased with a bone when she virtually threw him out, so that seemed to rule that out.

I was having similar thoughts. I realised that I hadn't thought this through properly and effectively. Communications with Garside had been cut off, which defeated my object. I decided to give him a day to stew in his own juice and so next morning I asked Amanda to call him.

She put him through.

'I understand you were trying to contact me, Mr Garside...?'

I left that hanging.

Nobby coughed and spluttered, now he'd been caught on the wrong foot and wasn't prepared for this conversation.

'I don't know what your game is, Moon, but I deny ever knowing anybody called – what was it...'

I finished the sentence for him, '...Anna Lemartine. No, what I actually wanted to talk to you about was making an offer to settle your claim against us.'

That caught him out again, he hadn't expected this. This was more like it. Anna Lemartine was banished from his mind and he now thought he was in the pound seats for a negotiation.

'You should contact my solicitors, Moon, they are handling those matters.'

'Of course they are, but I don't think you would want your solicitors to be involved, Mr Garside, and if I were you I would listen very carefully to our offer and the conditions attached to it.'

A frisson of doubt re-entered his brain again in the looming shape of Anna Lemartine. This was not the behaviour of a man on the defensive.

'I don't think you've grasped the seriousness of this, Moon. If there are to be any conditions it is *me* who will dictate what they are.'

I ignored that. 'Well, we have only one Mr Garside; we obviously don't want to be out of pocket in this matter so the condition is we will pay you, in damages, whatever we receive from the 'red top' newspapers like *The Mirror, The*

Sun, The Daily Sport, The Daily Star etc., for the sale of the rights to publish anything, or all, that is in the Anna Lemartine video.'

Nobby paused as the last word sank in.

'What video? I don't know what the hell you're talking about so stop playing games, Moon, otherwise the settlement goes up from half a million to a million.'

'The video of you performing with Anna Lemartine – you must remember her? The huge black lady in a gold-lamé top and purple hot pants who pushed an electric cattle prod up your bottom in the Fishermans's Wharf Hotel? *That* video! You must remember the occasion, unless it is a frequent occurrence in the Garside calendar.'

Nobby felt as though he had been punched in the stomach. Moon wasn't bluffing; there was no other way he could know about Anna Lemartine and those details – unless that black bitch had told him. There was still a chance.

'You're bluffing! I don't believe you have a video of any such thing. I want to see this alleged video before I agree to anything,' he ground out.

'Sure, I'll send a copy to you. Mr and Mrs N Garside... and what's the address?'

Nobby couldn't cope, his mind was awhirl. The thought of Tottie finding out about his activities with the pulchritudinous Anna was the last straw. 'I'll ring you back in half an hour,' he gabbled.

'Take your time Mr Garside, we're not in any hurry.'

He agreed to come to London the following day and I was left with the problem of where to meet him and show him the video. The office was out – too many people around; our house was definitely out – Zoe was around, and she would want to know chapter and verse. I scratched my head, then I got it. Bob Barclay! He had all the necessary kit in his offices and was as tight as a clam when sworn to secrecy. It meant explaining things to Bob, not everything but most of it. He jumped at the opportunity.

'Did she really do that to him? Bloody hell, the papers would go frenzied to get hold of material like that.'

'Yes, well that's as may be, but the purpose is to get him off my and CONDES' back.'

I phoned Garside and told him I'd meet him at the offices of Barclay Developments at 6.30pm and gave him the address. He grumbled that that was late and meant he'd have to stay overnight in the Big Smoke. I said he could come earlier if he didn't mind the whole of Bob's staff watching as well.

He was sitting nervously by himself in Barclay Developments smart reception area when I arrived at 6.45.

'You're late,' he snapped. 'I hope you haven't dragged me all this way on a fool's errand!'

'Haven't you got that the wrong way round, Mr Garside,' I beamed at him.

I took him up to Bob's office. Bob, ever the affable host, offered him a drink, which he refused.

'Let's get on with it!'

He sat down tight-lipped and tense. His eyes fixed rigidly on the blank massive flat-screen TV.

I poured myself a gin and tonic whilst Bob slipped the DVD into the player and switched on the television.

To lighten the atmosphere I thought I'd do a little introduction, after all I was the only one here who'd seen the video.

'Henri Coquelin Productions proudly presents Anna Lemartine as Fiona Fitzeveryone and Norbert Garside as Binky Mexborough in 'Colonoscopy', a venture into the dark recesses of semi-human behaviour.'

Garside sat rigid with apprehension, it slotted into place. The mention of Henri Coquelin destroyed his last remaining hope; Coquelin had set him up. Moon wasn't bluffing. He managed to mutter, 'Get on with it!'

Bob pressed the play button. The screen flashed and then revealed Garside lying on his bed wearing a sports shirt and slacks reading a magazine. We heard a knock on the door and when Garside opened it we saw the back view of a huge figure dressed in a gold-lamé top and vivid purple hot pants hurtle through and pin Garside back on the bed.

Quite clearly we heard her say, 'Hello honey chile! I'm Anna. Feeling randy, are we? Can't wait to get started? Well we've got a bit of foreplay to do before we get down to the main event.'

With that she tore his shirt open with both hands. Buttons flew in all directions and there was a ripping sound as the material gave way somewhere.

Garside flushed, angrily. 'OK, OK, for God's sake turn it off now. I've seen enough, you've made your point,' he cried.

Bob ignored him. 'You've got to be kidding, sunshine. I haven't set all this up just for the opening titles.'

We sat there in fits of laughter with tears rolling down our cheeks as Anna got to work with her electrical bag of tricks. Well, two of us did; the third sat rigidly in his chair, his face now ashen and his eyes glued to the screen as all his hopes of making a fortune disappeared in an exhibition of groans, moans and twitches.

It came to an end when she repacked her gear and disappeared out of camera shot and the screen went blank.

I looked at Garside. 'I take it, Mr Garside, that we won't be hearing from you or your solicitors again.' It was a statement not a question.

He didn't reply directly. 'How did you get hold of that?' he ground out. 'It must have been Coquelin, he set me up. It must have been him. You said something about Coquelin Productions – but why? Why do this to me? I thought he was a friend, or at least that we were on the same side.'

He put his head in his hands as if to shut off the outside world.

I began to feel sorry for him; he was such an empty person, all flash and bluster but there was nothing there behind it. He was a selfish self-centred bully. No warmth, no feeling, no attempt to really connect with people; and now he was jobless but, if he backed off from suing us, he would still have some dignity which he could call upon for his future.

I had to protect our business, but I offered him an olive branch.

'If you withdraw your lawsuit, we will give you a written undertaking not to pass this video to any third party. The only people who know about it, apart from the participants and the Comorantians who set you up, are Bob and I. Nobody else. I forgot about Jack Fourie, but he had no axe to grind. The Comorantians I can do nothing about, but I can't see that there's any mileage in it for them now that you are no longer an MP.'

'If I withdraw my instructions to sue you, I want the video.'

Bob shook his head at me warningly.

'You can have it after two years when all this fuss has died down.'

'That's no good!' he snapped. 'How do I know you won't make copies and circulate them once I've withdrawn the suit?'

'Look Mr Garside, you're not really in a position to make demands. Once and for all I tell you that I have never claimed that you were the third man. Your suit is dodgy at the best. Desmond Fitzpatrick and other members of the committee have no recollection of me saying that you were the third man: the minutes don't record that either, so what evidence have you got? Fitzpatrick is quite clear that I didn't identify you as the third man, as is Hugo Elmes, so not only will you lose but the 'red tops' will have a beanfeast at your expense.'

He glared at both of us, angrily. 'You think you're bloody clever, don't you, you fucking southern poofters!'

We waited; I didn't think it would contribute much if I pointed out that Bob came from Shropshire and I was as Yorkshire as he was.

He wasn't stupid and grasped the rationality of the situation without too much trouble. He had no choice.

'Alright!' he growled, 'but who's going to draw up that indemnity?'

'Your solicitors can – if you want.'

He thought about that for a moment and rejected the idea. Abromowitz and Co. were not going to be happy having him stop the case and deprive them of the fat fees they were anticipating, and the last thing he wanted was to reveal any details of the video to them – Jewish shysters! They'd probably blackmail him about it.

Bob noticed his hesitation. 'It's not going to be a complicated agreement and the names of the parties don't have to be disclosed; they can be added on signature. Why don't you jointly appoint some neutral solicitor and then get a third party – me, for instance – to brief them? I have no interest in this matter.'

I nodded. 'Good idea! That's fine by me, what about you Mr Garside – or do you want to appoint somebody to act for you in the briefing? You'd have to tell them the whole story, of course.'

'There's one other thing,' pointed out Bob, looking at me. 'We'll have to be careful with the wording to prevent Garside complaining that you're blackmailing him.'

I glanced at Garside; this hadn't occurred to him, but now Bob had brought it up, he realised that there wasn't going to be any mileage in trying to run that now.

In the end it was agreed that Bob would get his company solicitor to draw up the agreement confirming that Parties A and B would hold, in safe keeping, the 'Anna Lemartine video' and they undertook to ensure that no third party got access to it. Copies of it would not be made.

Party C would drop his lawsuit against Parties A and B.

At the end of two years Parties A and B would hand over the safe keeping of the video to Party C.

Bob told Garside that he would email him a draft for his approval and do the same for CONDES.

Garside was shown the door and when we were certain he was out of earshot we both burst out laughing.

'Can you imagine any newspaper publishing pictures of Garside with Anna? They wouldn't dare. OK you could put them on the internet, but you wouldn't get paid for that,' Bob chortled.

'No, but I still think they'd've bought the video and run a stories with the less lurid bits. It would refresh the Port Mahon – Garside – Kronoff saga.'

'What less lurid bits? His eyes were bulging out of his head most of the time!'

****

The Frog and Nightgown was very busy that Saturday. It was warm and sunny so the 'boys' had pushed two tables together in the courtyard. Zoe and I arrived at the same time as Pete and Merrylees. Still feeling particularly benevolent from sorting out the Garside problem I told Big Jessie to "fill 'em all up" and sat down to murmurs of astonishment.

'What? What?' I feigned amazement that my generosity should cause such a reaction.

Tony laughed. 'You, buying a round on the spur of the moment. You'll be struck off the list of 'Yorkshire's Miserable Gits' if you go on doing silly things like that and the word gets out!'

Lightning Source UK Ltd.
Milton Keynes UK
UKHW020732140319
339130UK00009B/558/P

9 781785 078712